Tattoo Your Name on My Heart

Simon Cann

Coombe
Hill
Publishing

Published by Coombe Hill Publishing
33 Melrose Gardens
New Malden
Surrey KT3 3HQ
United Kingdom
coombehillpublishing.com

ISBN: 978-1-910398-04-3 (paperback)
ISBN: 978-1-910398-05-0 (ePub)

A big thank you to:

■ Cathleen Small for her editorial input.

■ Lawrence Rippingale (lozeng3r.com) for the cover art.

one

"You need to call the police."

Boniface leaned back in his chair, forcing his head and shoulders still as he softly spun his seat from left-to-right-to-left-to-right, twisting at the waist as he waited for his potential new clients to consider his advice.

"I'd call the police now." Boniface reached for the phone, clumsily grabbing it by the side and dropping it on the edge of his desk toward the bassist. The handset bounced out of the cradle and tumbled to the floor.

Boniface reached across his desk to pull up the handset by its cord and looked up at the bassist, hoping he wouldn't notice his nervousness. Hoping the other man was accustomed to fans being slightly on edge around him.

"No." The bassist's voice was quiet, but his opinion was clear, his decision definitive.

This was a man who understood how to project his presence. A man who performed on stage—Boniface had seen him perform with the band several times. And when the bassist stood on stage—an imposing, muscular figure in his black leather trousers and black sleeveless T-shirt freeing his arms as they exercised complete domination of his instrument—he had a clear understanding of how his audience would perceive his physical presence. He was patient and understood timing; he was a man who wouldn't play a note if it wasn't the right note at the right time.

He might not be the frontman, but he was the leader of the band— the general who always stood shoulder to shoulder with his troops and who understood cowardice in the face of the enemy. He understood that if you flinched, you failed—and you can't fail when people have paid money to see you perform.

This was the man who had said no, and had communicated no.

Boniface sat forward, his frown questioning. He made eye contact with the bassist and waited before raising his eyebrows to suggest he was hoping for elaboration.

"We can't."

The bassist appeared to have said all he was going to say. It was as if those two words were a full explanation. Boniface looked between the bassist and the bassist's wife sitting beside him, wordlessly cursing himself when he realized that as he stared at the outline of her now-clothed figure, he was remembering what she had looked like when she was modeling.

"We can't involve the police," said the bassist. His tone had changed.

He wasn't pleading; it was more that he was trying to be conciliatory. "If we go to the cops, Boniface, it will take time for them to investigate." He snorted, his solid figure—still sitting—twitched with his indignation. "Seriously, Boniface, the cops have got better things to do. They're not going to jump just because I snap my fingers." His tone softened. "And before we make it official, we've got to acknowledge that some cops are bent, others are just plain incompetent, and some leak stories. There are huge amounts of poison being spilled about us, and we need to know what the problem is—we're not trying amplify the hate and the shouting." He seemed almost apologetic. "No. I'm sorry, the police aren't an option."

The bassist sunk back into the leather sofa, his right hand seamlessly joining his wife's left. The slightest tightening of his hand in hers conveyed reassurance, the only sign that the two lumps of flesh might not be of the same person.

"A private detective?" offered Boniface, standing and walking to the window, a brown strip that spanned two walls. He looked through the tinted glass across the side street and over the girls' school on the other side of the road, its inmates having departed several hours earlier along with most of their jailers, although the few remaining cars implied that some were still dreaming up fresh torments for tomorrow.

He turned to resume the conversation and sat on the broad windowsill with his back to the school. For the first time since Boniface had shaken hands with his prospective new clients, a suggestion of a smirk started to spread across the bassist's face. Not a look of joy, but a hint that he was amused by the absurdity of what he had just heard.

"Do you know a good private detective? One you could actually trust?" The bassist relaxed back into the sofa, as if he had decided that he had said all he needed to say to settle the matter—at least to settle that a private investigator was not the right option.

Boniface regarded the other man. It wasn't one simple detail that suggested he didn't work in an office, but more the combination: his off-duty bright shirt under under an old sandy jacket, the slightly too long but styled hair, and the almost waxy skin tone from rarely seeing daylight for thirty years. He tried to show some grace as he gave way to the potential client. "No. Not in this country. I don't know any good investigators."

The bassist continued. "I don't have time to go through the process of searching for a good one, only to find that we've hired a dickhead rather than a dick."

Boniface gave a charitable smile for the bassist's weak joke and changed tack. "You must know other journalists, apart from me—you've been in the game long enough."

"The ones I know are hacks."

Again, it wasn't what the bassist said, but how he said it that told Boniface this wouldn't be a fruitful line to continue, but he persisted. "I was a hack."

The bassist's wife noticed her husband's reaction, momentarily shutting her eyes as if preparing herself for a tale from the road that she had heard before. "Look, Boniface. When we were on the road, we'd set the journalists up with a groupie, perhaps several. They'd be so grateful we'd get a glowing review."

The bassist looked to his wife, as if silently acknowledging why the groupies that must have followed the band were always irrelevant for him. Without catching his gaze, the coiled spring inside her started to release, letting her body melt softly into his.

"Those journalists—if you can really call those sorts of people journalists—are not the sort of people I respect, and are not the sort of people I want knowing our problems." The bassist's voice took on a more businesslike tone. "Tommy rates you. He says you're the smartest guy he's ever met—and Tommy's no fool." He tilted his head forward so that he looked up at Boniface and pointed with an open hand. "You're the perfect cover: a serious journalist doing a serious biography."

As the two potential clients sat together, Boniface understood that the sofa had been a good decision. When he re-carpeted the office—for the second time in less than six months—Montbretia had suggested he dispose of the businesslike meeting table with chairs on either side and replace it with something more informal, in this case a sofa and low table. She had also persuaded him that filing cabinets just wasted space. It took her a few weeks to digitize his archive and a few more weeks for him to get used to accessing that archive through a screen rather than pulling out a stack of papers, but by the time he was ready to concede that she was right—and that he didn't need filing cabinets in his office—the carpet fitters were ready. One day while he was out at a meeting with a client, Montbretia supervised the carpet fitters and managed to dispose of all the filing cabinets in the office—apart from the one in her room—putting the matter beyond discussion.

Boniface pursed his lips, thinking how to word his next question.

The bassist grinned. "And don't suggest a lawyer—I'll shake hands and be counting my fingers, and I need my fingers." He mimed playing the bass guitar. Where most mimes are a crude indication of how a non-musician thinks an instrument should be played, muscle memory kicked in as the bassist reached for the neck with his left hand, the fingers on his right a blur of rhythm.

"You're the perfect cover, Boniface. A serious journalist writing a serious biography about Prickle. You have a history: If people google you, they'll know who you are, and you'll seem plausible—and Prickle were big enough to justify a decent biography. If we send in a detective, that suggests we think there's a problem, which will lead to more questions." He waited a beat. "You can go anywhere, find what the problem is, and figure what our options are." Another beat. "Find a way for whoever's got a problem to get out without losing face, and we're all winners."

Boniface went to speak but was cut off by the bassist. "Look. Just spend a day or two, and if you find nothing, we'll call it quits."

two

Montbretia stood by the conference room door, watching.

Boniface led his guests out of the office and to the elevator. The husband had the look of a confident man. He stood straight—not military straight, more *I'm used to being looked at* straight. His walk had the slight swagger of someone enjoying life, pleased to see every new person who came into his orbit.

When the couple arrived, Montbretia had been by the door receiving a delivery. The delivery guy recognized the man and mumbled "you're Danny..." before he crumbled. It wasn't clear who this man was, but the delivery guy seemed to think he was famous, and the probably famous man seemed accustomed to this reaction, offering a firm handshake and happily agreed to a photo—Montbretia as photographer, with the delivery guy's phone.

With the few words they exchanged, Montbretia could recognize his accent: south London, but slightly softened—it didn't quite have the full rasp. She had been living in London for nearly a year, and now she was able to differentiate between the nuances of south London, cockney, and Estuary English. Accents were so much easier back home in the States.

The husband threw back his head, laughing. His solid figure—stocky, but not overweight, wrapped in neat jeans and a patterned blue-red shirt held in by a well-worn sandy jacket—projected the sound of his laugh through the door as he slapped Boniface on the shoulder. She watched as the edge of a dopey grin spread over Boniface's profile.

The wife stood neatly, her feet together and her back—which was toward the doors Montbretia looked through—was perfectly straight, maximizing her height, but even with heels she was still shorter than Montbretia.

Shorter but more elegant, felt Montbretia.

She was dressed modestly: brown suede ankle boots, jeans that were fitted but didn't cut off her circulation, a white cotton blouse that followed every contour without any excess material billowing, and a light-brown suede jacket, matching her boots but fringed along each arm and across the back. Her jewelry was equally understated, with wedding and engagement rings, a single bracelet, and a small brooch on her jacket's lapel.

For all the elegant understatement, the one fact she couldn't hide was that her figure showed the perfection usually reserved for plastic dolls. If there was ever to be a sliding scale of zero to

I-wonder-how-much-surgery-would-cost-to-look-like-her, against which every woman could find her place, then on whatever measure you chose to consider the archetype, she was pretty much at the top of the scale.

Boniface stood straighter, his hand raised to offer his guests the elevator, and Montbretia took her last look. Her final glimpse was of the woman's hair. Montbretia had looked closely when she arrived—she hadn't meant to, but she was taller and looked down on the other woman. Although she couldn't tell for certain, Montbretia was sure that perfection like that—blonde hair that didn't look bleached—would cost a fortune. But each strand seemed to be a slightly different color, and the color of every hair was consistent from root to tip.

And no one pays to have the odd gray hair, do they?

They had gone. Montbretia's vision remained fixed on the space where she had been staring at the blonde woman with the soft gray eyes. As she pulled herself out of her trance, she realized that Boniface had gone, too. Where he would usually say farewell to clients by the elevator, he had apparently decided to escort this couple to the parking lot.

She sighed noisily, continuing to stare.

Her line of sight was broken as Boniface walked from the elevator and through the door. There was a lightness to his step she hadn't seen before, but she did recognize his slightly embarrassed, over-excited teenage boy look.

"You disgust me, Boniface." She exhaled heavily, intending him to hear. "You were sickening."

Boniface's grin spread.

"You're besotted with her, and you're treating him like your best buddy ever. Honestly, Boniface. This is sad." His grin continued to spread. "Come on—eyes back in your head. Tongue off the ground and back in your mouth. You know you didn't take your eyes off her ass?"

"But I had my back to you." Boniface enjoyed his minor triumph.

"I don't need to be able to see your eyes to know where you're looking. I've been here for a year—I can understand how Londoners greet each other, and I can tell where you're focusing by looking at the back of your head." Montbretia stared at Boniface. "You're not going to say I'm wrong, are you?"

Boniface looked down, chewing slightly on his lower lip as he shook his head.

"Who were they, anyway?" asked Montbretia.

"My teenage fantasy."

"Which one?"

"Both!" said Boniface. "Danny..."

"You mean your new BFF."

"Danny Featherstone," said Boniface, his tone lower, "is the bassist in a band called Prickle."

"Never heard of them."

"They're not really your thing," said Boniface. "Melodic, hook-laden, classic rock. They started as a blues band in the seventies, but in the eighties the founding singer left and Danny took control. He recruited a new singer—much better than the original guy—and pushed them in a tighter, more commercial direction." He paused. "I saw them...twice."

"That probably explains why I've never heard of them," said Montbretia. "And your new sexual fantasy?"

"There's nothing new about that fantasy." Boniface seemed wistful. "Dawn was perhaps my very first fantasy. She is a gorgeous creature who comes from a time when we didn't have the internet, and the only way for a teenage boy to see young ladies who got the goods out was in the newspapers."

"What do you mean, Boniface? She's your age—what was she doing posing?"

"Think again—she's ten years older than me."

"Wow," said Montbretia. "Life has been kind to her."

"Maybe. Maybe not. She comes from a time when sixteen-year-old girls could appear topless in the newspapers." Boniface shrugged. "It was great when I was a teenager...but I'm older now, and now, in retrospect, it just seems like..."

"Child abuse," offered Montbretia.

Boniface bobbed his head as if trying to construct the next sentence. "Yeah, but even though girls have to be eighteen now, I'm not convinced that topless women in daily newspapers are, you know, a good thing." He smirked. "Which isn't to say I've fallen out of love with the female form."

"While we're behaving like grownups, what do they want?"

"Tommy sent them."

"Tommy as in Tommy Newby?"

"The same," said Boniface. "Apparently, Danny and Tommy bonded over a love of vintage Bentleys, and when Danny mentioned to Tommy that he has a problem, Tommy sent Danny to us."

"And the problem?" asked Montbretia.

"The problem is Danny and Dawn are being trashed on the internet." Boniface stood firmly, his feet apart, his arms folded. "Prickle are head-lining a charity gig: Trying to sell tickets when you keep getting slagged isn't easy. After the gig, the band are taking a year off, and Danny and Dawn have been talking about doing some TV work."

"And the TV offers are sticky if the internet hates you," said Montbretia.

"Precisely."

"I get it, but what do they want you to do?"

"Not much, just talk to a few people, see if I can find what's going on." He pushed out his chin with an I-don't-know motion. "See if there's a problem that can be solved."

"But you're not a private investigator, Boniface, so please tell me they're paying us well." Montbretia watched as Boniface unconsciously flinched. "They *are* paying us?"

Boniface pursed his lips.

"Boniface?" Her question was more insistent than she intended. "What are we charging them? They're getting the full Boniface charm offensive, and this office doesn't come for free."

Boniface wrinkled his nose. "It's..." He exhaled. "There's..."

"Tell," demanded Montbretia.

"They've got a problem with the band's management." He paused, thinking. "They control the band's finances."

Montbretia shut her eyes. "You're saying we're not getting paid." Her voice was monotone. "You are playing at being a PI, and we're not going to get paid." She opened her eyes and watched Boniface, knowing he was mentally playing through every argument he could put forward, trying to predict her response.

"Two meetings. I can do it alone—I don't need you. By this time tomorrow, everything will be sorted." He stopped as if that was sufficient explanation, but continued when Montbretia remained silent. "And I'm not being a private investigator—there's a simple cover story: I'm a journalist researching Prickle's biography."

"So Prickle are some sort of rock gods—at least rock gods in your mind..."

"Prickle are headlining the Royal Albert Hall," said Boniface weakly.

"I still haven't heard of them." Montbretia shrugged, feeling slightly chagrined. "And she's something of a sleazy, low-rent former model—with a killer figure and great hair, if I do say so myself—and somehow they've wrapped you around their collective finger, persuaded you that all you need to do is meet two people under the guise of research for a biography of some band that no one else will have heard of, and the issue can be solved? That's it?"

She widened her eyes to indicate that she expected a response. Boniface seemed to assent, but with little conviction.

"And payment—at best—is goodwill of someone who has had a lifetime of lies from jerks, plus you get to stare at Dawn. If you honestly believe that this only needs two—or three or four—meetings, then we're going to be bankrupt by the end of the month." Montbretia turned into the conference room and sat at the large table, looking at the papers she had spread in front of her.

Boniface came as far as the doorway and stopped. "I...I promise not to involve you." He stepped into the room, looking at the papers. His tone changed: "You're working late."

"And getting paid. There's a novel concept." She softened her voice.

"Some Weissenfeld work. We're about to award the contract to an NGO to deliver the second tranche of aid in Somalia—I said I'd look over these papers for Chlodwig and give him a call in the morning."

"Paper?" asked Boniface. "I thought no one used that anymore."

"Ah, the missionary zeal of the newly converted," said Montbretia. "People still use paper to communicate, Boniface. What we," she pointed between the two of them, "don't do is store paper. We receive, read, digitize if it's for the record, and then recycle."

"Say hi to Chlodwig when you speak to him. I'll be in after...you know."

"I know," said Montbretia.

"And now I'm going to research a singer from the 1970s, so that I know as much as I can before I bang on his door tomorrow morning."

three

Boniface looked for a doorbell.

There was none.

He looked for a knocker.

There was none.

There was a corroded chrome letter slot with mounts at either end where a knocker would usually hang, but clearly it had been yanked off many years ago.

He stepped back and surveyed the front door—the sky-blue paint, which had probably been applied in the early 1970s, was now faded and chipped, and from the wear marks at the bottom of the door, Boniface guessed the door was habitually kicked open when it stuck in the winter. He stepped forward, rapped firmly with his knuckles, then stood back so as not to be aggressively filling the space when the door was answered.

Not that the knock had aroused any signs of life.

As he had walked along Bethnal Green Road from Bethnal Green underground station, before he turned north up a side street, he had wondered how to start the conversation. He still wasn't sure—so much depended on the attitude of the man he hoped would answer the door.

In his mind he went through the details Danny had told him and the additional information he had gleaned from the internet. Graham Barrington—Gray, as he preferred to be called—had founded Gooseberry, a tight blues/rock band, in the early 1970s. Due to a similarly named band, they had quickly changed the name to Prickle and hadn't looked back.

With Gray Barrington and his gravelly voice at the front, the band worked tirelessly, gigging around the UK and Europe. Typically, they would play more than 300 shows a year in a range of venues up to 1,000-seaters. Every show sold well—even if it didn't sell out, it would break even—and every album sold in respectable numbers over time, but never in sufficient numbers over a short enough period to hit the top of the charts.

In 1979, Gray was impressed with a 17-year-old bass player's feel for the blues and offered him the gig when the band's previous bass player left. And so Danny Featherstone found himself a member of Prickle.

Boniface rapped on the front door again, this time harder, and then pressed his ear to the peeling sky-blue paint. Somewhere inside someone shouted. He rapped again. Another shout. He stepped back from the door and turned to look down the street as he waited.

Fashions change, and with the advent of 1980s hair rock, Prickle's blues-based sound was increasingly at odds with what the mainstream wanted. Album sales slowed, and as their contemporaries started playing theaters and stadiums, Prickle began a midsized club tour. Gray interpreted this comparative lowly status as the band holding him back, and after accepting a deal with a US-based management company, quit the band for a solo career on the other side of the Atlantic.

Danny had explained, the solo career didn't work as Gray expected. The record label enforced a contract term on Gray requiring him to deliver two further albums. Having taken the US management deal but then being obligated to deliver two further albums in the UK, Gray had wrapped himself in legal red tape from which it took him three years to extricate himself. After three years, few people remembered him, and even fewer cared.

Even from two paces away from the front door, Boniface could hear the heavy footsteps descending the stairs. The heavy steps of the man who, as far as Boniface was able to divine, had spent the last 30 years in the musical wilderness, not earning very much money—or if he had earned money, apart from a few royalties from his 1970s recordings, it hadn't been from making music. There had been some gigs, mostly in pubs, some failed bands, some promises of work, a few irregular performances at small blues festivals, but nothing of any note as far as Boniface could tell.

A quick scan of their respective offerings on YouTube was enough to bring the distinction between Gray and Prickle into sharp relief. Gray had a few handheld videos shot in pubs, usual filmed on a mobile phone—in total seven songs. By contrast, Prickle—the band Gray had abandoned—had professional videos, stadium footage, bootleg videos of stadium performances, and a few TV specials.

The footsteps reached the door, and Boniface heard it squeak as it opened. "What?" The voice was raspy, angry, insistent.

Boniface turned, casting a gaze over the street. On each side of the street, the brick-built terraced houses—each adjoining both neighbors with no gap—formed solid walls with no front yard separating the residences from the sidewalk. The houses were what used to be called two-up/two-downs. Literally, two rooms upstairs and two rooms downstairs with the staircase from the lower floor to the upper horizontally bisecting the house.

When they were built, none of those four rooms was a bathroom. Then again, when the houses were built, Queen Victoria was on the throne, heating in houses was provided by fires, and electricity was an unheard-of notion.

During the Second World War, the Luftwaffe razed much of the East End of London. The terraced two-up/two-downs that remained were then labeled as slums—the lack of bathroom making them unfit for human habitation—and, in an irony not lost on Boniface the houses that survived the attentions of the Luftwaffe were demolished to be replaced by gleaming tower blocks, which soon became nests of deprivation and academies of crime.

Those terraces that weren't cleared as slums, now with indoor plumbing and gas-fired central heating, had become highly desirable, although as with everything from the Victorian era they required constant maintenance, and looking along the street Boniface could see that some of the properties were very well maintained. In short, gentrification was happening around—the incoming residents could afford to maintain and upgrade their houses. Those who had lived there for longer couldn't.

Gray's house fitted the latter category and was not maintained. Danny recalled that Gray had inherited his house from a grandparent, and it was probably that grandparent who had painted the front door sky-blue.

His house wasn't well maintained, and as Boniface finally looked at Gray, he could see that neither was the man who had first formed the blues rock band Gooseberry more than forty years ago.

Boniface knew that Gray was sixty-something years old, but as he pulled his thin toweling robe, which might once have been white but now wasn't, the short but wiry man behind the door looked seventy-something. What hair remained was dyed, cheaply. It had probably been dyed black but had faded to a dirty brown—its tone not helped by the lack of washing and the apparent absence of a comb in Gray's life.

"Gray? Gray Barrington?" The man might be Gray, but in none of the photos Boniface had looked at last night had Gray looked so old or been standing in a toweling robe.

The man behind the door grunted but didn't disagree.

Boniface put one hand forward to shake and held his business card in the other. "My name's Boniface...Alexander Boniface. I'm writing a biography about Prickle—I was wondering if I could buy you breakfast?"

Gray shook his head and let the door swing fully open as he leaned on the door jamb. Boniface looked through the door, which opened directly into the front room with a beaten-up sofa against the far wall, an old cathode-ray-tube television in the corner across from the sofa, and—piquing Boniface's sense of irony—a stack of paint cans, brushes, rollers, roller trays, dust sheets, and a stepladder spattered in many colors of paint.

"What's the chief prick and the little pricks up to now?" asked Gray.

"As I said," continued Boniface, "a biography of the band. I was hoping to have a chat since you are the guy who got the whole thing started."

"Honestly, Boniface," said Gray, looking down at the card Boniface had pushed in his hand, "you're less welcome than the Jehovah's Witnesses. You'd be doing me a huge favor if you'd just fuck off and let me get back to bed." He stepped back and started to swing the door.

Boniface put his foot on the threshold, blocking the motion of the aged wood. "Come on, let me buy you breakfast. Full English. A proper fry-up." He smiled. "Are you a tea or coffee man?"

"Seriously, you look like one of those poofy city-types that keep moving in around here and talk about how much *character* the street has. I don't like them and I don't spend time with them. I don't like you and I'm not going to spend any time with you, no matter what that kid Danny is up to." He seemed weary. "Just...just go."

Boniface removed his foot, and the door banged without closing properly. From the outside Boniface could hear soft flesh impacting the wood, followed by a squeak as the lower part of the door made its way fully into the frame, the latch clicking closed.

four

"We don't hold people by their ankles and dangle them out of windows."

Aaron Delcort chuckled as he sat across from the PR man who called himself Boniface, then winked at Fiona Aldred sitting to his left. "At least, not as a business practice. What we do for fun in our own time is a private matter, right Fi?"

He smiled broadly. The Boniface guy seemed to have a sense of humor bypass.

For a PR man, Boniface wasn't very chatty—there seemed to be no notion of that bonhomie he would have expected. Delcort pushed the corner of the other man's business card and scanned it again: *Alexander Boniface*, and immediately below, in smaller text, *Boniface Communications*, a company which apparently had an office in Wimbledon. It didn't give him much to work with.

He had never heard of Alexander Boniface—or Boniface, as he asked to be called—and he hadn't had time to check him out. Five minutes on the web would have been useful—even thirty seconds looking at a street-view of his office would have helped establish whether the address was kosher.

But you play the cards you're dealt, and Boniface had turned up and asked for a meeting about Prickle. Given the contractual difficulties with the band, he had asked Fiona to sit in with them—she was the lawyer; she could take over if there was no hint of any new business to talk about, no deals to be done. But if there was a negotiation, he was the man to lead.

"I'm sorry, you have us at a bit of a disadvantage. You know about us—we're PAD Management. I'm Aaron Delcort, the D in PAD; Miss Aldred, Fiona, is the A; and Haroon Patel..." He looked through the glass wall of the conference room but couldn't see his colleague. "Haroon Patel is the P in PAD, and we handle the affairs for Prickle—but we don't know about you."

An Asian man with rimless glasses, a pencil mustache, and the wisp of a beard perched on the peak of his chin passed. "Ah! That's Haroon, there. He handles the money, and Fiona looks after the legal matters." The lawyer by his side bobbed her head once, as if affirming his introduction.

Boniface was well dressed in a dark-blue suit with a subtle white stripe. He sat quietly on the other side of the table, seemingly listening intently. All he seemed to have brought with him was a phone, which he laid to his right. He inhaled softly and began. "There's not much to tell you beyond what I've said already. It's a bit of a labor of love for me...I'm writing a biography about Prickle." He paused, looking between Delcort and the lawyer. "It's in the very early stages, and I'm just gathering background information at the moment before I start interviews." He became hesitant. "Now, I know you've got some...challenges...issues, minor contractual snagging to work through. I don't how you want to describe it...but I was hoping we could open up some form of communication."

Delcort looked to his colleague. "Do you want to grab this one, Fiona?" He flopped back into his seat, hearing his bracelet clink as he dropped his arm, its satisfying weight gripping his wrist, then looked at Boniface, watching for the reaction he expected.

"Before we entered into our relationship with Prickle and Danny, we obviously undertook extensive due diligence." And there it was—Fiona had started talking, and from the slight shift in his facial muscles, Delcort saw that Boniface had reacted.

He liked taking Fiona to meetings with him. Other people always found her slightly disconcerting; she was never what they expected.

First, there was her appearance. She was tall, 6'1" he believed, but then there was her preference—no, make that consistent, unwavering choice—to wear heels, which gave her an additional four or five inches. Especially with what she called mega-heels. To him they looked like a throwback to the 1970s—the bastard child from a night of passion between a stack heel and a stiletto. While tall, she was skinny. Not left-to-right skinny—she seemed a normal enough width—but front-to-back skinny. If she turned sideways, the wind would blow past her.

Her hands were small and delicate. Framed by her brown shoulder-length hair with hints of red, her facial features, while mildly asymmetrical, were equally delicate. Apart from her nose, which was thin and protruding, with a prominent bridge giving it a near oblong profile.

But it was her voice that seemed to have got Boniface—it was not the sort of voice one expected to come out of that sort of body. It was deep. Very deep. But rich—suggesting a level of education and sophistication—and soft. Delcort watched as Boniface leaned forward at the siren call of that soft, rich, deep voice.

"We intended—still intend—this to be a long-term relationship with the band," continued Fiona.

Delcort sat straighter: It was time to add some detail that Fiona should have brought to Boniface's attention. "These guys aren't young anymore. We wanted our relationship to be like one of those houses you move into when the kids leave home. You know, there's still space for the kids to visit, but the house is more practical for your requirements as you age...because, you know, it's the last ever house you need to buy before you..." He shrugged. "You know..."

Fiona continued. "We sought warranties—basic assurances of facts—in a number of areas, and these were all readily forthcoming." This was the reason he made Fiona a partner—she was a great lawyer and went straight to the key point in any legal matter. He could hand her any document, and she would instinctively sniff out the weasel words slipped in.

She understood what was there for show and what was there to look crazy. She was the one who had explained to him why the riders in concert contracts specified a large bowl of M&Ms with the green ones taken out: If you turn up at a gig and there's a bowl of M&Ms with the green ones still there, then everyone can see that the contract terms haven't been met. And if the promoter doesn't bother with the simple conditions, then you can expect they won't have bothered with more complicated terms of the contract—for instance, all that stuff about the safety of the band while they are performing.

In addition to her awesome understanding, she was his secret weapon in any negotiation. She was happy to sit in a meeting and make sure every "i" was dotted and every "t" crossed. Send her in, and she would willingly lead the war of attrition, waiting for the other side to crack. She could read a contract and analyze it in five minutes, but she was happy to grind the other side down over five hours of negotiations, knowing their lawyer was on an hourly rate but that she was on staff and could wait all night.

"There's no need to get into the detail," said Fiona, "but let's just say these warranties are much of the root of our present discussions with our client."

"To repeat what I said before," said Delcort, chuckling and adjusting his diamond-studded cufflinks, "we don't dangle people out of the windows, but in this case we do have a legitimate grievance, and while this matter is outstanding we will comply with the contractual terms to the letter."

Delcort looked directly to the other man, who had pulled out a small notepad and was jotting. Boniface looked up from across the table. "And one of those terms allows you to freeze the band's finances because you control the bank accounts?"

Delcort twisted his cufflink the other way, playing back the words and the tone Boniface had used. There seemed to be no rancor, no angle or implication. It seemed to be a basic statement of facts, expressed as a question. He watched as Boniface made another note.

"This isn't doing you any good, is it?" Boniface sounded sympathetic. "You're paid a percentage, so if the band isn't earning, you're not earning. And if you're not out there hustling for more work, then your future earnings are going to be impacted." He paused, staring straight at Delcort. "I'm not missing a subtle nuance here, am I?"

Delcort went to speak and found himself cut off as Boniface continued. "If Prickle has ceased to exist by the time I finish my book, then I'm going to have trouble selling my book—it will have become as interesting as last month's newspapers." His voice brightened. "I'm talking to people—surely I must be able to put your perspective forward. If I could give a push...just to get things moving."

She didn't need to make a sound; Delcort had known her long enough to know that Fiona was silently groaning and was getting ready to stamp on Boniface's naïve stupidity. "I wish it were that simple, Mister Boniface, but you need to understand that our dispute is not simply about one little thing that needs to be fixed. We are dealing with so many contractual issues—contracts that date back many years before our relationship with Prickle ever began. Claims, especially by Mister Barrington, about issues from the 1970s where the contract terms were never documented and were not even mentioned during our due diligence. There are men turning up looking for payment in cash." She sighed; Delcort know these visits had distressed her. Heck, they had distressed him. "I'm not sure which is worse, these men or Luca's former wife. She is getting tiresome. Not that Luca seems to care—her behavior seems to amuse him."

"Look, I'm sympathetic to Luca's plight, but I'm not releasing funds," said Delcort, picking up where the lawyer stopped. "If he gets any gear, then that psychotic ex-wife of his will steal it again. She has no concept of *owned by Prickle*. As far as she's concerned, if Luca has touched or been in the same room as the gear, then Luca owns it, and so now after the divorce, it's hers."

Boniface grimaced and Delcort continued. "You're a wide-eyed optimist if you think you can sort this, Mister Boniface. There are just too many people and too many problems, and while this situation remains, we're not going to do anything to facilitate this biography."

five

"I've just been talking with the tallest lawyer in the world. Seriously, I've met shorter giraffes."

Montbretia stared at Boniface. They were standing at the corner of a residential street somewhere—Montbretia wasn't quite sure where precisely—in East London. The instructions Boniface had given were to get to Bethnal Green tube station and then walk. Walking wasn't usually difficult, but walking in brand-new, cheap, high-heeled ankle boots was.

As she came toward him, Boniface's eyes surveyed a side street—a solid wall of conjoined two-story houses with no front yards lined either side. "Let me get this straight, Boniface." She could hear the anger in her voice but didn't care. "All this job will take is two meetings, which you can handle—you don't need me involved."

She paused. He was looking down.

"But now you've dragged me across town—literally from Wimbledon in the west to Bethnal Green in the east—having instructed me to pass through some flea-bitten market on the way and deck myself out with what can only be described as 1980s hooker-chic. I'm not feeling it, Boniface."

He was still looking down, refusing to meet her glare.

"I told you this would go wrong, and now we're both working for a client that we shouldn't even call a client because they're not paying us. It's not good business." She waited a beat. "And to make things worse, it's one o'clock and I haven't eaten."

He lifted his head, his eyes scanning up and down, seemingly pausing and examining each separate item: the boots—red, complete with buckles—that pinched and were hell to walk in, the short tight black skirt, the flouncy top made of something scratchy with lots of cheap nylon lace, the random neon patterned jacket, a collection of mismatched scarves dangling from one wrist, and enough cheap bangles on the other to permanently lengthen her arm, all topped with back-combed hair and huge dangly earrings that she remembered each time she moved her head as their momentum slapped her shoulders and tugged her lobes. Thankfully, there hadn't been time to get her hair streaked, otherwise Boniface might have insisted.

"I'm sorry." He faced her directly. "I've messed up—this is bigger than I thought."

Montbretia glowered at him, feeling her anger ebb as she calibrated his reaction. He was sincere in his apology. He was contrite—even if he was hiding it well. If she pushed it, he'd just get angry, and to be honest, she couldn't remember why she was so angry...it wasn't as if she was having her pay cut. "Is this what the 1980s looked like?"

Boniface nodded slowly. "I'm afraid so."

"I feel like a streetwalker." His mouth twitched as he tried to maintain a serious look. "When can I put my own clothes back on?" She held up a carrier bag holding the clothes that she had changed from at the market when she went back in time to the 1980s.

"Very soon," said Boniface.

"I wasn't sure whether to get legwarmers and fingerless gloves."

"No. No need. You're fine." Boniface reached for the carrier bag. "Shall I take that?"

"Why?" Montbretia could feel the bristle of suspicion creeping up on her.

"I need you to do something," he said. His mouth smiled, but his eyes didn't. "And since you're dressed and ready, it would be a shame if you missed out on the fun and games."

Montbretia shut her eyes and willed her voice calm. "Go on."

"Up there..." She opened her eyes, looking in the direction Boniface was now tilting his head. "Number eighty-seven is where Gray Barrington lives."

She wrinkled her forehead.

"Gray Barrington was the founder and original lead singer with Prickle." The wrinkle softened as Boniface continued. "He may...or may not—I don't know until I've spoken to him—be the cause, or at least one of the causes, of Dawn, Danny, and Prickle's problems. Until I've spoken to him in a civilized manner, I won't know."

"You *can* do civilized, Boniface. It just needs a *little* effort." She noticed he didn't respond. "You brought me all this way and made me dress up, just to give you some reassurance?"

He was quiet. She felt her head leaning forward in expectation of a reply to her facetious question. Boniface noticed, wrinkled his nose, and with a shake of his head, no more than a twitch, confirmed that wasn't why she had been summoned. "I need you to get me in." His tone suggested humiliation. She waited for the explanation. "I spoke to him, he told me to...to go away."

"Ah."

"So I need someone else, someone he doesn't know, someone who can get us through the front door, and you're good at this stuff."

"This stuff? You mean good at dressing like a hooker?"

"Good at talking to people. Good at putting people at ease. Good at not confronting them and putting your foot in the door when it's being closed on you." His voice had become a whimper.

"And again I pose the question—why am I dressed for a 1980s

prostitutes' fancy dress party?"

Boniface shifted his weight from one foot to the other, his gaze looking down. "I just thought you should look as nonthreatening as possible."

"Well, I'm certainly threatening the eyeballs of the people of this street." Montbretia glanced down at the fluorescent orange, yellow, and green areas of her jacket. "But I don't see how this makes me less of a threat to him."

Boniface shifted uneasily again. "I just thought that this is a guy who doesn't...understand modern women. He doesn't understand current fashions—he sees them as threatening—so I thought it would ease the way past his front door if you dressed from an era where he actively participated."

"How old is he?"

Boniface pushed out his bottom lip. "Sixty-something, give or take."

"And he only likes women who demean themselves like this?" Montbretia held out her arms, looking down at her new clothes. "What are you saying? He's a misogynist?"

For the first time since she had arrived, Boniface laughed. "Quite the contrary—he likes women as far as I know. His problem is they don't like him." His look became more serious. "Look, I'm not suggesting he's a feminist—simply that, like many men, he's putty in the hands of a smart, good-looking girl who gives off the right signals."

"And if it gets hairy?"

"If he makes a grab for you, kick him and run—I'll be outside the moment you go through that door."

"You?" Montbretia failed to hide her incredulity. "You're not really renowned for your street-fighting prowess."

"He's an old guy."

"You mean, I'm more likely to save you from him?"

"So you're agreed it's pretty low risk."

"As long as you discount the risk I've already sustained by dressing like this and the risk of my further embarrassment."

Boniface grimaced.

"So I knock on the door. What's my story when he answers?"

A slow grin clawed its way across Boniface's visage. "Gray made some decisions which—given what happened subsequently—may now be regarded as less than smart decisions."

Montbretia grunted. "So?"

"You need to understand the scale of these decisions," said Boniface. "Gray quit Prickle and headed for the big money in the States, but that got messed up."

"I thought you told me Prickle were big."

"They became...but when he left they were just a hard-working band not earning much money, and with a small fan base."

"Oh," said Montbretia. "So where was Danny when this happened?"

"He was there—he was in the band," said Boniface. "And like the other guys, he thought the band was dead, but this is where he stepped up and took responsibility. There were gigs the band was contractually obliged to play, and Danny doesn't like disappointed fans so he kept the band together."

"Good for Danny," said Montbretia. "But don't bands get new singers all the time?"

"It was a rough time: The drummer quit to join Gray for his first solo album, their management ended their relationship with the band, and the record label dropped them." Boniface waited a beat. "The record label dropped Prickle but enforced a clause against Gray as the frontman requiring him to record two further albums for them."

"The record label kept Gray but dropped Prickle?" asked Montbretia, noticing the wry smile spreading across Boniface's visage. "Given that Prickle still exist and you're star-struck by them, I'm guessing that things turned around."

"I think more to the point, *Danny* turned things around. It took about 18 months, during which time Prickle recorded a new album with their new drummer and their second new singer, just to stop the band from sinking. They also found a new record label and got new management in place. The first track off Prickle's new album was 'Tattoo Your Name on My Heart,' a song Danny wrote to impress a girl he'd met who he was trying to show that he could be responsible and provide a secure income and home life."

Montbretia waited expectantly as Boniface continued. "'Tattoo Your Name on My Heart' was Prickle's first international mega-hit and was the song that broke the band in the States, making Prickle one of the few bands from the UK to break the States in the 1980s. By this time, the British Invasion twenty years earlier was a distant memory."

"Stop, Boniface! Don't tell me about the band: What happened to the girl?" Montbretia was exasperated; he never focused on things that matter.

"You tell me," said Boniface. Montbretia went to speak but stopped as his face softened. "You met her last night at the office. They've been married for nearly thirty years."

Montbretia went to speak again but stopped, again, gently holding her lower lip between her teeth and feeling her eyes beginning to mist. Her lip released as the smile spread across her face. "Aww."

"And thirty years later, all the material Prickle has put out since Gray left is considered classic rock. And this is where the *quid pro quo* bites Gray in the ass: Danny and Prickle have had the success that Gray thought would be his when he left the band." Boniface tried to hide a smirk. "Seems it wasn't the band holding Gray back…"

Boniface had stopped talking and seemed to be looking expectantly, his eyes darting toward what she presumed was Gray's house. "So, again I ask," said Montbretia. "After I knock on the door, what's my story when he answers?"

"You say you want to meet Gray Barrington—you've been listening to his stuff forever. Tell him your dad loved his stuff—something like that—and make sure you tell him you don't like the direction that Prickle went after he left. Tell him you much prefer the bluesier feel of the band's early songs. Once he's talking, tell him he should write a biography. When he agrees to that, you open the door and give me a shout, and your work is done. Within ten minutes we'll be having lunch."

"Really?"

"It's a plan." Boniface sounded slightly offended.

"A plan?" She sighed. "A plan says the man with the unresolved issues with his former wife, a hard-on for his current client's wife, and who's asking a girl in her twenties to act as bait for an old, lecherous, somewhat past-it rocker."

"You get a new wardrobe on expenses," said Boniface, winking as he turned toward Gray's house. "You're here and you're dressed for the part. Come on, it'll only take two minutes."

six

It's hard to know what is considered the front when you're talking about a circular building.

Logically, the front has the entrance that looks over the main road toward the Albert memorial; after all, this was the Royal Albert Hall. But Danny had qualified the front when he said "the steps," which implied the other front entrance, or as Boniface preferred to think of it, the back entrance. The entrance that didn't have the large hanging banners promoting the charity gig in two weeks, which Prickle would be headlining. Their first gig since Thad Stirling's untimely death.

Boniface understood why Danny and Prickle felt they had to perform. Thaddeus—Thad, as everyone had called him—had died three months previously from pancreatic cancer. He had been dead within a month of his diagnosis. When his widow, Penny, asked Prickle to get involved with the gig—a fundraising effort to support research into pancreatic cancer—there was only one answer, and so in two weeks Prickle would take to the stage of the venerable London venue, with a new singer, and pay tribute to an absent friend.

It might not have been the front, but the broad, shallow stairs leading up to the hall gave the best perspective of the building, and halfway down the stairs Boniface rested on the stone balustrade, watching as the figure of Danny Featherstone appeared, dressed much as he had been yesterday, but with a different, although equally loud, shirt under his old sand-colored jacket.

"How long did I take?"

Boniface pulled out his phone and checked the time. "Not that I was counting, but four minutes, thirty-six seconds. Thirty-seven. Thirty-eight."

Danny reached Boniface, the corners of his mouth twitching. "See, I said I'd be out in under five."

"You said under five, and a cup of tea." Boniface had meant to keep his jest light, but he felt a certain annoyance—he could have spent the last four minutes and thirty-eight seconds getting a drink for himself.

Danny's mouth twitched more noticeably, and he turned to look in the direction from which he had come. His head bobbed, as if scanning the far horizon, then after a moment or two he raised his hand and waved before turning back to Boniface, now grinning and saying nothing.

She appeared at the top of the steps, frizzy blonde hair, a crisp white cotton blouse, a short but not slutty black skirt with an apron, carrying a tray, heading toward Danny. "Your tea, Mister Featherstone."

"Thank you. And it's Danny." The bassist picked the teapot from the tray, poured the tea into a cup, and turned to Boniface. "Milk? Sugar?"

"Yes, and one, please."

He stirred, and then lifted the cup and saucer from the tray. "Thank you. I'll bring the cup back." The waitress turned and ascended the stairs as Danny passed the tea to Boniface. "It tastes better in porcelain." His goofy grin returned. "Where were we?"

Boniface sighed. "Don't I feel like a dick?"

"Tommy said I've got to treat you right. And I never disagree with anything Tommy says." He took two steps, turned, and rested against the balustrade, leaving space for Boniface to rest his saucer. "So. Where are we?"

"I've talked with Gray. You're right—he's an asshole and bitter and is causing problems, but I can't see that he's got the wit to arrange an internet hate campaign. He's not on Twitter, he doesn't have a website, and he's only got a dumb-phone." Danny slowly focused as Boniface continued. "That kid, Danny..."

"Everyone's a kid to Gray, but I find it hard to believe that you had a conversation with Mister Barrington without the words 'chief prick and the little thorns' spilling from his mouth."

"And I believe I have the honor of addressing the chief prick," said Boniface, distracted as a group of Japanese tourists ascended the steps, enthusiastically pointing at the building and pausing on every third step to take a photo. "The only time he said anything vaguely respectful was when he mentioned Thad. Seemed he really rated him as a singer, even if Thad was part of the conspiracy to brainwash *his* audience."

"How did you get in?" asked Danny. "I thought he'd tell you to do a range of physically impossible but sexually explicit activities."

"He did," said Boniface. "Montbretia got me in."

Danny continued. "I knew I liked her. So what else did Montbretia help you get out of Gray?"

"Not a huge amount. You're all unspeakable people. You were a joke for hiring Kit to fill his place."

"But Kit was only with us for five minutes—he didn't even record an album." He softened. "Five minutes, but we still get his fans turning up—they like to see where it started. We come on stage, and it's all a bit surprising for them."

"Well, Gray didn't like Kit. He thought you were smart replacing Kit with Thad, but apart from that, nothing." He took a sip of tea. "Well... there was one thing. He mentioned the name Billy Watkins. Does that mean anything to you?"

Danny paused, narrowing his eyes. "Never heard the name. What was the context?"

"Gray seemed to think that Billy Watkins—another kid—had something against Dawn and you."

Danny pushed out his bottom lip.

"That was what I got from Gray."

"I hope you thanked Montbretia."

"I did," said Boniface. "I took her to lunch."

The bassist stood, pulling up his shoulders to stretch his back. "What about PAD? Did they give you anything?"

"They're angry, if that's what you mean." Boniface paused. "They think you didn't disclose information." He felt a certain indifference to the overly pushy salesman and the tall lawyer he had met.

"They are angry." There was disappointment in the bassist's voice.

"Angry, but not trying to destroy you. That was my take," offered Boniface.

Danny rocked his head from side to side, seemingly contemplating.

"I could believe they might want to renegotiate your deal, but they didn't sound like they want to walk away. They're annoyed. They're frustrated. They hate all the claims that Gray has hit them with—claims that Gray didn't mention when we spoke—but apart from that, their big problem is Luca. What's happening with him?"

Danny relaxed. "Luca is perhaps the most talented musician I have ever worked with. Ever. His playing is sublime—he is technically brilliant, and his musicality is...I run out of superlatives." He paused, defocused, as if he was recalling the playing of the guitarist. "But everything else in Luca's life lacks structure. I think that's the polite way to phrase it."

Boniface felt a slight chill as the broad stairway funneled small gusts toward the concert venue. "Luca does the whole social media thing?"

Danny had the look of a slightly exasperated but still indulgent uncle. "There's only one way to get that phone of his out of his hands—give him a guitar. He's always holding one or the other."

"I'm just throwing this out there," said Boniface, hearing the caution in his own voice. "I got the impression from PAD that Luca had issues, and you know he does the social media stuff.... Is he the source of these stories that are out there?"

"No." Boniface was surprised at how definitive the response was. "Not his style. Luca is fearless—when he's got a problem, he tells me directly. Very directly."

"The wife," said Boniface. "PAD said there was a problem with his wife."

"Bing-Bing."

Boniface raised his eyebrows.

"Missus Parzani, Bing-Bing. Or Bing2, as it gets written." An amused look crossed his face. "Yeah. She's a fiery one, but she's not our problem. However, there is something you could help me with here."

seven

Boniface had the look of a boy with a new girlfriend who knew tonight was the night.

The night.

And he was about to have a shower and get out his best underwear. "I'm surprised you've got time to drag yourself away from your new BFF to come into the office." He didn't seem to notice. "Don't worry, I can carry on without you."

"Could you do something, please?" Montbretia could swear that Boniface had gone deaf since lunch. "It's Luca."

"Luca."

"Prickle's guitarist."

"Prickle, who are not our..."

Boniface cut across. "Prickle, our client." He still seemed unfeasibly joyful. "Prickle who have a gig in two weeks. A charity gig, and some organization is needed, and as you know, their management is refusing to undertake any work."

"Because of Mister Barrington, who likes to live in a time warp and thinks women forty years younger than him are impressed that he was in a band twenty years before they were born."

Boniface seemed to come down slightly from his high, but only far enough to be maginally empathetic. "Yeah, I didn't like him much either. But he was far more pleasant when you were there. Anyway..." He floated back to his high. "Luca has a problem and needs some help."

"Happy to do so," said Montbretia, watching to see if Boniface noticed the sarcasm, "once we have a contract in place and he's made his first payment."

"And there's our problem," said Boniface.

"Well, I'm glad you realize," said Montbretia, pushing her chair back from her desk, spinning to face Boniface, who stepped into her office. She was on home territory: back in her own office, wearing her own clothes—jeans, not as well fitting as Dawn's; white blouse, also not as well fitting as Dawn's; and sneakers—in combination, so much more comfortable than the streetwalker outfit Boniface made her wear to see Gray. And now, safely in her own comfort zone, she was happy to take on Boniface.

Boniface went to speak, then stopped. Waited. And then began. "Luca was made bankrupt two months back—he has no cash. So this thing with Prickle having their bank account frozen is hurting him the most. Danny and the other guys have got money in their own bank accounts—Luca doesn't."

"Well then, Luca should be the one chasing Barrington and that giraffe woman." Montbretia sat forward in her chair, readying herself to spin back to her work.

"Luca is a musician, not a businessman, and in any event, Luca has a bigger problem. Three months ago he got divorced..."

"Well, clearly you're the ideal person to counsel him, as I'm sure the former Missus Boniface would attest."

Boniface smiled. "Veronica and I divorced amicably—at least as amicably as you can when your heart feels like it has been torn out. Missus Parzani, however, has other problems." Boniface bit his lower lip, shaking his head. "At the time of divorce, a financial settlement was agreed. That settlement—not unreasonably—led Bing-Bing, that's the ex-wife, to have certain expectations."

"Why does this story sound like the story you told me about the managers?"

"Quite," said Boniface. "The trouble is, with his bankruptcy, Luca isn't in a position to meet his obligations."

"Ah," said Montbretia, sitting back.

"Ah, indeed. But where many people would get mad, Bing-Bing is getting even. She seems quite a feisty individual...and she's been looking for any asset that she can sell to generate the cash she believes is her right. It doesn't matter who owns the asset; if she can get hold of it, then she takes it and sells it."

"Oh."

"Luca had four guitars. Each was individually built to his specification. They took months to build—the tops were hand-carved from wood chosen for its resonance, the electrics were state of the art. I know nothing about guitars other than these cost about five thousand bucks each and were the tools of his trade."

"Were?"

"Yup. She bribed a crew member—ex–crew member now—and took possession. She sold the four for 250 quid each."

"Twenty-thousand bucks' worth of gear sold for one-thousand pounds?"

Boniface nodded mournfully. "All Luca now owns is the clothes he wears, his phone, and...well, that's it. She's taken the rest and sold it."

"And where do we fit in?" asked Montbretia.

"Luca needs help, but he doesn't want charity—he does have some pride—and Danny..."

"It's alright, Boniface, you can call him 'darling' or 'my true love.' I won't be offended. I realize you've moved on."

"Danny wants us to see if there's anything we can do to help the gear situation."

Montbretia flopped back in her chair, shaking her head. Boniface walked across the room and leaned on the windowsill with his back to the tinted glass. "We do PR, Boniface. Oh, and apparently you do a bit of private investigating." She felt her voice harden. "Since when do we do musical instruments?"

"This is simple PR," said Boniface. "The idea is to get some gear for Luca. The roadies think they can get some guitars, I said we'd see what we can..."

"We?"

"We." A look of smug confidence crossed his face. "See, you already think you're on board."

Montbretia sighed loudly and stood up, crossing her arms. Boniface didn't seem to notice and continued. "Spend five minutes on the internet—search for guitar amps—and find what the main brands are. Then call them and ask to speak with whoever does artist relations. Tell them that Luca Parzani is interested in their gear, and you'll find they will be eating out of your hand. It's a simple trade: They give him gear, he gives them publicity."

"Why am I doing this?" Montbretia felt her crossed arms gripping herself tighter.

In her anger, she missed the sotto voce comment Boniface made, but she could have sworn that he said "you virtually offered." By the time her gaze had burned out his retinas, he was more conciliatory. "Because you're good at it...and it's not going to take long."

"It's not what..." she muttered to herself, not even sure what she was saying. "What sort of idiot is Danny? I mean, I don't like being rude about your BFF, but why are we doing more when all we have done so far—if you look at what we've actually achieved—is fail?"

"Danny is trusting us because Tommy told him he should. And we're doing this because I feel we owe Tommy one, even if this is paying him back indirectly." He relaxed, his upright posture collapsing. "And Prickle are in a bind."

Montbretia dropped her crossed arms and leaned on the back of her chair.

"Besides, I get to hang out with rock stars and models. The fifteen-year-old boy who lives inside my head won't let me turn down this experience. Like every fifteen-year-old boy, I need to get it out of my system."

"Basically, you're a groupie, Boniface. And you know what sort of reputation groupies have?"

Boniface shrugged.

"And does the groupie understand the danger here?" When he didn't seem to be responding, she continued. "No one knows who's started this chaos. No one really knows the extent of whatever the problem is. Have you even checked to see whether we're just talking about a few drive-by posts on Facebook that the happy couple have taken out of proportion?"

"It's more than that," said Boniface. "Remember, we talked to Gray, and I talked to the managers. No one said there isn't a problem."

"But you still don't know exactly what the problem is." She spun her chair and sat down. "Anyway, what are you doing to help?"

Boniface looked sheepish.

"I'm taking advantage of my newly rediscovered independence and the generosity of my friend Gideon Latymer."

"You mean you're driving somewhere."

"Mmmhmmm." Montbretia raised her eyebrows, holding them until Boniface continued. "Danny and the band have found a new singer for the gig—they saw a video of him on YouTube fronting a Prickle tribute band and offered him the gig as a one-off. He's arriving tonight, so I'm going to listen to his first session with the band."

"Where?" Montbretia didn't even make an attempt to sound interested.

"Danny and Dawn's. Danny's got a studio where the band are rehearsing. And after that, I've been invited for dinner—Danny called Dawn while we were chatting earlier." He pushed up the ends of his lips with little sincerity. "It would be rude to let them down after I've already accepted."

eight

"The princess killer," said Gideon as he handed over the keys. "For your use. I retain ownership, so you can go bankrupt and it won't be repossessed. I'll also meet the cost of insurance—for you and any driver you nominate—as well as the maintenance, and I've had one of those bluetooth things fitted so you can use your phone...to do navigation or music or actually talk to people." He shrugged. "Montbretia will understand."

She understood, but she didn't love the car. "It's not a classic, Boniface. It's just old. But it is very sweet of Gideon." The night before Boniface's driving ban expired, there had been a knock at his front door. Gideon stood, holding the keys in front of him. He still felt a continuing need to apologize for his behavior when Boniface was implicated in a murder he didn't commit, and he hoped the gesture might demonstrate his contrition in a practical manner.

"Why princess killer?" said Montbretia slowly, when Boniface relayed the story the next day.

"It's the car—the same make and model, a Mercedes-Benz W140 with a 2.8 liter, straight six, petrol engine and automatic gearbox—that was carrying the then most famous woman in the world on the night she died in Paris." That alone was enough to ensure that Boniface always wore his seatbelt, and given that he had stopped drinking quite some time ago now, he could always be sure that he would be sober.

But he was still cautious about driving anyone who wanted to behave like a princess, and preferred to call it the barge due to the way that it wallowed. But the wallowing was not a problem; the car was comfortable and to date it had performed its intended function of transporting him from place A to place B with 100 percent consistency.

And this bluetooth thing was great.

One of the first things Boniface had done with Montbretia after they met was ask her to accompany him when he went to replace his phone. She had refused to let him buy a flip phone like his last model. Instead, she insisted that he buy one that could "you know, Boniface, actually do useful things."

And one of those useful things was maps and navigation. Danny had explained to Boniface that he and Dawn didn't so much live in a place—more at a GPS location, which happened to be near a narrow country lane. As they stood outside the Royal Albert Hall, he had put his finger on the map. "Navigate to here and you'll find us." As Boniface drove down the long, narrow, winding lanes of the Surrey Hills, he was pleased to hear the directions shouted out by his phone be relayed via bluetooth through the car's speakers.

He wasn't sure what route he had followed, since his phone told him to leave the main road, and he didn't know exactly where he was, but he knew that it was the Surrey Hills. There had been a big sign—*Surrey Hills, area of outstanding natural beauty*—and the road had then inclined upward, winding into a forest.

The directions had led him over the brow of a hill from where he could see the valley floor sweep below him and everywhere apart from the sky and a red-brick church was green. As he followed the road into the valley, he was directed from one narrow road, to another narrower, to one narrower still and with additional twists. And just to add to the fun, this narrow twisting lane was cut through its surroundings, leaving steep banks on either side. Steep banks with sandstone projections that had been smoothed by passing cars, and a canopy of trees enclosing the top of the route. It was nearly an hour and a half until sunset, but already Boniface had felt the need to switch on his lights.

Heading south, he reached a village. Shere.

Old is a relative term. In the UK, there are several measures of old—most are based around events in the history of the British Empire. There is, however, one measure of old on which all British citizens agree: Domesday.

With the Norman Invasion led by the man who became known as William the Conqueror, the British Isles were changed permanently. Having invaded and conquered in 1066, William set about assessing his new dominion. He wanted to know what was there so he could levy tax.

The survey, an inventory of the land, people, and assets—recorded in what the overrun population colloquially called the Domesday Book—was completed in 1086 and now stands as one definitive test of old. If your town or village is in the Domesday Book, it is old. If it is not, then you're just a jumped-up oik with new money and ideas above your station. If you can prove that your building is Norman—in other words, that it was a construct of the invading Norman hoards—then you can scrape a claim to being old. But younger than that, and you are just a kid, as Gray Barrington would call you.

Shere was officially old. However, while listed in Domesday, most of the architecture was a mixture of wood-beam Tudor and red-brick Victorian.

The tiny but picturesque village was only fifteen miles from the outer limits of London's sprawl, but Boniface knew it was the last recognizable waypoint on his journey. It took him 90 seconds to pass from one end of the village to the other, and only that long because the street was narrow and cars were coming the other way. As he left the village, he knew he had to rely on his phone to guide him, although, ironically, while the navigation system could still find the satellites in the sky that it needed for direction, he had long since left phone reception behind.

Relying solely on the voice of his phone, he followed the narrow strips of tarmac, occasionally passing driveways and once or twice turning at junctions. "In thirty yards, your destination is on the right," announced the navigator. Boniface took his foot off the accelerator and allowed the weight of the barge to slow his forward movement.

A stone-covered driveway came into sight, and Boniface turned right, crunching along the track, passing a brick house and drawing to a halt with a slight skid on the loose surface when he reached a cluster of cars.

He got out and stretched. "Come to where we're making music," Danny had said. Boniface looked around. In addition to the house, there were two barn-like structures: old brick footings with the main structure formed from blackened rough-cut overlapping planks. On the nearer, a row of LEDs gently winked around the eaves, reassuringly confirming that the valuable antique car—a passion shared with Tommy Newby, who had referred Dawn and Danny to Boniface—was under constant electronic vigilance.

He listened. Rock bands make noise, right? Surely that was half the point of being in a band, and Boniface couldn't see any neighbors who were likely to complain.

But all he could hear was birds chirping.

A door opened forcefully in the far barn, and a tall man with curly hair that reached halfway down his back walked out, stopped, and turned to face where he had come from. He shouted back in the direction he had just come from; with each syllable he gestured with outstretched arms to emphasize what he was saying. Boniface didn't recognize the language, but he recognized Luca Parzani from his photos and presumed the language he was shouting was Italian.

Parzani stopped, pulled the phone is his right hand closer, tapped on the screen, then started walking swiftly toward the cars. Every few yards he looked back over his shoulders and shouted something.

He reached the parking area and headed for an anonymous small beige Korean car. Boniface didn't know the manufacturer, but he recognized the type. It was the perfect rental car: totally anonymous—it would never annoy anyone so it would never get vandalized, and it always offered perfect reliability. He guessed that Danny was paying for it and had made the choice of model in case Bing-Bing tried to take possession.

Without acknowledging Boniface, Luca got in the car, reversed, spun the wheels as he began to move forward, and accelerated to the gate, turning left and disappearing.

Boniface followed the path Luca had just taken and stepped into the barn, taking a moment to get used to the dull light of the lobby. In front of him there was a small office-like alcove with a desk. Sitting, hunched over the desk, Danny was talking softly but quickly on the phone.

There was a sound of shuffling from the room to his left, and the lobby became darker as a figure stood between the large room and the lobby. "Boniface, right? Just Boniface. No Mister, no first name, just Boniface."

"That's it," said Boniface, looking up at the big black figure. He was shorter than the giraffe in her mega heels, but still about 6' 2", broad, and deep. In a fight, Boniface would want this guy on his side.

"I like your style, man. I'm Mel, and you know my brother Danny." He held a fist over his heart as he let his gaze indicate the alcove where Danny sat, releasing his fist and reaching forward to shake Boniface's hand.

He'd never put his hand in a vice, but Boniface reckoned he would feel less pain if he did. Mel was pure physical strength, but then again, he did hit things for a living. Typically, he would spend two or three hours a night hitting things, and hitting things constantly with all four limbs.

A heavyweight boxer, by contrast, might take twelve three-minute rounds. Thirty-six minutes. And much of that time would be walking around or hugging the other guy to stop him from throwing punches. Boniface would lay money on the drummer every time.

"Come in, man," said the drummer, turning back into the bigger room. "Have you been here before?"

Boniface shook his head.

"Welcome to where the music is made." Mel Grant led him into the room filled with instruments—Boniface surveyed his new surroundings, noting what seemed to be stations for five musicians arranged in a pentagon.

A drum kit stood on the farthest point. Boniface started counting the drums—there were at least fifteen, including two kick drums; at least ten cymbals; four cowbells; enough electronic pads, Boniface guessed; and what looked like an electronic xylophone.

He felt his feet hit the floor, but the sound was wrong. "Acoustic treatment," said Mel. "Listen." He clapped his hands. There was the sound of flesh slapping, but no brightness, no echo. "See the fabric?" He indicated the fabric-covered walls and ceilings, lit by small white lights on brushed steel rails. "Basically, there's a whole heap of rockwool behind there, which kills the reverb, so what you hear is the sound but not the slap-back that you're used to hearing in a normal room."

To one side of the drums, a row of five bass guitars stood in a rack next to a stack of black amps. On the other side, an old guitar was plugged into a small amplifier. The bassist's and guitarist's stations were each completed with a microphone with a long lead snaking across the room. At the fourth point of a pentagon was another microphone, its lead also running across the room, and no instruments.

"So where's the new guy?" asked Boniface. "I was hoping to hear him.

Are you still waiting for him to arrive?"

"Ah," said Mel. He grimaced, looking away as if checking whether they were being overheard.

"Uh oh."

"Where had you got to in the story?" asked the drummer.

"You found a guy on YouTube...he was arriving tonight, but I guess not," said Boniface.

"Oh, he arrived. He arrived," Mel sighed. "It goes like this: We saw this guy on YouTube who was based in Auckland."

"Auckland, New Zealand?"

"Is there another Auckland?" said the drummer, for the first time starting to look weary. "We saw his performances on YouTube: He wasn't Thad, but he had power and a good tone, and he sung the songs with conviction. He knew the words, and he looked like he could handle an audience, so we thought why not get him in for the gig?" He sat down on his drum stool, his huge biceps threatening each kit piece. "You know we've got a problem with our management?"

Boniface nodded.

"Right, so we made the arrangements to fly this guy over and put him up at a hotel. Danny got it sorted and paid for everything. Anyway, as the arrangements are being made, the guy says that he'll be flying in from São Paulo. We didn't care where he came from, so we made the arrangements and today we sent a taxi to pick him up at Heathrow, take him to the hotel, and then bring him here at five PM once he'd had a chance to rest and have a wash."

Boniface stepped over to a stool by the rack of basses and sat.

"When he arrived, he looked whiter than the guy in the video, his hair was longer, and boy had he put on weight. But, y'know, we only saw a video on YouTube; people change, and we couldn't be certain when the video was shot.

"But he could sing?" asked Boniface.

"The guy in the video? Oh yeah, he could sing. This bozo?" The drummer looked down, shaking his head at the memory. "The lisp and the thick Portuguese accent we might have been able to deal with. We might have been able to work with the mumbling. But he didn't know what a tune was—seriously, there was no melody—and he thought he had a great falsetto: I can still hear the screaming now."

"I'm sorry, I'm not understanding," said Boniface. "You make it sound like this was a different person."

"It was! The guy had sold the gig on eBay. Sing at the Royal Albert Hall with Prickle. This guy from São Paulo is a complete Prickle super-fan; he paid ten-thousand bucks for the gig and was totally overawed at meeting his heroes. The pity is that he couldn't sing, his heroes were mightily pissed, and as you've seen from Danny, the search for a new singer is now pretty urgent."

"So what's happened to the guy?" asked Boniface.

"Newt..." Mel pointed to the three rows of keyboards stacked on a triangular stand, as if to indicate the keyboard player Newton Jubb at the fifth point on the pentagon. "Newt was so appalled with the whole situation that he took the guy back to his hotel and will then take him to Heathrow, pay his fare home, and wait until he is gone."

nine

Boniface sat at what he guessed was probably an interior designer's idea of a perfect table for a country kitchen.

If pushed—and in the same position—he probably would have made a similar recommendation: long, unvarnished oak, with wooden chairs on one side and at the head, and a bench on the other side. It married the basic requirements for form and function.

His biggest gripe, as he sat in one of the wooden chairs on the side of the table, was the lack of padding. Already his bum was feeling weary.

Not that he really cared about the discomfort of his bum; it was just that the discomfort was distracting him.

Distracting him when he had an opportunity to sit and look at Dawn.

She had been standing since he arrived, tending to the dinner that she was cooking, and as she walked around the kitchen—stirring, adding a pinch, looking and assessing, increasing the heat, decreasing the heat—Boniface sat back and did what the teenage boy inside told him to do: admire. Who cares if you're on a hard seat if you get to see your teenage fantasy up close?

Well...teenage fantasy but clothed.

As had been the case twenty-four hours previously, Dawn's choice of clothes was unfussy but stylish: jeans that fitted—a marginally different shade from yesterday—a white T-shirt that fitted without any stretching or bulging, wedding and engagement rings, and a single bangle, also different from yesterday's but equally unadorned. When she found him—chatting with Mel Grant in the studio—she had kissed him. It wasn't the kind of kiss that the teenage boy inside his head wanted—just a peck on the cheek—but it seemed to hold genuine affection. "Come and have something to eat," she said.

He didn't need to be asked twice. In fact, he probably stopped listening after the word "come".

"I'm sorry for dragging you away from the boys," said Dawn, turning toward Boniface. Something inside him melted as her gray eyes seemed to involuntarily open to express regret, while the smallest tilt of her head reassured. It was a simple enough gesture, but it left Boniface feeling that all his strength had left his body.

If Dawn was talking, that was probably a sign that he had been silent. If he had been silent, then that was a sign he had been staring. Staring when he should have been asking questions, trying to get to the bottom of...trying to understand what the problem was...before the latest problem.

"No worries," he brightened. "To be honest, I was glad to get out of there—it seemed pretty tense."

"They all looked so...serious, and I heard Luca shouting," said Dawn. "I've never seen my bear get so angry." Her voice was a whisper. "He was so hurt. You know, Thad..."

Boniface nodded, not saying anything, but keeping eye contact, knowing where his eyes would land if he didn't force them away.

There was the sound of a soft, moist plop on the range behind Dawn and she turned, grabbed a wooden spoon, and focused her attention back on the main pot.

"So while Danny and the others are in the studio making noise, what does a normal day involve for you?" asked Boniface.

She kept the spoon slowly stirring the pot in front of her as she turned her head toward Boniface. "A lot of the time, I'm off taking pictures." She tilted her head toward a large print of a Gothic tower topped with battlements, shot against a blue sky with puffy white clouds. The trees around the tower only seemed to reach one-quarter of its height, giving it a sense of size. "That's one of mine."

"Wow." Boniface stood and placed himself directly in front of the print, looking at the detail of the stonework edged with red brick. "Stunning building, stunning photo." Dawn flushed slightly, rapidly looking back to her pot and stirring with renewed vigor. "Where is this?"

"About four miles in that direction." She jutted her chin forward. "Four miles by foot or horse. Farther if you drive—all the roads go north/south; only the locals understand how to go east or west."

"Where did you get it printed?" asked Boniface.

"Here." Boniface felt his head twist too quickly, letting Dawn know that he was surprised at her skill. He stumbled to recover. "I didn't know the printing systems you could get at home were that good."

"They're not, at least not at the consumer end. But if you spend some money, then..." Her voice trailed off as she bent to look in the oven. "And I'll let you in on my dirty little secret." She wiped her hands on a cloth as she walked over to Boniface. "This wasn't the first time I shot this tower, and it wasn't my first print. In fact, it wasn't the second or the third or the fourth time—for either."

Boniface stepped to the side to allow Dawn to face the picture directly. "I'm sorry," he said as she moved closer than he expected, brushing his arm, and then wondered why he was apologizing.

"You see there?" Dawn pointed toward the top of the tower. "It's a bit noisy—I tried to balance the sharpening and the noise reduction. If you step back to here..." she put her arm around Boniface's waist and her other hand on his closest shoulder to softly move him back, "you can't see it, but if you move here," she glided him forward, "you can see it's just a bit overdone on the edge of the octagonal tower." She dropped her arm, returning to the range as Boniface wiped a bead of sweat from his forehead. "But there's an emotion in that picture—a vibrancy—that I love, even if it's not perfect."

He pulled back his seat, noticing a tremor in his hand, and sat. "So... your dirty little secret?"

Dawn giggled. "It's part photography, part exercise. I go out three, four days a week taking pictures. Sometimes I walk; sometimes I borrow a horse and ride. I can spend weeks taking the same picture every day, because every day the light will be different, the landscape changes, the plants change. You can never get the same picture—you always take a new and unique picture."

She reached into a cupboard.

"Fresh today." She placed a loaf of bread on a breadboard on the table. "And then I sort through the pictures and print my favorites, but there are so many choices—different papers, different inks, different settings—so every print can come out different. Many times I've taken a shot thinking it was the best I've ever taken, then I've come home and printed the picture. When you go from this," she held her fingers to indicate a small square, "to this," she held her hands apart, unwittingly thrusting her chest forward, "you notice things."

"You would notice," said Boniface, sliding his chair toward the table.

"I come home, I print out the picture, and it'll be great...I mean *really* good, but there will just be something. Something small, so I'll go back to the original image, process it a bit more, print it again, and it will be better, but..." She made an odd sound as she grimaced. "So the next day I'll go out again and take the same photo, then come home and go through the same process. It can be like a meditation—you just keep focusing on one thing, constantly repeating, and in the end..." she pointed with her eyes toward the picture of the Gothic tower behind Boniface, "in the end, you live with the imperfection."

"So where do you go to take your pictures?" asked Boniface.

"All over—I guess you'd call my territory the five-mile radius from here." She grimaced. "Funny. I was born twenty-five miles away, but it's like a different world. It was a different world—I never knew about this place. It was only when Danny and I got married that someone suggested the church at Albury. Do you know it?"

Boniface felt his head confirm that he didn't.

"You should," said Dawn. "If you go back to Shere, turn left and follow the path across the fields. You'll soon find it—it's in the grounds of Albury Park. It's old—very old, Domesday old—although like all old buildings, it's been added to. The last guy was in this sort of Catholic sect, and he didn't want the peasants near his house, so he built this new Protestant church in the village, then he built a Catholic church for his sect, and then he got Pugin—I looked him up; he's the guy who did the interior of the Houses of Parliament—" Boniface felt his eyebrows raise, "to convert one wing of this tiny Norman church into a mausoleum, and it's stunning. I won't describe it—you need to go. It's not used as a church anymore, but a charity looks after it so you can visit at any time. When you get there, you'll see why we fell in love with the place and had to get married there, and that's how we discovered this area."

She laughed softly. "The funny thing is, even with so many churches, this whole area used to be so lawless. All the old houses around here have disproportionately large cellars from the time when people would do a bit of rustling, do a bit of stealing, and then hang out in the hills. It was so remote up here that no one got caught." Her voice brightened. "Anyway, are you ready for some food?"

"Definitely," said Boniface.

"Well, cut yourself some bread—I told you, it's fresh, it didn't come from a supermarket."

"I'm sorry," said Boniface, flushing slightly. "You mean it's your own bread."

"I didn't grow the wheat and mill it, but I did make the bread today. And the vegetables in the soup were all grown here." She placed two large steaming bowls with carrots, peas, onions, and spinach floating in the dark liquid on the table: one in front of Boniface, the other where she sat.

"Thank you. It looks amazing," said Boniface. "And all grown by you?"

"Grown and cooked by me," said Dawn.

"Should I go and call?" Boniface pointed loosely in the direction of the studio.

"No need—they'll come when they're ready. When the boys are working, they never know when they're going to be finished, so I prepare something that's going to be ready when they say 'NOW!' but which won't spoil if they spend an extra hour rehearsing. Soup is good because it's not too heavy if they're eating late at night—there's nothing worse than fat rockers."

Boniface took a mouthful. "It tastes even better than it looks."

"Thank you." Dawn smiled. "I didn't know whether the new singer was going to be a vegetarian, so I didn't include any meat." Boniface matched her ironic grin. "Anyway. Tell me about your investigations—Danny mentioned you were busy today."

"Yeah. Strange day," said Boniface, leaning forward to cut a slice of bread.

"You can dunk," said Dawn, pointing between the bread and Boniface's soup. "So what made the day strange?"

"As you would expect, it's no one's fault, and everyone blames everyone else, and no one seems to know what they've done that's a problem. But the thing that's odd is this one name came up, and no one seemed to recognize it."

"Oh?" said Dawn.

"Billy Watkins," said Boniface.

There was a small crash as Dawn's spoon hit her bowl, splashing soup over the table.

Boniface looked up to see her face flush, her chin trembling. "I'd better go and check on the boys," she said as she stood, leaving her soup.

ten

Danny slid out of the black Audi A8 and stretched, feeling the stiffness that comes from a fitful nap grabbed on the sofa in the studio alcove. "I ache, Sven," he said, leaning on the car door and talking through the open window. "Really ache. I'm getting too old for this shit. All I had to do was walk to the house and up the stairs, but..."

The drum roadie, who was always keen to drive, nodded. "And if you hear anything from Reuben, call." Sven nodded again, the large stretched piercing in the center of his earlobe, lined with dark-colored bone, looking like a fulcrum on which his head moved. "I'll be back in five."

He took the stairs two at a time, both flights, reaching the landing outside Boniface's office, where he peered through the wired safety glass in the door. He lightly tapped with his index and middle fingers on his right hand—a brief rhythm resonated, and within a few seconds Montbretia's face appeared from a room on the left with a slightly confused look.

Her frown fell away, replaced by a broad smile as she recognized him, cantering for two steps and slowing as she reached the door. Cantering... he looked at Montbretia's ponytail, the ends flicking across the shoulders of her white cotton blouse as her head twisted.

"I was wondering who would knock like that," she said, pushing the door and leaning to hold it as he entered. "And now I know. Is he expecting you?"

"Nah, I just dropped by—it's only a flying visit." Montbretia left the door to swing as she turned toward Boniface's office. Her step was light but confident as she bounced three steps in front of him before leaning around Boniface's door and knocking once.

"Visitor for you." She stepped back and was gone before Danny had his foot into Boniface's office.

"We didn't have a meeting scheduled, did we?" Boniface stood up quickly—the look of confusion giving way to a businesslike greeting. "I haven't got anything new to tell you, although we're working hard to get something sorted for Luca, and there are a few people it would be good to talk with. Anyway..." he indicated the deep leather sofa facing across the room. "Please sit. Do you want a tea? Coffee?"

"No...no...nothing for me," said Danny, remaining standing. He caught his reflection in the window cutting through the center of two walls—if the band weren't going to tour for a while, then he was going to need to exercise. Who was he kidding—he already needed to exercise. "I just wanted to apologize for last night. It was a complete…you know…and I just ignored you and…"

Boniface visibly relaxed. "It's not a problem—really—you had quite a *challenge* to deal with." He paused and then continued, his voice darker. "Have you sorted things out?"

Danny snorted. "The first half, yeah. The big issue, no." He moved to stand more clearly out of Boniface's personal space. "Our would-be new friend is on a plane and should be in Brazil around now. Luckily, because of our dispute with PAD, a contract hadn't been drawn up for the guy, hence he had no legal claim against us. I paid for the flight here and the hotel, and Newt paid for the flight home last night." He sighed. "So that's done. The big problem is that I haven't found a singer for the gig, but I'm working on it."

Boniface said, "Well, if…"

"Thanks, man, but I really came here to say sorry," said Danny. "I'm on my way to the Albert Hall again. There's a lot of stuff that PAD would usually sort. I've got Sven—Mel's drum tech—driving me. He loves driving—and he loves people's reaction when they see him in the car."

The confusion crept over Boniface's visage.

"He's tattooed and pierced," said Danny, pointing to his ears, nose, and arms as if that explained the situation. "People don't expect to see a guy like that driving a dull businessman's car." His tone became more matter-of-fact. "And it's good to have him with me—he can check out the practical stuff for this gig."

Danny moved to the door and looked back. "What went on with you and Dawn last night?"

He could have sworn that Boniface blushed.

"When?" asked Boniface.

"I mean, did she seem alright to you?"

"Yeah," said Boniface. He paused, seemingly replaying something in his head. "But thinking about it, she did seem a bit…I don't know…there was an odd reaction."

Danny frowned and cocked his head.

"I mentioned that name to her: you know, Billy Watkins." Danny listened. "She seemed…" He shrugged. "Disconcerted?"

"What did she say?"

"She didn't. She went outside."

"That's probably when she came in," said Danny. "I was on the phone. She was cat-like, you know, nuzzling up against me. But that call took an hour." He looked up, feeling a small jolt. "You weren't on your own for all that time."

"No. Mel came in for some food. We had a good chat, and after that I left—I figured you were busy, so I didn't disturb you when I went." Boniface straightened, his voice slightly strained. "Why? What did

Dawn say to you?"

"That's the thing," said Danny. "She didn't. I was on the phone—she just came and purred around me, then went." He rested on the doorframe. "By the time I had made all the calls I could make, I was so wound up that I didn't want to go back into the house and wake up Dawn as I thrashed around getting into bed, so I crashed on the sofa in the studio."

He stood away from the doorframe, pushing his shoulders forward to stretch the muscles in his back. "It's not the first time I've slept there, and the next morning is always a little bit less pleasant than the time before." He let his muscles relax. "I guess I must have kipped there for about three hours and finally gave up at about six, when I went inside. I made us some tea and took it up to Dawn, but she wasn't there."

Boniface showed a look of surprise.

"That's not totally unusual—it was after first light but before sunrise, and sometimes she goes out early to take photos. But it didn't look like she had slept in the bed, and she hadn't taken anything with her as far as I could see." Boniface frowned and Danny answered the silent request for elaboration. "She left her phone, which is not totally unusual—coverage is so spotty in the hills that sometimes all you're carrying is a heavy clock. She didn't seem to have taken any cameras." He exhaled deeply. "It's as if aliens came down and took her."

Boniface stood silent.

"So she didn't say anything to you?" Boniface shook his head. "I guess she'll be home by the time I get back, but I just wondered..." He stood up straight. "Look, man, I've got to shoot, but if you hear from her, give me a shout. Let's stay in touch."

As he passed, without breaking stride, he tapped a rhythm on Montbretia's open door. "See you, Monty."

eleven

Veronica Rutherford felt the pressure at the bridge of her nose and softly massaged the throb with a thumb and two fingers. She sighed as she released, opening her eyes to focus on her breakfast companion, her ex-husband.

He was doing that thing he did when he started to get excited— leaning forward, his head tilting forward and back imperceptibly, with his eyes opening wider. He wanted her reaction. He wanted her help.

She checked her watch. Ten AM. Far too early. She should have still been at home with a coffee and the papers, but instead she was in a restaurant that catered to the breakfast-meeting crowd. Or rather, in a restaurant where—since there would be staff preparing for lunch—you could get something to eat if you knew the manager, and because this was three minutes' walk from her office and served good enough food, Veronica knew the manager.

She resettled herself in her chair, giving a gentle tug to the seams of her dress just above her hips, feeling the material straighten around her shoulders. "Please tell me you haven't got the hots for her and this isn't some desperate attempt to play the hero."

Boniface seemed almost hurt; he had obviously been expecting a different response, and as he scrambled to deny the implicit accusation she continued. "From what I've heard, they're utterly devoted. It's not even the stuff of romance novels—there are no obstacles to their love."

Her ex-husband paused, then seemed to deflate, his tone slightly disappointed. "They talked about doing some sort of a reality TV show—you know, at home with..."

Veronica felt herself frown involuntarily.

Boniface's tone remained subdued. "I didn't know how to tell them it would be awful telly. Really tedious. After the first five minutes, you'd figure they were never going to fight—nothing like the Osbournes. And then they're class traitors. They've left their roots but haven't been fully accepted on the next social echelon. Remember, Danny is mates with Tommy Newby—he's not the sort of guy you invite 'round when you go and meet the Ambassador."

The restaurant sat where the top end of Shaftesbury Avenue met New Oxford Street at a 45-degree angle, and it mirrored that angle, with two glass-fronted windows converging toward the east of the building. The large windows let in light, which cast deep shadows but also meant that one diner would be framed by a halo of light. In this case, it was

Boniface who was backlit, casting his visage into gloom—physically and metaphorically.

"But the TV series isn't today's problem. You're fiddling, and you're going to break something that isn't broken."

"No. It *is* broken." Boniface was cautious but firm in his assertion. "Dawn is missing."

"Dawn wasn't there when Danny woke up, you said. You also said that Danny said this wasn't unusual. And, to quote yet another fact you told me, Danny doesn't know when Dawn left because he was sleeping in an outbuilding. In other words..." She took a sip of coffee, becoming increasingly frustrated with the delay of her scrambled eggs. "In other words, Dawn might have gone for a walk five minutes before Danny woke up, and could be home by now."

Boniface deflated further. "She could." He leaned forward. "But even if she does come back, you didn't see her reaction last night." Veronica remained silent—with the slightest twitch she indicated for Boniface to continue. "I mentioned this guy Billy Watkins, and it was like...it was like she had a seizure: She dropped her spoon—into her soup, which splashed halfway across the table...not that she noticed it—and she dashed out of the room. This wasn't a mild reaction; this was...I don't know...I don't want to say fear, but it was certainly a primeval reaction. This was something she couldn't control. This was something that made her react physically and emotionally." He sat back in his chair. "This is something that matters."

Veronica looked at her former husband. He certainly looked rational. He had dressed himself properly—but he always did wear good suits, and this was a good suit. He had obviously washed. He was feeding himself. Nothing seemed wrong or out of place, but one small incident with a woman he had only met 36 hours earlier seemed to be driving him.

"If it didn't matter—if it wasn't something to be worried about—then Danny wouldn't have turned up at my office this morning. He didn't need to see me in person—if he wanted to apologize, he could have called. He could have sent an email or a text. There's any number of things he could have done—especially since his time is limited at the moment. But instead, he went out of his way and came to see me."

Boniface could be laid-back. He could be trusting. Laid-back and trusting to the point that it seemed that he didn't care, but something seemed to be niggling him. "What do you want from me?"

Veronica had a sinking feeling as she heard the words drop out of her mouth. The dread dissipated as she heard his response. "A bit of common sense? Some thoughts about who might have some background on Dawn? She would have been modeling about thirty years ago, so have you got any ideas of someone who might have been around then who might have an idea about what's going on?"

"Thirty years ago, you and I were still at school, and dinosaurs roamed freely in the hills." She rested her head on her hand and defocused. "I guess the guy who would know about models would be a photographer."

Boniface nodded once.

"Do you remember the fat guy with the mustache who used to be on staff?" She hesitated. "Terry Meyerson, I think his name was?"

Boniface's grimaced. "I remember. Obsessed with his bowel movements; he couldn't start work until he'd had a good shit and then described his output in nauseating detail. Some people read the runes, others read tea leaves, but Terry predicted the future based on the texture, color, and shape of his bowel movements."

"And the contents of today's mustache would form the topic of tomorrow's bowel movements." She grimaced. "If you've got the stomach for it, he's probably the one to ask first."

Boniface pulled out his phone and checked the time. "He's a photographer; he won't be up yet. But that's a good idea—I'll go and see him this afternoon."

"My pleasure," said Veronica. "I'm just pleased to have a chat that doesn't end with you asking me to dig through our archives."

"Ah," said Boniface. "Now that you mention it, since we're talking about pre-internet history, dinosaurs, and all that, could you have a quick look and see if you can find anything about this Billy Watkins guy? See if there are any links to Dawn?"

twelve

Boniface left Veronica and walked down Shaftesbury Avenue, the main artery of London's theater district and the fastest route to find another person who was there when the dinosaurs were wondering about their continued evolution.

Gray had been pretty dismissive about Kit, but then he would be—Kit was the singer who had filled Gray's place and helped Danny when Prickle made good on their contracts after Gray walked.

Kit had a very powerful, almost operatic voice, but he didn't last long in the band—only about a year. There were no albums released with him performing, but there were a few TV shows and live performances that had been uploaded to YouTube. "Funny thing," Danny had said to Boniface as they chatted outside the Royal Albert Hall the previous day. "Kit was the first guy to sing 'Tattoo Your Name on My Heart'. We nearly recorded it with him, but when he told us that he wanted out, we felt it better to get the new guy in who could tour with us in support of the album he sung on. That new guy was Thad, so it turned out good for all of us. And Kit was there when it mattered—he was always honest with us, and we've stayed great mates."

According to Danny, Kit loved the performance side of being in the band but hated everything else—in particular, he hated being in a band that was constantly on the road. The touring fatigued, and so he quit. Instead of being in a band, he went on to perform on the West End stage, becoming one of the leading stars of musical theater.

Boniface reached the theater, named after a long-dead English actor, and a mirror image of the theater at the other end of the block. What had once been white stone faced onto Shaftesbury Avenue. Posters advertised the show and highlighted its star: Kit Flambeau. The name Christopher Edington, which his birth certificate still showed, was an otherwise forgotten memory following a suggestion by Danny when he felt the band wanted to reflect that their new singer had more fire than the last guy.

Boniface turned right, following the side street on the edge of the theater. Immediately the change was visible. No longer stone-fronted, the side and rear elevations of the theater were red brick with yellow painted concrete details around the doors and windows.

The street had also changed. He had left the bustle of the tourist trap and was now heading into the seedier side of Soho, at the seedier end of Soho, knowing that if he kept walking he would find the building that had housed London's first strip bar offering full-frontal nudity. Now this area was a magnet for low-rent brothels populated by trafficked hookers, sleazy strip clubs, and money exchanges. It was a strange convergence, but thinking about it, both areas probably attracted tourists equally.

Boniface turned right again to find the theater's stage door—a black lump of wood that was intended more as a fire exit than as an entrance for stars. He grabbed the scuffed steel knob and heaved the door, stepping into the gloom lit dimly by an exposed incandescent bulb.

"I'm sorry, sir," said a voice to his right. "The box office is at the front." Boniface looked to the voice: A small man with loose gray skin that had lost its elasticity, wearing a white shirt with small straps on the shoulders to affix epaulettes, dropped his newspaper next to a cap on the shelf beside him. He stood from his stool, as if this added authority to his implied instruction.

"Oh, hi," said Boniface. "I was wondering what time Kit Flambeau arrives."

"He's not here, sir," said the gray-faced man.

"I get that," said Boniface. "It's 10:30 in the morning, and the performance isn't until 7:30 this evening. What I want to know is when he arrives."

"He arrives when he arrives, sir." The guard was apparently being polite—he was certainly using the words a polite person would use—but he seemed unable to care about Boniface's question.

"Okay, thank you," said Boniface and turned, pushing the fire door to leave.

As he heard the door being yanked shut behind him, Boniface felt the stab of his eyes adjusting too quickly to the daylight and became aware of the noise of the city: people shouting, bicycle couriers blowing their whistles, black cabs driving past, construction workers thrashing masonry with mechanical tools, and a van with the word Gas on the side beeping every four seconds for no apparent reason.

He stood with his back to the door, letting his vision track along the stores with a view of the stage door: a Lebanese restaurant, a money broker, a convenience store, a euphemistically named massage parlor with a minicab office above, a betting shop, and directly opposite a bar with a sign advertising its suitability as a place for users of a high-profile gay hookup phone app to meet.

There seemed only one sensible choice, and he set off for the convenience store.

"Hi, how are you?" he said to the Indian-looking man behind the counter just inside the door, the whiff of burning incense filling his nostrils.

"Good morning you, sir," replied the man, his white-toothed grin like a beacon in the gloomy store.

"It's a lovely day, isn't it?" said Boniface.

"Good morning you, sir," said the other man. Boniface was sure the thick accent was Indian.

"It feels like spring," said Boniface.

The other man continued to smile broadly, nodding vigorously. "Good morning you, sir."

Boniface paused. "I wonder if you can help me?"

"You want newspaper?" asked the other man.

Boniface shook his head.

"Cigarette?"

"No. Thank you, no," said Boniface.

"Whisky?"

Boniface laughed, shaking his head.

The other man kept his head still, his eyes moving from left to right, exposing eyeballs bloodshot at their extremes before he ducked under the counter, returning a few seconds later. "Girlie girls?" He held up a magazine.

Boniface shook his head once, and the other man ducked back under the counter, returning a moment later. "Asian?" He held up a magazine with a naked Japanese-looking girl who appeared to be no more than twelve. Boniface felt a sickening feeling in his gut and pulled a sour face.

The man ducked again, coming up with another magazine. "Granny?" he asked, holding up a magazine picturing a thirty-something woman with sticky fluid around her mouth, the number 69 prominently emblazoned in the top-right corner of the magazine.

"I don't think it means that...oh never mind..." said Boniface.

The shopkeeper dropped the magazine to the floor and began flicking through the next in his stack. "Big girl?" He found the page he was looking for and turned the spread for Boniface to see. "Big girl," he said with some pride, puffing out his cheeks.

Boniface slowly shook his head. A look of shock started to cross the other man's face, and he ducked back under the counter. There was some rustling, and he returned. "Poo poo wee wee?"

Boniface shut his eyes, slowly shaking his head. He opened his eyes, pointed at the stack of magazines that had accumulated on the counter, and waved a finger over them while shaking his head.

There was the sound of plastic strips lightly slapping together and shuffling feet. A slightly older man, also Indian-looking, with the addition of a thick black mustache, came. "Good morning, sir."

"Morning," said Boniface, feeling slightly weary. "I wonder..." he addressed the man with the mustache directly.

"Yes sir, how can I help?"

Inside Boniface felt relief. He wasn't sure how he would mime this question to the first man, charming as he may have been apart from his interest in selling a wide variety of pornography. "The theater across the road—you can see the stage door."

"That is correct, sir," said the second man, grinning broadly like the first.

"So you see when the cast arrive? At least, you must notice when the big star arrives—there must be a crowd of autograph hunters, people wanting their picture taken with him..."

The man with the mustache nodded. "Oh yes, sir."

"What time does he turn up?" asked Boniface.

"Four o'clock, sir." His head kept nodding. "Lots of people."

"That's great—that's all I need to know," said Boniface, leaving the store and pulling out his phone. On the third ring it answered. "Could you set me up to write a piece about the theater?"

thirteen

The street was becoming familiar. This was Boniface's third visit in just over twenty-four hours.

The brick-built terraces lining each side of the street were unchanging, but this wasn't surprising. Little around here had changed for the last 150 years, and as he turned the corner onto Gray's street, Boniface expected Gray to be similarly unchanged.

He rapped his knuckles on the peeling sky-blue paint and listened.

Silence.

He balled a fist and beat the door three times. At times like this, he would like Mel Grant with him to do some serious hitting. There was a voice inside, muffled. Boniface remembered how long it took Gray to answer the door the day before and waited, expecting to see the no-longer-white toweling robe shortly.

Footsteps came down the stairs, and someone cursed under his breath as he fought with the door. There was Gray, looking like he did when he first answered the door yesterday. "Can't you just piss off, Boniface? I told you yesterday I'm not that sort of girl—I'm not going to sleep with you."

Boniface tried to keep his face straight but failed. "Can I come in?"

"No." Gray didn't even consider the question. "I've got my reputation to think about. What would the neighbors say? Imagine what would happen if I die in a car crash tonight—they'll say 'he would get friendly with anyone in a suit,' and I'm not having that."

"Yesterday's offer of breakfast still stands."

Gray wrinkled his nose, seemingly unconvinced but willing to be persuaded.

"Come on," said Boniface. "Come and have breakfast."

"Nah," said Gray. "What do you want?"

Boniface accepted defeat and moved to the right of the door, leaning on the front of the house so he could see the other man while he half-hid behind the door. "Something you said yesterday…"

"You mean when what's-her-name was here?"

"Montbretia."

"Yeah, Monty. Where is she?"

"Back at the office, working."

"Shame."

"You mentioned the kid. Billy Watkins."

Gray remained silent; his body language stayed quiet, too.

"Who is he?" asked Boniface, letting his gaze follow the line of the street and focus in the distance.

"Just some kid at the place I play poker."

"You any good?"

"What?" asked Gray.

"Poker? Do you win?"

"I'm on a streak I don't want to be on at the moment." Gray seemed to have offered more than he wanted.

"Perhaps get another game," said Boniface.

"I've got to win back what I owe here first."

"Gotcha," said Boniface. "So where is your game?"

"Haggerston," offered Gray.

"Yeah, yeah, yeah, Haggerston," said Boniface. "Is that the one by the..." he moved his hand as if drawing a straight line on a piece of paper in front of him. "Next to the..." he horizontally cut the air with four ascending cuts. "With the..." he twirled his finger in front of him. "You know, that one."

"If you mean is it the one next to the Halal butcher and the dog-grooming parlor, then yes."

"So this kid Billy, he's at the poker place in Haggerston. Does he play?"

"No." Gray was slightly incredulous. "No. He's like a junkie begging cash. I'm not sure why Ernie tolerates him."

"Oh, it's Ernie's place—why didn't you say?" said Boniface. He moved on before his bluff was called. "So what's Billy's beef with Prickle?"

"Dunno." Boniface waited. Finally, Gray relented. "He knows I used to be in Prickle, he knows big-tits Dawn is married to Danny, he thinks she's a whore. I mean, we're all whores—we all do stuff for money, he's doing stuff to buy drugs—but he seems to have a real problem with Dawn."

He stopped, seemingly having given up all he knew.

"Do I need to talk to him?" asked Boniface.

"What? Because he said something nasty about your new mate Danny? Or have you got the hots for Dawn?"

It was the second time Boniface had been asked that question that morning. It was becoming uncomfortable. He kept his voice soft. "I just wondered whether there's an angle for the biography. You know, I wondered whether he's significant."

Gray snorted. "He just a junkie kid, Boniface. Leave him alone. And leave the biography alone—I mean, who actually cares about the pricks? And now, if you'll excuse me..." He snorted. "Whether you excuse me or not, I'm going back to bed, but before I go, one request: Please don't wake me up tomorrow. In fact, I really don't think I need to see you again."

fourteen

When Boniface implied to Gray that he knew Haggerston, technically that was what people called "a lie."

Of course, he knew *of* Haggerston, but as far as Boniface could recall, having lived in London for his whole life, he had never been to Haggerston.

And he didn't have a clue who this Ernie guy was, but he was grateful for the information from Gray.

When he got to the end of Gray's street, he called up the map on his phone and found where the top end of Bethnal Green meets the bottom of Haggerston. He searched on Google for a Halal butcher in Haggerston, found one—actually, found several, but started with the one with several good reviews—and checked back to the street view. Sure enough, there was a dog-grooming parlor in the same row. He set the map to navigate and started walking. Expected distance: 0.8 miles. Expected time: 16 minutes.

The farther he walked from Gray's house, the farther into the sprawling mass of urban north London he walked. The less it appealed, the faster he walked, arriving in well under 16 minutes.

Boniface looked at the row. As Gray and his map had suggested, there was a Halal butcher. Looking through the window, there was a butcher dressed in a white coat and white hat who seemed to be concentrating on turning a large piece of meat into many smaller pieces with the assistance of a big blade.

Next to the butcher was a black wooden double gate giving access to an arch under a building. Then came the dog-grooming parlor that Gray mentioned, which seemed to be more of a general pet shop that also groomed dogs—whatever the case, it didn't look like an enticing place to take a prize pooch.

After the pet shop, there was a Chinese takeaway, presently closed, although whether it was permanently closed or due to reopen later in the evening was unclear. Lastly, there was a convenience store that seemed to specialize in toilet paper, cigarettes, and alcohol. Above this, there was the sign for a cab firm.

Nowhere looked like a gambling den run by someone called Ernie.

There were few enough people on the streets. None looked like they could be the "junkie kid" Billy.

Boniface played Eeny, Meeny, Miny, Moe and decided to start with the Halal butcher.

He was struck by how clean the butcher's shop was, how organized it felt. The man in the white coat and hat was still concentrating on the piece of meat, but it was much smaller than when Boniface had first seen it.

"How can I help you, sir?" The butcher put down a cleaver as he turned to face Boniface.

Boniface paused, not certain how to preface his question. "Do you know a kid called Billy who hangs around this area?"

Boniface thought he saw the butcher's eyes flick to his knives. "Billy? Billy who? Is he a customer?"

"I don't know," said Boniface. "I was told he hangs out at the...club... the gambling...and wondered if you might..."

Unlike Gray, the butcher didn't seem keen to want to fill in any gaps Boniface was leaving.

"You know, the club?" Boniface asked.

"If you're asking me about gambling, then you may have some misunderstanding about my faith, sir."

Boniface flushed. "Sorry—I'm not looking to gamble myself, I'm looking for someone who does. I'm trying to..." Boniface held his hands as if gripping a steering wheel and bearing left, "guide him away from gambling. Do you know the place?"

"As I said, sir, my religion."

"Thanks anyway," said Boniface as he left, heading down the street.

The pet shop/grooming parlor had a sign saying "gone for lunch, back at 2." The Chinese takeaway had a stack of flyers for other restaurants piled with the mail inside the door—it looked like more than a few days' worth of mail.

Boniface took a look at the convenience store and, remembering his last experience with a similar store across from the theater a few hours earlier, decided to check out the cab office first. Continuing around the corner, he found seven cars parked at varying angles and at different distances from the curb, all Japanese or Korean in origin, all a shade of brown, all with plates noting they were more than fifteen years old, all with a Christmas tree air freshener hanging from the rearview mirror— apart from the car that lacked such a mirror—and all showing dents, scratches, and bad repairs.

There was an open door that looked like the door you would find on a cheap residential property thirty years ago—brown wood, with a semicircular arc of glass at the top. From the look of the door, it had been fitted thirty years ago and had not been varnished since. The door opened onto a small lobby, no more than three feet square, the walls covered with woodchip wallpaper that had been painted—but not recently, as the dirt marks showed.

Boniface looked for a sign or some directions and, finding none, allowed his eyes to follow the dirty streaks on the wall, turning right onto a staircase. Standing outside the door, he leaned forward, craning his neck into the lobby. His nose was assaulted by the odor of chemical air fresheners, takeaway food, unwashed men, and poorly maintained plumbing.

He looked from the stairs to the street and back to the stairs. It seemed fairly obvious to him that—lacking any other handrail along the stairs—as people came down the stairs, they would slow themselves on the wall, and no one had ever bothered to clean where everyone steadied themselves.

Boniface pulled his head out of the lobby, took a deep breath of clean air, and stepped in, following the stairs to the top, where they turned awkwardly into a long, thin room. The blinds—probably the same vintage as the front door—were closed, but through the broken slats, sufficient light fought its way into the building. But it seemed that when it got there, the light became disheartened and died of disappointment, leaving all of the surfaces a murky, indistinct purple/brown color.

He took a moment to try to understand the architecture. He guessed this had probably once been an apartment or the upper floor of a house, but someone had seemingly adapted it to be the cab office. What he guessed had been the front room had the wall between it and the corridor at the top of the stairs removed. Clearly the wall had been structural, so it had been replaced by a beam to hold the roof.

On the far wall, across from a low table that was probably even older than the front door, was a row of chairs—the sort of chairs you would have found in a doctor's waiting room in the 1970s: square seats, thinly padded, covered in dull green vinyl, and interlinking with the seats to either side. The seats were worn, with the fire-hazard foam stuffing coming through the tears.

Boniface couldn't see all of the seats—three were occupied. Each occupant looked similar but with minor variations: small, dark-skinned, unwashed hair, thin nylon jacket, indistinct trouser color matching the wall coverings. They talked in a low but fast babble in a language Boniface didn't understand.

"Hi," said Boniface. The man on the right looked up—the other two continued talking. The man said something. Boniface wasn't sure whether he was talking to him or continuing his conversation with the other two.

"English?" asked Boniface.

The man lowered his head and began to engage with his compatriots.

Boniface looked at the wall separating the front and the back room, where a large window had been inserted. On the other side sat a man who looked similar to the three in front of Boniface—he held a microphone and was also talking in a language that Boniface didn't recognize.

However, where theirs was a low, constant babble, this man was talking more forcefully—it sounded like he was angry.

The man put the microphone down. "English?" said Boniface, looking through the glass between the notes and postcards pasted on the other side. The man shrugged and looked down at the desk in front of him.

A phone rang. The man behind the glass reached out his hand and put a receiver to his ear. "Haggerston Cabs. Where do you want to go?" he said in a thickly accented voice, looking away when he caught Boniface's eye.

As the call continued, Boniface surveyed the structure. Where the front room had suffered a merger with the passageway, the back room, even with its window into the front space, still retained its separation and was accessed through a doorway from what remained of the passageway. Boniface walked to the door and waited for the call to end.

He felt his nose burn slightly. There had been an unpleasant smell when he first stepped in, but he had acclimatized to that. However, there was something more here—chemicals singeing the hairs in his nostrils. He turned his head to the bathroom with its door perpendicular to the back room.

The bathroom suite was the kind of pink that was only available in the 1970s—or the decade that taste forgot, as most people tended to think of it. There was a bath stacked with boxes, a sink with dust that Boniface could see from where he stood, and a toilet—with a white plastic seat that had yellowed. The yellow clashed with the pink. The floor in front of the lavatory pan looked as if there was a plumbing leak. At least that's what Boniface hoped the source was.

The phone clicked, and Boniface spun to face the controller. He seemed better fed than the other men and had washed his hair more recently. "Where's the poker club?"

"No poker club here." The voice was accented but softer than Boniface had expected.

"Sure, but where? It's up here somewhere." Boniface let his hand drift to point in the general direction of the street.

"No."

"How long since you had your last tax audit?" It was an immutable law that any business where most of the income came in cash would be twitchy about their taxes. Even the most honorable of businesses—and Boniface suspected this business might not fall into that category—would be wary of officers of Her Majesty's Revenue and Customs banging at the door. Even if they had done nothing wrong, there's always a room for error, interpretation, and huge amounts of time to be wasted.

"It's a bad place." Boniface was disappointed that the only card he could play hadn't elicited more, and he waited for elaboration. "Very bad place," continued the other man.

fifteen

Boniface had seen the black gates as he passed. He had assumed they were something to do with either the Halal butcher or the pet shop, which was still closed for lunch. But according to the controller in the cab office, this was where the poker club was.

And that was the limit of the information Boniface could force out of the other man, apart from being told again that it was a very bad place. It might be bad, but it wasn't as if Boniface wanted a game.

While not particularly well maintained, the wooden gates filling the arch had a certain look of solidity to them. Boniface pushed lightly; they moved but were clearly locked. He tried the wicket gate—the door cut into the right gate. Applying the same pressure he had applied to the main gate, he found that the wicket gate swung easily with a smooth swish of the hinge.

Careful to lift his foot and duck his head as he passed through the gate within a gate, Boniface found himself under the arch—a tunnel formed from the red-brick wall of the butcher and red-brick wall of the pet shop, and the roof from the floor above that joined the buildings. He felt his foot twist and looked down to find cobbles giving an uneven path leading out to a small courtyard with two figures: One had noticed him.

Boniface found his footing and proceeded through the tunnel— keeping to the right to avoid a stack of paint tins, dust sheets, and a stepladder against the pet shop wall—and walked out onto the small courtyard, a neat cobbled square open to the sky and extending behind the pet shop and the butcher shop with an iron rail guarding a concrete staircase leading under the back of the butcher's building. Two large wooden beer barrels stood outside a closed glass-paneled door, obscured by a curtain on the inside.

Now that he was closer, the two figures seemed bigger.

The guy on the left, maybe in his thirties, was slim and about the same height as Boniface, with black lace-up boots under his frayed, dirty jeans and a sleeveless denim jacket covering a shapeless bottle-green sweater. His hair was raven black—the sort of raven that finds a way to create his own dye, probably to cover another color failure—and his face scarred from acne that still exploded across his cheek. He drew heavily on a roll-up, pulling his lips around the cigarette before forcing the air out of his lungs.

He didn't move to look in Boniface's direction.

The other guy did.

As Boniface looked at the dark skin, he could see a young Mel Grant. He had the same basic bone mass and potential for muscle as the drummer—if he spent five hours every day hitting things—but at the moment, he looked less fit. However, Boniface didn't feel the need to test the streetfighting readiness of the teenager who was letting his stare silently judge Boniface.

"Hey," said Boniface, feeling slightly uneasy.

The black teen raised his eyebrows. He may have been the younger of the two standing outside the door, but he seemed to be the guardian.

Boniface weighed up which name to throw. "Billy mentioned I might be able to get a game."

The teen's eyes opened slightly, questioning. "Billy?" From the accent, this guy could definitely be Mel's son—or a cousin born a few streets away in South London.

He looked toward the white guy, still sucking on his roll-up, then back to Boniface. "I'm sorry, sir, there must be some mistake." He stood and as Boniface looked up, recognizing a figure as big as Mel Grant's, he understood the conversation was over.

"My mistake. Sorry for the intrusion." He took two steps into the tunnel, then turned, reaching into the top pocket of his jacket. "If Billy does turn up..." he walked toward the large black youth, holding his out his business card, "perhaps you could get him to call me. He won't be disappointed."

sixteen

Boniface wasn't quite sure what he had been expecting when he found that Terry Meyerson had a studio in Camden.

The word "studio" can be interpreted in so many ways, and Camden means different things to different people. To some, Camden means TV studios, internationally renowned markets, a range of hip gig venues, and a strong connection with the alternative culture.

To others, it's another part of London that you never want to go near.

Boniface wasn't surprised to find that Meyerson's studio wasn't in Camden Town, but instead was within the municipal borough, and so qualified as being in Camden on a technicality. The surrounding light industrial units suggested there would be a reasonable-sized studio but that it wouldn't likely be a high-end establishment.

A cheap but rust-proof plastic sign directed Boniface between two buildings—each lightweight corrugated steel. Up two concrete steps, the front doors were aluminum-framed with glass panels—two doors that met in the middle badly. Boniface looked at the doorbell with another plastic sign—"Please ring"—then back to the right door, which had not fully shut.

He pushed. It opened. He stepped in, letting the door fall behind him.

The lobby had the feel that it had been left by the previous resident. The blue nylon carpet tiles showed the trail of passing footsteps, and the Blu-tack on the wall reflected the extent of posters that had once hung. Now, the Blu-tack demarcated the limits of the less faded areas. And the desk at the front showed four corner holes around a similarly lighter-shaded oblong where a previous occupant's nameplate had been removed.

And the previous occupant's receptionist had also since departed. The dusty detritus left on the desk suggested no replacement.

There were two doors at the other side of the lobby. One led down a white painted concrete-block corridor, lit with a buzzing strip light. The other didn't. Boniface turned his head down the open corridor and, seeing only more blue nylon carpet tiles, returned to the other door, which he pulled gently, finding a small well on the side of a larger room. A male and a female voice were audible from within the main room.

Cautiously, Boniface stepped into the large room with a high ceiling, finding himself reminded of a school gymnasium without the wooden floor. At the far end was a white screen pulled from a roll at ceiling height and turned through 90 degrees as it met the floor. Two banks of lights focused toward the white strip, as did two space heaters. A fat man stood in the center behind a camera on a tripod at eye level, and a woman stood a quarter-turn further around, with a makeup brush in her hand.

Boniface felt his foot scrape against the floor.

The woman gasped, dropped her powder brush, and ran toward the door Boniface had just entered through, her heels clipping as she passed. The photographer slowly winched himself to an erect position and turned through 180 degrees as he walked backward in a small arc to reveal another woman—naked from the waist up, and if Boniface was being honest, somewhat chubby—who let out a small yelp and crossed her arms over her chest, her eyes darting as if searching for somewhere to hide.

The photographer turned back to the model. Boniface could hear his low mumblings and attempts at reassurance as the chubby girl blushed. It took a few moments, but she was soon nodding with more certainty, although her arms remained firmly fixed across her chest.

He turned to Boniface as the makeup artist returned and, seeing the distress of the model, ran a few steps to her, turning to the photographer as she passed. "I'm sorry about that—the door's locked now."

"Didn't you used to be Alexander Boniface? Last I heard you melted down…" The belly was fatter than last time—the shirt no longer had any chance of circumnavigating the girth and reaching the top of his trousers, and the mustache had lost color and shape, but this was Terry Meyerson. As he stepped forward, Boniface could see that the other man had eaten a burger at lunch. "Terry," he said holding out his hand. "Good to see you." He flicked his eyes to the model who, helped by the makeup artist, was slipping on a blouse. "Can we have a quick chat?"

The fat man flicked his head up, pointing to the door through which Boniface had entered, and ushered him through the lobby, down the strip-lighted corridor, and into a side office. Like the corridor, the walls were whitewashed concrete block, but with a row of framed photos on each side.

Boniface glanced. He recognized some of the shots—some of the most iconic images that had accompanied the news over the last thirty years: a policeman dying in the streets, having been attacked when he tried to save a five-year-old who got caught in a riot; three grandmothers with tears in their eyes as Princess Diana's gun carriage passed; sports-men—the England cricket team, Boniface thought—being driven around London in an open-topped bus. "Are these yours?"

"Mmm." His face softened. "I've been around for a long time, Boniface—if you wait long enough, you get lucky."

"These are good pictures. Really good pictures," said Boniface straightening. "I was…"

The fat man cut Boniface off. "I'm sorry—this girl's already paid, and she's on her lunch hour. She's got to go back to the office and tell them she went shopping." He raised eyebrows, shaking his head with a look of amusement. "Give me ten minutes to finish this thing, and then I'll be with you."

He reached the door and turned back. "There's a bottle of scotch in the desk drawer—help yourself."

seventeen

"What did he look like?"

Ernie Norton sat back in his vintage desk chair—deep green buttoned leather over dark wood—listening to the spindle squeak as he coaxed his chair from left to right, then rolled it back and kicked his feet on his desk as the seat slowly tipped.

"He wasn't a gambler," said Jojo. The big black teenager dressed in combat pants and a sweatshirt was thinking.

Jojo Brooks was young, and like many kids from what sociologists laughingly liked to call the wrong side of the tracks, he had no fear about using violence. But unlike his contemporaries, somewhere down the line Jojo had learned about consequences—this made him cautious. He didn't lose his bravery, but he thought ahead, which meant he didn't cause trouble except when he wanted to and when he was content to accept the consequences.

And he wasn't one for bravado. Where most teens brag—and brag about things they don't understand—Jojo listened. When confronted, he shut up and waited for the other guy to talk first. More often than not, the other guy found this intimidating—and it was—but in truth, Jojo wasn't trying to intimidate, but rather to find out.

"What does a gambler look like, Jo?"

Jojo paused, weighing the question. "There are two types of gamblers who turn up here, Mister Norton."

He was respectful too, thought Ernie, and he liked that.

"The first sort of gambler is the professional. The guy tries to do this for a living. They've got their whole story settled—they do whatever they need to do to look cool. It's like their heads aren't attached to their body."

"Huh?"

"Below the neck," continued Jojo, "they're still. There's no heartbeat. No movement. From the neck up, everything moves like when they show a bullet fired in the movies. It's all in slow motion. The neck moves slowly. The eyes move like they're on drugs."

"Like a swan, but in reverse," offered Iain Irvine, sitting in the corner behind Jojo, his high forehead in front of his slicked-back thinning gray hair reflecting the few beams of light that had got into the room, casting the contours of his face into deeper contrast.

"Nah, man," said Jojo. "They don't fly and crap on your head." He laughed with Irvine, then turned back to Ernie. "Swans have their legs going like this." He rapidly dog-paddled with his hands. "These guys are slow and dead."

"The others," said Ernie, tugging on his collar.

"The chancers. They're all swagger. They try to look like the big man—walk up all confident, like they've just ridden into town." He patted his shoulders firmly. "It's the shoulders and the hips that give it away. They put one shoulder forward and drop the other hip." He looked to Iain Irvine and carried on explaining. "It's like a chick, but a chick stands up straighter so her bum wiggles and her tits stick out further. And girls have shorter steps—these blokes stride."

Ernie dropped his feet to the floor, feeling the moment of the upward tilt push his body forward. He stopped its movement by resting his elbows on his legs. Clasping his hands together, he looked over his desk at the big teenager. "So this guy? This..." he looked at the business card on his desk, lit from the brass banker's desk lamp with the green shade. "This Boniface?"

"He just walked. Like a normal person. He had a suit; it was like he was going to the office."

"Maybe he works in an office?"

"No. It was his eyes. He was looking everywhere—it was like he was trying to take in every detail. He wasn't playing the big man." He paused. "It was like he was sizing the place up for a job."

"And what did he say?"

"Billy said I could get a game." He looked up. "Something like that. Definitely 'Billy.' Definitely 'get a game.'"

"And Billy was there?"

"Standing right beside me."

"Did Boniface recognize Billy?"

"No."

"Did Billy recognize Boniface?"

"Said he'd never heard of him."

"So this guy, Boniface, says 'Billy says I can get a game,'" said Ernie. "What did you say?"

"I'm sorry, sir; there must be some mistake."

"You didn't ask him anything?"

"Didn't want to give him a hint about anything."

"Smart." Ernie sat straighter and sniffed. "How did it end?"

"He said 'sorry to disturb you' or something like that and walked away. Then he turned back and gave me his card and said if Billy turns up, he won't be disappointed."

"What does that mean?" He looked around Jojo to the third man. "Do you know, Irv?" The two were silent, but he could hear them shifting slightly. "And how did Billy react to this?"

"You know Billy; he's a junkie. His eyes flashed, but this Boni-whatever-his-name-is didn't see. I told Billy it was nothing, and he went off looking for a score."

"Have you called the number here, Irv?" Ernie tapped his finger firmly on the card, the knock echoing in the darkened room.

"Yup." Iain Irvine stood up. Cypriot born to Scottish parents, he had a love of the sun, and when he couldn't return to the land of his birth, he worshiped sunbeds. His double-breasted light-gray suit with a heavy stripe showed a slim figure, and even in the low light, his white shirt contrasted against his tanned hide mottled with age spots. "They do PR. That's what the American girl I spoke with said. Boniface wasn't there— she could get him to call when he gets back if I wanted." He shrugged. "They usually get business by personal referrals, apparently."

Ernie sucked air through his teeth.

"It seemed like a lot of work and a lot of detail for a fake number, but I'll check them out on the internet tomorrow when I release my next torrent of shit about Danny and Dawn."

"But it still doesn't answer the question, does it?"

Jojo Brooks and Iain Irvine glanced at each other, then returned their focus to their principal. "Who knows about Billy? Who told this Boniface about Billy?"

The two seemed to relax.

"And my question is, has our little songbird been singing? I should probably ask him."

He looked at Jojo. "Just a hunch, but if this Boniface returns, I want a word with him. A *word*."

eighteen

"I'm sorry. It took longer to get her settled than I thought."

"Not a problem," said Boniface, sitting in the chair behind the desk. "She's not your usual subject." He indicated the walls, and a few prints he had found on the desk that he looked at while he waited.

"Unfortunately, increasingly this is what I'm doing," said Meyerson. "The world of the smudger has changed. Hell, we're not even called smudgers anymore, are we? There's that new breed: the paparazzi." He paused. "But you can't just blame those guys. It was coming—the paper got rid of the staff photographers, I got older and fatter, we went digital... it all changed."

He dropped onto a lime-green hessian-covered sofa. "I guess the biggest thing was that I didn't have the energy to keep getting up early and working late. So I started doing more studio work, and now you see my empire." He made a sweeping gesture. "In many ways it's better—I've got a lot of sources of income. I do a bit of teaching—you know, spend five hours in a professional studio with a pro photographer and a model—I've been digitizing my old archive, and a lot of that's now available through the photo libraries...."

"Good income?" asked Boniface.

"Not really." He stopped. "Well...it's not good if you compare it to what I might get paid for a day's freelance work. But if you think that it's a photo I shot thirty years ago that is still bringing in income when I'm asleep, then it's bloody good money! And it's consistent—it's a small amount every month, which balances out one of the other things I do: portfolio building."

Boniface frowned.

"Like the one that gave you an eyeful."

"My eyes aren't that great, Terry, but all I saw was an embarrassed chubby girl—and not chubby in a good way."

The photographer sighed loudly. "They come here thinking if they get their gozangas out, that's the way to change their life. They figure all they need is a portfolio, and the phone will start ringing. They dream they'll be rolling in dosh by summer." He dropped his voice. "Take that one out there. She's twenty-three and has decided her life is shit—she didn't work at school, and now she's in a dead-end secretarial job. The trouble is she's got too much facial hair, doesn't have a personality, and the body's gone, if it was ever there. There are girls of eighteen who are far better—and she's got the damage from an extra five years of bad diet, lots of drinking, and not looking after herself."

Boniface stared at the fat man.

He held up a hand. "Guilty as charged. I am living proof of how bad living robs you of your model-like figure. I tell you, put me on lettuce leaves for a week, and I look like Cindy Crawford."

Boniface raised his eyebrows, questioning. "Does shooting portfolios for these wannabes make money for you?"

The fat man snorted and his mustache wobbled. "It's break-even paywise, but some of them are useful if I need a model for the photography days here. Where I make the cash is on the occasional referral to agencies. I tip 'em the wink if I see a good one, and they slip me a few notes." He shrugged. "Supply and demand. In the old days, before silicon, the girls who could supply more were always in demand. But now, what they want in the business is really simple—a natural girl in front of the camera. Pretty, but not too pretty. Can't look too sexually aggressive. If I find one of those and make the referral, then it's pay day for me. Double if she actually signs up."

Meyerson stopped talking, seemingly thinking about how much he might get paid for his next referral.

"So baby-face Al is all big and grown up, and now calls himself Boniface. You got—not famous—what's the word...? Renowned. Notorious? What happened?"

"I got drunk. I embarrassed people. I went to work with Gideon Latymer handling press for the Department of the Environment. I got drunk. I embarrassed people. My marriage ended."

"I'm sorry. Vron was such a sweet girl," said Meyerson, with a note of regret that sounded sincere.

"Yeah. It's a tough one—but we're still on good terms. It was her who suggested I chat to you. You probably heard that after the marriage ended, there was that whole damaging-a-tree-with-a-car-while-drunk thing and the meltdown, so now I'm on my own."

"I heard some of it," said the fat man. "But it seemed pretty tame stuff in comparison with what we got up to in the seventies." Boniface was sure he pulled in his stomach before he asked his next question. "You said Veronica suggested me?"

There was hope in the question.

"I'm chasing something from the past," said Boniface. "I'm doing a biography—it's a bit of a labor of love, and I need some background." He paused, waiting until he was sure Meyerson was listening. "Do you remember Dawn Featherstone—Dawn Vickery, as she was then—and the group M-Stub8?"

A look slowly spread across the fat man's face, morphing into relaxed tranquility. "Dawn Vickery. The last of the torpedo-tit girls." His eyes were closed. "I remember Dawn. I photographed her—I've probably got those pictures sitting waiting to be digitized."

Boniface waited—he didn't want to think what was passing through Meyerson's mind.

"What can you tell me about the band?"

Meyerson seemed lost—floating in a bubble of bliss.

"And do you know where any of them are?"

Meyerson opened his eyes slowly, moving as if he were coming around from a general anesthetic. "What can I tell you? There were four girls; it ended badly."

"Tell me what you know," said Boniface.

"There were four of them—they all started off being photographed for the papers, and someone thought it would be a good idea to make them put on clothes and sing. It was just a racket—the rumor was they got session singers in and mimed the live performances." He shrugged. "Anyway, there was Dawn. She was the pretty blonde with..." He held his hands in front of him. "She was the one the men chased, but she was always...reticent."

"About men?"

"No. In general. She always stepped back." He looked up, a look of enthusiasm on his face. "I'd love to shoot her again. You know, I could do a then-and-now spread. Properly lit—really tasteful and arty."

He was lost again, his eyes defocused.

"Lorna. She was a sweet girl.... Such a pity about her death—that was what finally ended the band. Then there was Carmen. She was the really wild one, the man-eater, but she's probably drugged out of existence now. I heard she had been doing really filthy porn—you know, where they actually hurt the girl. Proper hurt, not acting hurt. But that was just a rumor, so don't quote me."

"I won't," said Boniface.

"And last there was Jilly. Jilly with the wonky headlights." He held his hands in front of him, then raised one and lowered the other. "You never could shoot her head on—the left one would be staring you in the eye while the right would look at your shoe. This was before Photoshop, of course, so you had to hoist up one side with a bit of sticky tape and shoot from an angle. Nice girl, though. Still sends me a Christmas card every year."

"Seriously," said Boniface. Meyerson nodded. "Where does she live? Have you got an address?"

The fat man levered himself to his feet and walked out of the room, turning right. Boniface could hear drawers being opened and closed, and Meyerson returned. "Leyton."

"Leyton, East London? Leyton five miles away?"

Meyerson half-smiled. "Yeah. There's the address."

Boniface stood. "Terry—it's been a pleasure. We really should get together soon."

"Don't forget, I'm always available for work—if you want me, or if Veronica ever has an assignment that could use my skills." He pointed to the pictures hanging around the walls. "I can do more than just flabby girls."

nineteen

"For crying out loud, Boniface." Veronica immediately regretted the sharpness of her tone, but from the way Boniface was loitering in the doorway—seemingly not wanting to commit to actually coming into the room and nonchalantly pretending that he was just passing—she felt justified.

Like you just pass the fifty-eighth floor in an office block. When you don't work there. When you've got no other friends in the office—and indeed, arguably, a number of enemies.

In short, he was after another favor; he knew he was chancing his luck. He knew he would get shouted at, and he knew that if he stayed by the door, he could run and avoid the conversation; but if he was sitting in front of her desk, there would be no avoiding the torrent of abuse that he knew she could heap upon him.

That's torrent of abuse as he would tell it—in reality, all he would be subject to would be a simple statement of the basic facts.

He half-stepped into the room and began, casually, as if he was mentioning the weather. "Did anything ping with Billy?"

Veronica felt a surge, an overwhelming desire to do physical harm. "Does our divorce not mean anything to you, Boniface? *Anything*?"

Boniface had the look he got when he was calculating the odds—when he was playing verbal chess, trying to figure out what he needed to say to make sure the conversation reached the point he wanted it to reach in three moves, rather than saying what he wanted to say.

Veronica knew that he knew she knew what he was doing, and given his hesitation at the door, he would be guessing that whatever he said would be criticized.

So he seemed to be choosing to do no wrong instead of trying to do right, and was waiting without replying.

Which, given how Veronica felt, was probably the right play. Boniface would never be a poker player—you could always read his tells—but he knew this, and he knew strategy, and he knew the tactics to deploy to achieve the strategy, so he didn't need to worry if people could read him.

He just needed to avoid poker players.

"I haven't had time, Boniface." She was angry that he was making her feel guilty for not having finished looking into this Billy Watkins.

Boniface had that look he got when he was about to be understanding.

"Don't tell me it's alright. Don't patronize me and say it's okay while you start feeling frustrated inside. If you want to help, tell me what I'm looking for and I'll find it. But just remember, as you said, this is before the internet age, at a time when we used—shock, horror—typewriters. Someone needs to look through files or fire up the old microfiche to find this stuff."

Boniface remained quiet.

"What's my priority here—apart from, you know, doing the job that I'm paid to do, and not abusing the resources of my employer? You know, I'm meant to be the editor of a national newspaper—the one who says yes, no, and that's a stupid idea, stop chasing it, now go and do something more productive...."

She looked around her office. Unlike her staff, who sat at their workstations in the middle of a big room, she got an office with some degree of personalization: a chair of her choosing, and not the latest in ergonomic design, which only confused her and broke her nails—no, a proper chair upholstered in leather and made for her comfort. She got a desk: not too wide—it was a charming piece of vintage cherrywood, not some bombastic statement that was bigger than Boniface's car. She even got real plants—in this case, Japanese maples, which seemed to get exchanged every few weeks with very similar versions of the same species.

"I've got you into that theater," she said. "You've got an appointment at three-forty-five. Ask for Morag Sullivan."

"What do we know about Morag?" Boniface was keeping his tone light.

"That her name is Morag. That she was kind enough to agree to meet you this afternoon."

She looked over her gold-rimmed half-moon glasses: Boniface trembled like a scolded child. A shake of her head and she felt her auburn mane ripple. When it settled, she continued. "You do understand—you do remember, you used to work in the business—that we have deadlines here. I can't just say to my readers, 'Sorry there's no news today, I was sorting out some stuff for my former husband—here are some pictures of kittens that we grabbed off the internet instead.'"

Boniface shrugged one shoulder and muttered, "Might raise your circulation—kittens are very popular, especially cute ginger kittens."

Veronica waited for his smirk to fade. "I'll leave you to make your pitch for that new strategy to Mister Kuznetsov." She paused. "I'm sorry—my proprietor, your friend, Vanya." She continued, her voice softer, conciliatory. "How's it going? Did you see fat Terry?"

"I did, and he gave me a name and an address," said Boniface.

"Related to the theater?"

"No—it's another lead. I need to see this Morag Sullivan to get in there to see Kit Flambeau."

"But he's a musical theater guy—goes on TV when they need a rather camp but slightly vivacious guest. What's he got to do with all this?"

"He was a member of Prickle for a short time."

Veronica mouthed "oh" as Boniface continued.

"I figure he must know if there were any unresolved issues—he dealt with the aftermath of the original singer, Gray Barrington, walking away." Boniface sighed. "Danny thought...no, Danny doesn't think—Danny loves everybody. Danny wondered out loud who might be bitter and causing the problem, and Gray's name came up. I spoke to Gray, and even twenty-five years later he seems angry, and I get the impression he's got some unpleasant mates...so I'm just putting two and two together, and so far I've got thirty-eight. I'm hoping Kit can get me down to about thirty-six or thirty-five. I've just got dead-ends. All I want is some little hint."

He moved to stand outside the door but leaned in, a somewhat mournful look across his face.

"I'll call you if I find anything on this Billy," said Veronica.

Boniface mouthed the words "thank you" and was gone.

twenty

It was an odd haircut.

Rising vertically at the sides, but with tight curls on the top. And the brown-blond-silver looked dry, very dry—don't-touch dry, like twigs, kindling ready to ignite, somewhere that no bird would nest because there was no comfort.

Boniface was aware that Morag was talking, but he really hadn't been paying attention—the conundrum of the architecture of her hair needed to be resolved first.

She led him through a door—from the front of house to the back of house, public to private. He stopped thinking about the hair for long enough to take in the difference. Where the front of house was velvet-covered to the dado rail, well-tended dark wood, and soft carpet, this side was concrete, walls painted army-surplus colors with paint probably acquired as a job lot left over from the 1940s and bought on the cheap in the 1950s.

Which was probably when they bought their lightbulb. Boniface could swear there were still traces of paint on it—a wartime practice not to give the Luftwaffe any help. Post-war austerity had then dictated that the paint be scraped off rather than a new bulb purchased.

He checked the time on his phone and looked along the corridor. The fire door at the end looked familiar, as did its guardian, who didn't seem to recognize Boniface from his earlier visit.

Morag continued to talk.

Boniface wondered whether it was too soon to look at his phone again, wondered whether she might find it rude, which it would be. The door at the end of the corridor opened, and a figure entered backwards.

"Thank you, thank you. I love you all." The voice was light, affected. Some camera flashes bounced in the gloom, and as the door shut, the sound of excited voices was muted.

Morag leaned forward conspiratorially and muttered, "Kit's very theatrical."

Kit had the round face of a man who had lived the good life and had never missed a meal, and the cravat and handkerchief of a man for whom a certain panache was worn like a second skin.

"Darling Morag. How are you today?" He turned to Boniface. "I'd certainly remember you if we had met." His voice was rich, resonating, with slightly camp inflections that Boniface was sure he was effecting. "This is a very special treat you have brought, just for me. You are such a darling, Morag."

"Boniface," said Boniface. "And I was wondering if we could have a quick word before you get busy."

"Darling, Boniface. You can have a slow word." He pulled his shoulders back, forcing out his chest, fluttering his eyelashes as he looked down.

"Theatrical," mouthed Morag, giving Boniface a "told you so" look.

"Two minutes and I'll catch you," said Boniface to Morag, who looked slightly shocked as Boniface followed Kit into a room off the gloomy passage.

Boniface let his eyes take in the room. Utilitarian white paint had been uniformly applied within the last five years. The only color came from a spray of flowers where the plastic had yet to be removed and a rail of what Boniface presumed were the actor's costumes.

Kit caught Boniface's surprise. "Yes, darling. This really is what the star gets." The word "star" was laced with irony. "But it's much nicer than what the other poor souls are forced to endure."

"You're busy, so I'll get straight to the point: Prickle," said Boniface. Kit raised his eyebrows, then gave up. "I've been asked by Danny to write a biography of the band. I'm at the early research stage, and I'd like to schedule some time to sit down with you properly, but at the moment, there's something I'm missing."

Kit nodded.

"The bad blood with Gray. You were there. Beyond the obvious—Gray quit and left the band with a whole bunch of contractual engagements to fill—what happened?"

"Ah, Prickle in 1984," said Kit, the flamboyance returning. "They were the best of times. They were the worst of times."

He sighed and looked up. Suddenly, Boniface could see plain Christopher Edington talking to him. "I knew Danny was pissed at Gray, but I didn't see anything beyond that. It happened before I arrived. And to be honest, I had my own issues." His voice seemed to catch. "I was coming to terms with being gay."

"You make it sound like a bad thing."

"No, no, no," said Kit, brightening slightly. "But it's tough when you're eighteen—biology largely determines that we're brought up by heterosexuals, and no matter how loving and how supportive, heterosexuals tend to work with the basic expectation that their offspring will be... well, straight. And you're conditioned that anything not straight must be bad—queer never meant good."

The singer leaned against the dressing table as he continued. "Things were different then. When I was born, homosexuality was illegal."

Boniface felt a slight shock register over his face.

Kit continued. "Homosexuality was illegal until 1968, and after that the age of consent was twenty-one. When I joined Prickle I was eighteen, so if I wanted to be a gay man, I would have to break the law—and if you were caught you were regarded as a sexual deviant, not due any respect in the justice system."

He smirked. "It's funny looking back. A short while after I joined, Mel joined, so we had a black guy and a gay guy—we were the most politically correct band before they had even invented political correctness."

Boniface reflected on the other man's wistful recollection and tried to push the conversation back to the topic. "But was Gray mentioned?"

"The management grumbled occasionally but then decided to drop the band, so it was pretty irrelevant." He looked around as if a prompt on the floor might give him a hint. "I'm not sure what I can add—I joined when I was a kid. I was still living at home and hated being in a new place each night. We'd get to a grotty little bed-and-breakfast, and pretty much my first question would be 'where's the gay bar?' It was alright for the others, but I never found any gay groupies."

"What about Dawn?"

"I was there before Dawn." He looked at Boniface expectantly, stifling a joke. "Night. That comes before dawn, right? Seriously—she came on the scene when I was on my way out. She was lovely—if Danny had married her sooner, then I might have stayed. She was my friend—perhaps the only real friend I had—but she was damaged."

Boniface waited for elaboration, staring directly at Kit.

"Lorna. All that bad business." He shrugged. "I think Dawn was pleased to have someone who she could chat with who she knew wasn't trying to get into her knickers or exploit her." His face brightened. "I still remember when Danny first played 'Tattoo Your Name on My Heart.'"

Boniface cocked his head, silently asking for the story.

"He strummed it on that acoustic guitar he used to carry around." The thespian was lost in his memories for a moment or two. "I cried, Boniface. Big soppy tears. There's Danny—he's a very personable guy—but he's a guy. He doesn't do feelings—unless he's talking about vintage Bentleys."

Boniface waited.

"Danny had all these new songs, all these big choruses to get the audience on their feet punching the air, and 'Tattoo' had a huge chorus, but when you listen to the words, when you hear the emotion of a guy with an acoustic guitar spilling his heart—I lost it and blubbed." His voice was meek. "It's a boy telling a girl he loves her. And she believed him." His eyes misted.

Boniface watched as the other man blinked away the moisture, then straightened. "One last question. Does the name Billy Watkins mean anything to you?"

"William Watkins," said Kit. "I know lots of willies...but no William or Billy Watkins, I'm afraid."

twenty–one

Rafferty kicked his ball. Hard and without much skill, which wasn't that surprising when you are five and your football pitch is your grandmother's kitchen. That limited skill being further compromised by hyperactivity, currently provoked by the greenish-yellow sweets the man next door had given him about thirty minutes ago when he came to tell Rafferty's grandmother about his trip to Singapore, and which—unknown to Rafferty, the traveler, or the grandmother—contained quinolone yellow, or E104 as the Europeans liked to call it.

The ball knocked a vase on the window containing a single fluted daffodil, and the flower, vase, and water headed for the floor, with glass smashing and small fragments radiating like an army of dagger-wielding ants.

As the glass hit the tiled floor, two-year-old Jade, Rafferty's half-sister, screamed, then through her tears started to tell Rafferty how naughty he was. Savannah, seven months, Jade's full sister and Rafferty's half, continued crawling from the hall into the kitchen, and when Jade went to slap Rafferty for his naughtiness, got caught by her older sister's swing and started screaming too.

Jilly turned off the gas, removed the pan from the heat, and resisted the temptation to tell Rafferty that he was a little bastard. Even if he was, literally and metaphorically. That could come later—first she needed to get the kids away from the glass, and second, she needed to clean up the mess.

"Stay there!" Her voice was loud enough to give Rafferty a reason to pause, but only pause. Jilly could see his eyes focusing on the football— the football that had rolled to the other side of the room. She took three small steps and reached the siblings. With each step, she felt the grinding of glass between the floor and her slippers.

"Naughty, naughty, naughty, naughty!" Jade ensured blame continued to be ascribed to the guilty party. Savannah just kept screaming.

Jilly reached and grabbed the crawler, pulling her close and inspecting her hands for any slivers. Not seeing anything, she pulled the baby's hands over her cheek, feeling for anything more dangerous than dirt.

She looked down at the other two: "Out!" She threw her head in the direction of the hallway.

"Football, football, football." Rafferty was jumping up and down. "Football, football, football."

"Naughty, naughty, naughty, naughty!" Jade hadn't paused.

"Stop. We will have quiet in this house," said Jilly. The baby screamed. "Including you, miss," she said softly, pulling the baby closer and kissing her. "We'll feed you in a moment." She looked down at the two siblings standing in front of her: "Come on, out. It's very dangerous in here."

Rafferty moved to pass his grandmother. She held out a leg to stop him. "No, Rafferty. You two stand there," she pointed to the carpet in the hall, ending at the edging strip where the kitchen tiles began. "Come on, both of you, now."

"Can I get..." began the five-year-old boy.

"No. I'll get it for you—it's very dangerous with the glass. Now come on, both of you, onto the carpet."

Reluctantly, the two moved the short distance, turning to face into the kitchen, leaning and trying to maximize the portion of their bodies that was in the kitchen while keeping their toes behind the edging strip. "You stay there," said Jilly, feeling that it would be easier to train a sheepdog as she took a soft brush from the closet and pushed the glass fragments to the side, clearing a path for her to retrieve the ball.

She grabbed the ball and returned to the two who seemed—with the exception of their toes—to be completely in the kitchen. She shooshed them back and squatted, looking from one to the other. "It's very, very dangerous in here, so no coming in here until I've cleaned up. Alright?" Rafferty made a grab for his ball—his grandmother was faster and held it behind her, releasing the firmness of her grip on the baby to balance. "Is that clear?"

Both children nodded.

"Now, Rafferty. You can have your ball back—but no more football in the house. Alright?" The five-year-old cracked first and nodded his reluctant agreement to the deal before his grandmother returned the untethered wrecking ball. "Now, both of you go! I need to clean up."

As the kids turned, the phone rang. Jilly looked at the caller's number and sighed. "Hi babe, are you on your way?" She looked at Savannah and said, "Yes, it's your mother—she's calling me to say she's coming home soon...yes she is."

The baby gurgled as Jilly stepped into the hall, closing the door on the half-swept broken glass and other Rafferty-induced chaos that was keeping her from feeding her charges. She turned away from the closed door, passing the pictures of her children when they were young.

A lot had changed since then. The older, James, was now traveling, as they liked to call it. As far as Jilly could tell, that was a way of having an excuse for getting really drunk, taking a lot of drugs—most of which would be illegal in the UK—and, during those periods when the drugs and alcohol didn't have a detrimental effect, having a lot of sex with anyone who wouldn't say no. She looked at Savannah and frowned— some other mother would have to look after the results of their daughter's stupidity, even if her son had been equally culpable.

She and Pete, her now ex-husband, had named Kayleigh after the song. It was a favorite of both of them. She had been an incredibly cute kid, but as she grew up she found she had inherited her mother's figure, but super-charged through the growth-hormone-rich diet that everyone unwittingly ate in the 1990s when they consumed cheap TV dinners.

Kayleigh had always been popular with the boys, but it was only when she was fifteen—as Jilly held her hand in the waiting room before that first abortion—that Jilly found James had been setting her up with his friends. There seemed to have been a barter system—if you had a sister that James could have sex with, then he had a sister with a very pleasing figure who would reciprocate. Any boy who didn't treat her like a princess—albeit a tainted princess—had her big brother to answer to. As Kayleigh filled out, James's circle of friends grew, and the extended families of his friends were called to lay down their teenage women.

The first grandchild—Rafferty—came when she was 19. The father was still a matter of debate. She married before her second kid was born—but only due to an unfortunate miscarriage. That guy hung around long enough to father Jade and Savannah, but he had left two months ago, leaving Kayleigh on her own with the three kids.

"They're running me ragged, babe," said Jilly to her daughter. "What time are you coming home?"

There was a ring at the door before Jilly could hear the answer. "Oh babe, really..." She pulled the crook of her right elbow more tightly around the baby and reached for the door with her right hand, levering it open while keeping the phone pressed against her ear with her left hand. "Babe. No. This is the third man in five days."

She paused, listening, observing the man standing outside her front door. "No babe, of course I love the kids, but they're your kids." He was dressed in a blue suit—a good suit that fit—and with a sensible haircut. He didn't look like the normal double-glazing/cavity-wall-insulation salesmen that often turned up at this time of day. "Babe, of course you're entitled to a life, but your kids need a mother." And he seemed quite happy to wait while she chatted. "That's too late, babe, what are you expecting to do—wake the kids up and take them home?"

She could hear Rafferty in the front room, or rather, she could hear his ball bouncing off the walls. Jade ran to see whether there was anything interesting at the door and stood, looking between her grandmother's legs, holding on tightly to her right leg. "Okay, babe. One drink, then get here as soon as you can."

She clicked the button to end the call and placed the receiver on a shelf under a mirror just inside the front door before turning to the man. "Hi."

"Hi—you must be Jilly? Gillian Crossley as was, now Gillian Walker."

She twitched, not knowing whether to acknowledge or deny.

Jade started rocking back and forth, knocking between her grand-mother's legs with her head.

The man was relaxed, offering a door-to-door salesman's row of teeth, but something about his demeanor suggested he wasn't here to sell. "I'm glad I found the right place—Terry Meyerson gave me the address. I should introduce myself: My name's Boniface, and I've been asked to write a biography about the band Prickle. Obviously you will have known the band from your M-Stub8 days. More significantly, you will have known Dawn, who married Danny."

A football banged into the hall behind her. She ignored it, watching the man who called himself Boniface. "I was hoping you might have a bit of time when we could sit down and chat."

The football knocked the side of her head as it passed over her shoulder before leaving the house through the open door.

"Do I look like I've got time?"

Boniface stepped back, grimacing, and picked the football out of the flowerbed before rolling it past Jilly's feet to Rafferty. "Are you the next David Beckham?"

"Did you really need to do that?" Jilly's voice was a whisper. When Boniface returned a look of shock, she explained. "Now he's going to break my house even more before his mother arrives." She looked down at the baby. "Even you know that, don't you my angel?"

She talked to the baby for a moment or two, bouncing her as the infant gurgled, then looked up. "And why would I want to talk? You know the story—Dawn got away. I still see her every now and then on TV. She's done well—she lives in the country in a big house. I don't envy her the money, but it's shame she didn't reach back and help some of us she left behind. I guess she's got new friends now."

She didn't expect a response and went back to talking to the baby. When she looked up again, Boniface seemed to be waiting as if she had paused in the middle of a sentence. She elaborated. "What does Dawn tell her new friends? They're all lords and ladies in the country—hunting and fishing every weekend. Do they respect her? Or is she just tolerated, then groped by the husbands who are bored with their wives and fanta-size about screwing her?"

Boniface seemed to be amused. Maybe he was humoring her. Perhaps he just didn't want to argue. "What about your time in the band?"

"There's not much to say that hasn't been said a million times. We were like sisters—it all ended the night Lorna died." She felt her bottom lip tremble. "But that's a load Dawn has to carry." Her voice trailed off. She inhaled sharply, her voice becoming steadier. "None of us knew how to deal with that pain, that guilt."

Boniface remained silent but tilted his head, raising his eyebrows expectantly.

Jilly shook her head, then blurted. "It was Dawn and Carmen—they were with Lorna. We were at a party and they went out for a smoke—I stayed back with some guy. They were playing on the bridge—Dawn wanted to dance on the balustrade and encouraged the other two to follow her. Dawn and Carmen got off, before Lorna..."

She wiped the tear from her eye.

"They called the police, the river police, everyone, but it was thirty hours before they pulled Lorna's body out of the Thames." She sniffed. "Dawn went inside herself—she couldn't talk. Carmen, she found other ways to keep blotting out the pain, and look at her now."

Jilly stared into the distance, jolting as Savannah screamed. "That's how it ended, and I haven't seen Dawn or Carmen for years. I don't think I can help you."

She shut the door on Boniface, sat at the foot of her stairs clutching Savannah, and sobbed while Jade watched.

twenty-two

There was a beaten-up Ford parked outside the black gates. Boniface wasn't sure which model it was, but it had that I-don't-earn-enough-to-care-how-I'm-judged vibe about it. The self-affixed sun visor and go-faster racing stripes running down the sides both pointed to a lover of all things 1980s.

Boniface pushed the wicket gate—the gate within the gate—and stepped onto the cobbles.

"What are you doing here, Boniface?"

The aggressive tone seemed familiar, but he didn't immediately recognize the small wiry man in front of him. Boniface looked down at the thinning hair—even in the dull lighting obviously dyed—and grinned. "Hello, Gray. I didn't recognize you with your clothes on."

"You got me in trouble—I've just been to the headmaster's office to have a word about my attitude problem. They don't give out detentions here—they tear your bollocks off." By the glass-paned door, the large black teenager lifted himself from the barrel he had been resting on.

Boniface stepped back to look at the other man—white dungarees spattered with paint over an equally paint-spattered dirty white T-shirt. "What are you doing, Gray?"

"I'm moving my gear—di'n't you see the car outside?"

The large black teen stared at the two men.

"You got me in the shit, Boniface, and now if you hang around here, you're going to cause problems for yourself." He cast a swift look behind him, then continued—his voice soft, his lower jaw fixed, his speech rapid. "Turn around and go, or they'll make you regret it."

"Mister Barrington," the black teen reached them, blocking out the light from the far end of the tunnel. "You must introduce your friend. Who is he?"

"He's no one, Jojo, no one." Gray cast a swift look back. "He came in the wrong door—he's just leaving now."

The black teenager let his gaze fall on Boniface, locking eyes. He waited.

"Gray used to be in a band," said Boniface. "I'm writing their biography—I was hoping we could chat."

The teen turned his gaze to Gray. "So he's a business associate of yours?"

"I am," said Boniface.

The teen slowly looked back to Boniface. "Then I must apologize for our earlier misunderstanding. Please do come in."

twenty-three

"I offered him a comfortable seat," said Jojo, continuing with some satisfaction, "in the room under the butcher's."

"That's good," said Ernie, resting on the side of his desk, tugging the collar of his shirt and then the lapel of his jacket. "Did he say what he wants?

Jojo shook his head. "Nah, man. He talked to that Gray guy."

Ernie sat up straighter. "He spoke to our little songbird?"

Jojo dropped his head once. "Gray said he didn't know him, but Boniface said he used to be in a band and he's writing a book about them."

Ernie stood and walked around his desk, dropping into his chair on the other side. "What do you think he wants, Irv?"

Iain Irvine sat in his customary corner, listening. "Two visits in one day—it's not an accident. He can't want nothing." Irvine turned to the black teenager. "He didn't give any hints."

"Nope. But you told me"—he turned to Ernie—"to hold him, so I put him in our best room." He paused. "He ain't wired. And he hadn't figured there's no phone reception down there."

"Am I the only one who doesn't like this?" said Ernie. "Think about it. Visit one—he asks for Billy. Visit two—Billy doesn't get a mention, but he sees Gray and says he's writing his biography. It's like he's two different people."

"Is he the guy that Gray told us knocked on his door?" asked Iain Irvine.

"Of course he is; who else would it be?" Ernie felt his voice catch in his throat. "Just Gray didn't tell us what a nuisance he is."

"What d'you want me to do, boss?" Jojo looked like a coiled spring who was coiling himself tighter.

"Is Wes around?"

Jojo nodded once.

"I'm going to have a pleasant chat with Mister Boniface. You boys can accompany me. I'll talk to him, but you need to communicate the message. We don't need to break anything, we don't need him to piss blood, but we need a bit of humiliation, we need a bit of pain so he remembers us tomorrow, and we need anyone he meets to notice his bruises."

"So the face," said Jojo. "I'll go and find Wes." There was a flash of brightness as Jojo opened the door onto the corridor outside, stooping under the doorframe as he left. As the door shut, the gloom he preferred returned.

"There's one thing, Irv, that no one seems to be mentioning."

Iain Irvine looked up.

"He calls himself a PR guy—he gives his PR card. But what's a PR guy doing looking for people or writing books? It doesn't add up to me." He exhaled. "I hate when people make me think this hard."

twenty-four

Veronica looked at the keypad, trying to remember what pointless logic Boniface had used for the security code. It didn't take long to remember that this time the choice had lacked any real sophistication. She hit the keys 2-4-6-8-3-5-7-9, waited for the click, and entered, turning into the first office on the left where the light was on.

"Hi Monty!"

"V-ron-ron!" Montbretia stood and hugged Boniface's former wife. "How are you?" Without waiting for a reply, she stood back and held her visitor at the shoulders. "And thank you for my tree."

Veronica laughed. "I wasn't quite sure what to get you."

"Well, you can be assured that yours was the only tree," said Montbretia, sitting back in her seat and gesturing to the only visitor chair in the room—the single-seat version of the sofa she knew was in Boniface's office. "It was lovely. Not what I expected, but then again, I'm not sure what I expected as a housewarming present...."

Veronica turned her back to the window crossing the far wall of the office and lowered herself into the chair. "I know you don't like flowers—and I wasn't quite sure what was appropriate, especially given..." she lowered her voice "...the circumstances."

Montbretia lowered her head. "It was very thoughtful." There was a pause, Veronica thought she could hear a sniff, then Montbretia looked up—her face a mask of joy, her eyes moist. "I wasn't expecting to become a house owner—and definitely not a house owner in London—but with Ellen..." Her face dropped, and the moisture because a small tear pooling in her left eye, slowly beginning its course down her cheek. "It's Ellen's anniversary in six weeks."

Veronica sat quietly, watching the younger woman as the memory of her late sister momentarily consumed her.

"Everything changed that day." She was cautious but firm. "I hadn't expected to stop traveling at that point, but after Ellen...I did. I didn't expect to be working, but when Boniface asked me to help out for a few days, it seemed like a good way to earn some cash. Days became weeks, and...here I am. And of course, there's the work I get from Chlodwig and Weissenfeld Shipping. We're about to deliver the second tranche of aid to Somalia, so if Boniface sucks I've got Chlodwig, and when Chlodwig gets too serious, there's Boniface. And I get to own a house and live in London—tired of London, tired of life, right?"

Veronica relaxed into the chair. "You're looking busy—what's he got you working on?"

"Work that earns the business money?" said Montbretia, the sarcasm bleeding through.

Veronica winced. "I thought he understood that he needs to keep earning money to keep the business afloat."

"So did I," said the younger woman. "So did I."

"I can hear the annoyance—let's change the subject." Veronica watched as Montbretia affirmed. "So what fool's errand has he got you spending you time on, safe in the knowledge that it will generate no income?"

"Amps," said Montbretia. "Guitar amplifiers, you know for..." she windmilled her arm as if a rockstar hitting a guitar on stage.

"I didn't know you knew anything about the subject."

"I don't," said Montbretia. "Or at least, I didn't until a few hours ago—but actually it seems simple." She shrugged. "Heads, cabs, stacks, and combos."

Veronica cocked her head, narrowing her eyes.

"A head is an amplifier. It's the box with the amplifier in it," said Montbretia. "A cab—or cabinet—is the speaker cabinet, and apparently the boys think twelve inches is perfect."

Veronica felt her eyes tightening.

Montbretia seemed to notice. "I'll spare you the fruit of my research into different tubes... Apparently this is all in pursuit of *the tone*. The tone, which no one can precisely describe, nor can they give a consistent recording of what exactly they mean—you go through YouTube, and everything is 'this microphone doesn't give the full sound' or 'this room is wrong.' It all sounds like a scam to me." She snorted. "And apparently feedback—you know, that horrible screech—can be good." She flopped back into her chair, which gently oscillated.

"So where do you fit in the world of *amps*?" asked Veronica.

"You will understand that because these things have valves, are constructed from marine ply, and are wired up by hand, they cost a lot of money."

"Suppose so."

"This means that the main market for these things is weekend warriors. Tubby accountants—boys that wear bad suits but have sensible haircuts—who want to, and I quote"—she made a sign of horns with each hand, holding down her middle and ring fingers with her thumbs while extending the outer fingers—"'rock out at the weekend,' provided they're in bed by 10:30. And the way to market to this audience is with slutty women wearing spandex and too much makeup."

"I think the way to market most things is slutty women," suggested Veronica.

"Opinion is split as to whether the sluttiness of the woman is in direct proportion or disproportion to how well an amp will deliver *the tone*. There's also some debate about whether blondes or brunettes have an effect, but all seem to agree that larger breasts are necessary." She shook her head, disbelieving. "Don't argue with me, I'm just the messenger. I'm only telling you what the internet told me."

"I think you have found the big dilemma for all marketers."

"But for guitars and amps, there is another way," said Montbretia, gaining fresh energy. "You can get a professional to endorse your stuff, and this is where I come in. Luca...he's the guitarist with this band, Prickle—I take it you've heard about them from Boniface..."

Veronica acknowledged wearily.

"Rather surprisingly, Luca is actually regarded as something of a guitar god. And from what I've heard in the last hour or so, he is actually quite good." Montbretia pushed her jaw forward, grimacing. "Again, I'm just telling you what the internet told me, but apparently in the world of the guitar, once you have got *the tone*, then you need to do *the solo*. To go with the solo, you need the face. I knew about the horns..." she held her hands up, making the sign of the horns again, "but I didn't realize about the face."

Veronica felt a slight nervous twitch cross her face.

"As I understand," continued Montbretia. "The song will be playing, the guitarist will be going strum, strum, strum, but when it's solo time, he needs to show that he is suffering; he needs to convey the emotion."

"He can't just do that through, you know, playing?" asked Veronica.

"Oh no. First, he needs to stand as if he's been shot and is clutching his wound. And then, the face." She frowned. "There's something about shredding. I'm not sure what it is—I think it just means playing very fast. Whatever it is, Luca seems to have a really good ear for melody, harmony, and just shutting up when he's not needed, where all the others just go on and on and on. And people seem to love Luca, but Luca needs new gear—Boniface had some bizarre story about his ex-wife selling off everything he owned...."

"I missed a trick in our divorce, didn't I?" said Veronica. "Then again, I'm not sure that Boniface had much worth selling. Ironically, he did have some Prickle CDs. He probably still does—I wasn't going to keep them."

"Seriously? He actually did like them?"

"Yeah. A lot. Went to see them live several times."

Montbretia looked uncertain. "Well, don't tell him I said this, but I've been listening to a lot of *rock*, trying to understand this whole amp thing, and Prickle really are better than most of them. They've got tunes, melodies you can actually hum." She blushed slightly. "I was in the bathroom with this tune going round in my head—it was only when I got back here that I realized it was one of Prickle's."

Veronica leaned forward and whispered. "Your secret is safe with me."

She sat up straighter. "And talking of him, I haven't heard him stomping about, so I guess he's off chasing his youth."

Montbretia nodded. "I tried him on his mobile about five minutes ago. There was no reply; it went straight to voicemail. That's not unusual—it's not as if he's going to be in any physical danger. It's mostly his dignity that he's going to hurt...and the bank balance."

There was something strange in Montbretia's delivery. "You look worried," said Veronica.

"No," said Montbretia too swiftly, blushing as she seemingly realized her over-defensiveness. "I'm not worried about Boniface—I just think he might be...going in the wrong direction."

Veronica waited for the younger woman, letting the silence encourage her to talk.

"Boniface thinks this is about Prickle—he thinks it started with people saying things about Prickle on the internet." She sighed. "There's a level of that with every band, but nothing out of the ordinary for Prickle."

"So..." said Veronica slowly.

"It's not Prickle that are getting the hate, or even Danny—it's Dawn. She hasn't seriously been in the public eye, at least not more than a few TV shows here and there, for over twenty years, but the hate that's been coming at her from what looks like one or two people is just..." She seemed unable to form a word. "It's just horrid." She paused, seemingly having articulated her concern to her own satisfaction, and then slumped back into her chair. "So what brings you here, V-ron-ron?"

"I think you know why I'm here." The younger woman deflated. "What you're really asking is what fool's errand have I been obliged to perform this time?"

Montbretia affirmed.

"And the answer is, he asked me to check out someone for him. But if he's not here, I'll go and see if he's at home—and if he's not there, I'll let myself in and wait. It's getting dark, so he won't be that long."

twenty-five

Ernie Norton walked out of the glazed door, obscured with a dark curtain loosely held on the inside, and stepped into the cobbled courtyard, every surface a subtly different hue of darkening gray now that the sun, which only briefly reflected off the surrounding buildings, had disappeared many hours since.

Passing between the two barrels, he turned to his left and descended the staircase, disappearing under the rear of Abdul's butcher shop into a warren of exposed brickwork and aged concrete.

Wes and Jojo followed, both youths pumped with adrenalin, but both understood—Ernie had labored the point and threatened—that their sole role was to stand still and glare silently.

Stand still and glare until Ernie had left the room, after which he wouldn't really care enough what was going to happen.

He paused outside the door—the beige/gray tone contrasting with the dark blood dried across the foot of the kickplate. He waited. Jojo leaned forward, drew back the bolt, and pushed the door open, then stood back to allow Ernie to pass through.

"I don't believe we've had the pleasure, Mister Boniface."

The other man sat on an old wooden chair, his suit slightly rumpled, his shirt ripped, and—he knew from talking with Jojo—lacking buttons.

He was never sure when concern changed to fear. There was something in the anticipation—in not knowing what was going to happen. Once the first fist landed, once there was actual pain, then there was certainty—it became a matter of survival. Once you're in survival mode, you'll say anything, do anything to survive. When the man on the chair was in survival mode, then Ernie didn't need to be there—when someone will say anything to survive, then what they say is useless. All Ernie wanted to hear was the truth, and someone who was afraid, truly afraid, would be willing to bargain with the truth to avoid whatever future consequences their mind had conjured.

He heard Jojo and Wes shuffle in behind him. Jojo came second—he always stooped under the door, breaking his step. Ernie listened as the door slammed, holding back until the youthful feet stopped scraping, confident that one youth was now positioned on either side of the door.

Keeping his body still, he watched Boniface, noting the increase in the speed of his eyes—his pupils darting, down, to Ernie, back up, left, to the door, to Wes, up, right, to Ernie, to the lightbulb with its thin wire cage, to the top-left corner, to the bottom-right corner, to Wes, to Ernie, to Jojo, from the top-left corner down to the bottom-left corner, and back to Ernie, then dropping to his feet.

Boniface had been in the room for thirty minutes. For someone not used to incarceration, that was a long time to sit in a room with concrete-rendered walls and a concrete floor, only having an uncomfortable chair with one slightly short leg to sit on. It would be unpleasant to start with, but after thirty minutes—thirty minutes in a room where the only interior decoration had been the blood, piss, and shit of previous occupants—you would usually deduce two things. First, that there was no way out apart from the door. Second, that the only reasonable response to deduction number one was fear.

The only matter to be decided was how Mister Boniface was going to react to that fear.

"Why are you messing with my little songbird?"

From his reaction, this wasn't the question Boniface was expecting—or perhaps it was the question, but phrased in a way he wasn't expecting. In any event, the reaction was as he hoped and immediate—panic and confusion. Boniface was almost relieved when he started talking. "You mean Gray?"

Ernie noticed that this was the point where he paused.

This was the moment when Boniface was trying to determine how Ernie would react.

His voice was different when he continued—more confident, but far less authentic. Ernie looked at his eyes. In that pause, Boniface had relaxed and decided that his fears were unfounded. It was one thing not to respect Ernie, but it's stupid not to respect your fears.

"There's obviously been a big misunderstanding." Boniface was talking as if he was chatting to a cop—he was serious but believed they were on the same side. "I'm writing a biography about the band Prickle—I don't know if you've heard of them. Gray was the founder and the original lead singer, so he knows a lot that would be really good for the book. I was hoping he might have some old photos."

So this was how Boniface was going to react? With bullshit. Ernie wouldn't feel so bad about leaving him with Wes and Jojo if that was the other man's attitude. If he had started with the truth—or even made an acknowledgement that there was a truth to be told—then he might have reconsidered, but now...it didn't seem much point.

"A biography? And yet you haven't had the civility to talk to me?" He spun on his heel, slowly pacing around Boniface. "If there's money involved, then you should be paying it directly to me. I see no reason for middlemen who will want to take their cut or who might accidentally lose the money before it reaches me."

Boniface had the courtesy to introduce a tremble in his voice when he continued. "I'm sorry, I didn't know I needed to...Gray didn't..."

Ernie exhaled, continuing his pacing. "While I acknowledge that there was an apology—of sorts—wrapped up in your last few words, I'm still left wondering what else you haven't asked. What else should I know?"

Boniface seemed to change course. "It's been hard with the band's management problems...I didn't know I was...and I haven't—I mean there's no—at least not at the moment..."

"No what?"

"Money," said Boniface. "I'm not paying Gray for the biography."

"Let me get this straight," said Ernie. "You're not meeting our little songbird's debts and you're also trying to say there are management problems, which mean it's not your fault. But we're talking about my band and I find that a bit...confusing."

It was as if Boniface genuinely did not understand what he had just heard.

"For someone who says he's an author, you seem to be very persistent." Ernie stopped his circling, now standing face-on to Boniface. "But here's the interesting thing—you say you're an author, but the business card you left says you're a PR man. It doesn't stack up. And neither does it square with your first visit here."

Ernie stood back. "I don't issue threats and I definitely don't issue ultimatums—they just encourage people to do stupid things that they didn't really want to do in the first place—so I'll just say that I hope this is the last time we will meet in a business context." He turned to Wes and Jojo. "Will you two gentlemen be kind enough to escort Mister Boniface off the premises? Our business here is concluded."

Jojo opened the door and Ernie stepped out. The door slammed behind him as he followed the concrete and brick leading him to the stairs up to the courtyard.

twenty-six

The deadbolt turned.

The deadbolt turned the other way—of course he wouldn't have known that bolt was already unlocked. Unless he had called, and why would he?

Veronica leaned forward, picking up the bottle of whisky next to her handbag, and poured another measure. A large one.

The key tapped around the top lock and eventually found its home, zipping into the empty space before turning.

The door opened. Steps. The door closed. He knew she was there—either that or he thought very careless burglars had passed through—but he said nothing and didn't come into the room.

She heard the bathroom door open, and then there was nothing. There was no squeal of the door shutting. No sound to imply he was urinating.

Nothing.

She took a sip, replaced her tumbler on the table, and called: "Conventionally, when one has guests, one comes in and says good evening."

No response.

"Boniface?"

Veronica stood and walked through the lobby to the bathroom, cautiously rounding the final corner, letting Boniface come slowly into view. She gasped "what happened to you?" and ran forward, stroking Boniface's cheek with the back of her hand.

Boniface remained stationary, leaning on the sink and looking in the mirror. "Apparently I tripped over."

"And broke your fall with your face?" She almost sniggered, quickly lifting a hand to her mouth. "What happened? Did the big boys at the theater argue when you said you didn't like the color pink?"

"Ha, ha," said Boniface mirthlessly. "The unlicensed minicab driver who brought me back was scarier—the door had a broken catch and was held shut by one of those stretchy things with a hook at each end. Apparently he's getting it fixed tomorrow."

He raised a hand to his cheek, revealing a jacket seam under his arm that had been pulled apart, and then turned to face her, showing a ripped knee, his breast pocket pulled off the jacket, and grime stains scraped up his chest.

"You look like shit, Boniface. Perhaps it's time for you to start drinking again, darling." She stopped, not believing what she saw. "Where are your buttons?"

"Over a very wide area. But at least Jojo satisfied himself that I wasn't wearing a wire." He sighed heavily. "Not that Jojo would know what a recorder looks like—all he's seen are cop shows with a big clunky lump of wire taped to the cop's chest so that you know he's wired."

Looking at him straight on, the damage to his face looked worse than she had first suspected. His upper lip was cut and swollen. His left cheekbone was grazed, and his left eye would probably be black by tomorrow. "What happened to your cheek?" She heard the panic in her voice as she realized that the three-inch straight mark on his face was a gash.

"Wes—or rather, Wesley's knife. The knife was bigger than him." His hand moved to his left ear. "He started on my ear—trying to scare me. It worked. Then he was playing the big man—trying to scare me even by rubbing the blade on my cheek." His face loosened. "I think it scared him more than me when he cut the skin."

"Have you called the police?"

"No. And we're not going to, and we're not going to document...this." He indicated himself. "If we call the police, then I can't... And by the way, you're only seeing the edited highlights." He pointed around his face. "There's more below, but I don't think anything is broken."

Veronica ran forward, clinging to him, feeling the tears start to flow.

"Ow," whispered Boniface. "I hurt all over."

Veronica jumped back, tears flowing faster. "What hurts most?"

"Everything—but apparently I'm lucky. Ernie doesn't want me pissing blood tomorrow."

"Do you want a whisky?" asked Veronica.

"Thank you, but no. That's the thing about not drinking—you don't drink, even when you want one."

"Then you should have a bath—a long soak. When you get out, you can tell me all about it." She looked into the sink in front of the mirror. "Use the bathroom in your room—I'll clean up here."

twenty-seven

"I don't trust Boniface." Ernie ran a hand over his rough cheek. "Even after Jo and Wes have talked to him, I won't trust him. His story doesn't make sense—I can't even figure it from his perspective."

He inhaled deeply—a moist sound cultivated by fifty-five years of smoking.

"I don't trust Billy. Junkies are never reliable."

He paced the short distance from his desk to the door, turning and continuing to talk. "And I definitely don't trust Gray."

He reached his desk—a chunk of wood that was older than him and wider than he was tall—and rested on it. "As for those bastards at PAD Management...they're slippery. I've dealt with a lot of villains, but that bloke with the jewelry and his idea of truth..."

Iain Irvine remained motionless in the corner—his liver-spotted hide glistening in the few rays of light that Ernie hadn't scared out of the room. "Do you want me to handle this?"

"Yeah," said Ernie. He stood again and slowly began to pace around his desk. "But more than that, I want to know what their angle is. How does Boniface fit with Billy and Gray—is he onto us? And why did he seem to know about PAD?"

The muscles in his upper lip remained taut. Irvine spoke. "I'll apply some pressure—legal, of course. I am your lawyer, after all—in the right places. I'll go round first thing in the morning—I'll take Jojo or Wes to make sure that I articulate the message clearly."

"Make sure the message gets through," said Ernie. "But remember, this is about applying heat—not burning."

twenty-eight

About an hour after returning home, Boniface, wrapped in a white toweling robe with his damp hair combed back, shuffled into his front room and dropped onto the sofa diagonally opposite Veronica.

"For the record, I still hurt."

"Aren't you meant to make some joke about the other guy?"

"I believe that's the form—but they were both younger than me and clearly enjoyed their work. And I saw them walk away after they dropped me so delicately outside their boss's fine establishment, having doused me in cheap gin and left the bottle next to me so that anyone who passed would think I was drunk."

Veronica took a sip of her whisky, replacing the tumbler on the table in front of her. "So tell me what happened—start from when you left me."

Boniface exhaled, his mouth a tight circle. A tight, painful circle. "Kit. I saw Kit Flambeau. Nice chap, but he gave me nothing. Nothing. And for all the flamboyance—when you turn off the audience, he's a very quiet guy."

"So where next?"

"Fat Terry—he sends his regards, by the way. If ever you need his skills, just call." Veronica winced and Boniface continued. "He had the address for one of the girls who sung in the band with Dawn. Jilly Crossley, as was, now Gillian Walker."

"I don't remember the name," said Veronica. "I remember the band—or at least, I'm familiar with the story of the end. They were the lot where the girl fell in the Thames and drowned."

"Lorna," said Boniface. "The poor girl's name was Lorna Roscoe."

"If we could do today's forensic tests, then I'm guessing we would have found a lot of illegal substances in her system."

"That would be my guess, too," said Boniface. "And like you, I didn't know Jilly's name until Terry mentioned it, but then again, she didn't know who I was, so that made us even." He winced as his stomach muscles tightened. "When I got there she was having a bitch of an evening, and to be honest, my heart wasn't in it."

"That's not like you, Boniface."

"Quite the contrary," said Boniface, slowly maneuvering to face her more fully, "I give up quickly when there's no prospect of victory. When I got there she was having a row with her daughter on the phone and there were these three grandkids—a babe in arms, a clingy two- or maybe three-year-old, and this little bastard, Rafferty, who seemed to make everyone's life hell. I'm guessing she had been with the kids all day and the daughter had just dropped the kids on her for the rest of the night, so she was pretty cantankerous, and there was this image Terry left in my mind."

"I don't think I want to know about Terry's image."

"Do you know how hard it is to talk to somebody when all you can think about is their wonky headlights?" Boniface held his hands in front of him, raising one and lowering the other.

"That aside," said Veronica dismissively, closing her eyes.

"She seems to think Dawn was culpable—no, not culpable...but not without responsibility—for the death of Lorna."

"Did she elaborate?"

"Not really—but I didn't want to push. She seemed ready to snap with those kids, and I think I shocked her the way I sprung Lorna's death on her. From her reaction, I could believe that she sat down and wept after I left."

"So is there a link here—someone has an angle on Dawn about Lorna's death, Dawn gets windy and does a runner?"

"But why would Dawn suddenly run twenty, maybe thirty years later?" He relaxed back into the sofa, wincing as he released his weight into the padding. "And why would she react so badly when I chatted with her?"

"Call—see if Dawn's home—ask."

"Can't," said Boniface flatly. "If she's not home, all a call at this time of day will do is worry Danny even more."

Veronica started to disagree, then gave way. "You talked to Jilly—where next?"

"Jilly was in Leyton, so I jumped on the Central Line, got off at Bethnal Green, and walked up to Haggerston."

"Haggerston! Without an armed guard or police escort."

"It's not that bad."

"Allow me to get a mirror for you." She paused. "Why Haggerston?"

"Prickle's former lead singer Gray mentioned this club—he said this was where he had met the elusive Billy Watkins—the guy whose name scared Dawn. So I went to see if I could find Billy, and you know the rest. Well, apart from me scraping myself off the floor, crawling to the taxi office, cleaning myself in the dirtiest bathroom in London, and riding in the cab from hell over here."

"This is the Billy you wanted me to look into?"

"That's the one," said Boniface, feeling some enthusiasm for the first time since he met Ernie.

"Well, it's been a wasted beating you've taken: Billy's dead."

twenty-nine

Montbretia surveyed the wreckage.

Boniface called it his face. She called it what it was—wreckage. And apparently there was more damage under the suit, not to mention damage to yesterday's suit.

Yesterday's suit had been blue. Apparently that suit was no longer. It had sustained injury while undertaking duty on the front line and had later died from those injuries when Boniface got home. He and his former wife had paid tribute at the funeral.

Today's suit was charcoal gray, although it was unclear why Boniface felt the need to waste another suit, especially when what he should be wearing was cotton wool to protect himself from any new bumps. And if he was going out, surely he should be wearing jeans like her—clothes intended to sustain at least some physical stress.

She handed him a blister strip of paracetamol and a plastic bottle of ibuprofen. "You can take them together—they're different types of painkillers. The Tylenol"—Boniface frowned—"sorry, what you call paracetamol is probably better for pain, and the ibuprofen is an anti-inflammatory. Which you need."

He grunted.

"Have you eaten?"

Another grunt, but less committed. "I'm not letting you go anywhere until you have, but first..." She walked to the kitchen, filled a glass of water, and returned, placing it on his desk before leaning over to pick up the paracetamol and push out one tablet from the blister pack, dropping it on the desk in front of him. "Extra strength; you only need one." Then she picked up the plastic bottle, pressed on the top to open the childproof cap, and fished out a round tablet that she dropped next to the first. "Take. Now."

Boniface grunted, took a sip of water, then put both tablets in his mouth and swallowed before taking another sip and replacing the glass on his desk.

"You don't have to thank me," said Montbretia. "Just tell me what Veronica said about Billy Watkins."

"He's dead," mumbled Boniface.

"You said that. She didn't just say, 'He's dead, bye,' or even, 'He's dead; wow, it looks like you've got a shiner coming'—which, by the way, you have—'bye.'"

Boniface took another sip. "Veronica found a guy called Billy

Watkins. He was a few years older than Dawn and was born a few streets away from Dawn."

"That's hardly conclusive."

Boniface shrugged, then closed his eyes, seemingly trying to block out the pain. "It's not, but it was New Addington."

"So? Where is it? What does that mean?"

"You've been in London for a year—there's a reason you've not heard of New Addington," said Boniface. "It was one of those areas they reinvigorated after the war. They used the greenbelt to circumscribe the urban sprawl, but they managed to fit this small island within the permitted zone. The idea was to build a vibrant community in the middle of what was effectively countryside, but which was actually in London."

"I'm already guessing..."

Boniface seemed to want to soften his face, but as he did he put his hand to his cheek. "They built the estate, but by the time they got round to building the transport they had run out of money, so it never happened—meaning no one in New Addington could travel to work, so no one got a job and crime rose, social security rates went up, gangs started to...you get the idea."

"But that still doesn't prove that Billy is Dawn's Billy—surely the guy could have got out of town. There must have been some roads."

"It doesn't prove—but this Billy stayed around New Addington. His criminal record tells us he didn't travel far from home, and Dawn told me she was there until she was 16, so it's not totally unreasonable to make an assumption."

"What happened to Billy?"

"Car crash in 1994. He died. The passenger—a woman—survived. That's all we know." He looked overwhelmed by the effort—as if his weakened body was having its energy sapped as he forced his brain to retrieve information and lay out a series of basic facts in a logical order.

"So you're going to leave it alone now?"

"Of course. If Dawn's back. If not..." He shrugged and seemed to regret the movement.

"Have you seen a doctor?" He moved his eyes—slowly, as if they hurt too—and focused on her, without the energy to keep his eyelids fully open. "Seriously, Boniface. You should."

"I'll be fine." He talked without moving a facial muscle—expelling oxygen without allowing his lungs to move his chest.

"And what did the police say?"

"Are you and Vron ganging up on me?" If he hadn't been so weak, Montbretia expected there would have been anger in his words. He tried to expel air through his nose, but seemed to find only discomfort, so he stopped. "We're not going to the police about any of this. Danny doesn't want the publicity or the embarrassment for Dawn. No one wants a potential nonissue—which this could turn out to be—becoming a matter of legal record."

"You reckon somebody beat the living..." She let the thought hang as she reformulated her words. "You think somebody did this to you over a nonissue?" She waited, not really expecting a response. "Do you even know what *this* is?"

"Do you?" His voice was quiet but accusing.

"What I know is this presented as a problem that Dawn and Danny had. They came in here—this room," she moved back from his desk into the middle of the room, "and, according to you, said that they—they, both of them together—had a problem."

Boniface's eyes made the slightest movement—this seemed to be an acknowledgement requiring the least physical pain.

"That's not what's being said on the internet," said Montbretia. "Dawn is the one getting the kicking...Danny and Prickle are secondary."

Boniface half-smiled. "But here's the thing—I go looking for the guy whose name scared Dawn, and everything I find relates to Prickle. Just before my pounding, Ernie said some crazy stuff—I don't quite remember what he said; I had other thoughts going through my head, and it wasn't really a matter of proper etiquette to ask if I could take notes." He leaned on his desk, wincing slightly. "There's a link—I don't know what it is, but there's a link." He moved his head to face Montbretia directly. "And I'll see what Danny thinks about it when I get down there."

"You're going there?" Montbretia could hear the concern in her voice as its pitch lifted.

"Yeah."

"Do you really have to? I really think you..."

"I have to." Boniface was moving slowly, but he seemed to be hiding any pain.

"Is Dawn back?"

"I'll find out when I get there." His tone indicated the conversation was at an end. "And when I get there, is there anything I can tell him about the amps for Luca?"

Montbretia brightened. "I found a company that love Luca and would like to talk about endorsement—they're called Zeimetz Tone Engines. I'll print out the details before you go."

She paused. "But once you've talked to Danny, please leave this alone. Walk away. And if you can't walk away, then call the cops."

thirty

Montbretia had insisted on going to fetch him a bacon sandwich. "With a face like that, you need food, Boniface. When did you last eat properly?"

He had complained, but not too loudly: It hurt, and if he was honest, once Montbretia had put the idea in his mind, he wanted a bacon sandwich but didn't want the hassle of going out and waiting in a line. Nor did he want people staring at his injuries while he stood in line.

She made him a cup of tea before she went out, which had reached drinking temperature when she returned with his sandwich. She didn't need to, but Boniface felt it was better to give way on some small things while digging his heels in for the things that mattered. His final sip of tea washed down two further painkillers, and before he left she wrapped two additional tablets in a tissue, slipping the wrap into his jacket pocket with instructions to take them at some point. "You're not going to overdose on six tablets," she said. "The injuries that those kids have inflicted on you will do you far more harm than a few over-the-counter pharmaceuticals."

And with those words, she had escorted him to the barge—the Mercedes permanently lent to him by his friend Gideon—which he then let drift him down to the Surrey Hills.

For this visit, he had two advantages that he hadn't had on his first trip. First, he at least had a clue about where he was going—he still clicked up the navigation thingy on his phone, but at least with this journey he recognized one or two familiar landmarks. Second, it was morning—before midday. With each minute, the sun got higher, and while this didn't add much to the ambient temperature of the early spring morning, it did bring an additional brightness as the sun's rays penetrated the dense canopies in the woods and copses, giving pools of light and pools of darkness to the narrow twisting road—a groove digging its way through the sandstone banks that he passed in the Surrey Hills.

In daylight it was much easier to see the cars coming in the opposite direction from some distance, but there was a new hazard: ramblers. Those that stood in the sun or moved were easy to spot. Those that saw a car and withdrew to the shadows became invisible specters waiting to jump out at him when his only hope of not killing them was to throw the steering wheel in the opposite direction. And as he threw the steering wheel—even with the power steering—he remembered the less than subtle message that Wes and Jojo had given him last night.

The Mercedes skidded on the imperfect surface of the road. The turnoff into Danny and Dawn's drive came upon him faster than he expected; she didn't say anything, but Boniface was sure that the woman giving him directions on his phone now thought a little less of him for not paying sufficient attention. He dropped the car into reverse, rolled it back twenty or thirty yards, and turned onto the stone driveway, pulling up in the small group of cars between the three buildings.

Luca was sitting just outside the kitchen door at a cast-iron table— white with patches of rust and enough space for four chairs, although there were only two. He had a cup of coffee in front of him and his phone in his hand. With the delicacy of movement that was only available to surgeons and musicians, Luca tapped out a message on his phone with his right hand while picking up his coffee with his left. The coffee returned to the table as the Italian continued to focus on his message—or more likely, messages.

Boniface eased himself out of the barge, slowly standing and wondering if this is what old age would feel like. At the studio door, he noticed Danny and raised his hand in greeting—the bassist returned the sign. Then Boniface pointed to Luca, tapped his wrist where most people wear a watch, and held up a splayed hand. Danny gave him two thumbs up and disappeared into the studio.

"Luca, hi. I'm Boniface."

Boniface held out his hand, ready to shake the Italian's. The guitarist continued typing with his thumb, then looked up and gently slapped his left hand across Boniface's outstretched palm as he started typing again. "Are you our new daddy? You seem to be around a lot.... Or should I call you uncle? Zio Boniface." Luca briefly lifted his eyes to scan Boniface as the Englishman pulled back the other chair. The Italian continued in his heavily accented voice. "Did you fight our last daddy—is that when you got hurt, Zio?" He seemed to want a reaction, but not a response.

Boniface cautiously lowered himself into the chair, feeling the hard iron patterning refusing to give any comfort to his back, arms, and legs. He sat as still as he could, and in modulated tones asked, "Have you heard of Zeimetz Tone Engines?"

"Of course. I'm not stupid, Zio. I use guitar amps for a living." The guitarist didn't look up from his phone.

"What do you think of their gear?"

The guitarist reached for his coffee, keeping his focus on his phone, gently rocking his head from left to right. "Some of the best."

"They want you to endorse them."

Luca looked up from his phone, his eyes widening, his long wavy hair settling after the sudden movement. "So you're not my uncle, but Santa Claus."

"I'm not the hero here," said Boniface. "It's you they want. I'm just passing the message."

"Now I know you're kidding."

The pain across his back and legs was too much—the concentration of his weight onto the narrow metal patterns of the chair was hurting and what he really wanted were feather pillows delicately supporting him. Circumspectly, Boniface willed his body to the vertical, walking behind the chair to use it as a support while he kept his gaze locked with the Italian's. "Seriously—they've got some nice shiny new gear, and they'd like to lend it to you. Permanently."

The Italian put his phone on the table and leaned back in his chair before taking a sip of coffee. "What do I have to do? You know I don't have sex with men."

"They're after a simple endorsement deal. You use the gear in public, and they have your picture in a few ads." The Italian showed no emotion as Boniface continued. "As a start, they'd like a video of you trying the gear for the first time—you know, plug in, turn some knobs, strum, and make warm noises about how good it sounds. You can shoot it in my office if you want—Montbretia will call and arrange a time." He pulled a card out of his breast pocket and dropped it on the table. "Here's the address." He released his other hand from the chair and stood straight. "And if you tweet about the stuff, I'm sure Zeimetz won't complain."

The guitarist dropped eye contact and picked up his phone.

thirty-one

"The other guy?" Danny raised his brows to widen his eyes. "Sit down." He sat on the edge of his desk and pointed to the sofa—the sofa where Boniface presumed Danny had slept on the night that Dawn disappeared.

The bassist's attire seemed to be his standard non-stage wear, but with a different shirt and no jacket. He had a sympathetic look as he seemed to study Boniface's visible injuries, and remaining quiet, he lifted his hand—pointing without accusation—identifying each individual wound.

"You might not use words, but your actions imply you don't see me as the streetfighting type."

The bassist laughed. "Tommy told me you were a good guy—he didn't tell me about your hobbies. What happened?"

"Long story," said Boniface. "I'll get to it."

The bassist shrugged. "Is Luca okay?"

"Very okay, I think," said Boniface, enjoying the softness of the sofa after the battering of the iron chair. "We've got him some amps—Zeimetz Tone Engines."

Danny rocked back on the desk, his lower jaw hanging. "How did you pull that off? Those amps have got quite a reputation. Hand-built in...I'm going to go out on a limb—Luxembourg, isn't it?"

Boniface tried to nod but felt talking might hurt less. "Zeimetz have got a new model that they were going to launch last week. They had another guitarist ready to endorse the gear, but he got arrested on kiddie-fiddling charges two days before. They needed to move quickly, we got lucky, and Montbretia sweet-talked them."

"That great!" said Danny. "Really great. Well done, Boniface." He paused. "What does Luca have to do?"

"A few photos. A hand-over video. Use the stuff live. Maybe a workshop." Boniface tried to shrug. "Maybe he'll tweet about it."

"He probably has already," said Danny. "And he's cool with all this?"

Boniface moved his head up and down, feeling the tension in his neck pull with each movement. He looked up, noticing that Danny's face seemed to have changed. The mood in the room was different.

Danny leaned behind him and flicked the door.

The dark-colored utilitarian lump of wood—which probably met the latest fire standards for offices—swung, thudding into the doorjamb, the latch clicking to confirm that the door would not open without human intervention in the area of the handle.

The sound in the alcove office slowly decayed, leaving a space unlike the oasis in the next room. Here, harsh white walls with hard, reflective surfaces were a contrast to the other room, with its soft fabric masking acoustic baffles and gentle lights to comfort.

"She's not back." Danny's voice was small. "I've checked—and checked again. She hasn't taken anything—no cash, no cards, no jewelry. She definitely didn't sneak in last night. I was waiting—I didn't sleep."

Looking at him, Danny didn't look too bad for his lack of slumber. Then again, he had probably spent most of his working life with unconventional sleep patterns.

"I sent out the roadies—Sven and Reuben—on horses to look. Trouble is, no one knows this area like Dawn—she's always out walking, riding, taking pictures, talking to people." He paused, exhaling heavily. "She loved the area from the first time we came here—someone recommended the Norman church at Albury for our wedding, so we drove down here one afternoon." He brightened slightly. "About 18 months after we released 'Tattoo Your Name on My Heart,' the royalties came through. I asked her: 'What are we going to do with the money?' She had one response—buy a house in the Surrey Hills. Somewhere where we can raise kids. Somewhere where we can grow old. Without Dawn, there would have been no 'Tattoo.' Without 'Tattoo,' there would be no income and Prickle would have died. I would have had to get a proper job and a boring wife. So it was my pleasure to buy this house with that money."

Danny was looking down, hiding his eyes.

"Of course, there were never kids. Some call it a sadness—and I'm sorry about it; Dawn would have been a great mother—but how can I complain about anything when I've got a wife I love and who loves me, and we live here?"

"I saw Kit." Boniface wasn't sure whether to change the subject, but he guessed that Danny didn't want to lose face and cry in front of him.

"What?" Danny replaced the maudlin introspection with incredulity.

"Because he was around and he might have a clue about something you don't think is relevant."

"She's my wife, Boniface. I think I would know whether someone is a good person to talk to—and Kit isn't. Lovely guy, but not relevant here."

Boniface could hear the simper in his voice—he knew he was only asking the question to hide his embarrassment. "Have you found a singer for the gig yet? What about Kit?"

Danny's voice was slight. "I'd love Kit to sing for us, but the set is too long—it'd put too much strain on his voice—and anyway, he's already working that night."

The room fell silent—the two men looking at each other.

Boniface broke the noiseless entente. "And you're sure you don't want to talk to the cops about Dawn, or go to the press, or whatever?"

There was a rip of anger in the bassist's voice. "Dawn would hate the intrusion—years later it would still be like a scar you need to put makeup over. She remembers things." His voice softened—a tone of disappointment. "I thought you understood this."

"I thought I did," said Boniface quietly. "But when I started asking questions, you can see the results..." He unbuttoned his shirt to reveal more bruising over his chest. He felt the accusation in his voice. "Are you sure there's nothing else?"

Danny trembled. It wasn't anger that Boniface could see. This was a man who'd been awake too long and had been worrying too long, who'd just had the PR man he'd asked to help instead suggest that the worst-case scenarios he'd been thinking about—all those still-awake nightmares that he dismissed as ridiculous, all those unfeasible possibilities that only happen to other people—well, perhaps they could be happening to him. He started slowly. "I trust my wife."

Boniface wondered if that was all Danny wanted to say. A simple incontrovertible statement that encapsulated a basic truth but also reflected the entire basis of his life.

"Does she have secrets? Perhaps—but they'll be..." The bassist waved a hand in the air as if mimicking a butterfly. "But I don't need to know everything—I trust her, she tells me what she wants to tell me. You've met her—she's a good person, right? What's the worst that she could tell me?"

He dropped his head, catching it with his right hand, and sobbed.

thirty-two

"I didn't know what else to do," said Montbretia, opening the door for Boniface. She seemed twitchy, on edge. "I'm sorry—I put her in your room. I couldn't think..."

Boniface moved slowly, cautious not to knock his injuries on the door as he awkwardly slipped past Montbretia and started walking toward his office. "It's not a problem—I'll..." he reached the door to his office, trying to give Montbretia a reassuring look as she disappeared even though he wasn't sure what the problem was.

"This is an unexpected pleasure." Boniface watched the baby giraffe move her legs, readying to lift herself to the vertical. "Please don't stand. These sofas are far too low to get out of, especially when you've got heels." Boniface offered his hand to shake, casting a glance at what was probably better classified as small tower blocks strapped to the feet of his guest before feeling the delicate skin of her small paw momentarily slipped into his.

Leaving his guest where she sat gave Boniface the opportunity to orbit and observe the lawyer, an opportunity not afforded to him when he had visited PAD Management's offices on Denmark Street twenty-four hours earlier. In the intervening period, Boniface hadn't felt the need to revise his observation that she was long and skinny—she would probably always be—although she did seem to settle her frame into the sofa with surprising grace. However, there was something about the face.

Most people have a nose attached to their face. Fiona Aldred, the A in PAD Management, seemed to have a face attached to her nose. A slightly asymmetrical face, which in combination gave the appearance of something that Picasso may have produced in an experimental phase when working with human beings.

It wasn't unattractive—quite the contrary, it was certainly interesting, and if he wasn't in so much pain, Boniface wondered whether that interest could actually reach alluring—but nonetheless it was an unusual face that gave him too many things to think about. It also looked like an angry face, or if not angry, then certainly stern.

Still, an angry lawyer was preferable to a weeping bass player and a missing former model.

"Mister Boniface."

He had forgotten the depth of pitch of the quiet voice.

"Please, just Boniface."

She seemed to acknowledge this but did not correct herself, instead continuing: "PAD Management is a professional firm." Her volume lowered as she articulated each word individually. "The practices that are presently being adopted are outside the expected norms of behavior."

Boniface felt his eyes narrow and his head cock instinctively.

"I feel we were far more frank with you yesterday than was necessary, or indeed may have been appropriate, but I hope we illustrated to you that there are some very real—although not insurmountable—problems in the relationship between PAD and Prickle. But even so, we are not looking to end the relationship."

Boniface was unsure why he was being told what he already knew and had clearly understood at the time.

"We believe that the talent and experience we bring to the relationship has led to results and will continue to lead to results beneficial to both parties."

Boniface felt an overwhelming urge to call her Fifi but resisted. "That was my understanding following our meeting, Fiona."

The lawyer stared at Boniface. "Your lawyer would seem to suggest otherwise. Those *gentlemen*," the word dripped contempt, "who accompanied him seemed to be of a similar opinion."

"What lawyer?" asked Boniface.

The lips on Picasso's experiment pursed. "Aaron Delcort was pushed. Very roughly." Her tone fired accusations. "That sort of behavior is simply not acceptable under any circumstances." She relaxed slightly. "As far as I can tell, I didn't get threatened because they thought I was just the secretary. It's not every day you find yourself the beneficiary of ignorant sexism."

Boniface waited a moment or two, attempting to communicate that he was considering, then continued with a softness he hoped would lead Fiona's attitude to a calmer place. "I don't have a lawyer. I haven't asked anyone to call on you or to..."

"You will forgive my skepticism." There was a newfound force in the lawyer's voice. "While I'm grateful for my own personal safety, I find this denial rather hollow given that it is quite clear you are working for Prickle."

Boniface felt the confusion returning, and a need for more painkillers.

"Beyond Mister Irvine," continued the lawyer, "what about this?" She held up her phone, pointing to the screen. "While we may have a dispute with Prickle, we still like to keep up to date with them, and Luca is very keen to document every moment of his day. Apparently Zio Boniface—*Uncle* Boniface—has kindly supplied him with some new amplifiers made by Zeimetz Tone Machines. That seems a very generous action for a man who claims only to be writing a biography."

"There's a..." started Boniface.

"Shh," said the lawyer, getting to her feet and looking down at him.

"Let me be clear. We don't take well to threats—our next response will be to involve the police and to seek injunctions where necessary. As you will understand, that may have a reputational impact for your business."

She stepped back, seemingly judging the office. "As I've said, we believe we bring considerable talent to the relationship with Prickle. From what I've read about you, I'm not sure that you have the competence in this area or the resources to match what we offer. And if you do want to take the business of Prickle, you can be assured we will be looking for a considerable financial payment in settlement of our losses."

It only took her long legs two steps to reach the door, where she looked back. "One other thing." Boniface looked up. "Your lawyer. He isn't."

thirty-three

Boniface reached his office door in time to see Fiona Aldred step into the elevator.

"I really am sorry," said Montbretia as Boniface walked into her room and carefully lowered himself into the seat by the window. "She's..."

Boniface waited. When Montbretia offered nothing further, he threw out a few suggestions. "Tall?" Montbretia wrinkled her nose. "Skinny." Montbretia seemed to consider the description. "Odd." Apparently Montbretia couldn't dispute that characterization. "She might be odd, but I think she's competent, although perhaps a little misguided at the moment."

"Misguided?" asked Montbretia.

"I think there's some confusion," said Boniface. "I told Luca about the amps."

"I know," said Montbretia. Boniface frowned. "He tweeted about his amps and his new Uncle Boniface."

Boniface deflated. "Seems to be something of a theme here... Anyway, Luca is expecting a call from you when you're ready to make arrangements for the hand-over to be filmed, or whatever it is Zeimetz want." He leaned forward, feeling the pain. "Thank you for getting that sorted—in the world of Prickle, it is important."

"Talking about the world of Prickle, how was Danny?" asked Montbretia.

"Rough. Dawn's not back and he's not sleeping, which isn't that surprising."

"So that's the end of our dealings with them—apart from getting the amps to Luca?"

Boniface felt his head turning from left to right and back.

"So did he agree that you should go to the cops?"

"No."

"The press?"

"No."

"What did you agree on, Boniface?"

"Nothing. He wasn't in a state to agree to anything, and I didn't want to push him."

"You should have—you should have pushed him."

"He was in tears."

Montbretia let out an exasperated sigh. "And that is why you should have pushed him. If it matters enough to cry, then it matters enough to call the cops—especially because the evidence is only going to fade." She indicated the bruising and the cuts on his face.

"It's not important," muttered Boniface.

"He's been pushing you to help him—and it's in his best interest that everything is sorted—and when you get an opportunity to move things forward, you duck." She looked away, leaving the room quiet—the only sound coming from outside, where a delivery truck was reversing into the school grounds.

Boniface began softly. "I'm going to chat with Jilly again."

"The granny?" There was no approval in the question. "She's already told you to go away once. Do you think your war wounds will make you more appealing?"

"I want to see if she's a bit more amenable today. Hopefully I can get to her before the kids have worn her down."

"As an idea it's bonkers, but I'm not going to stop you." Her tone was resigned. "But please take some more painkillers before you leave."

thirty-four

"It's you again." She pulled the baby closer as she looked him up and down—her cynicism turning to concern. "You looked better yesterday." She squinted, as if looking at the detail of an oil painting. "A lot better."

"I felt better yesterday." The face of a granddaughter appeared between her grandmother's legs, her hands sturdily gripping a limb. "I came to apologize for yesterday—I got you at a really bad time and I intruded. And I was stupid to return the ball."

Her face softened. "Raff's at school, so it's calmer here. Us three girls together." She smiled at her two granddaughters, then pointed her head toward Boniface, questioning. "So what happened—who did you upset?"

Boniface looked down, feeling sheepish and not quite sure how to respond.

"Are you going to keep being a pain in the bum until I talk to you?" asked Jilly. He raised his eyes and twisted the side of his lip. "Do you want a cup of tea then?"

Jilly was already leading into the house before Boniface could respond. He followed her into the kitchen, where in one swing she flicked on the kettle and placed the baby in a high chair. "Savannah needs some lunch, so your tea will be a couple of minutes."

Boniface looked at the two-year-old still clinging to her grandmother's leg. "If you need another pair of hands..." Jilly turned to face him, a slight look of shock. "Let me wash my hands and I'll get straight on it."

She pointed to the sink and turned to the fridge. As Boniface dried his hands, she placed a small jar and a plastic teaspoon on the table next to the high chair where the baby sat. "Put this on." She handed him an apron from the back of the door. "Don't argue; that's a nice suit and Savannah will be wearing a bib, so you'll be even."

"This kitchen looks very new," said Boniface, sitting in front of the baby and unscrewing the cap of her food. "And it's all very clean and shiny. Do you have an army of people who come in to scrub and polish every night?"

"Ha!" Jilly threw back her head and laughed. "No—it is new. My ex is a plumber—I paid trade prices for the units, and he and two of his mates fitted it. They did the bathroom at the same time." She raised her eyes upward. "Turns out that in divorce he's not that unreasonable... Plus, he knew the grandkids would be spending a lot of time here, and he wants the best for them."

She looked over at her granddaughter swallowing another mouthful as Boniface cautiously removed the spoon. "You're good with kids."

"They see a kindred spirit—they recognize one of their own," said Boniface. "It's us kids against the world; no sense in fighting among ourselves."

"Any of your own?"

Boniface shook his head. "You've probably heard the story...my wife, now ex-wife, and I worked, I drank a lot, *a lot*, it was never the right time, I drank some more, I went to work for the government, I melted down, it all became ugly, the marriage ended. Good terms—but no kids."

"I'm sorry," she said quietly, watching Boniface feed her younger granddaughter.

"I've been talking to a lot of people over the past couple of days—one name came up which seems important." Boniface watched as Jilly's eyes brightened slightly. "Billy Watkins. Have you heard of him?"

"Heard of him. Met him," said Jilly softly. "He was the devil. At least as far as Dawn was concerned, he was all things that are evil rolled into one."

Boniface lifted another spoonful of puree and concentrated on the moving mouth in front of him.

"He turned up to an M-Stub8 gig one night. When I say gig, it was an appearance at a nightclub in somewhere like Stevenage, Letchworth, or Welwyn Garden City. One of those poxy commuter towns about thirty miles north of London. The Friday night crowd would be out on the prowl—those that pulled would go to their car and shag. Those that didn't would come and watch us lip sync while they leered and made the kinds of suggestions that only teenagers who have never had sex can make. The first we knew about Billy was when he took some kid out—the kid made a comment about Dawn, Billy fractured his cheekbone, and Dawn froze."

"Nice guy," said Boniface lightly. "The kind you'd want to invite round to meet your mother."

"He turned up quite a bit after that—it always upset Dawn. She'd known him from where she grew up and never wanted anything to do with him. He started chasing Carmen to make Dawn jealous; all that did was make Carmen unhappy and let Dawn get away." Her voice became reedy. "And then Lorna died and we fell apart. Carmen stayed with Billy—she didn't have anywhere else to go. We all clung to whatever driftwood was floating by—seems Dawn got lucky and grabbed a bit of solid oak."

She turned and faced out the window, her older granddaughter tugging at her leg. "So what's Billy done now?"

"He's dead," said Boniface.

"Dead?" She sounded almost relieved. "Does Dawn know? She'd be... well, it would be something she didn't have to worry about. She really was that upset whenever he turned up."

Boniface paused before he continued, his tone noncommittal. "Do you know where Carmen is these days?"

"No." Jilly seemed apologetic. "I last saw her a few years ago—I don't think the years have been kind. I only got half the story—she was in a car crash, a bad one, left her in a coma. After she left hospital, she self-medicated and worked the streets to pay for her habit. She was in a squat for a while, and I think she did some porn—the really unpleasant stuff. When we spoke, she was in a hostel trying to pull her life together again."

She stood up straight, picked up a cloth, and came over to the baby, wiping her mouth. "Was that nice? Say thank you to Uncle Boniface." She turned to Boniface. "That sounds a bit odd, Uncle Boniface."

"Savannah wouldn't be the first person to call me that today," said Boniface.

Jilly picked up the baby, resting her over her shoulder and gently patting her back. "Don't get me wrong—I'd like to see you come round here and feed her every lunchtime...and perhaps you could take Rafferty to the park until he's about 35—but I don't know anything more. It was a long time ago, and lots of those memories still hurt today."

thirty-five

"Boniface!" Montbretia answered the phone. "Please tell me you're not in a hospital somewhere—I freaked when I saw your number come up. I thought someone might have lifted your phone off your dead body."

She dropped into her chair.

"So where are you?" She pushed the handset under her chin, clicked her mouse, and called up a map onto the screen. "Leyton—I thought you went to see Jilly." She paused, listening, watching as the map focused in on Leyton. "Oh. Jilly's in Leyton. Did she tell you to go away again?"

Montbretia clicked from the map view to the street view, dragging the cursor through the streets of Leyton in East London. The streets looked similar to the streets she had walked through in Bethnal Green when Boniface had dressed her up as a hooker from the 1980s and made her knock on Gray's front door. Perhaps these houses were more modern and maybe a bit larger. They certainly had front yards, so you couldn't bang on a door as you walked along the street.

"You fed her grandkids! I never had you as the Mister Mom domestic-tranquility type...you get too upset when your suit gets splashed in the rain." She continued listening, pulling the phone tighter under her chin, typing in internet searches as he spoke. "Sure, I can find—or at least look for—someone. Who are you interested in? Carmen Gallagher. Was in M-Stub8 with Dawn and Jilly."

She looked at the images appearing on her screen. Most were scanned from newspapers and magazines dating from the 1980s, but some were of a higher quality. There were pictures of her on her own—mostly, but not all, in a state of undress—and some pictures with the band, all clothed but dressed in a way that felt familiar given how Montbretia had dressed to visit Gray.

"Carmen Gallagher," she said to Boniface. "What am I looking for?" She clicked through more photos.

There was something striking about the woman—she stood out. Her skin was perhaps slightly darker than the other girls—with a name like Carmen, Montbretia wondered if one or both parents might have been Spanish—and her hair was darker: thick and rich with a curl that seemed natural. But what reached out from the screen and grabbed Montbretia was the woman's confidence.

Carmen was forward, Carmen was fearless, she lacked any form of self-consciousness, she roared, she had an animal-like sexuality, she was provocative, bold, assertive, vigorous, full-on, unabashed, unrepentant.

Whether she was clothed, naked, or somewhere between, she was always smiling—not that fake model smile, but the smile that begins at the mouth, covers the whole face, and makes the eyes shine with complete joy. Smiling, shouting, cooing, and enjoying herself. Where so many models look as sexless as a three-year-old's plastic doll, Carmen—with or without clothes—always seemed to transmit the message that she *loved* sex.

"You want me to find her current location...might be a hostel in central London. Well, don't get too specific, Boniface. I'd hate to have an easy afternoon or to have any confidence that I can find an answer before you get back."

She scanned a few articles. Mostly old perverts with their own webpages reminiscing about the models from when they were teenagers—she decided not to look too closely in case Boniface's name was there. "Isn't this Lorna character important—might there be something in how she died? Yeah, I get that she's dead so she can't tell us anything, but what I'm saying is perhaps there's something related to her death and why Dawn disappeared."

The question seemed to make Boniface grumpy.

"Okay, okay. You can tell me why Carmen is important when you get back." She exhaled, pushing out her bottom lip. "So I'm looking on the internet and I'm not seeing any contact numbers—where do I start? Okay...I'll call Veronica for newspaper archives, but do we have a clue which hostel? Okay, I'll get on the phones."

thirty-six

Boniface decided to take the stairs. He was still in pain—and suspected he would be in some discomfort for a week or more—but he needed to stop behaving like an invalid, and it was only two flights of stairs. In any event, he hurt a lot less than he had this morning.

He stood outside the door and punched in the key code.

It was strange—usually the lights would be on. If not all the lights, then at least some. Switches were a thing of the past: All the lights in the office were on motion sensors coupled with timers. If you walked from one end to the other, the lights would come on, and then—according to some bizarre rules set by the electrician who did the fitting—the timers would progressively switch the lights off.

Theoretically, if you sat very still for a very long time, then all the lights would switch off, but the reality was that one or the other of them was always moving, so there would always be a light on somewhere.

Boniface opened the door and stepped into the main corridor, letting the door close behind him. The lights in the corridor clicked on, confirming there hadn't been a power cut. He stepped forward, and the sensor at the far end picked up the movement, firing more lights into action. When he passed the kitchen, there was a click and the light came on—he needed to call the electrician to fix that. There was no need to register someone passing. When he went into the kitchen to make tea, then he wanted light. When he passed, he wanted dark.

There seemed to be one thing missing: Montbretia.

He stepped into her room, lit only from the dull light outside, filtered through the tinted glass—a hangover from the 1970s. There was a buzz, and the light fired, revealing a floor covered with papers, scattered pens, and a broken mug, with what might be coffee splashed across the wall.

"Hello." A small voice came out from behind Montbretia's visitor's chair. "Has she gone?"

Boniface moved as quickly as he could to the chair and dropped to his knees, ignoring the pain as he maneuvered himself to look through the gap beside the chair, and into the space where Montbretia was sitting. "Hello," he said, looking at the figure sitting with her knees under her chin, her arms wrapped around her shins and pulling her legs toward her body. "Has who gone?"

"The woman who shouted."

"What woman who shouted?"

"The scary woman who shouted."

"I didn't see any woman—shouting or not."

"Go and look. Make sure she's gone." It wasn't a polite request. Montbretia had issued an order.

Boniface stood slowly. Maybe he should try not to kneel down on a hard surface for a day or two.

He walked into his room—the light flicked on—and checked behind his sofa and under his desk. No one, shouting or otherwise. There was no one in the meeting room—including under the long table. The two client rooms were similarly bereft of people, and both the kitchen and the reception area were empty.

He reached Montbretia's door before turning and checking the fire door, which was locked, and then checked the front door, which was properly closed.

"There's no one here," he said, looking down at Montbretia, who was still sheltering behind her chair. "Do you want a hand up?" He reached down. After a few moments Montbretia grabbed his hand and pulled herself to the vertical. She pushed the chair forward with her knees, slipping through the gap, and hugged Boniface. "She was scary and she shouted. Very loud. And she threw things."

"It's not like you not to fight back," said Boniface. "But please don't think I'm not grateful that I don't have to buy new carpets again."

"I don't like fighting on home soil. And I couldn't injure myself—one of us has to remain capable, and it's not you at the moment."

"I can feed babies. What further skill could I need?" asked Boniface mock-huffily. "Who was she?"

"I don't know. She was scary and shouted and threw things. Isn't that enough for you to identify her?"

"Probably," said Boniface.

"What did she look like?"

"Shorter than me. Slim. Angry. Long dark hair, straight. Asian, perhaps, Thai, maybe, but probably Filipino."

"Alone?"

"No—there was a big dumb lump, but he didn't say anything."

"Did she say what she wanted?"

"You mean in between throwing things?" Boniface nodded. "The gear—she said it was hers."

"What gear?"

"The gear—the gear for Luca." She stepped back and lifted her shoulders, then sighed deeply. "Has she really gone?"

"Mmm."

"She got really angry when I said the gear isn't here." Montbretia looked up, letting her hair fall over her face. "Who is she, Boniface?"

"I don't know, but my guess is you just met Bing-Bing, Missus Parzani, Luca's former wife."

There was a look of surprise on Montbretia's face. "Why did she...?"

Boniface raised his shoulders slightly. "My guess? Luca tweeted about the new amps, she saw the opportunity for him to make further reparations but didn't realize the gear hasn't arrived, and you got in her way."

"Really?"

"It's my best guess," said Boniface. "You still look shaken—let's get out of here and get some lunch."

"We can't leave," said Montbretia. "She'll be back. The last thing she said was, 'You'll be sorry.'"

"It was just an empty threat. Come on—let's get something to eat. If you're not here, she can't hurt you."

thirty-seven

Montbretia and Boniface left the first flight of stairs, turning onto the second flight leading up to their office. "That's a good place for lunch," said Boniface. "Good food. Not too heavy."

"I told you you'd like it," said Montbretia. "Now do you understand why I wanted to go there?"

"I do," said Boniface, reaching the landing and falling silent.

Montbretia walked around him, then noticed where he was staring. "Did you lock the door?"

"You say that as if locking the door would have stopped the glass getting kicked in." They looked through the lower half of the door to the glass—which had previously filled the pane, but which was now shattered and scattered over their carpet.

Part of the wooden frame that had held the pane had been twisted but not fully broken off, and was stopping the door from closing. "You wait here," said Boniface, gingerly pulling the door.

"No," said Montbretia, stepping into the passage and following Boniface as he pushed himself against the wall to avoid the broken nuggets of glass. "Did you set the alarm?"

"It was only a quick lunch," said Boniface, walking into Montbretia's office.

Her desk drawers had been removed, their contents tipped in a pile on the floor on top of the already scattered papers, and the empty drawers stacked roughly on the desk. He looked more closely: The faces of two drawers had been pulled from the rest of the drawer. The chair—her earlier buttress against invaders—had been tipped over.

"It's that bitch," said Montbretia. "She said she'd be back."

Boniface led into his room to see the sofa tipped over and the desk drawers open but not removed.

"So I tell you not to keep anything in your desk—I scan every document for you—and it's my desk that gets emptied."

Boniface quietly led into the conference room to see the table had been turned over. He poked his head into the two client rooms to see similar, and then looked in the kitchen, which seemed exactly as it had been when he'd last looked in.

"I'm telling you, Boniface. It's that bitch—she said she would come back. She said I'd be sorry." Boniface watched Montbretia. She stood straighter, uncurling her shoulders. She inhaled deeply. "I'm calling the cops."

"No." Boniface's voice was quiet, but the speed was reflexive. "Don't call them. Not yet."

"If not now, then when?" Montbretia's tone suggested her frustration at Bing-Bing was transferring into anger at Boniface.

"Apart from the door, there's no real damage. If, repeat *if*, it's Bing-Bing, then that will just be embarrassing for Danny and the band."

"What do you mean no damage? And who cares about embarrassment?"

"I mean this is a mess that will take us both..." he exaggerated the word *both*, pointing between them, "a while to clean up. But it will take far longer to talk to the police. And we all care about embarrassment—think how we'll feel if we call the cops and they can't prove it was Bing-Bing."

Boniface watched as Montbretia's face twitched.

"We need to get out of here," said Boniface. "It's not safe with all that glass, and I'm not leaving you here. Give Luca a call—don't tell him about this, but say we want five minutes to talk about the amps, away from Danny. While you do that, I'll call the carpenter."

thirty-eight

"May I just officially state for the record: The Surrey Hills are gorgeous. Why haven't you told me about them before?"

Boniface seemed to have decided that Montbretia's question was rhetorical.

"Is this place real? I mean, do people live here—it looks like a film set. You know, the kind of place where there's some busybody old woman who figures who committed the murder before the detectives. Then she just says 'hmm' when they ask and brings everyone together to confront the murderer...in the library."

"They do shoot a lot of stuff around here," said Boniface. "But these are real places. Real villages with real people. People actually live and work here."

"Wow," said Montbretia. "I'm coming down on my bike."

"The third best way to get around," said Boniface.

"Third?"

Boniface tilted his head forward as he steered along the narrow lane, flinching when the barge drifted close enough to sculpt the sandstone banks. "You need to understand the geography of the place."

"And you do?" Montbretia was not convinced.

"No," said Boniface. "But Dawn does, and she told me."

Montbretia accepted defeat and went back to looking out the window as Boniface continued. "There's the main road that goes through the bottom of the valley. And from this central road, there are spurs that jut off."

"Are we on a spur now?" she asked.

"Yeah," said Boniface. "And the difficulty with the spurs is that if you want to go from place A on one spur to place B on the adjacent spur, and you want to drive, then most of the time you have to go all the way out to the central spine and back again. And as you will have figured, that gives you a long journey along narrow, twisting roads."

"Narrow, but pretty—it's just so green out here, Boniface."

"It might be," he said, his tone unaltered. "However, if you're driving, your attention tends to focus on not wrecking your car on these sandstone banks."

"Okay," said Montbretia hesitantly. "But that still doesn't tell me why a bike is only the third best way to travel around here."

"You will have noticed the hills," said Boniface.

"I saw the sign," said Montbretia. "You pointed to it—it had the word *hill* on it. But they're not exactly massive hills, are they?"

"You mean, we're in the hills, not in the mountains," said Boniface. "And the thing with these hills is they're pretty irregular, so to answer your question, the best way to travel around here is on foot. The distances aren't huge, and you can go directly from one point to another without needing to come out to the central spine."

"You are aware that bikes can follow footpaths?" asked Montbretia.

"I am," said Boniface. "But they have wheels that can buckle and tires that puncture, which is why they're not as good as walking or the second best way to get around: horses."

The tree cover cleared, giving a view of the late afternoon sky but little sight of the surrounding land, which was separated by tall hedgerows on the sides. The road twisted again before inclining downward, passing through another tunnel formed by trees, giving way to a clear stretch of asphalt, lined below the height of the road by a row of red-brick houses with deep-pitched roofs.

Boniface slowed the barge and turned to the right into a large parking lot, its uneven surface covered by gravel.

"Where are we?" asked Montbretia.

"Exactly where you told Luca we would be."

"You said 'the pub in Peaslake.' I thought that was...code." She looked around. "Where are we?"

"Peaslake," said Boniface and pointed at a wide two-story building, rendered in white, with dark-brown roof tiles. "And that is the pub."

"But how will Luca know that this is the right pub?"

"Because it's the only pub," said Boniface. "I don't want to overstate the case, but with that row of houses," he indicated the row that they had just passed, "and those houses over there," he pointed to the houses on the slopes of a hill about 50 yards away—a mismatched collection of red brick and some mock-Tudor woodwork dotted between enough trees to suggest these building had just escaped from the woods, "that is the whole village. Come on, I'll take you to the heart of the metropolis."

Boniface led Montbretia out of the parking lot. "Where's the sidewalk?"

"There isn't one," said Boniface, leading Montbretia past the pub with a large red-brick chimney seemingly glued to the outside wall on top of the white render. The road forked as it reached a junction, forming a small grass triangle with a sign declaring that you were indeed in Peaslake. Boniface took two steps forward, indicating in turn the village stores, a small, squat building with a glass frontage divided into individual panes; the village war memorial, a simple stone cross; a red telephone booth; and a red letter box. "And here ends the official tour of Peaslake."

"That's it?"

"It's a village."

"It's...it's beautiful." There was a lightness to Montbretia's voice. "Tiny, but beautiful. I don't care what you say, Boniface. I am so coming back here on my bike. How did you find it?"

"I took the wrong road when I left Danny's." He turned back to the pub. "Let's go and sit down while we wait for Luca."

The two settled with a cup of tea and a mineral water, taking position on a not particularly comfortable sofa with a clear view of the door. "There he is," said Boniface as Luca came through the door, his long hair looking somehow out of place in an English village that seemed to have lost track of time somewhere around the mid-1930s.

Three people—two men and one woman—all in their sixties or seventies headed toward the door, blocking Luca's path. Their senses of style could not be more different. The rock god in jeans and a leather jacket, his flowing mane and the swagger. The pensioners' prevalent color of choice was beige; their style of dress—to be kind—could be described as elasticated easy wash.

Montbretia heard the end of the conversation. "Bella." The Italian was holding the older woman's hand to his lips—his gaze fixed on her face.

"Is he flirting with her?" she asked, keeping her lower jaw immobile.

"Don't be jealous," said Boniface. "Your turn will come."

Luca was beaming, holding the door for the three pensioners. As the woman passed, Luca's face dropped, and he released the door onto her two male companions before he turned toward the bar. Spying the barmaid his shoulders went back, his chest puffed out, and the edge of his grin returned.

"Are we going to have this with every woman in the bar?" asked Montbretia, her jaw becoming tighter. "I ask that because I think that dog over there is a bitch," she nodded toward a damp and muddy golden Labrador lying next to her master.

"I said your turn would come," said Boniface. "I'm just not sure whether you're in the queue before or after the Lab." The barmaid put a drink in front of Luca. He made a comment and she blushed, her cheeks getting redder as Luca continued talking. Finally, the guitarist picked up the glass, pointed to Boniface, winked at the barmaid, and continued chatting with her.

"According to Mel—Prickle's drummer—around this time of day he'll be looking to find a woman for the night using that fearsome combination of social media, his natural charisma, his complete lack of self-consciousness, and desperation."

"Desperation?" asked Montbretia.

"If he doesn't hook up with a woman who can provide recreation and a bed, then he has to spend the night in the hotel that Danny is paying for—and it's a pretty grim, tedious box out by the main road."

"Why doesn't Danny let him stay at his place?"

"Apparently—and I'm just repeating what Mel told me—Luca is very uninhibited and is very proud of his body. This combination meant there was far too much chance of *accidental* nudity—you could find that he'd come down for breakfast, get a coffee, sit outside and have a smoke, and the idea of putting on clothes wouldn't have crossed his mind."

"Oh."

"Danny could cope—he's been touring with the guy for years. But he didn't want to inflict that on Dawn."

"Zio Boniface." The guitarist was standing on the other side of the low table in front of Boniface and Montbretia's sofa. "You need to pay Chloe for the drink." He lifted his glass as if it explained fully, then turned toward the bar. "Chloe, bella." The barmaid blushed again.

Luca dropped into the chair opposite Montbretia, taking her hand and focusing his full wattage on her. "So, Uncle. Is this my next present that you're bringing me to win favor?" His gaze remained on Montbretia. "Are you trying to show me that you're a cool uncle?"

"This is Montbretia—who you should thank for sorting the Zeimetz Tone Engines deal."

"Ciao, Montbretia," said Luca without letting his gaze slip. "So she is my present. She is a very beautiful present, Uncle. Thank you. I will be sure to show her my full appreciation for all she has done to help me."

Montbretia pulled her hand away.

"Fiery," said Luca, a look of delight exploding over his face.

"We've got a slight problem," said Boniface. "Over here, Luca." He snapped his fingers, twice, and for the first time since he had sat down, Luca relaxed his gaze on Montbretia. "Bing-Bing came to try to take possession of your new amps."

"Which haven't arrived yet," added Montbretia.

A look of glee spread over Luca's face.

"She was pretty abusive. She got very aggressive."

A look of serenity crossed Luca's face. "She's a woman who knows her own mind."

"Then later," continued Boniface, "while we were both out, the office got trashed."

Luca shook his head—there was a slight rustling as his mane settled.

"You do see the link, Luca?"

"You're wrong, Zio. It wasn't her," said Luca. "Bing-Bing didn't trash your office." He paused. "You clearly don't understand strong women, Zio Boniface."

"There's strong and borderline sociopath," muttered Montbretia, falling silent as Boniface caught her eye.

The guitarist smiled at Boniface. "I like strong women. I like women with an opinion. I like women who will stand up for themselves and tell me what they want." He leaned forward, lowering his voice. "Take

Chloe." He threw his eyes toward the barmaid. "She is pretty, yes?"

"A bit young for me to be looking," said Boniface.

"Look at her, Boniface, she is pretty." Boniface shrugged as the guitarist continued. "But she's not interesting. She would just lie there and let me have sex with her."

He looked back at the barmaid.

"She *is* pretty, but where's the fun in that? I want to be surprised. I want to be excited. I want to be thrilled. I don't want..." He spread his legs, tensed every muscle in his body, and then relaxed. "Where's the fun in that? I'm sorry if that's what your wife likes, but for me..." He shook his head. "No. Give me my equal. Give me someone with spirit."

He stared up at Boniface, his eyes accusing. "Don't you like a woman with an opinion, Boniface?"

"But Bing-Bing took everything you owned and sold it. She took all your guitars and sold them. There were some beautiful handcarved pieces. Does that...?"

"Those are only objects, Uncle. She wanted my attention. She divorced me to get my attention. That's all she's doing." He raised his eyebrows, delivering the words as if he was stating elementary facts. "She wouldn't destroy your office—it wouldn't get my attention."

thirty-nine

"You need to introduce that guy to Gideon—they could share stories."

"Share women more like." Boniface walked briskly around the side of the pub toward the parking lot. He could hear Montbretia following a step behind, seemingly surprised by his sudden decision to move.

"Why are we leaving? We haven't finished our drinks, and Luca's still on the prowl." She ran a step to draw level with Boniface. "I mean sure...I found him kinda creepy in a charming, oily sort of way, but you're moving as if you've left the gas on and if we don't get home in five minutes the house will burn down."

"Don't you see?" Boniface didn't wait for an answer. "We've got a problem."

Montbretia ran for another step, drawing level with Boniface as he turned into the parking lot.

"If it's not Bing-Bing—and I found Luca's rationalization totally plausible, even if I do want to wash some images off my brain with bleach—then that means it's someone else."

"So? It's someone else?" Montbretia reached the passenger door of the barge as Boniface dropped inside the car.

"I'm saying you were right," said Boniface, starting the car as Montbretia sat. He started moving backward before her door was closed.

"Right about...?" She yanked her door shut. Boniface put the car into gear and spun the wheels as the tires bit into the loose gravel surface.

"That whatever we're into is dangerous." He turned onto the road, heading in the direction from which they had come. "There's a USB thumb drive in that glove compartment—"

"So if you're agreeing it's dangerous, then are we going to the cops?"

"No." Boniface was accelerating—pushing the car faster than he felt comfortable pushing it in such narrow lanes. "We don't have time to explain the problem—the problem for which there is insufficient evidence—to flatfoots and wait for them to catch up. We need to do something now."

"Is this what you're after?" asked Montbretia, holding up an object.

Boniface flicked his eyes to the object Montbretia was holding—a silver plastic USB stick on a black lanyard—and immediately returned his view to the road, giving a single nod.

"What shall I do with it?"

"Put it round your neck."

"Done," said Montbretia. "Do you want to explain where we're going?"

"We're going to send out the bat signal. We're calling International Rescue." Boniface turned on the car's lights and accelerated.

"I don't understand, Boniface. Why are you driving like a loony and why don't you just use your phone?" She pulled out her phone and held it on the edge of his peripheral vision. "Use mine—just tell me who to call."

"I bought the drinks with a credit card," said Boniface.

"You know, that's legal. You don't go to jail for using a credit card or for buying three drinks in a public house in the English countryside."

"Yup, but there will be an electronic trace."

"There's a trace of your whole life somewhere."

"Precisely—but there mustn't be a trace for where we go next."

"Now you're talking in riddles. Where are we going?"

"Guildford is the closest town—it's close but far enough. And there's a university with lots of people, and we should be able to find an internet connection, which is when that gizmo round your neck will come into action."

"What? Wearing a necklace gives me superpowers? It makes me invisible?"

Boniface relaxed. "In a way it does. It anonymizes your connection on the internet, making you virtually untraceable—virtually, not completely, hence we're going somewhere that we've never been before and where we'll never go again."

Montbretia was breathing heavily through her nose, seemingly not able to decide which question to ask first out of the many that seemed to be bouncing around her brain.

"Why do we need this cloak-and-dagger stuff?"

"For Leathan's protection."

"Who's Leathan?" asked Montbretia.

"Leathan is...Leathan," said Boniface. "The point is, you don't know who he is. But more to the point, neither does anyone else know what Leathan looks like."

"So?" Her tone was more confused than accusatory.

Boniface sighed gently. "If it hasn't clicked already—if Bing-Bing didn't break our door, then Ernie did. Ernie who organized for my face to be rearranged last night. Ernie who doesn't know what Leathan looks like. And Leathan is good at dealing with this sort of challenge."

Montbretia paused before asking her next question. "I still don't see why we can't just call this Leathan or send him an email."

"Because those can be traced, and the reason that Leathan isn't living here is that he upset a few people. If we make him traceable, then he might end up dead, and dead is no use to us."

"So how do we contact him?"

"Facebook."

"But you're not on Facebook."

"I am. I'm a 14-year-old girl in Nebraska called Madison. I post about kittens, gummy bears, One Direction, and...well, all sorts of stuff I don't care about."

"It sounds a bit creepy," said Montbretia.

"It is. But with this identity, I post on my friend's page, and she is Leathan. I post that I've bought a new packet of gummy bears, and I'm about to eat them, and Leathan comes running. Or at least he picks up a phone that can't be traced, when it is safe for him, and if the Facebook logs are ever traced, no one knows who made the original posting or who read it."

Montbretia sat quietly as Boniface continued to thread the barge through the country lanes of the Surrey Hills. "I've been here for a year, and suddenly you tell me there's this guy called...what was his name?"

"Leathan. Lee...thn," said Boniface, emphasizing each syllable. "And you haven't heard about him because we haven't had a problem of this size before."

"Oh," mouthed Montbretia. "But isn't this all a bit ad hoc...Facebook postings and the like?"

"It is—that's why we're sending up a flare now. I'm relying on Leathan not being in trouble and checking the internet. Depending on what state he's in, he could call in five minutes, but he might not see the message for five weeks."

forty

"Are we going to every pub in the Surrey Hills?"

"This is only the second pub." Boniface let the barge wallow along the marginally less narrow lane, with a few less twists and permanent hedgerows replacing sandstone banks, until he reached a whitewashed brick house with Tudor beams.

He scanned the walls—the waves in every plane and the lack of any right angles told him that the building was old. There were three similarly constructed buildings—all clearly built at a time when tarmac roads were unheard of and the internal combustion engine would have been viewed as witchcraft worthy of the most serious consequences.

"Where are we?" asked Montbretia as Boniface let the barge drift around the lefthand bend, taking another left in front of the pub he had seen from the main road: another low-standing brick-built whitewashed building, but more modern than the wobbly houses they had just passed. This had some form and structure—this had a well-maintained slate roof. This had right angles.

"Sutton Abinger." He paused. "I can tell you're glad you asked."

The parking lot was maybe three times the length of the pub, but with only a handful of cars and a few motorbikes. The kind of motorbikes that were only run on weekends or when the owner could be sure there wouldn't be any rain. Certainly not the kind of bike that would appeal to a member of a motorcycle gang.

They had been sitting for less than five minutes when Mel Grant joined them. His tan leather jacket highlighted the rich, deep tone of his skin. "Hey Mel." Boniface stood to shake the drummer's hand. "I don't think you've met Montbretia."

"Haven't met—but I've heard good things about." He shook her hand. "Good to meet you, Montbretia. I hear you've sorted some amps for Luca. I should get you fixing my endorsements."

Montbretia flushed and mumbled something as the drummer sat.

"Why the secret squirrels, Boniface?"

Boniface winced. "Not secret..."

"You want me on my own—in a pub that's just that bit further away—and it's not secret?"

"Not secret," said Boniface. "Discreet. I don't want this conversation going beyond us—I don't want anyone to know we're having this chat."

"I'm not sure if that's better or worse," said the drummer, leaning back in his chair.

Although the pub was old, somehow the furniture and décor were the wrong sort of old. The tables and chairs were all the same theme that appeared in many pubs: thin stick furniture and varnished dark wood. Tables that were never quite level, meaning whenever they got knocked—which happens when you get a group of people around a table talking and drinking—the drinks got spilled. And spilled alcohol then flows off the edge of the table and onto the deep red carpet with blue diamonds outlined in yellow.

"I spoke to Danny this morning," said Boniface. "He seemed fragile. I don't want to add to his worries, which is why I'm asking you. All I want to know: Is there anything I should know?"

The big man's face relaxed. "I told you, Boniface. Danny's my brother." The drummer clenched his fist, beating his heart twice. "Genuinely I have nothing to tell you—not that I would blab if there was something."

Boniface let his head rock backward and forward, silently acknowledging the drummer's words but wondering whether silence would encourage the other man to elaborate.

"He's under a lot of stress. He feels it's his responsibility to find a singer, and without the management to help, that's a lot of work. And there's the cash—having the bank account frozen is a major worry. But I think the big problem is finding a singer. He's asked everyone—he asked David Coverdale, but he's got a throat problem. He asked Paul Rogers, but he's booked for another charity gig in New York that night. I'll tell you how extreme it's getting—he even thought about asking the guy who sold the gig on eBay."

Mel was repeating excuses. In Boniface's experience, when that happened, it was time to ask some more questions.

"But is there more—is there something I don't know?"

"Why should you know more?" Mel's attitude had changed. Suddenly the relaxed, easygoing guy was on the defensive. Questioning. Wondering. "What's your role here?

"I'm trying to help find what the problem is Danny wants solved."

"What does that mean, Boniface?"

"Is there a problem with Dawn?"

The drummer fell back in his chair, which groaned with the momentum of the highly evolved body mass hitting it square on. Boniface was sure he could hear the wood starting to crack.

"I was the person he first played 'Tattoo Your Name on My Heart' to." A broad row of white teeth showed. "'Do you think she'll like it?' he asked."

Boniface leaned forward and went to rest on the table. Looking down, he saw the thin film of spilled drinks trickling like a stream running downhill and decided against leaning on the table.

"I thought it was a brilliant song—but more than that, there was this guy spilling out his emotions, trying to tell a girl that he loved her. We didn't realize it would be the song that would break us globally. We didn't realize that it would be the song that would make their relationship. We didn't realize that the song was the key."

Boniface sat up straighter as the drummer continued, his voice soft. "But it wasn't the song that won over Dawn. It's great song—she loved it and still loves it, and she was bowled over by the romantic gesture of this guy standing there emotionally naked, just for her. What got her—what won her—was the commitment."

Boniface felt his brow crinkle.

"Danny put everything into that song. He told her everything. But he also put everything into the band—into what the kids today would call *our career*. The day that Dawn first heard the song was the day that she realized Danny was totally serious about how he was going to make money to exist as a grownup. He proved he didn't want to behave like Luca. He wanted normal things that everyone wants—a house with the mortgage paid, a car without finance due, money for kids, holidays, pensions and savings. This wasn't a dream—this was a plan that Danny was putting into action. And that's all Dawn wanted: Mister Average, Mister Dependable. The honest, hardworking guy who loved a girl for herself, not because she was an appendage to his lifestyle, and not because of how she looked."

Boniface looked at Montbretia wearing the same white cotton blouse with brown buttons that she had been wearing all day—even when she hid behind the office chair, even after lunch when she managed not to splash herself. The cuff was now dirty where she had smudged her makeup as she mopped a tear listening to Mel's story.

"I was the best man at his wedding. I stood by him at the church—have you been to the church?"

Boniface shook his head.

"You should—stunning building, and it's only a few miles from here. Over a thousand years old. Ask Dawn; she'll give you all the history."

The drummer was looking down, seemingly lost in thought, then raised his head. "I was his best man—it was my privilege. It was my joy. Danny is my brother, and with that marriage I gained a sister, and I've been with them nearly every day since. I love them more than..." His voice trailed off, his eyes misting.

A few drinkers were talking at the bar, but Boniface was fixed on the big man.

As he began to speak again, his voice caught. He coughed and continued, his voice more steady. "They are two different personalities, but they work together and they communicate without words. He'll do anything for her. He won't treat her like a kid—but he will lay down his life. There's total trust."

"Have you seen her in the last couple of days?" asked Boniface.

"No, but that's not unusual. We play; she does her thing. She's got her own work—you've seen her pictures. You only get pictures that good by working hard."

"You're sure there's nothing there?"

The drummer leaned forward. His voice quiet, respectful. "You're coming from a good place, man, but I'm not comfortable with these questions. If you want to know something, you need to speak to Danny; you need to speak to Dawn. I won't tell Danny we had this meeting, but this is the end of the conversation."

forty-one

Boniface and Montbretia turned right out of the pub into the parking lot.

In the canopied lanes it would be dark. In the steeper-sided valleys—like the small valley with the pub where they met Luca, although *valley* was too strong a term for natural dip in the terrain—it would be getting dark. But out here with the comparatively flat, open space in front of them, without any woods or copses to bring shade, there was still sufficient light in the early evening.

Montbretia stared across the wooden fence and over the field that ran parallel to the parking lot and then farther.

When she had gone to the bathroom, she'd read a note about the pub where she and Boniface had just met Mel, the muscular drummer from Prickle. Apparently, parts of the building dated back to the sixteenth century. For such an old building it seemed incredibly well preserved—or maybe the main public areas were modern? Eighteenth century or something like that?

Boniface's pace was slower than normal—slower than it had been when they walked back from lunch. Something during the conversation with Mel had started niggling Boniface—he had never been able to walk at full speed and organize facts into a logical order. The slowed pace was one of the few signs she could recognize when something was troubling him.

But she wasn't sure what was making him think. Was it the love story? Had it tugged at something deep in his subconscious? Had it made him think about his marriage, which had ended but not quite ended? Was there some incongruence in Mel's story? Or was it the simple fact that Mel seemed unaware that Dawn was missing? Boniface only found out by accident when Danny thought she'd be back. Maybe Mel didn't know what was going on.

Boniface opened her door, then walked around and got in on the driver's side, firing up the engine before closing his door and putting on his seatbelt.

"Turn it off," said Montbretia.

Boniface looked toward her, a frown crossing his brow.

"The engine—turn it off. We need to talk."

The engine died.

"Please tell me that you're not going to screw this up."

"What?"

"Your conversation with Danny." She calibrated the tiny movements across his face—tightening micro-muscles, a slight loss of skin color in his cheeks. "You said he was fragile this morning. If Dawn's not back he's going to be even more fragile, and the last thing he needs is you accusing him or upsetting him, or wondering out loud if..." She became aware that her voice had been getting louder. She began again, softly. "What are you going to say to him?"

"I haven't even decided..."

"You have," she whispered. "You had decided before Mel left us." She lifted her voice. "I'm not disagreeing—it's probably the right thing to have a proper conversation with Danny—but before we go in, would you like to think about what you're going to say?"

"I'm going to ask him about Ernie."

"What in particular?"

"I'm going to ask him if he knows Ernie. If he does, I'm going to ask him what Ernie wants."

"And how are you going to react to what he tells you?" Boniface remained impassive. "Think about it—if there is a link, what's he going to tell you?"

Boniface pushed his jaw to the side.

"If he doesn't know Ernie, but there's still a link between our office being broken up and Ernie, then what can he tell us?" She paused. "I don't know what's going on—but I'm just saying, think what Danny might say if he doesn't know what's going on."

Boniface moved his mouth as if chewing air. Words didn't follow.

"And don't forget that pressure may be being applied directly to him. Heck—think what kind of pressure he's under with Dawn gone."

The mention of Dawn seemed to jab Boniface like a needle.

"So think hard: What are you going to say, how are you going to say it, and what do you really want to know? Remember, you're not being a journalist here. You want to encourage him to talk—not force him to defend himself."

He fired up the engine.

"And what about Carmen—don't you want to know about her?"

"In due course," said Boniface. "But for the moment, Danny is my priority."

forty-two

Boniface let the barge drift right and float over the stone driveway before coming to rest with the small group of cars that seemed to have made a tradition of congregating behind Danny and Dawn's house. This evening, there were only two cars—Boniface recognized neither.

"You'd better wait here," he said, then stopped himself. "I didn't mean stay here in this cage—I mean, I'd better go and see Danny alone."

"I already understood," said Montbretia.

"Do you want a coffee?" asked Boniface, casually. "The kitchen's just there." He pointed to the back door next to the table where Luca had sat that morning. "I'm sure they wouldn't mind if you helped yourself."

"I'm fine," said Montbretia. "Go and talk to Danny. And please don't mess it up."

Boniface closed the door and caught sight of someone he hadn't seen before.

Something screamed rock and roll.

Something also screamed not in the band. Or at least, not in this band.

Where Danny and Mel were on the less desirable side of 50, they were still in good shape—Mel more so than Danny, the more physically demanding role giving him a much better workout. However, this wasn't just about shape, this was long-term decisions, and the guys in the band seemed not to have made choices that they might be regretting now. This guy was different.

The tattoos covering each arm were as effective at covering his skin as a coat of gloss paint. Boniface couldn't quite be sure where the T-shirt ended and flesh began. He pondered—he hadn't seen Danny or Mel wearing a T-shirt. Maybe they had similar tattoos.

What they didn't have was a massive hole in their earlobe lined with some sort of dark material. The piercings on the man's face seemed minor to Boniface, but the stretched earlobe seemed...permanent, and not really something that could ever be covered. Boniface found himself staring as he neared. "Danny around?"

"In there," said the pierced, holed, and tattooed individual, in a hard-to-place Scandinavian accent. "My wife..."

Boniface looked back, not sure about the statement.

"My wife...I saw you looking." He held his arms, proudly displaying them. "My wife is a tattoo artist." Boniface tried to keep his face straight as the image of a body with no space between the tattoos took root in his brain. "Perhaps you would like one? Or your friend?" He tilted his head in the direction of Boniface's Mercedes.

"I'm fine, thanks," said Boniface, slightly distractedly. "But the ink is incredible. Such detail."

"I know," said the living artwork, continuing to walk toward the parking lot.

"How you holding up?" Danny was sitting on the sofa in the studio office as Boniface entered.

The bassist said nothing, communicating with a few indistinct hand gestures and facial twitches that could be interpreted as freely as an ink splodge. Boniface carefully maneuvered himself onto the desk, sitting where Danny had been sitting when the two chatted that morning.

"Ernie," said Boniface. "Ernie Norton."

Danny remained silent, his visual communication ending.

"Do you know him? Know the name?"

Danny pushed out his bottom lip.

"Any clue?"

A slow turn of the bass player's head.

"He seems to think he owns the band."

"He doesn't, and I don't know him." Danny's voice was controlled—a musician delivering the exact performance required. "How did you come across him?"

"Gray."

Danny exhaled, his exasperation visible, almost tangible. "I told you on day one that he's the root of the problems. This Ernie might be some bloke that Gray shot his mouth off to. Gray did that back in the day, and I'm sure it still happens."

The bassist returned to noncommunication mode, melting back into the sofa.

"But Ernie's more than some bloke Gray met in a pub—he's responsible for my face, and he broke up my office this afternoon." Danny stared as Boniface continued. "That's a lot of reaction for some bloke you don't know."

"What can I tell you, Boniface? However you want to phrase it, I don't know this bloke. That's not an endorsement of the man...that's not to suggest that I'm not concerned about your well-being, but it's not really the thing that has kept me awake." His voice fell. "I'm only concerned about one thing: Dawn."

"No news?" asked Boniface, his tone sympathetic.

"None."

"And you're sure there's no connection? You still reckon it's a coincidence—Gray mentions Billy; I mention Billy to Dawn and she disappears; I mention Billy to Ernie, who you don't know, and I get pummeled. You don't see any connections?"

"Why would I?" There was anger in Danny's voice.

"Because if I'm wrong, then Dawn has disappeared for another reason. A reason that is hidden from both of us—or at least, it's hidden from me." The annoyance on Danny's face didn't seem to be calming as Boniface continued. "People don't choose to disappear to get away from happy situations. You don't see it in the headlines: Happy housewife with a blissful marriage runs to get away from her happiness."

"Now you're being crazy, Boniface."

"But there's something here that I don't know," said Boniface.

"Whatever it is, I don't know either—and you seem to be implying I'm lying or it's my fault. You're meant to be helping, Boniface, not accusing me." He breathed heavily through his nose. "She's my wife. I love her, and I want her back."

A phone rang. Both men stared at each other. "That's mine," said Boniface, shaking himself free from the short staring competition and thrusting his hand into his pocket. He answered. "Hold on." He looked at Danny as he stood. "I need to take this. I'll be outside."

forty-three

He became aware, slowly.

His heart was beating faster. Not pounding, but a few extra beats per minute. Enough that he noticed.

As he held his phone, he could see a tremble in his hands. Maybe not unrelated to the increased tempo of his heart, but he still became aware and noticed it wasn't just his hand.

It was unlikely the temperature was any cooler than when he had entered the studio, but walking from inside to the outside, he could feel the drop. He pulled his jacket instinctively, then leaned against the wall just outside the door and spoke. "Leathan."

In his previous visits, he hadn't paid attention to the density of the woods or their proximity to the house. Danny and Dawn really did have a fairytale cottage—even if it was rather bigger than a cottage—in the middle of the woods. But maybe it wasn't a fairytale; perhaps it was the stuff of nightmares.

"It's urgent—I'm in deeper than I realized." He heard his own voice and turned away from Montbretia. He knew she was still sitting in the car, but somehow he didn't want to make a full confession about his lack of caution, even though she was out of earshot. "When does the train leave?"

He heard movement in the lobby of the studio.

"Okay...you need to get your passport." The steps inside became steps outside as Danny appeared. "I understand: *a* passport, not necessarily *your* passport." He felt himself starting to uncurl. "I'll be there when you get in.... Yeah, I know the procedure." Boniface slipped his phone back into his pocket and looked up at the bassist.

Danny looked sheepish but seemingly had no curiosity about Boniface's interruption. He held up his hands as if surrendering. "I'm sorry, man. It's tough, and I know you've got my best interests at heart." He looked more closely at Boniface's wounds. "And I know you've taken some blows for me. But I ain't lying: I love and trust my wife."

Boniface tried to find the words, but Danny continued. "Look, man. I thought he was a crank, but some kid turned up today."

"Kid?" asked Boniface. "Are we using Gray's idea of a kid or...how old was he?"

Danny's face softened. "Gray's idea of a kid—I guess he was early thirties, but I couldn't be certain. Hard-life twentysomething, maybe." He seemed to be lost in thought. "How he looked and how he appeared seemed at odds—I couldn't make it out."

Boniface tried to unscramble the description as he waited while Danny recalled each element one slice at a time.

"He dressed young, but young from the 1990s. Boots, old jeans, white T with a sleeveless denim jacket."

"That's hardly a look exclusive to an era."

"That was when this look was last common," said Danny. "We had lots of fans who dressed like that—at first I thought he was one. He seemed to know who I was."

"You spoke to him?"

"Yeah. I sent Sven to get rid of him—Sven can look quite aggressive with his tattoos and the holes in his ears—but this kid was quite insistent, so I went to speak to him." The tension seemed to dissipate slightly. "And up close, he wasn't pretty—I'd say there have been a lot of drugs over a long time. I'd say he ain't long for this planet with that level of usage. His skin had that look when all the energy has left it and his hair...it was dark, but was that sort of look you get when teenagers are experimenting and just mix everything together, and it just comes out the color of ick."

"So what did he say?"

"He wanted to see Dawn, but he wouldn't say why." Danny started hunching, pulling his fists tight. "He was...you know...tetchy...on edge... aggressive. Like he was wound up or needed his next fix. But there was more—it might have been fear, maybe nerves or anxiety. Whatever it was, it came out as aggression."

"What did you tell him when he asked to see Dawn?"

"I said she wasn't around."

"Which is true."

"But he thought I was talking bull, so I said she's gone to stay with her sister in Canada who's sick, and I don't know when she'll be back."

Boniface sucked air through his teeth. "If you're going to lie, don't elaborate. Don't get too specific—just give one detail."

"Thanks," said Danny sarcastically. "Why didn't you tell me that earlier?"

"He called you on it?"

"He said she doesn't have a sister. Then he was off. He took a couple of steps, turned, said 'I hate liars,' and was gone. I sent Sven to have a look—but he had gone."

forty-four

When Boniface got back in the car after talking with Danny, he went to say something to Montbretia, but then paused, as if trying to marshal his thoughts before he began his sentence.

He hadn't begun to speak as he nosed the car out of the drive and onto the narrow lanes of the Surrey Hills, drawing a smooth line along the middle of the road, equidistant between the high-sided embankments, and moving without the urgency he had shown earlier.

On the ground, as they threaded through the forest, it was night, but in the blinks of darkening blue sky that she saw as the trees occasionally yielded, it was clear that the day hadn't fully departed yet. It was dark enough to be dangerous. Dark enough to require Boniface's full concentration. But not yet dark enough that you could fully call it night.

Montbretia remained silent as Boniface navigated out of the Hills and back to a main road she soon recognized as the A3—the main artery into and out of southwest London: starting near the center of London just south of the river and soon becoming three lanes each way, finally ending at Portsmouth, the military and civilian shipping town on the south coast.

It was an easy route: All Boniface had to do was stay on the main road until they got to Tibbet's Corner, the junction—named after a highwayman who may or may not have existed, but who had now passed into lore as fact—on the A3 at the corner of Wimbledon Common. Here Boniface would take the road into Wimbledon and to the office.

It was an easy route and there was little traffic around, but Boniface had remained silent for the journey. Silent. He hadn't even cleared his throat.

Montbretia wasn't sure what was keeping Boniface quiet. It might have been his chat with Danny. It might have been the phone call—it was surprising that Boniface hadn't told her who called. Or it might have been that he was feeling rough so he was concentrating on his driving.

It might have been all three.

Whatever the cause, he was thinking. At several stages in the journey his breathing became heavier—almost as if he was inhaling, holding, then exhaling. He seemed to be holding his breath as they passed her turn—but this wasn't a problem; Montbretia was happy to go back to the office to pick up her bike. If she didn't, that meant public transport tomorrow—two buses.

He was still thinking as they approached Tibbet's Corner. The junction was an easy one—three lanes split. One lane turned off up to the intersection where they would join the road leading into Wimbledon. The other two continued, passing under the intersection and following the trail to London without interruption.

Montbretia waited for Boniface to think about the junction—he was in the middle lane, not the lane that filtered off. The car remained in the middle lane continuing into the underpass and avoiding the junction, exiting on the other side and continuing toward London. Montbretia waited to see if Boniface reacted. The car continued passing the Royal Hospital for Neuro-Disability, which apparently had once been called the Royal Hospital and Home for Incurables, only recently changing its name to its more hopeful current one.

"We're not going to the office, then?" Montbretia ended the quiescence. She knew Boniface needed time to think—time to process and play through every scenario, time to integrate whatever he had just been told with whatever he was thinking, with whatever hunch was buzzing around at the back of his head like a fly banging on a closed pane next to an open window...it knows there's a way out, but it doesn't have the brain capacity to know to move to the right and then fly.

But thinking had moved to acting, and clearly acting involved her.

"If it's not Bing-Bing, that leaves one person, and something Danny said is niggling."

Montbretia wondered whether it was time to suggest the police again, but waited. Boniface seemed ready to elaborate, at least a little.

"It's time to tell them we surrender. Time to tell them we're beaten." Montbretia felt her head jerk to look at Boniface, who was still focused on the road. "It'll give us some breathing space, which is what we need at the moment."

"What about this Leathan friend of yours?"

"Oh, he's coming," said Boniface. "But I want to roll out the red carpet for him."

forty-five

"Without wishing to be too crude about this, Boniface, where the hell are we?"

"Haggerston."

"To repeat. Where the hell are we, Boniface?"

"You can ask me as often as you want, but it won't cause us to miraculously move from..."

"Boniface." Her volume was quiet. Her tone stern. "Where—in the broadest sense—are we? Think politics, not geography."

He pointed down the street: on one side, terraced houses, the other and sweeping away from them, a housing estate—the projects, as Montbretia insisted on calling it—cheaply constructed low blocks of high-density housing run by a combination of the local authority and a social housing project. One side of the road had been called a slum and flattened; the other somehow survived. "You see at the end—a small row of shops."

"Just."

"Take it from me, there's a butcher and a pet shop that would like to believe it's a grooming parlor."

"You're taking me shopping?"

"It would be preferable, but no." He reached into his jacket pockets and pulled out his phone, his wallet, a small notebook, and a pencil. "Between those two is a black wooden gate—a fair size; it's big enough to get a van through."

"I'll believe you," said Montbretia, taking the contents of Boniface's pockets as he pushed them into her hands. "Wouldn't it be easier to park outside—then you could show me?"

Boniface twisted, trying to reach into his trouser pockets with his fingers. "You're staying out of sight." Slowly he disentangled his office keys from his pocket before twisting the other way to rummage in his opposite pocket.

"Why am I staying out of sight?" asked Montbretia. "And why are you giving me the contents of your pockets—I thought you said you were surrendering?"

"I didn't say we were surrendering," said Boniface, handing over the last few scraps he had pulled from his pockets. "I said we would tell them that we are surrendering."

"You mean lie," said Montbretia. "Lie to the people who did that to your face." She paused. "This is where we are?"

Boniface rocked his head forward.

"How can I express in words—words that you will understand and react to—that I think this is the stupidest thing you have done. Ever."

"I think you just did," said Boniface.

"No. I said understand and *react*. React as in decide not to do the really stupid thing." She paused as he continued to search through his pockets—now beginning a second check of each. "Stupid for you and stupid for me. You're leaving me here in what must be said is not the most salubrious location within this grand city."

"I wasn't sure how to raise that aspect of my plan, so thank you for that." Boniface smiled weakly. "If I'm not back in an hour, then call the cops. Tell them there's a knife fight, not guns—we want them to come in, not to put up a cordon and negotiate." He opened the car door. "The keys are in the ignition." He stepped out. "Get in the driver's seat. Lock the doors and stay safe. If it gets too hairy to stay here, then drive."

He gently shut the door before she could argue and began the short walk, arriving to find the small wicket gate within the larger gate ajar. He pushed the smaller gate fully open, pausing to survey the tunnel.

The painting equipment he had seen yesterday was gone, giving an unobstructed cobbled surface leading up to the door with its concealed glass. Lazily hunched on the barrel to the right of the door was an unwelcome vision: Wes.

Physically, Wes was unprepossessing—shorter than Boniface, he didn't look particularly muscular, but he had a sneer, worked on for years and which Boniface suspected would now be as hard to shift as a speech impediment.

The teenager said nothing, choosing instead to fix his unwavering gaze on Boniface.

"I need to see Ernie."

The teenager's stare remained.

"We had our fun yesterday, and now the grownups need to talk." Still no response. "Do you really want to tell Ernie that I came here to give him what he wants, and then you turned me away?"

The stare remained, but the confidence in the eyes momentarily flickered. "Waiting room." He flashed his gaze to the stairs leading under the butcher's shop.

Boniface let his head shake once.

"Ernie's office for this discussion."

The teenager remained impassive, keeping his vision fixed on Boniface.

"If I don't call home within an hour, then it's goodnight Saigon—they send in the napalm—if that's not something of a mangling of history." Wes looked at him with his best dead-eyed stare. "I'm not sure if you're trying to be scary or whether it's just a matter of you not having a clue about what I just said."

"Jacket," said the teen, snapping his fingers.

forty-six

Boniface looked around the room as the light disappeared. The harsh strip light in the corridor had been replaced by the yellow glow of a single lamp, which even at its brightest struggled to form a pool of light.

Boniface buttoned his cuffs, slipped on his jacket, and began to button his shirt. "I got the message."

He looked at the face—gray skin with old-man stubble, exaggerated with deep shadows—visible across the dust mote–filled half-light.

There was movement in the gray face. It might have been what passed for a smile—Boniface couldn't be sure.

"I would have preferred a carrier pigeon."

A small sound from the other man, a raspy chuckle.

"My preferences aside, I received the message loud and clear, and I don't want another message."

A tilt of the head seemed to be the extent of any form of reciprocation.

"Clearly we got off on the wrong foot," continued Boniface, looking for somewhere to sit but seeing nowhere. "I'm hoping we can rectify any misunderstandings." As his eyes became accustomed to the dark, he strained to see what was on the walls—it might have been framed boxing posters or it could have been movie posters. Then again, given the lack of light, it might have been crumbling plaster creating interesting patterns. "And in this spirit of understanding and cooperation, I have a simple question: What can I do for you, Ernie?"

The man behind the desk didn't hesitate. "Leave my band alone. Stop trying to make money off my act."

The door opened. Boniface's eyes spasmed with the light rushing like a burst water main. In the corner away from Ernie, he thought he could see someone sitting—thinning, slicked-back hair and a suit—and then the door was shut and whoever had entered rapidly crossed to Ernie.

A whisper. A grunt by Ernie. Then, as quickly as the person had entered—Boniface couldn't even be sure whether it was a man or woman—they had gone, with a brief burst of light confirming to Boniface that there were three people left in the room.

"When I was here yesterday—the first time—I saw a kid. Who is he?

Ernie grunted, the hint of self-satisfaction showing in the shadows around his mouth. "He's a junkie who thinks he can be helpful."

"Could I talk to him?"

"He's not here," said Ernie. "He's probably getting off his head on krokodil. Why the interest?"

"Someone thought they had seen him."

"I doubt it," said Ernie. "Now. Back to my band."

forty-seven

It was only when Montbretia released her hold on the steering wheel to feel for the key in the ignition that she realized she had been gripping the wheel—with her nails digging into her palms—since Boniface had disappeared from her view.

The car fired immediately and started to move without its driver taking her gaze off Boniface as he now walked toward her. Her eyes swiveled, taking in the mirrors, and she pulled into the center of the road, feeling the acceleration push her back against her seat. Boniface heard the car before he saw it—his head jerked until he locked onto the vehicle and moved swiftly, crossing the road as Montbretia pulled up.

There was a satisfying clunk as she released the central locking, and the passenger door opened at once, with Boniface slipping into the passenger seat. He was pale, but the tension around his eyes that had been present before he got out of the car had dissipated.

She hit the gas and the car started moving. Boniface finished closing his door, then pointed as if giving directions—the tremble in his right hand becoming more pronounced as he extended his arm.

"Mmm hmm."

"I've agreed to give him the band." As they came toward a junction, Boniface indicated the left turn.

"I say this with love, Boniface, but wasn't that immensely stupid?" Montbretia accelerated out of the junction, feeling calmer as they got farther away. "You've agreed to give him the band...but the band isn't yours to give."

"That's alright," said Boniface airily. "I've also agreed to procure anything that I don't already own."

Montbretia felt the need to look at Boniface and shout at him, but kept the barge moving steadily along the backstreets of northeast London, somehow feeling safer as each street seemed to lead to a slightly less minor street, which might eventually lead to a major road she might recognize. She fought the urge to turn but couldn't still her tongue. "And again, I say with love: That is even more stupid—Danny will never agree. Please tell me you know what you're doing."

She kept her concentration focused on the road, but somehow Montbretia knew Boniface was smirking. "And if you want me to top the stupidity table—catastrophic stupidity, you would probably call it—I made a deal but I don't understand what Ernie thinks he's doing." She shot him a look—he was smirking, but his face fell as they made eye contact. "He's trying to steal Prickle's back catalog. But that won't make him much money if he doesn't keep Prickle gigging, and he says he doesn't care if Danny, Mel, Luca, and Newton all die tomorrow. They're not in his plans."

"So let me get this right." Montbretia felt a calmness in her voice—if she understood what Boniface was saying he had just done, they were past the stage where panicking would achieve anything. "You've shaken things up, knowing that they will react, but you don't have any idea what you're going to do when they do react."

"I do," said Boniface as the car reached a junction.

"Home?" asked Montbretia.

"Saint Pancras—Eurostar terminal," said Boniface. "I didn't just go and see Ernie for the heck of it. What I've done will get him talking—there was another guy in with him, and we don't know how many other people there are in this venture. They're going to talk for a while, and hopefully they'll still be talking when Leathan gets in there."

"Leathan gets...in...there?"

"That's the idea," said Boniface, leaning forward and opening the glove compartment before starting to reload his pockets. "We know Ernie and his friends are our problem. Leathan will help us fix it."

"How?" Montbretia realized she was giving Boniface too much scope to be evasive. "I mean, what's this Leathan's history—why did you call him?"

Boniface groaned quietly. "When I was a journalist, it was acceptable to break the law a little. Do something cheeky, and that was fine."

"Really?" asked Montbretia.

"It was a different time—it was called showing initiative," said Boniface. "But there were things you couldn't be caught doing. It would be too embarrassing for the paper, not to mention perhaps beyond my skillset. But that didn't mean you couldn't outsource. I outsourced to Leathan. He was efficient, he didn't get caught, and he was productive. And for what I've got in mind, I need to do a bit of outsourcing."

"In short," said Montbretia, "you're telling me that he's a crook."

"Who amongst us has not broken the law?" asked Boniface. "There are good criminals and there are bad criminals. Leathan occasionally does bad things for a good reason." He patted his pockets, seemingly making sure everything had been returned to its rightful home. "I just hope Leathan's up for it."

forty-eight

"It might be something out of a horror movie, but I still like it," said Boniface, looking up at the dark-red brick Victorian gothic structure. "They used to call this the cathedral of the railways."

In front of them, four floors of red brick detailed with sandstone, all topped by a slate-covered mansard roof with gable-fronted dormer windows protruding. A square clock tower with a tall square spire and four small round spires on each corner stood at the far end of the building. "Turn by the clock, and I'll jump out round the corner."

Montbretia pulled up, avoiding three black cabs. Boniface's door was open before the car had drifted to a halt. "You're leaving me here? Alone? Again?" She winked. "Seriously, can't you just call him and tell him where to meet us?"

Boniface put his foot on the asphalt, grabbed the front pillar, and turned back to Montbretia. "His phone will have been switched off hours ago, before he got on the train." Montbretia's face didn't relax. "This is risky for him—being at a specific place at a predictable time. He needs to see me and be confident that I'm not being followed. He needs to be sure that no one is waiting for him. If I'm talking with someone—you, for instance—he'll freak."

"And when he sees you...is that when you have the big tearful reunion?"

"Once he has seen me—once he is sure it's safe—then he'll call."

"Call?"

"Yeah." Boniface relaxed. "You can put batteries back into phones." He stood on the road, leaning into the car. "We'll pick him up at a place where Leathan is sure he's not being followed—I'll call you."

"I'm beginning to feel like a chauffeur. I'm driving a Mercedes—all I need is a cap and a blue blazer, and I'm set." Boniface shut the door on Montbretia and headed for the station, stepping inside the Victorian architecture and finding a modern cream-painted steel-framed skeleton supporting the body's vital organs: commerce. A cathedral to transport had become an ecumenical meeting ground, inviting those who worship at the church of shopping to come join.

And to make them feel welcome, on the ground-floor level, between the cream-painted steel structure and the sandblasted red-brick skin, rows of glass units had been created. Home to faceless food and clothing chains as prevalent as cockroaches, plus those stores that you never quite know what they do but that seem to exist exclusively in public-transportation hubs. Apart from a few coffee shops, most of the units were closed for the night.

Boniface followed the signs to international arrivals, casually coming to rest about thirty yards away from the exit with his back against a cream-painted pillar. He scanned his fellow greeters—some individuals, some groups, some looking bored, others excited—everyone looked worthy of suspicion, and no one looked suspicious. All were gathered in a loose semicircle around the frosted-glass doors under the electronic display announcing that the next arrival was due in two minutes.

It looked so normal, apart from the upright piano.

Boniface had noticed this trend—leave a piano somewhere public. It seemed to be an idea taking hold; he had last seen one in Heathrow airport. A kid—eleven or twelve—resentful of having been dragged out of her house, resentful of not being trusted on her own, sat at the piano. Her parents—the mother plain, the father overweight—seemed not to notice or had long since stopped trying to communicate or take an interest in their daughter's passions.

She began playing an etude: the highly structured piece fully resolving with a simple melody as addictive as cocaine. The first time he heard it, Boniface thought it was sweet. The second time, he noticed a minor mistake. The third time the etude was repeated, he was bored with the tune. And by the fourth time, he wanted to find whoever thought leaving a piano was a good idea and suggest an alternate location for the instrument.

He tried to stare casually at the cathedral roof: glass supported by dark-gray steel spanning the entire width of the building, and the imposing clock—so big that he could see the minute hand move—at the far end. There was a sigh of air as the pneumatic struts pushed the doors open to allow a wave of people to flow from the customs hall that greeted newly arrived passengers.

At first a few drips—younger, self-important passengers. People with places to go and people to see, apparently, and practical footwear. But soon the drips became a wave of humanity, pleased to be released from their captivity in a steel tube traveling at 180 miles per hour for more than two hours.

Boniface looked through the passageway that was now spilling a flow of people. At each end, automatic doors gave the impression of a bad airlock, although he wasn't sure which side was infectious—or who was being protected from whom. Still, it was reassuring to know that only a single narrow retail unit had been sacrificed to allow passengers to get from their trains.

The passengers continued. Some dressed for comfort—their wardrobe a collection of elastic, soft fabric, and manmade colors. Some dressed to be seen—straight lines, very tight where they needed to be tight, and patterned to give a message. Whether they dressed for comfort or for show, there was one consistent factor: luggage. It may have only been a clutch purse with the heavy lifting delegated to someone else, but no one had empty hands.

Apart from one man.

Boniface caught the side of his face and averted his gaze.

One man—black leather jacket, jeans, black sneakers, and no luggage. Leathan swam in the middle of a shoal of people, his speed average and his movements slow, with his head rotating from left to right. The only fast movement was his eyes—fixing on a target, then jumping to the next and the next. He veered away from Boniface, the only acknowledgment a meeting of the eyes, which the train passenger held for a moment longer than a stranger would.

Boniface watched as Leathan passed about ten yards away to his left, then he took the righthand side of the expanse, soon finding his way back out. "North of where you dropped me—walking north." Montbretia answered on the first ring as Boniface started to pass the brushed steel and glass of the new part of the station, crudely bolted onto the gothic monument.

He checked behind—a quick jolt of his head over his shoulder, followed thirty seconds later by a stop to check his phone, giving him the chance to look in the reflection of the large pane and see whether he was being followed, not that he was good at this sort of thing.

The barge wafted up, and Montbretia reached across to open the door.

"Forward and left," said Boniface as he sat. "Under the tracks, then turn right."

Montbretia pulled out, carefully navigating the left turn. "Is he here?"

"Yeah, yeah. I went left; he went right. Right at the end."

Boniface's phone rang. He answered without speaking, listened, and hung up before pulling up a map. "Next left, then first right."

"Leathan?"

"Mmm."

"And?" said Montbretia as she pushed the car around the left bend, transitioning from a main road to a residential street with low blocks on either side—to the left, near-purple brickwork with concrete sills and lintels, to the right, near-orange brickwork with red tile sills. The wall and steel fence both said "we expect crime." Along the center was a strip of asphalt, marked with residential parking spaces on one side and a no-parking yellow line on the other. She slowed as the car approached a speed hump.

"And now we drive around this one block. Slowly—this sort of speed. Leathan will find us once he's sure we're not being tailed."

forty-nine

Leathan looked down at the plasticized cardboard container resting on the plastic table, its lid open to reveal what was to be dinner. He reached his fingers through the greaseproof paper and grabbed a chicken leg, taking a large bite with the side of his mouth while using apparently poor table manners as an excuse to scan the room.

It was a small restaurant—calling it a restaurant was probably an exaggeration. It was a chicken shop—nothing more—but as he bit, Leathan found that it was a surprisingly good chicken shop.

There was still a small crowd milling in front of the counter next to the glass and steel warming the food. Between the counter and the grills, there were two guys. He would call them men, but they were little more than boys—Indian perhaps, but unlikely. More chance they were Pakistani or Bangladeshi.

Both spoke atrocious English but were working incredibly hard and were very attentive to their customers. He hadn't quite understood when the offer was made, but slowly they overcame the language barrier, and Leathan understood that he was being offered chicken cooked to his tastes so he could specify just how spicy and which herbs he wanted.

He was too hungry to wait, but he liked the attitude. The immigrant spirit unlike the English, who just sat around and complained. One of these guys would be a millionaire, maybe both. The only question was how quickly. From their English, they had been here less than six weeks. However, Leathan was sure that within six months, they would both be speaking the language like a Londoner. Within eighteen months, at least one would be self-employed, and within five years, one would be millionaire. He could then afford to celebrate his twenty-fifth birthday in style.

Leathan watched as the man at the head of the line—well, huddle—took his food. A cardboard box carefully placed in a plastic bag. He had seen him come in: Most people were in groups, so someone on his own stood out. The man passed over some change and turned, leaving through the main door with his meal.

He continued his survey. What struck him most was how clean the place seemed. Clearly there was heavy foot traffic, but he couldn't see grease or the detritus that follows human beings who are not forced to clean up their own mess. The mirrors on either side reflected; there was an absence of fingerprints and accumulated dirt. Even the cards for local cab firms, a fixture in every other fast-food restaurant, seemed to have been cleaned away.

The tables were all clean. He looked at the diners—groups of two or three, and one of five—all clustered around their tables, engrossed in rowdy conversation. No one had that look people get when they don't want to lean on the table because they're not quite sure what the previous occupant left.

Three men at the table opposite, all in their early twenties and dressed in cheap hoodies, stood. The guy behind the counter who hadn't been serving was there before the last of the three stood up. The garbage was in a black plastic sack, the table was sprayed and wiped, and the plastic bench seats wiped. Seemingly pulled out of thin air, a mop appeared to wipe the floor. He was gone within thirty seconds, and the table was occupied by two women who didn't miss a word of their conversation as they sat and began eating.

"So why am I here, Boniface? What exactly do you want me to do?"

"Help." Boniface sat meekly on the other side of the table—he seemed to appreciate the warmth of the chicken shop as he crossed his arms, gripping the sleeves of his shirt.

Next to him sat Montbretia. "Call me Monty," she said as they got out of the car. She was shorter than he had guessed, but her hair was longer than he had expected as he looked at her from behind. She had been driving when Leathan got in. The car was on the second loop of the block and slowing as it approached a speed hump. Leathan opened the door without waiting for the car to stop—without even waiting to see whether they had noticed him.

Montbretia seemed unfazed by the new occupant and had then driven smoothly, making rapid progress and not drawing attention, while keeping the passengers comfortable. Having worked her way through a warren of back streets, she had found several places to eat—Leathan had chosen this one, and Montbretia had found a tight spot where she parallel-parked without incident.

Boniface, however, fussed and had insisted that she take his jacket. So now he looked cold, and she looked swamped by his gray suit jacket covering her white blouse.

Leathan grinned. "You bring me to this cheap chicken shop and ask me for help."

"It was your choice, Leath—I'll take you to the Ritz if that's where you want to go. But you wanted somewhere anonymous so you could feel safe, and apparently a noisy chicken shop is it."

"You got me there," said the new arrival, his eyes alternating between scanning the room, scanning anyone passing who was visible through the plate-glass window, and catching a glance of his food in an attempt not to smear it over his face. "Give me the problem again. Start with this Ernie—he sounds like a medium fish in a tiny pond."

"But he seems to want a different pond," said Boniface. "He

wants—for lack of a better term—to own the band. As far as I can tell, he wants to take possession of Prickle's sources of income."

"Once a thief," offered Leathan.

"That's what I thought, but Ernie doesn't want the musicians. For a band like Prickle, that's an odd choice—no individual musician matters. But he needs a band that is out working—playing gigs, doing TV slots, being interviewed—in order to generate the publicity to sell the music that makes the money. Prickle are a working band—as soon as they stop, ninety-five percent of their income goes away overnight."

Boniface hesitated, seemingly considering something he hadn't thought about before. "He might have an angle, but from what I've been able to tell, he doesn't have the competence to make money from a band—he's way out of his league, and he doesn't have the contacts to help him."

"But you say he does have a musician."

Boniface exhaled. "Gray. Graham Barrington. He founded the band and was the lead singer, but he left nearly thirty years ago. It's not as if he brings an audience or has great connections."

"But there is a connection, right? Or rather, two."

"And that's where I'm really confused," said Boniface. "Gray mentioned this kid Billy Watkins who has hung around at Ernie's place—Ernie says there's a kid who's just a junkie. But when I mentioned the name Billy Watkins to Dawn, she disappeared."

"You say that as if you think she took herself out of the picture—you don't think there's a kidnap going on here?" asked Leathan.

"I think she ran," said Boniface. "And while it's tearing up Danny, I'm sure we'll find something made her run."

"And is there a connection between this Gray and Dawn?"

"Not that I've found."

Leathan took another mouthful and continued speaking before finishing chewing. "Gray has no money—although he does own property, so capital but no income—and yet he's managed to run up a gambling debt."

"It's not just that," said Boniface. "As far as I can see, he's still running it up, but he's paying in sweat. You get my point."

"I do," said Leathan.

"I don't," said Montbretia.

"You would expect someone with Ernie's finishing-school manners to deal with any debts in a practical manner," said Boniface.

"Isn't he doing that—you said Gray was probably doing some decorating."

"I think," said Leathan, "that what Boniface is suggesting is that we might expect Ernie to break Gray's legs to give him an incentive to repay the debt."

Montbretia's face registered shock.

"But instead," continued Boniface, "Gray is being encouraged to gamble more and so fall further into debt. In other words..."

"Ernie wants Gray in debt because he wants something from Gray. I get it," said Montbretia. "I still don't get how this relates to Dawn."

"Which is why Leathan is here."

"You're pretty hopeful that I'm going to agree with whatever you've got planned." Leathan finished his chicken and licked his fingers before wiping them on a paper napkin. "So what can I achieve now, tonight?"

"About an hour ago, I went to see Ernie to announce my surrender. I told him he could have whatever he wanted, I wouldn't stand in his way, and I'd help him get whatever I didn't have."

Leathan leaned back, dropping his napkin into the cardboard box and shutting the lid. "A strategy—and I use that term loosely—which is not without risk. If I may look at your actions in another light, we could even suggest that you've broken stuff in the hope that something happens."

"Yeah," said Boniface. "And I'm rather hoping you can get in there and find out what's happening."

fifty

Montbretia held the Mercedes steady, letting it find its own way along the back streets of northeast London. A subtle nudge here and there on the steering wheel, and the car maintained a perfect line down the street, low revs keeping the engine quiet in acknowledgement that it was midnight and they were passing through residential streets.

"Once past—slowly—and then park quarter of a mile up," said Boniface. "It'll be on the left in a moment, Leath."

Montbretia flicked her gaze. Both men seemed to sink down in their seats, pushing their faces up against the window.

"Pet shop, black gate, butcher," said Boniface. "That black gate is the entrance to Ernie's empire." The lights in the surrounding stores had been extinguished, with the exception of a few twinkles confirming that the refrigerated displays in the butcher's shop were still chilling. Around the black gate a lazy yellow light drifted, like fumes exhaled by a crowd of smokers. The wicket gate was not fully closed—its outline also etched in yellow light.

Montbretia flicked another glance. The two men's heads were moving slowly with perfect synchronization, seemingly each having their gaze locked on the gate. She let the car drift, neither accelerating nor decelerating—the engine tone remaining constant—as she watched the trip meter; the tenths of a mile turned over for a second time, and she looked for somewhere to pull over. Within 45 seconds of passing the gate, the car was stationary, the engine cut and its lights out.

Boniface turned and frowned. "It's a residential street, Boniface. A running engine is going to draw attention, and the lights illuminate the plates, so unless you want someone to notice us and to get a description..." She let the end of the explanation hang.

Boniface reached into his pocket and pulled out his wallet. "How much money have you got?" he asked Montbretia, grabbing all the paper money in his wallet and handing the bills to Leathan without counting and without breaking eye contact with Montbretia. "And your key to my place."

Montbretia wriggled her hand into a pocket, making three dives before all of her cash had been retrieved. She held out her hand to Leathan. "Count it first," said Boniface. "This is a loan, not charity."

"I, on the other hand..." said Leathan as Montbretia started counting, "don't really care about those fine differences. I just need cash."

"Twenty-seven pounds and thirty-two pence," said Montbretia

holding out one hand to Leathan but looking straight at Boniface and fiddling in another pocket with her other hand.

"Thank you," mouthed Leathan.

Montbretia hooked her nail under the split ring and began to work Boniface's two door keys through the steel trap. The ring snapped shut as she liberated the two pieces of metal, holding them out for Boniface. "For him," said Boniface, throwing his eyes toward the passenger in the back seat. "He needs somewhere to go when he's finished here." He turned to face Leathan. "We'll find somewhere else for tomorrow night if you're still around."

Leathan took the keys silently, pushing them into a pocket.

"Anything more we can do for you?" asked Boniface, his gaze fixed on the man in the back seat, who was a lot less talkative than he had been in the chicken shop, preferring to communicate through body language alone.

Currently he seemed to be saying "I don't want to communicate" as he reached for the door handle.

"Take care," said Boniface.

"I have done this before." Leathan seemed to expend the minimum energy necessary to make the sounds.

"And look how well that turned out," said Boniface. "You're living in a different country constantly looking over your shoulder, sleeping in a different bed every night, and putting a new SIM card in your phone each morning." He paused; slowly Leathan's head lifted, his gaze toward Boniface. "Take care—you're no use to us dead."

In one continuous movement the door opened, he stood, the door closed silently, and Leathan started walking away from the car and away from Ernie's.

"He'll circle round," said Boniface as Leathan's figure came into view, his head down as he moved through the shadows.

"What's this about a different bed every night?" asked Montbretia. "You make him sound...I mean, can we trust him?"

"We can trust him."

"But leaving the country, a different bed?" She sucked her teeth. "I mean, he seems alright, but so do most crooks you meet."

"There are people you can trust—there are people you don't trust but have to work with. I trust Leathan. I told you, when I was a journalist and needed something that was just outside my reach, I called Leathan."

"I'm not questioning his skills," said Montbretia. "More his...I keep coming back to him sleeping in a different bed each night. Why did you bring it up?"

"Not to get this reaction," said Boniface, his voice was low but his mouth pulled tight. "I just wanted to remind him that he's not... invincible—things go wrong." He leaned back against the door. "We're mates. We were drinking buddies. Sometimes you need to use slightly stronger language to illustrate a point for a friend. It's not a criticism—I just made a point using shorthand."

"Drinking buddies," said Montbretia, not quite sure whether the term sat well with Boniface.

"What term do you want me to use?" asked Boniface, seemingly picking up on her hesitation. "Two heterosexual male friends who, in the past, frequently consumed too much alcohol together. What label should I apply?"

"So Veronica knows him?"

Boniface hesitated; there was a second of tension in his jaw, and then the softening of his face that usually preceded the admission of an error. "I think it would be fair to say that she's not a fan."

"Give me something positive about him, Boniface. Everything you tell me just digs a deeper hole."

"You're blowing this up," said Boniface. "Veronica doesn't get on with Leathan, and let's be fair here, Leathan ain't Vron's greatest fan." He leaned forward, resting on his elbow, his hand open, chopping the air for emphasis. "Veronica's problem with Leathan wasn't so much a problem with him—it was a problem with me. She didn't like what I did when I was with him. But what I did was my fault..." he brought his hand to slap his chest, emphasizing his guilt, "it wasn't Leathan leading me astray."

"Okay," said Montbretia cautiously. "Different bed each night..."

"I gave Leathan a lot of work. He even did a few bits after I started working for Gideon at the Department of the Environment."

Montbretia felt her eyes go wide and her head crane forward, wordlessly posing a question.

"You would be surprised what nonattributable information can help," said Boniface. "When I had my...incidents...and went to straighten myself out, I wasn't in a position to feed Leathan any more work, but he hooked up with an investigative reporter called Sam Cartwright." He paused, staring straight into Montbretia's eyes. "Sam is a good journalist. Hardworking. Honorable. Always wants the facts. Always after stories that matter."

"So why did he want Leathan?" asked Montbretia, trying to keep her tone light.

"Leathan is good. Leathan is dedicated. Leathan will do dangerous stuff. Leathan gives a monkey's about human beings."

Montbretia felt chastised. "Oh."

Boniface softened his voice. "Sam was doing a story about organized gangs in London—not small-time criminals like Ernie, but the new breed of international criminals that are coming to London. In particular, Sam was focusing on human trafficking—human trafficking for the sex trade. He had a story about a Bulgarian gang that was running brothels across

London and all the major cities. It wasn't just that this gang trafficked in the girls—modern-day slaves by any other name—it was that they also stole other trafficked women. These women might have been brought into the country to work as domestic servants, but the Bulgarians got hold of them and made them work as whores." He exhaled. "Forget about Leathan, go and talk to Gideon; he'll tell you just how deep the problem is in this country and how horrific the conditions are for these people. I know you saw stuff in Turkey, but this is where the people you met end up."

"So how did Leathan get involved?"

"Sam wanted an inside man—someone who could give him better evidence."

Montbretia felt her face freeze.

"The Bulgarians are tightknit—the gangs don't let outsiders in, and as you've figured, Leathan isn't Bulgarian and wasn't on the inside. However, there's a lot of local knowledge that's needed, and that's where Leathan got in."

"He was working *with* the gang?"

"In order to get the story—which would then be followed with passing all the evidence to the police," said Boniface. "Leathan did some good work, but the trouble is that to get the evidence, Leathan had to see a lot, and that's where his problem came." Boniface snorted. "I call it a problem—Leathan did the decent thing, and the problem is now his."

"What happened?" Montbretia's voice was a whisper.

"Remember, I was in treatment at the time this happened, so I'm not clear on some of the details, but what I do know is that Leath got attached to a girl—I don't know who…I don't know how attached. It got to the point where he couldn't let her suffer, so he rescued her and blew open the part of the operation he knew about. There were police, arrests, and subsequently there have been convictions."

"So he did a good thing—what's the problem?"

"The problem is the Bulgarians. If they find him, he's dead. And we're not dealing with a small organization here—their tentacles stretch across Europe, and they've got a lot of people on their payroll. So Leathan's reaction was to skedaddle and drop off the grid, hence we communicate in odd ways—he doesn't leave an electronic footprint behind him, and he sleeps in a different bed each night."

"Oh," mouthed Montbretia.

"It puts a different gloss on your impression of him, doesn't it?" said Boniface.

Montbretia nodded slowly.

"So do you see why I think he's got a pretty good idea about right and wrong?"

Montbretia could feel her head still nodding.

"And at this point, I think we should leave Leathan to do what he does. He's got money and he's got the key to let himself in." Something changed in Boniface's tone. "Do you want to go home?"

"I'm not sure I'd sleep—I'm too wired...scared...anxious, so I..."

"I was hoping you'd say that," said Boniface. "If you're still twitchy, you can stay at mine—that way you'll be there when Leathan gets back. But before we go home, there's somewhere I want to go first."

fifty-one

"Isn't it a bit late?"

"You mean, isn't it a bit early," corrected Boniface. "Our problem isn't waking him up; our problem is whether he's back home yet. And anyway—it's not my problem, it's yours: You're knocking on the door. You're my lucky charm for getting in to see Gray."

Montbretia had pulled the car to the curb, diagonally across from Gray's house, before killing the engine and the lights. A few streetlights offered some illumination along the two brick rows with doors and windows punched into the walls.

"I'm not dressing like a hooker from the 1980s again," said Montbretia as they got out of the car.

"Some might say that wearing an oversized man's jacket has something of an eighties vibe," said Boniface. "Especially in the way you've turned back the cuffs. I think it'll be just Gray's thing."

Montbretia muttered under her breath. "The street's quiet."

"Yep." Boniface cast a glance along the brickwork rows—a few upstairs windows showed lights, and one downstairs window. "But we only care about one house, and I'm guessing from the glow that he's watching TV."

Montbretia pushed out her bottom lip.

"You know what to do," said Boniface quietly.

"Actually, Boniface, I don't."

"Make something up and get us in—we need to talk with Gray." He grinned. "And if you have trouble, just throw in the word threesome."

Montbretia raised her eyes and turned toward the door as Boniface flattened himself against the front wall.

She tapped the door lightly with her the tip of her index finger. Boniface heard a voice inside. "What?"

Montbretia pushed the flap in the mail slot, looked through, and then lifted her mouth to the opening. "Hey, Gray," she purred.

Boniface heard the TV go quiet. The glow of the front window faded, to be replaced by yellow light as an incandescent bulb lit. There were footsteps, and the door opened—a squeak as the expanded wood rubbed on the frame.

"Hi, babe," said Gray. His voice gravelly, his enthusiasm clear, his hopes clearer.

Montbretia lifted her foot over the threshold and turned to face Boniface, winking with her eye not in Gray's line of vision as she moved into the house. "Fancy a threesome, Gray?"

He was still stuttering as he turned to see Boniface standing in his door. "What happened to your face?"

"What happened to yours, Gray?"

"Jojo or Wes?" asked Gray. "Or did he bring in outside help?"

"Jojo and Wes," said Boniface.

"Ouch." The older man sounded sympathetic. "Must have hurt... must still hurt. But I did warn you, and you were determined to keep bullshitting."

Boniface stood in the middle of Gray's front room, which due to the location of his front door was also his entrance hall, and looked back at the former lead singer of Prickle. "Oh, do come in," said the singer, in a tone that was probably intended to be sarcastic, but that just sounded grumpy.

"Thank you," said Boniface, managing to get the sarcastic note Gray was looking for. "Is this where we're sitting?" he asked without looking at Gray. He caught Montbretia's gaze, then pointed with his eyes to the beaten-up sofa leaned up against the back wall of the room, indicating she should sit. He saw her hesitation.

First a bristle at the implied order, which soon changed to an understanding that Boniface wanted her sat for strategic reasons.

Then there was the look of horror in her eyes as she looked down at the beaten piece of furniture. The 1970s olive/tan stripe, fashioned out of a fabric that was probably over 90 percent nylon—the rest being grime. It was frayed, ragged, and torn and seemed to have been fixed by the last road crew who had passed through with pieces of silver duck tape. Boniface dropped onto the sofa, feeling it thump against the wall, and cast an irritated look at Montbretia, imploring her to sit. Tentatively, she moved to position herself—her body lowering as if it were being lowered into a bath of acid.

"Why don't you get yourself a chair," said Boniface as the singer turned into the room, having wrestled the front door shut, careful to avoid the stack of paint cans that had increased in size since Boniface's last visit.

"Make yourself comfortable," said Gray, again failing with the sarcasm as he walked diagonally across the room, exiting through the far doorway.

He returned a moment later with a dining chair, unsurprisingly of 1970s vintage with a winged oval wooden back and frayed leatherette-covered seat. He placed it in front of the television and sat. "Your face looks bad—you really did upset the boys, Boniface."

Montbretia was still looking around herself at the sofa: she had a look that said she was unsure whether it was damaging to her long-term health. Instinctively, she pulled Boniface's suit jacket tightly across her chest. Boniface looked down at the carpet—the color of indifference—and hoped Montbretia didn't follow his gaze.

"But I'm not pissing blood—apparently on Ernie's instruction—which I believe is a good thing."

Gray looked slightly self-satisfied as he sat back in his chair, straightening his dirty white T-shirt. "Why are you here?"

"Because we're your friends," said Boniface. "Friends call round. Friends drop in and say 'hi.' Friends just have a chat…"

"I get it," said Gray. "Now tell me why you're here and then get out of my world forever." The natural aggression in his voice was far better suited to these sorts of exchanges.

Boniface felt his face harden, his voice lose its lightness of tone. "Why does Ernie think he owns Prickle?"

"Because I do, and he reckons I'm going to sell Prickle to him."

"You own Prickle?"

"Stands to reason—I founded the band. I never gave away my rights, so I own them. And if Danny wants to fight me in court, then my lawyer assures me we will win."

"Your lawyer?"

"Yeah."

"You've got a lawyer, Gray?"

"Yes, Boniface. I have a lawyer."

Boniface paused taking in the room—it would have been regarded as being in need of some sprucing up thirty years ago. Now…now, Boniface couldn't even figure where to begin. He pointed to the large television behind the singer. "You're the last man in the country with a cathode-ray tube TV—everyone's gone flat screen—and yet you can afford a lawyer."

He let the observation hang.

Gray used a fingernail to loosen something caught between his teeth, continuing to talk and perform dentistry simultaneously. "He's a good guy—he knows his stuff, and he can be really aggressive."

"Who is he?" said Boniface calmly, his tone temperate, his attitude mollifying.

"Iain Irvine," said Gray.

"And he's been meeting people for you—talking about the situation?"

"Suppose so," said Gray, looking suddenly out of his depth.

"But he's a good lawyer?" asked Boniface with little conviction, more in the style of a cat toying with a mouse.

"Oh yeah," said Gray.

"Do you know where he gained his law degree?" asked Boniface.

"Why would I know that?" The aggressive tone was back.

"Just for my own interest," said Boniface, letting his face soften. "I'm always interested in where these people learn their trade."

Gray shrugged, pulling up his legs under his chin, his feet on the seat of his chair.

Boniface deepened his voice and tilted his head—his best empathic look. "You know Ernie's a criminal."

Gray shrugged again. "We're all dancing on the wrong side of a non-white line."

Boniface went to speak, then nodded his acknowledgement. "But it's a case of degrees. Ernie's more of a criminal—Ernie has people who make sure you trip up as you leave his fine establishment..." Boniface indicated his injuries.

"He ain't been criminal to me. And I find it hard to believe that your past is completely lilywhite...pure as the driven and all that."

"I've made a few mistakes," said Boniface quietly. "But what I've done isn't relevant. What is relevant is what you and Ernie are intending to do next."

fifty-two

"Shouldn't we go and see Danny? Tell him there's a lawyer."

Boniface shook his head and stirred his peppermint tea. Montbretia stood on the other side of the kitchen counter, staring intently. He looked at the clock on the microwave. "Have you seen the time? It'll be three before we can get there." He squeezed the teabag. "If we turn up, it'll freak him out—no one turns up at that time of day in person, except with bad news. And if Dawn's not back, then we've just increased his level of panic needlessly."

Montbretia's stare was fading and she glanced down at her rooibos, chasing the teabag around her mug. A South African—who had tried to start a chat in a coffee shop line and had asked for a date before the barista delivered her coffee—had told her she would like it. Montbretia had bought a box of rooibos teabags, but from her lack of enthusiasm, Boniface doubted the South African was right, and doubted the South African would be mentioned again.

"And what's the point in telling him? Danny's still got the same problems whatever we tell him." Boniface lifted his teabag out of his mug and dropped it into the food scraps recycling bin. "Anyway, that guy ain't a lawyer."

"What guy?"

"This Iain Irvine that Gray calls his lawyer. He's not a lawyer."

"You know him?" asked Montbretia.

"No." Boniface picked up his tea, walked around the counter into the lounge area of the room, and sat on the farther sofa, carefully placing his cup on a coaster. "But when I saw Ernie tonight, there was someone in that room with Ernie, and I'm guessing that was Irvine."

Montbretia, still wearing Boniface's jacket with the cuffs turned back, joined Boniface on the perpendicular sofa, placing her rooibos near to his peppermint. "Why did you ask where the lawyer gained his qualification?"

"Because this guy's behavior makes him sound like the *lawyer* who turned up to see PAD Management this morning—the one who took some heavies and started pushing them around. According to Fiona, the trainee giraffe with the deep voice, this guy ain't no lawyer. While I may not agree with everything Miss Aldred says, I think she's quite astute and would do the research and get that kind of detail right."

Montbretia took a sip of her tea and pulled a face. "It's too sour for me."

"Milk? Sugar? Honey?" offered Boniface, becoming increasingly unsure that his suggestions were helping.

"I'll suffer this—perhaps it's an acquired taste," said Montbretia. "So this guy who isn't a lawyer...I don't see what the significance is."

"The qualification, or lack of qualification, is a sideshow. What matters is this seems to be where the action is. Ernie's a crook—but he's got a so-called lawyer on his payroll, and as far as we can tell, that lawyer isn't a defense advocate. But more than that, Gray seems to think there's a legal claim, and PAD seem to think there's a legal issue..." Boniface stared into space, contemplating as he took a sip of his tea. "Ernie's a crook, so why is he acting as if he thinks he's got a legal case?"

Montbretia leaned forward. "But you can't fight a case without a proper lawyer, can you? This Iain Irvine can't stand up in court unless he's a proper lawyer—that would be..." she smiled, "fraud, or something—I need a lawyer to tell me the correct law that would be broken."

"It's not that simple. First, I'm guessing that Iain Irvine isn't a complete numpty—he's already been able to cause enough problems, even before fists flew. Second, and probably more importantly, there's the question of whether he might just be successful. Say Gray does have a legal claim—say there's something that Danny didn't pin down, or can't prove that he pinned down, all those years ago. And there's a third aspect here—say that Irvine ties Prickle up with litigation. That can last for years, which could destroy the band—Luca needs to earn, no singer's going to join if they're not getting paid... You get the idea."

"I thought this guy was just a low-life running a card school with the odd beating thrown in just for fun. That's quick money."

"And that's where I think we've underestimated him. Ernie just needs to wait. And if he gets bored of waiting, then he slaps a few people or makes a few threats. But he's not just threatening—he's like a pirate ship drawing up beside you. If they get one rope over—so what. Two ropes—okay. Three ropes holding you—there might be trouble. Four—start worrying. Every new rope—every pressure point is another advantage. The only question is what he's going to throw a rope over next."

"Well, if he's that smart, then shouldn't we be doing something?"

"I am doing something," said Boniface. "I'm sitting here waiting for Leathan." Montbretia frowned and Boniface continued. "There's no point in putting your trust in a guy and then not trusting him."

"But should we go and fetch him, something like that?" There was a hint of desperation in Montbretia's voice.

Boniface shook his head. "We could be seen—if Ernie makes the link between us and Leathan, that's bad for all of us."

"But we can't do nothing." Montbretia's voice had the hint of a whine.

"I'm not going to do nothing—I'm going to try to get some sleep, and so should you. The spare bed's made up. I'm not doing anything until I've heard from Leathan...or I've heard that Leathan's dead."

fifty-three

There was a noise.

Boniface wasn't quite sure what it was—he had been asleep, and the noise was in a different room. Perhaps something made of metal being knocked.

He rolled over, pulling the duvet tight, but dared to open one eye to look at the clock. It was still dark, and at best—best—he had been asleep for ninety minutes. He let his feet fall to the floor and his toes wriggle in search of slippers. It might not be much, but he wanted some protection for his feet.

He stood and walked around the bed, the only illumination coming from the streetlights pushing around the edges of his curtains and a faint yellow glow from his door. He leaned into his bathroom, put his hand around the door and grabbed a toweling robe, wrestled to find the sleeves as he walked into the passageway, and managed to tie the waist as he walked into the main room where he had sat drinking tea with Montbretia not long enough ago.

He became aware of the smell and looked at the items that had been spread over his kitchen counter. "I didn't have any bacon." He looked at the loaf of sliced bread standing vertically on the counter. "Nor bread."

"But Ernie did," said Leathan, turning to him, a smug grin firmly plastered. "And if you can't steal from a criminal with impunity, who can you steal from? I found all I needed for breakfast and figured it was time to get out of there." Leathan pointed at the pack of bacon and then looked up to Boniface, his eyebrows raised, questioning.

Boniface nodded. The other man pulled out the grill pan and carefully laid some more slices of bacon before returning the pan, noisily.

"There's a cab office just down from Ernie's..."

"I know."

"Thought you might. I got a cab, and the driver told me an interesting story when I said I wanted to go to Wimbledon. Apparently he drove someone well-spoken to Wimbledon yesterday. A guy in a suit but who looked like he'd been in a fight. Apparently the suit was ripped and the guy looked like he had received quite a beating..."

"Fancy that," said Boniface. "So you got in."

Leathan's grin was back. "The simple lines are the best. Imply you're a brother criminal doing work on their manor, and say you've come to pay your respects and to ask what taxes will be levied for safe passage."

"And it worked?" asked Boniface, although the bread and bacon

"It got me in." Leathan's tone was matter-of-fact. "And I've met Ernie."

"And stolen his bacon."

"Yeah." Leathan grimaced. "Ernie may seem like a bit of an anachronism—an essentially harmless, toothless tiger—but he's found a way to be relevant. He can administer pain, but he outsources the administration—and speaks very highly of his staff. Apparently these fine gentlemen from Brixton and Battersea..."

"I think I've met them," said Boniface.

"Well, then, you will know that they are very willing to take on work. Both sides seem to feel there's an advantage to using dark skins to do damage to light skins."

Boniface could feel his visage posing a question.

"It plays straight to the stereotype—a white person saying 'they were black' always sounds racist if you go to the cops, even if the cops are the biggest racists of the lot. But still you get into the 'how black' and 'what sort of black' conversations, and the cops don't know what to do because the pattern of crime doesn't fit their usual expectation of internecine gang wars."

Leathan pulled out the grill tray and started turning the bacon. "And Ernie's smart here—no one expects him to send in a bunch of black guys." He paused, finishing the turning, then placed the pan back under the grill. "The difficulty for us is that Ernie has these guys around for a reason."

The visitor walked to the end of the counter and leaned, resting on his hip and crossing his arms, watching Boniface. "Ernie has a problem—there's an influx of new criminals. Big gangs doing really unpleasant stuff."

"But that's not news for you, Leath—those gangs are why you left."

"Yeah—but Ernie probably doesn't have the advantages that I did..."

"You mean a French mother who taught you the language?"

"Helps," said Leathan. "But I was more thinking about my winning personality and the fact that I didn't have a business. Ernie can't just take his business to Paris, or Prague, or...wherever. So he's trying to adapt."

"Please tell me he hasn't been reading books."

"Nah...but he's being clever. He sees that certain areas are a no-go for him—the big ones are drugs and prostitution. These are the areas where you need the contacts and the logistics to get the merchandise into the country, and this is where the Albanian and Bulgarian gangs are dominating."

"Again, this isn't news to you," said Boniface.

"True. But at the moment, Ernie has an entente-lacking-cordiale with these guys. Basically, he's not stepping on their toes, and they're not breaking his toes. But he's worried about the gambling."

"How so?"

"At the moment, he makes his money through gambling. It's easy-ish money, and the new boys in town don't care about it. But it's a small step for these new boys to decide they want to get into gambling, and if they do—even with his army of South London thugs—Ernie won't be able to win that battle. And he knows it, so...he's expanding."

"Into music," said Boniface. "So Ernie thinks he's going to be an impresario. Thinks he's going to be like one of those folk-hero managers from the sixties: half silver fox, half thug hanging people out of the window by their ankles. He sees that as glamorous, does he?"

"Nah—Ernie's logic is quite good here. He reckons he can run a semi-legitimate business and make an income. But the clever part is that he reckons the earnings will never be so big that the Albanians, the Bulgarians, or whoever would want to get involved. Why would the gangs do something that makes them fifty thousand quid over a year, which has to be split ten ways, when they can do the same amount of work in a month and earn a million by trafficking in a bunch of girls?"

"I hate to admit it," said Boniface. "But there is some sensible logic there."

"Indeed," said Leathan. "And as part of this, he has recruited Gray."

"We know this."

Leathan nodded and continued. "He encouraged Gray to gamble and has rolled up huge debts."

"We know this, too."

"And he has offered Gray a way out."

"We had figured that."

"But have you figured what Ernie's going to do with Gray?" Leathan started looking around as if he had lost his keys or his phone. "Where do you keep your whisky?"

"There is none," said Boniface. "No whisky, no alcohol."

"None! Not even for guests."

"None," said Boniface. "Come on, Leathan. You of all people know how readily I would accept a drink. I'm sober now, and it's much easier to stay sober if there is never, ever any temptation."

Leathan shrugged dismissively.

"I can call Veronica if you like. She will have some whisky—and you know it will be very good whisky."

"There's only so much disappointed disapproval I can take in one lifetime. It would pain me—and it would pain your former wife—so let's not. I'll have a cup of coffee instead."

"The kettle's there," said Boniface, bobbing his head forward.

"How does Vron react to your new plaything?" He looked directly at Boniface—the glint in his eye that had always been there when he was trying to be provocative. "Very cute—I commend you on your selection."

"We're not in...there is no *us*," said Boniface.

"Really?" Leathan seemed half joking, half surprised. "So you won't mind if I have a swing."

"I mind if you upset, offend, or hurt her, but apart from that, Montbretia is her own woman. She's quite capable of telling you to get lost—she doesn't need my help for that." He sat back in the sofa. "Now, tell me about Gray and Ernie."

"Sorry," said Leathan, exaggerating the O in sorry. "I didn't realize it was a tetchy subject—case closed, end of discussion." Boniface stared and Leathan exhaled. "Ernie wants to put Gray in as lead singer of Prickle. He figures the only guy that matters in a band is the singer—everyone else can be replaced, so he wants the only living singer under contract, and then he'll fire the rest of the band and get some cheap session guys who have no rights. Once that's set up, he'll exploit the back catalog like crazy."

"That explains a lot," said Boniface. "Gray gets encouraged to run up the gambling debt, which can be paid off with assets in Prickle, and his legs don't get broken so he can perform with the band."

"Couple that with the lawyer he's got who's applying pressure to Danny and the management, and you could see this might work."

"Lawyer?" asked Boniface. "Iain Irvine?"

"You didn't think to mention him before I went in," said Leathan, an edge of exasperation grating his voice.

"New information—we paid a visit to Gray after we dropped you. What he said makes more sense now."

"I say lawyer," said Leathan. "But the way they're behaving, I think Ernie fancies Irvine as his consigliere."

"And Irvine?"

"My guess—Irvine sees himself as the heir apparent, not that he's that different in age."

There was a creak of floorboard in the entrance hall, and the door opened partially. Montbretia, her hair mussed, stepped in, knocking her shoulder on the door as she tied a toweling robe tight. "You're back," she said groggily to Leathan; her voice was tired, but the relief in her tone was clear.

She moved to the other sofa. As she turned her back to Leathan, he stared at Boniface, raising his eyebrows questioningly. He indicated the toweling robe and Boniface's robe, silently making an accusation based on their similarity.

"Your keys," he said, pointing to the end of the counter as Montbretia sat.

"Thanks."

"Although I see you managed to get in without them." He walked to the grill, pulling out the pan. "Will you join us for breakfast, Montbretia?

Bacon sandwiches."

"That would be nice," she said. "I'll stay at this hotel more often if this is the service I get." She turned to Boniface. "I thought you didn't have any bacon—and I know you didn't have any bread."

"Leathan used his initiative."

Leathan placed three plates with bacon sandwiches on the low table, then dropped onto the sofa next to Montbretia. "I knew Boniface wouldn't take care of you."

"Thank you," said Boniface, reaching for the nearest plate. "So did you find anything else?"

"There's something that Ernie's not saying. He implied he has leverage, significant leverage, against Danny."

Boniface cursed as he chewed his sandwich. "Did he mention Dawn—even in passing?"

Leathan shook his head as he chewed.

"That's bad," said Boniface, putting his hand over his mouth. "That means problems for Danny through Dawn. We need to find her or find how Ernie and Irvine are using her as leverage." He looked over at Montbretia. "Eat up."

She frowned.

"We've only got one avenue that we haven't explored."

Her frown deepened.

"Carmen. I know it feels about a thousand years ago, but what did you find when you started calling hostels yesterday?"

Montbretia swallowed her mouthful. "I found nothing. A long list became a long list with about three hostels crossed off."

"Then we need to start knocking on doors."

"Am I okay to stay here and kip on the sofa?" said Leathan. "It's been a while since I slept, and you know I prefer not to go out in daylight."

"Take the spare bed," said Montbretia. "I'll change the sheets."

"No need—I'm fine," said Leathan. "I'll kip here. You two get going and find this woman."

fifty-four

"Oh, to be in Lambeth just after the night sky has cracked and is suggesting that somewhere—just somewhere—there might be a sun."

Montbretia sneered at Boniface, pulling her jacket tighter as she felt the bite of an early-morning breeze that had found its way from the North Sea and straight up the River Thames.

"Do I look sufficiently like a lawyer?"

Montbretia clapped her arms across her chest. "You'll do."

"And you don't think we've had enough trouble already with fake lawyers?"

"You're not really a fake lawyer—you're just..." Her voice trailed off.

"You didn't promise anything, did you?"

"I barely got a word in edgeways—as soon as they've found a way to say no, the calls ended."

"You didn't say there definitely *is* money?"

"I struggled to mention the subject with the speed the phones went down. It went 'I'm sorry, we can't disclose the identities of any residents past or present'—*click*."

"Okay, let's keep implying and let them extrapolate."

Montbretia looked at the façade of the office block—it had a certain facelessness. The brick frontage of orange-colored, wire-cut bricks produced cheaply in a factory for the minimum price seemed to have refused to weather in the forty years the building had been standing.

Two men came out of the entrance. Neither was a typical office worker. Their jeans were encrusted with filth, their footwear was indistinguishable—it was simply a dark color at the end of their legs. And their coats—such as they were—were tied with string for one and a length of plastic for the other. One man talked loudly, the other mumbled—neither seemed to be taking account of the other as they conversed.

Boniface had a look of sadness as he watched the two pass. "I guess we're in the right place. Does the address on your list say number forty?" He pointed to his eyes at the number forty on the tattered awning over the front door.

Montbretia pulled the list from her back pocket. "Forty it is."

Boniface pushed the brushed aluminum–framed glass door and stepped in, holding the door for Montbretia as they entered a reception area, which was only the reception area by virtue of the fact that it was the first place you reached in the building. To the side, a double door had been propped open, giving access to a corridor with offices on each side.

"Are you sure, Boniface? This looks like an office to me."

Boniface's voice was quiet, just above a whisper. "It probably was a few weeks ago, but while it's unoccupied and in need of complete refurbishment, landlords often let homeless charities use places like this."

Montbretia looked around and sniffed—a combination of institutional cooking and unwashed human filled her lungs. "Why would they?"

Boniface halfheartedly shrugged. "Buying their place in heaven. Also, if you've got people here, then they take care to a certain extent—it's cheaper than security guards. And as you will have noticed, the place needs to be completely gutted anyway, so it's not a huge deal."

A figure came out of the second door on the right, walking along the faceless corridor toward them. Montbretia guessed he was probably only around twenty, but he had that look when someone had been homeless—they could be anything between fifteen and fifty. She could see him taking in Boniface—the suit was conspicuous. "You couldn't spare us a tenner, could you?" he asked Boniface.

"Not unless you've seen Carmen Gallagher—and if you can take us to her now, there's fifty in it for you."

"Give me twenty and I'll ask around." He seemed better clothed than the two who Montbretia had seen leaving, but he didn't seem to have any respect for Boniface's personal space.

"I'll keep looking," said Boniface, stepping away and starting to move down the corridor.

"Is there an office here?" asked Montbretia.

"Up there," said the chancer over his shoulder, without breaking step.

Boniface was at the end of the corridor as Montbretia turned back. She ran the two steps to catch up as he tapped lightly on the door and confidently walked in. "Good morning," said Boniface. Montbretia followed him through the door. "Boniface," he held his hand to his chest, indicating himself, then indicated to Montbretia. "My colleague, Monty Armstrong."

"Lucy," said the woman behind the desk. Something about Lucy reminded Montbretia of herself. Lucy had shoulder-length brown hair—about the same length that Montbretia's had been when she arrived in the UK. She was slim—slimmer than Montbretia, slimmer to the point that Montbretia thought *issues with food*—and maybe two inches shorter. She also had that look of someone who was unaccustomed to exercise, or even, given her pallor, being outside.

Montbretia surveyed Lucy's office and hated it—peeling wallpaper, frayed and ripped carpet, and a strip light hanging by its wires that struggled to add to the gray light filtering through the filthy net curtain over the window. Then the realization came that this wasn't unpleasant because the homeless charity couldn't afford to undertake the maintenance—this was unpleasant because this is how the office was when the last paying tenants were here.

Boniface pulled out his phone. "I wonder if you can help us—we're looking for someone." He held his phone up for Lucy to see. "This is the most recent picture we have of her, but we also have pictures of her back in the eighties—she was a model then."

Lucy looked closely at the pictures as Boniface flicked through.

"Her name is Carmen Gallagher, and she's about forty-eight years old. We're looking for her in connection with a legacy."

Lucy paused, looking to Montbretia. "Did you call yesterday?"

Montbretia nodded.

Lucy sympathetically tilted her head—a look she was probably well practiced at delivering. "As I said, we don't disclose our residents—past or present."

"Does that mean she was here?" said Boniface.

"I didn't say that."

"True. But you said you won't disclose residents past or present. And since you won't disclose, that must mean she was here. If she wasn't, then you wouldn't be bound by a duty of confidentiality." Boniface seemed triumphant.

"We don't disclose details about anyone." Lucy gave a weak attempt to communicate an apology by scrunching her face. "In any case, our records are pretty sparse, and, newsflash, not everyone gives us a full name or their legal name. So if you want to take it that she's been here, go ahead—I'm saying nothing. If you want to take it that she hasn't been here, go ahead—I'm saying nothing." Lucy stood mute, but with the trace of a self-satisfied smile forming.

"I get that," said Boniface, continuing as if he hadn't really noticed that he had been rebuffed. "Look, as I said, I want to talk with Carmen about a legacy. We can meet somewhere public that suits her, she can bring a friend...you can be there...I just want to talk."

"It's still the same answer, I'm afraid," said Lucy.

Boniface jutted out his chin, admitting defeat. "If she does happen to get in touch, could you ask her to call me—here's my number." He reached into the breastpocket of his jacket, then pulled his fingers out as if there was a trap. "I'm sorry—I don't have a card. I'll have to write it down for you," he said, pulling his notepad out of his inside pocket. "I just got the suit back from the cleaner."

Montbretia stared. He always had cards in his top pocket. Always.

Boniface finished scribbling his note and ripped out the page, placing it on the desk. "I just want to have a chat with Carmen." Lucy's face soured slightly as she stood, not touching the page. "Thanks, Lucy. It was good meeting you."

They followed the corridor toward the door. "You didn't tell me you had a recent photo," whispered Montbretia.

"I snapped it at Jilly's." He took out his phone and held the picture for Montbretia, who reached over to steady his hand as they walked. "It's good to see her with her clothes on."

"It's a photo of a photo, Boniface."

"I know. What was I meant to do? I didn't want to ask and have Jilly say I couldn't take the picture, so I snapped it while she wasn't looking."

His phone disappeared into a pocket as they walked out of the main entrance. "You were a bit harsh in there, weren't you?" said Montbretia.

"Yeah. But all lawyers are assholes, right?" said Boniface. "I had to be true to character. If I claimed to be a lawyer, she might have doubted, but if I behave like one, she'll believe I am."

"And what's the story about getting your suit back from cleaner?"

"It suddenly dawned on me that I can't give them my card: It says Boniface Communications. If she twigs I'm a PR guy scamming as a lawyer, then we'll never find Carmen."

Montbretia pushed out her bottom lip, weighing up the other option. "Suppose so. Where next?"

"First, I think we should get some cash—I feel we're going to want to pay for information before too long. Then we go to the next on the list. And then the next."

fifty-five

"How many hostels are there?" Boniface stirred his tea.

"Fifteen in Westminster. Well, fifteen that wouldn't admit she was a resident and wouldn't confirm that she wasn't." Montbretia spread butter over her toast. "That fifteen also excludes any hostels where Carmen didn't fit their entry requirements."

Boniface frowned as he took a sip of tea.

"Different hostels have different requirements—some only admit young homeless, some won't admit you if you have a reputation for violence or if you've got a criminal record. And not every hostel has a website or comes up when you Google, so I'm not sure I've found everything. But of those ones that I did find, the answer is fifteen in Westminster."

"And we've been to seven so far."

"In Westminster. More in Lambeth, of course."

"Of course." Boniface looked down at his silent phone lying on the Formica surface, then leaned back to survey the café. It was small—two tables, both arranged as booths. He occupied one with Montbretia; the other was empty.

Most of the custom seemed to be office workers getting a coffee or something to eat at lunch before scurrying off for a day's work. And from the stacks of various rolls and the amount of sandwich fillings being prepared by the four staff behind the counter, Boniface guessed lunchtime would be busy, too.

"And after Westminster," said Montbretia. "I mean...what happens if we don't find her in the remaining eight?"

"Then we go wider. Ever wider concentric circles." He twisted his face—he wasn't quite sure how to communicate *what other options do we have*. "We keep going, and hopefully we get lucky."

"And if we don't?"

Boniface smiled softly. "If we don't get lucky, then life is...suboptimal." He snorted. "Not that it's much better than that at the moment—I'm not sure I wanted to spend my day going round hostels." He looked up at Montbretia. "Not that you wanted to spend your day dragging around homeless shelters, either."

Montbretia bit into her toast with little enthusiasm. "I would say it's not what I had planned, but that would only be true because I didn't have anything planned."

"Why don't you go home? You sound more bored than I feel, and you look like you could do with a bit more than ninety minutes' sleep."

"It's tempting, but I left my keys at your place, so I'd have to go past there to pick them up."

"So?"

Montbretia's lips winced and twisted. "Leathan's there."

Boniface waited, forcing his face into the best expectant look he could given his lack of sleep and his lack of enthusiasm.

"He got...well...while you were getting changed...I'm not...but..."

"Leathan?"

"With you?"

"Mmm."

"And he said this?"

"Mmm hmm."

"To you?"

"To me."

"Right," said Boniface and paused. "What exactly did he say?"

"Well...it's this whole different bed each night thing." Boniface waited. "He sort of implied that maybe I could supply a bed—just for tonight. Not tomorrow, because...you know..."

"And I'm guessing he also suggested that a body to keep him warm might be nice."

"More implied...but that was my understanding." She sat up straighter. "I can handle Leathan—hell, I might even find him cute in certain circumstances. But I only met him yesterday, and it's too early in the morning. I need a cup of coffee before I have those kinds of conversations." She seemed to relax. "Do you want to split the rest of the list?"

Boniface pondered. "Nah...safety in numbers, and one of us is bound to be more inviting to her. The point is to get Carmen talking, not to scare her."

"And you're sure there's no other way of doing this, Boniface?"

"I'm all ears—if you've got an idea, then shoot." He waited a beat. "We've got cash and we're making noise—the best we can hope for is we get close and someone blabs." He exhaled deeply, the jet of air rippling his half full cup of tea. "If this is all about Dawn's past, then it must be related to Lorna's death—why else would she run? Carmen's the only person who I know was there and with whom I haven't spoken. The only other person who seems to know is Ernie."

Montbretia's face soured. "I'd prefer it if we didn't pay him a visit." She put the last lump of toast into her mouth, chewing as she talked. "I still think we should split up—we could cover four hostels each and be back here in an hour, maybe ninety minutes."

Boniface's phone rang. "I don't recognize the number."

fifty-six

She wasn't sure whether to trust this bloke.

Boniface sounded like a ponce's name. And to be frank, he sounded like a bit of a ponce on the phone, but if there was money, then it might be worth talking to him. Provided he didn't require pain and/or humiliation in exchange for the cash... Provided it didn't require her to commit another crime.

And the meeting place seemed safe enough. It wasn't a side street where she was looking for a parked car. It wasn't a hotel near Kings Cross where they charged by the hour and wouldn't care if a murder was committed as long as you paid in full, up front, in cash, and then left the room so that it could be rented to the next punter.

It was a café in Westminster. A café she knew by sight but had never been in. The sort of place where people who work in offices go to buy sandwiches or rolls made with Italian-sounding bread, thinking it made their lunch better or healthier. But at the end of the day, bread was bread, whatever you called it.

She walked past the window, slowly but not too slowly.

There was a man sitting in a booth with a woman sitting opposite him. He looked like he could be a Boniface—thirtysomething, confident—but she couldn't see his face well enough, she guessed around six foot but he was sitting, looked after his hair, and had a decent suit. The woman sitting opposite him twisted as she passed—Carmen sped up and only caught a glance of her, mostly seeing the chestnut hair that flicked as she turned.

She didn't look like she was being held against her will.

She didn't look like she was the muscle, there to bundle Carmen into a waiting van.

In fact, she looked like the woman that Matt at the shelter said had turned up with this Boniface bloke this morning.

Carmen kept walking, stopping when she was about thirty yards past the café, where she waited, watching the entrance as people passed. After about ninety seconds, a girl with curly blond hair loosely tied back walked in. Carmen walked back, slowing as she again approached the café, making sure the girl was standing at the counter.

The blond girl was—and as she stood, she blocked the passage between Boniface and the door. If Boniface made a lunge, then blondie was going to get hurt. Rules of the jungle, unfortunately, honey.

Carmen pulled the door and stood, her foot keeping the dark

wood–framed glass door open. She took in the room, her eyes darting: three men behind the counter, blondie ordering, two tables—both probably fixed to the ground—one empty, the other with the man who was probably Boniface and the woman with the chestnut hair, a rear exit probably leading to the bathroom.

Boniface—assuming it was Boniface—made eye contact and started to slide out from his seat. The woman remained but turned her head and smiled.

"Hi. I'm Boniface." He leaned forward offering his hand, careful to avoid the blond. "You must be Carmen—it's so good to meet you."

She shook his hand once, withdrawing hers quickly, looking to see whether anyone else appeared.

"What do you want to eat?" Boniface had stepped back, leaving Carmen where she had been standing, and indicated to the menu boards.

"Umm…I'm not really sure," she said.

"Have you eaten yet today?" asked Boniface.

She shook her head.

"Full English?"

She nodded.

He turned to the guy closest to the grill. "Full English, please, for the lady."

"No black pudding," she said softly.

"No black pudding," relayed Boniface, then turned back to her. "Tea? Coffee?"

"Tea."

"It's builder's tea, but it's alright," said Boniface quietly, leaning forward. He talked like a wine snob, surprised at the quality of supermarket wine.

She nodded.

"And a cup of tea." He turned back and went to sit. "Please. Join us."

The woman slid across the bench seat to make room. "Hi. I'm Montbretia. Call me Monty," she said, offering her hand as Carmen cautiously moved closer. Carmen shook and carefully moved beside the woman who called herself Monty, sliding up the bench to sit squarely behind the table and diagonally opposite Boniface.

Matt at the shelter had said his face looked knocked about, and now, sitting across the table, Carmen could see that Matt was right: Boniface had a fat lip; several bruises displaying various shades of black, blue, purple, green, and yellow; roughed-up skin over one cheekbone; and on the other cheek a long, straight cut, the sort you get from a blade.

She pondered: If he was that smart, then why had Boniface got injured?

One of the guys behind the counter with a white shirt, black trousers, and white apron brought a mug of tea over, clunking it on the table and leaving.

"Quite a weapon, isn't it?" said Boniface, indicating the heavy white porcelain mug with the steaming brown liquid. "You could do quite some damage with that—scald someone, then clout them with it. They wouldn't fight back."

He didn't seem to realize he was describing her new emergency escape plan.

"Do you want to order something for later? A sandwich or something that you can take with you?" asked Boniface.

Carmen wasn't quite sure what to ask for.

"No hurry," said Boniface. "Think about it. Whatever you want—you can decide later."

The man in the apron returned with a large white plate, placing it in front of Carmen before pulling a knife and fork rolled in a napkin out of his top pocket. "Enjoy your meal," he said, turning away to leave Carmen looking at her filled plate, taking in each item: sausage, baked beans, bacon, two fried eggs, two fried tomatoes, fried bread, mushrooms, and hashbrowns.

Carmen unwrapped her cutlery and started to slice her bacon. "There, as I promised: breakfast," said Boniface.

"You said there was money," said Carmen, starting to chew her bacon, noticing that blondie had left.

"No, I said legacy," said Boniface. "And I may have allowed you to form the wrong impression—the legacy is M-Stub8's legacy." Carmen took another mouthful, her gaze fixed on Boniface. "But there is something for you." She opened her eyes wider, questioning. "I talked to Jilly Crossley—she thinks you're clean and you're pulling your life together. Is that right?"

"I'm clean," said Carmen, chewing. "Been clean for two years."

Boniface tilted his head as if he was listening intently.

"As for pulling my life together...that's harder. I don't have any real skills, and to try to get training at my age is hard."

"There are *no* offers?" asked Boniface.

"Who wants to take a chance on a former porn actress with a criminal record? I even thought about...you know...doing some more porn. But given what I've put my body through, there's not much—I'm at the extreme end of things." She cut into a hashbrown. "Do you know what the gangbang record is?"

"As in...?"

"As in the number of men one woman will have sex with in a single session."

Boniface shrugged. "It must be a big number, or else you wouldn't ask me."

"Mmm," said Carmen, biting into her hashbrown.

"Fifty," said Boniface.

"Do you want to guess?" she said to Montbretia.

"Seventy-five," said Montbretia tentatively.

"Just shy of one thousand the last time I looked." She looked between Boniface and Montbretia and saw disbelief. "I was asked if I wanted to have a go at breaking the record." She snorted. "They figured instead of just breaking the record—you know one-thousand-and-one, one-thousand-and-two—that we should smash it or set a whole new record for the largest number of double penetrations or triple penetrations."

"No." Montbretia's mouth was wide, the shock etched into her face.

"It's more appealing than the other offers."

"Worse than..." said Montbretia, her voice only just above a whisper.

"At least some of that stuff you might do for fun—the stuff I don't like is the pain...you don't want to know...and having guys crap in your mouth. Chocolate logs were never my thing...and never will be." She winced. "So do you get some sort of idea why porn isn't really an appealing option either?"

Boniface sat silently, then took out his wallet, opened it, and placed a £20 note on the table. He took a second and deliberately placed it on top of the first. Then a third, fourth, and fifth. Each note laid methodically and without hurry. He put his wallet away and looked up at Carmen. "Yours."

She reached forward, and he slapped his hand on the pile. "Yours for talking. And if we like what you say, we can help you—might even be able to find you a few bits of work. I'm not saying we can get you a change-your-life job—but a few days here and there so that you can tell people you've done some work. Maybe even help you get a reference."

"How do I..."

Boniface cut her off before she could ask the question. "How do you know you can trust me?"

She nodded.

"You don't." He paused—he seemed pleased with the answer he had given, even though it didn't help. "But what we do is this. I ask a question—just one. You answer. I give you the first twenty. Okay?"

She nodded again.

"We talk a bit more. When you think you've earned the balance of the cash, you say. Clear?"

"Clear," whispered Carmen.

"I'm not saying I'll pay you at this point—maybe I pay you nothing, maybe I pay you everything, maybe I'll pay you some—whatever I do, you'll get to see whether you can trust me, and from what you tell me, I'll see whether I can trust you. Fair?"

A single bob of the head.

"Ready?"

Another single bob.

"Billy Watkins," said Boniface. "Did you know him?"

Carmen felt her face flush and her stomach lurch. She dropped her head, unable to look at Boniface or the woman who called herself Monty.

She wasn't sure how long it was, but when she looked up, she could feel her eyes stinging. "I knew Billy." Her voice was hoarse.

Boniface lifted the top £20 and placed it on the table next to her. "You had a relationship with Billy?"

"Mmm hmmm." Carmen wiped her nose with the serviette. "He was the only man I've ever loved...the only man who loved me."

"Tell me about it—start from the beginning," said Boniface softly.

"I was in this band, M-Stub8—that's what you want to talk about?"

Boniface nodded, once. His head tilting as he leaned forward.

"There were four of us: me, Dawn, Jilly, and Lorna. We were all models...glamour models. They put us together in this band—we were awful, but it was a laugh."

Boniface remained still, watching. Listening.

"One night, we were doing this appearance, I can't remember where—some hole, Luton maybe—and Billy turned up. He was after Dawn—he knew her from way back...I don't want to say *love at first sight*, but you know when you see a guy and your heart just...you become aware.... You don't know why, but you know you've stopped breathing." Carmen looked at Monty. "You know that feeling."

Monty shrugged. "The last bloke I met recommended some South African tea. The only reason for my heart to stop was boredom."

Carmen laughed. "That's funny!" She leaned toward Monty. "Billy wasn't like that—he had a look about him...he was a guy that would fight. In fact, that night he did throw a fist. He was pure animal, and I was hooked. But as I said, he was after Dawn, and he didn't even speak to me." She turned back to Monty. "Seriously, he recommended tea—like..." She held up her mug.

Monty bit her bottom lip.

"Billy turned up a few other times, and we did get chatting—in fact, it was more than chatting—but he was only hitting on me to make Dawn jealous." She took a sip of her tea, and giggled "tea" under her breath before she continued, her voice becoming lower. "Dawn told me some things about Billy—they were quite...strong...serious accusations... But I didn't believe her—I thought she was just playing a game with Billy." Her voice took on a mournful tone. "I now know that everything she told me was true. Everything."

She reached under the table for Monty's hand and grabbed it, gripping it firmly. "We were like sisters, and it all ended the night Lorna died." She gripped more tightly, wiping a tear with her other hand. "None of us knew how to deal with that pain, that guilt. Jilly felt the loss—but you could see she blamed me and Dawn. It wasn't our fault..." She sniffed. "We weren't innocents—we encouraged Lorna to get up on the balustrade and dance with us—but we got down first and told her to get down, but she wouldn't. And then she slipped." She let out a sob. "We knew she was dead—we saw her hit head as she fell. It's the sound of her head hitting the balustrade that I hear when I wake up in the middle of the night. It was that sound that made me want to block out the world with a needle."

She wiped her tears with her fingers, breathing heavily. "Dawn went inside herself—she couldn't talk. Me, well, I found other ways to keep blotting out the pain. We all grabbed hold of what we could reach—I got Billy, and for once, he seemed to want me for me. He treated me well—I stopped having to show flesh, and life moved on. I lost contact with Dawn and Jilly, and life with Billy was good."

Carmen let go of Montbretia's hand, wiped her tears with her serviette, and brushed back her hair. "We were a family—me, Billy, and little Billy."

"Little Billy?" asked Boniface.

"Billy had a son: William. He was a nice lad—bit of a tear-away, but I liked him."

"How old was he?"

Carmen paused—running through dates. "I was there for his fifth birthday. I missed Lorna and the girls like crazy, but a kid's birthday gives you a different perspective. I would have been about twenty-two then, and you start thinking, you know..."

"Did it last?" asked Boniface. "You and Billy?"

"It was a bit on-and-off to start with. We'd be on; it was good. We'd be off; I'd have to work so I'd get my tits out. Billy would get angry—he didn't want his mates seeing me in the papers, so he'd come and have a go. One thing would lead to another, and we'd get back together. It would be good, then it'd be bad, then...you get the idea."

"I get the idea," said Boniface quietly.

"Then Billy's mum died. That hit him—that hit little Billy, who spent a lot of time with his nan. But it sort of brought me and Billy closer—we still rowed and were on-again-off-again, but we were more on than we were off." She looked across the table at the pile of cash. "I think it's time to pay."

Boniface picked up two £20 notes, showing each individually to Carmen, and placed them on top of the first note. "Part payment for part of the story. How did it end with Billy?"

"We were on and off, but mostly on. But we were out of it quite a bit—he was drinking a lot, I was doing a range of stuff, and that took up a lot of time."

"How long had you been together?" asked Monty.

Carmen paused, doing the sums in her head. "Little Billy—he was less little—he would have been about eleven or twelve, so what's that? Seven years?"

"Seven," said Montbretia quietly.

"I can't even remember where we were going, but Billy and I were going somewhere. We were both under the influence, and he was driving fast. One minute he's driving, the next the car's wrapped around a bridge, and I'm unconscious. Apparently it took forty-eight hours for Billy to die from his injuries. It took me a month to get out of hospital."

Montbretia gasped quietly. "And then?"

"What one of my counselors might have described as recreational drug use became self-medication, became addiction. Billy's family wanted nothing to do with me—not that they had ever wanted much—and I went back to work. I was seven years older—I was thirty, which in those days, in glamour-girl years, was more like 300, so I had to get involved in...you know...the dirtier stuff, so I took more to block out what I was doing...and you know how the story goes."

"What happened to the kid?" asked Boniface.

"Don't know," said Carmen. "His family—his father's family—took control. I never saw him again." She had the look of someone ready to leave the confessional. "I think that's the full hundred."

Boniface passed over the last two £20 notes. "Who was little Billy's mother?" he asked.

"Is there any more cash in your wallet?"

fifty-seven

"Do we trust her? Do we believe?" Montbretia was putting voice to the questions that were still swirling in Boniface's head as they walked through the doors into his apartment block, the light filtering through the glass panes in the doors soon losing its strength as they stepped across the marble-chip floors.

"I can't see any reason why she would lie." Boniface stood to allow Montbretia to ascend the stairs first, watching as she grabbed the brass handrail. "I'm not sure that I want to believe what she said, but would she really come up with that much of a story? You know, just keep talking with that level of detail?"

"By the sounds, she's done much worse for cash," said Montbretia, reaching the landing. "But that doesn't mean she was lying."

Boniface drew level and pulled out his keys. "Step quietly—we might as well leave Leathan if he's asleep." He slipped his key into the lock and held the black door open, following Montbretia into the apartment's lobby, which grew darker as he shut the door behind them, the only light pushing around the edge of the closed door to the main room.

Montbretia stood by the door, carefully placing her ear against it before turning the handle.

She stepped in and let out a small yelp.

Boniface followed swiftly and found the cause of her distress.

It took a moment to recognize the figure out of context, and another beat to recognize the danger. Boniface was more used to seeing Jojo Brooks standing outside Ernie's club, rather than leaning against the window in his front room. He was also conditioned to think of Jojo as one who used his fists, but the rusty pistol he was casually holding—as if it was the most natural thing that could be in his hand apart from his cock—suggested he might have other options.

"Sorry, Boniface," said Leathan. He was sitting on the sofa, his back to the door, facing Jojo, and didn't turn to apologize.

"Yeah, sorry, Boniface." Boniface turned to see the source of the second apology—the man standing behind the counter in the kitchen area. A figure Boniface half-recognized but had trouble placing out of context. Tall, gaunt, weathered skin with liver spots, and thinning hair combed back.

"I don't believe we've been formally introduced," said Boniface. "Mister Irvine, I presume?"

"The pleasure's all yours," said the other man.

"You were in Ernie's office yesterday."

Irvine ignored the comment. "Sit. Both of you." He indicated the spaces by Leathan. Montbretia sat next to Leathan, who was wearing jeans and white shirt with a buttoned-down collar, and Boniface took the perpendicular sofa.

"I'm sorry," mouthed Leathan with a look that was somewhere between apologetic, angry, and frustrated.

"Imagine our surprise when a driver from the cab company down the road came to tell us that he had just delivered someone to the same address as the guy who tripped on his way out. It didn't take us long to figure—two people, one address—and then there was the bacon. It's hard to say you came in good faith if you leave with my breakfast."

Leathan smirked.

"I'm a lawyer," said Irvine, apparently changing the subject. Leathan's smirk became a look of confusion, and he shot a glance at Boniface. "And as a lawyer, I think about contracts. There are four elements to a contract. Do you know what those four elements are, Mister Boniface?"

Boniface shook his head. Jojo looked bored and fiddled with the gun. Apparently he didn't care about contracts either.

"They're quite simple—it's probably what you would guess if you thought about it. The first part is the offer—like your offer to procure Prickle."

Irvine stood up straighter and walked out from behind the counter. "The second element of a contract is acceptance of the offer. You made an offer to Ernie, and Ernie accepted it."

He forced a look of pleasure across his face. "Now, most people think that's enough. But that's not a valid legal contract. Do you know what's missing?" He looked at Montbretia. "Do you?"

Montbretia shrugged. "It has to be written down?"

Irvine's mouth moved to become a rictal grin. "Good guess, but no. That's a very common misconception but it's not correct—a verbal contract is just as valid as a written one. No, there are two further elements—the first is that the contract must be legally enforceable. In other words, there must be consequences." He paused, letting his gaze linger on the three seated people. "And the fourth element—the one people always forget—consideration."

Irvine walked to the steel-framed window and stood toward the end away from Jojo before he continued. "Consideration. By which the law doesn't mean kindness—the law means payment." He looked at Leathan. "And with that bacon, we believe you have received suitable consideration to establish a valid contract. So let me now return to the third element of the contract and talk a bit about the legal consequences of not delivering on your contract, Mister Boniface."

"Bacon," said Boniface.

"Don't whimper—you offered the band. You're not going to tell me that you made an offer which you couldn't make, or that you were just bluffing." He stared at Boniface. "Good, so don't now start quibbling about the consideration."

"I..." Boniface stopped talking.

"You're going to deliver Prickle to us, Mister Boniface. And just to make sure you understand how serious we are, we're going to add a deadline. That way both sides"—he pointed to himself and then to Boniface, then back to himself—"can be clear about what's going on. So you have until midnight."

"Midnight," said Boniface.

"That's over twelve hours to do what you said you would do," said Irvine, checking his watch. "And if you don't meet our deadline, then Mister Featherstone—everybody's mate, Danny the bassist—will suffer. His wife may be missing—oh yeah, we know about that too, and we don't believe she's in Canada or wherever Danny told Billy she was—but we can still make her feel pain, unimaginable pain...pain that will destroy Danny from the inside."

He tilted his head at Jojo, who flicked the pistol in a move he had probably learned from a rap video, and walked in front of Irvine toward the door. Irvine remained still. "I presume you're that Leathan guy—the one our Bulgarian friends are hoping to meet." He shrugged as he started toward the door. "Maybe that makes things a little more urgent?"

fifty-eight

"Well, gentlemen. That was a rather disappointing interaction. What are we going to do now?" Leathan hadn't expected Montbretia to be the first to speak, but she had. And she seemed less downcast than him and Boniface.

Boniface, who sat back on the sofa, hopefully strategizing.

"You've gotta tell Danny," said Montbretia, who seemed to be far keener to act than the two men.

"Mmm," said Boniface. "But what am I going to tell him? What did Irvine *actually* threaten us with?"

"That he'd hurt Dawn," said Montbretia, talking over Leathan, who sat motionless apart from a small twist of his head as the conversation ping-ponged across him.

"And how is he going to do this?" asked Boniface. "I know that's what he said—what I'm trying to get at is what did he threaten to do? How is he actually intending to make good on his threat—especially as he doesn't seem to know where Dawn is either."

Montbretia stood up, removing the gray hoodie she had been wearing when she came in. Her voice was soft, encouraging. "What are the options? How could Irvine and Ernie hurt Dawn? How would that hurt Danny?"

Boniface mirrored Montbretia's calm tone. "Only one option I can think of—by going after her son. Hurt the kid, and Dawn feels pain that Danny can't fix."

"Excuse me." Leathan felt the need to break his silence. "When did we learn this little detail—that there is a son?"

"Carmen," said Montbretia.

"So you found her," said Leathan. Montbretia and Boniface nodded in unison. "Well done." He paused. "So who is the son?"

"I've seen him," said Boniface. "The first time I went to Ernie's place, he was hanging around there." Leathan felt his face register the confusion his brain felt. "It's worse than that, Leath. My blag to get in was that Billy had sent me—Billy Watkins, who was standing there. Billy Watkins, who I didn't recognize." He sighed, falling back into the sofa. "Which goes some way to explaining why I got beaten. They were on to me immediately."

"Hold on," said Leathan. "I thought Billy Watkins was dead."

"He is," said Boniface. "Billy Watkins Senior, his father, is dead—he died in a car crash with Carmen next to him. One name, two people."

"And you reckon Ernie's figured the Billy connection and he intends to use Billy Junior as leverage against Danny?"

"I don't know." Boniface leaned forward, resting his chin on his splayed hand. "I don't know, Leath. I really don't know."

"What's not to know?" Leathan stood up, moving toward the counter separating the kitchen from the main part of the room.

"Why did Dawn run?" asked Boniface. He looked up at Montbretia. "Any clue?"

"You mentioned Billy—she ran. Or at least, that's what I understood." She gave a slight shrug.

"Right. But if you're a mother, wouldn't you want to see your son?"

"I would," said Montbretia.

"So she must have thought Billy was Billy Senior, the father," said Boniface. "There was no reason for her to know he was dead, and that ignorance kind of makes sense if she cut herself off completely...which would be another reason to believe Carmen's story."

"But do you think Carmen's wrong? Do you have an alternative version?" asked Montbretia.

"Well, not an alternative version, but..." his voice trailed. "It doesn't fit with what Danny...implied."

Leathan started to fill the kettle. "I'll put the kettle on—you elaborate."

"The one thing we know to be true is that Danny and Dawn are the real thing—proper, true love."

"That's what everyone says," said Montbretia.

"Not even a hint to the contrary—wouldn't you agree?" said Boniface. "Yeah."

"So, if it is true, why doesn't Danny know that Dawn has a son?" He looked between Leathan and Montbretia, neither responding. "But put that aside—Danny and Dawn don't have kids. Danny was pretty discreet, but he implied that they had been through all the medical procedures...and the problem seems—I say *seems*, because he's never going to say outright—to be with Dawn. So if she can't have kids, then the kid can't be hers—and if the kid's not hers, then that explains why she ran when she heard the name Billy Watkins, since there was only one Billy as far as she knew."

The room fell quiet—apart from the noise of the kettle starting to heat the water.

"You know what you've got to do." Leathan watched as Boniface looked up to meet his eye.

"I knew what I had to do the moment the words came tumbling out of Carmen's lips. But I don't know that it's the right thing to do." His voice became almost pleading. "I can't tell Danny he's got a stepson if I can't prove that it's true."

"But take the alternate view," said Montbretia, moving back to the sofa and sitting where Leathan had been sat. "Are you really saying you're going to do nothing?"

Boniface exhaled. "I've got to do something—I just haven't figured what that something is."

"Yet," said Leathan, leaning on the counter. "I guess the question is: How much do you believe this Carmen?"

Boniface snorted and ran his hands through his hair. He looked to Montbretia for agreement as he said, "She's more than plausible."

Montbretia nodded, seemingly not having anything else to offer.

"You've got to lay it out for him," said Leathan, resting against the end of the counter.

"But if it's true, Dawn didn't tell Danny for a reason. We can't prove Billy is her son without her DNA."

"Nor can Billy or Ernie or anyone else without Dawn's DNA," said Montbretia.

"But hold on," said Boniface. "We've got to assume that Billy is Dawn's son and make sure that no harm comes to the kid. You heard Irvine's threat."

"He's not our responsibility," said Leathan. "You need to look after Danny and Dawn."

"Think about it," said Boniface. "Whatever the situation, how does Danny get up in the morning if he is responsible, however indirectly, for harm coming to his wife's child—probably her only child? And how does he make a decision about giving away the band if he doesn't know for sure whether the kid is Dawn's."

"That's why they invented coins, Boniface," said Leathan, pulling a piece of silver out of his pocket and flicking it.

"Okay. You've convinced me. I don't know what I'm going to say, but whatever it is, I need to say it to Danny," said Boniface, standing. "Can I trust you two here together?"

He passed the kitchen counter as Leathan said, "Sure."

"You're not going to get yourselves held up at gunpoint." He reached the door and turned back, much as Irvine had done. "And Leathan—don't try to proposition Monty. You met her less than twenty-four hours ago, and I need you both on good terms when I get back."

fifty-nine

Boniface let the barge glide through the narrow country lanes of the Surrey Hills.

He didn't remember the route he had taken—he had navigated by muscle memory and electronics as he dedicated his conscious mind to the task of considering every permutation and each option. He knew he would have gone up Wimbledon Hill, through the village, and along the edge of the Common passing between the windmill and the Embassy of the Holy See before turning left at Tibbet's Corner onto the A3. Once on the A3, he would have followed the three lanes until he turned off and passed through the village of Ripley, shortly to turn south through West Clandon and climb to Newlands Corner, where he would have seen the panorama of the valley created by the Hills spread in front of him before descending and turning right into the narrow country lanes meandering through an occasional hamlet, until eventually he reached the house that was becoming familiar: Dawn and Danny's house.

Except without Dawn, it was hard to call it her home.

Danny saw him arrive from the kitchen and came out to greet him. Boniface was shocked at how rough he looked—the shock must have shown on his face. "I ain't slept," were the bassist's first words. "Not since she left."

"Have you eaten?" asked Boniface.

"Scraps. I can't keep it down—my gut's tied in knots."

"You could shave...have a bath..." Boniface surveyed the rocker's appearance. For a man who earned his living presenting an image, he seemed to be utterly unaware of how he looked from the outside.

"Thanks, Boniface. You've driven all this way to tell me to find a bar of soap." Danny indicated toward the kitchen. "You feel it's my personal hygiene that's keeping my wife away, do you?"

"I'm sorry," said Boniface, stepping through the kitchen door, pausing at Dawn's photograph of the Gothic tower that he had admired shortly before he mentioned the name Billy Watkins. "I'm just a bit distracted. Something on my mind that I'm trying to get straight."

"Sit down," said the bassist, clicking on the kettle.

"You'd better join me," said Boniface, pulling back the chair he had last sat in when he had dinner with the other man's wife on the night that Danny had met the prospective new singer. Boniface indicated the other side of the table. "Don't worry about the tea...other things are more important."

"Now you're worrying me, Boniface," said Danny, pulling back the bench on the other side of the table.

"You remember when we last spoke I asked you about Ernie Norton?"

"Gray's friend...comrade...business partner...whatever."

Boniface said, "You said you didn't know him."

"And I still don't know him."

"Maybe you should," said Boniface softly. "Maybe you will." He paused, looking for signs on Danny's face to suggest how he might react. "He's the root of your problems, and he's trying to unleash a whirlwind of torment for you."

"If he wants to do that, why doesn't he come here and face me?" asked Danny, his body stiffening as he sat up straight. "Face me, man-to-man."

"Because he's sent me instead," said Boniface. "He has figured—correctly—that I'm not going to refuse to pass on his message."

"You really are starting to scare me, Boniface. What is this message?" Boniface looked at the bassist, who was gripping the edge of the table, the color having drained from his face.

"He's proposing a deal. Not a nice deal, but a deal."

"Come on, Boniface. What is the deal?"

"He wants the band. He wants to own Prickle—every copyright, every contract, every source of income, and in return for that, he will be kind to Dawn."

The room fell silent apart from the sound of the kettle and Danny's breathing—a deep inhalation, silence as he held the breath, a long exhalation, and a pause before the cycle began again. Boniface fixed his focus, waiting until Danny finally broke the still. "You told him no?"

"I told him nothing." Boniface's tone was reassuring. "The decision isn't mine to make—either way."

Danny's left cheek twitched.

"But there's more."

"More?"

"He's threatening your wife, Dan, not you."

"If he lays a finger..." Boniface held up his hand to stop the bassist before he made a list of threats, only half of which he would intend to carry through on.

"You need to listen." Boniface's voice was just above a whisper. "And you need to stop thinking about revenge—if you're off dismembering people limb by limb, then you're not here protecting Dawn."

Danny stared at Boniface and exhaled deeply.

Boniface began slowly but deliberately, pausing after he had uttered each phrase. "I'm going to lay out the story as I have been told. I'm telling you so that you know what the threat is. I'm telling you so you know what people are saying. I'm not claiming this is the truth."

Danny remained still.

"Okay?" whispered Boniface.

"Okay," mouthed the bassist.

"The kid that turned up the other day asking for Dawn—the one that seemed like a strung-out junkie..." Danny nodded his head as Boniface continued. "There's a chance that he's Dawn's son."

The room was silent again.

Boniface watched Danny, checking the emotions playing across his face: anger, hurt, disbelief, understanding, rage, acceptance. Finally he whispered, "It's not true...he can't be."

"I spoke to Carmen—you remember Carmen Gallagher; she was in M-Stub8 with Dawn." Danny blinked his eyes as if to affirm. "She says that Dawn did have a son."

"Bullshit."

"She says that Dawn told her." Boniface watched, calibrating the reaction across Danny's face—perhaps hearing for the first time about his and Dawn's greatest desire: a child. Maybe realizing that his wife may have lied to him.

Boniface continued. "Carmen says that she had a relationship with the kid's father—a relationship over several years—and this guy said Dawn was the mother."

Danny's eyes glistened; his lower jaw trembled as it tightened. His lips opened and closed as if sipping small amounts of air. "It's..." He stood, turning away from Boniface, one hand clutched across his stomach, the other lifted to his face. When he spoke—still facing away from Boniface—his voice cracked. "I don't care if there's a kid—I just want my wife to be safe. I want my wife home." His voice trailed off, to be replaced by sobs.

Boniface stood and walked around the table to Danny, putting an arm around the other man's shoulder.

"I know, Dan, I know. We all want Dawn home—but we need to focus. We need to deal with this issue—I'm pretty certain that once we sort out Ernie, then all your other problems will disappear."

"What they're saying, Boniface. It's all lies." Danny's voice was a whimper.

Boniface took Danny's head between his hands, forcing the other man to look at him. "To do the best for Dawn we need to focus. We can't prove whether the story is true or not..."

"I don't care if it's true. I love my wife whatever, and she loves me." Danny's voice was pleading.

"Focus," said Boniface. "Ernie has given us an ultimatum and a deadline: midnight. He wants the band and all the rights and earnings that flow from the band. You, Mel, Newt, and Luca will be out, and Ernie will put Gray in as singer with a bunch of session guys. That's his plan."

"That's just stu..." Danny pulled away, visibly angry. "That's crazy—that'll never work."

Boniface clapped his hands. "Focus. That's what Ernie wants—the threat is that he'll hurt Dawn. To quote, *unspeakable pain* if you don't comply."

"It's a lie. This kid's a lie. There's nothing to hurt us with." Danny's face was reddening; his voice was reaching a crescendo. "Tell him no, Boniface. He can do what he wants. But there's no kid, and he's not having the band."

Boniface returned to the other side of the table and sat. He motioned to Danny to return to his seat. The bassist was breathing heavily, his shoulders pulled in as if taking the stance of a prizefighter.

Reluctantly Danny sat, and Boniface began softly. "I'm having trouble believing what I've been told, but let's just play through the options. Say this kid is Dawn's. Say she gave birth when she was fifteen—years before she met you."

Danny snorted.

"Just...pretend, for one moment, that this kid matters. Think of the options. Ernie could wheel out the kid and sell the story to the papers. Wife of a rich rock star ignores her child and keeps him secret for thirty years. Think how Dawn would feel if that story were plastered over the newspapers day after day after day. And as a secondary issue, think of the blowback for you and Prickle."

Danny's voice was quiet but firm. "The story ain't true, Boniface. My wife doesn't have a kid. We went through every test you can go through with some of the leading gynecologists around the world—I cannot say this any more clearly: Dawn cannot conceive."

"I hear you," Boniface's voice remained calm. "But just imagine that there's a possibility that there's a perfectly reasonable explanation for this, and the kid *is* Dawn's. If Ernie murders this kid, procures his death, or makes the kid suffer—permanently injures him, gives him some funny pills that make him blind or lose a limb, sends him to jail, whatever—think what that would do to Dawn if she is his mother." Boniface sucked his teeth. "Ernie's mean—he could make the kid suffer and also go to the press."

Boniface noticed that Danny didn't seem to be responding. Danny didn't seem to have heard.

When he started speaking, the warmth had drained from his voice. "If she doesn't have a kid, then there's no story. Right?"

He paused, his eyes boring into Boniface, challenging him not to respond to the rhetorical question.

"I love my wife. I trust my wife." He paused, breathing heavily. "These aren't just words, Boniface. This is the basis of our whole relationship. I'm not going to undermine everything we have together and say I don't believe her." He inhaled deeply. "You can tell this Ernie to go and play with himself. If the kid gets hurt, it's on him, not me."

His gaze remained fixed on Boniface.

"And just so we're clear. If Dawn did have a kid, I wouldn't care—I'd still love her completely. And as for the idea of using a kid to get at me... how much bad press could an illegitimate kid cause? I'd love her to have a kid! Seriously—if the kid were hers, then as far as I'm concerned he's my son, and I'd throw open our doors to him." He continued, his voice smaller. "And if my wife has lied, I don't care—she will have had her reasons."

Boniface sat up straighter, keeping Danny's gaze. "You're sure, Dan?"

"If it's a choice between who lives, me or Dawn, then I'll lay down my life like that." He slapped the table, hard, the echo bouncing around the hard surfaces in the kitchen. "But if you want me to be worried about some chancer when my wife's missing, I don't care. Let this Ernie guy do his worst."

sixty

"I know why Dawn ran, and I know where she is."

"Where?" Montbretia felt a combination of joy and enthusiasm, tempered with caution. She had been sitting on the sofa perpendicular to the sofa where Leathan sat, but was now on her feet as Boniface made his announcement. Leathan remained seated, but turned, his arm flipped over the back of the sofa as they both faced the new arrival.

Boniface stammered momentarily. "I don't know where she is *now*, but I know where she will be—and you're going to find her." He pointed at Montbretia.

Montbretia went to speak but stopped. It was as if her brain had been slow in processing what her ears had heard and was still trying to resolve how the two facts—Dawn's location and Montbretia finding Dawn—related to one another.

"What did Danny say?" asked Leathan before Montbretia could resolve her internal dilemma.

"Not good," said Boniface, holding his hand over the kitchen counter and dropping his car keys. "In some ways it was a complete waste of time going to see Danny—he's too distracted. All he can do is sit and wait for Dawn...he can't not be there if she comes back."

"Can't he go and look around the nearby area?" asked Montbretia.

Boniface dropped onto the sofa next to Leathan. "You don't find a moving target by moving—you find them by waiting at a point they may pass, and that is what Danny's doing."

Montbretia twisted her lip and flopped back on her sofa.

"But while I agree that he can't leave the house, I'm not sure that he's right about what we do about Billy," said Boniface.

"So you did ask him," said Montbretia.

"For all the good it did." Boniface sighed softly. "Danny is certain that this Billy isn't Dawn's son. Can't be Dawn's son. So Danny isn't going to take any action to stop Ernie hurting this kid—if that is Ernie's plan."

"Even if..."

Boniface cut across Montbretia. "There is no 'if' as far as Danny is concerned. For him, the matter is not open for debate—he will not bow to blackmail, since he believes the threat is fundamentally false. That's what trust in a relationship does for you."

Montbretia looked at Leathan—he seemed relaxed, leaning back on the sofa, as if unwilling to take a lead. Instead, he was waiting for Boniface.

When Boniface continued, his voice was soft. "I had quite a bit of time to think on the way home. We seem to have two options: Either we let the pieces fall and see where they land or..." he paused, a look of mischief crossing his face as he looked between Montbretia and Leathan. "Or we reject Ernie's offer."

"The sensible option must be to stay out of this, Boniface," said Montbretia. "Look in the mirror—you can see what Ernie does when he gets upset."

Leathan scrunched his nose but remained quiet.

"Unfortunately," said Boniface, "Ernie has threatened me directly, which, by the way, means he's threatened you, because he'll hurt you if that's the only way he can find to get at me."

"There's only one option, Boniface," said Leathan. "We need to hurt Ernie—take out Irvine or hurt someone who's close to him."

Boniface winced slightly. "If we were on one of those corporate team-building away-day things, in the spirit of always giving positive feedback, I'd say I love your creativity."

"But as we're not," said Leathan, "can I take it you think my idea is shit?"

"No, no...I like it," said Boniface. "I like the vindictiveness. It appeals. It's just...well...it's too criminal, we don't have the time, and we don't have the firepower."

"I was thinking about a kidnap," said Leathan.

Boniface shook his head, not disguising his disappointment. "The trouble is, we don't know who—or what—Ernie cares about, and we don't have time to do the research." He paused, seemingly thinking. "This needs all three of us. Are you..."

Montbretia and Leathan nodded slowly before Boniface finished his thought.

"There are three people who might get hurt," said Boniface. "Billy, Dawn, and Gray. We each find one, get them to safety, and then I'll go and see Ernie and throw the deal back in his face."

"Not Danny," asked Montbretia. "We don't need to tell him to move?"

"No. Ernie thinks he's got him by his hold over Dawn." He fixed his stare on Montbretia. "And on the subject of Dawn—can you go and find her and make sure she stays safe?"

"Sure," said Montbretia, pushing her jaw sideways. "Where is she?"

"Ah..." said Boniface, turning to Leathan without answering Montbretia. "Can you find Billy? Whether he's Dawn's son or not, he certainly seems to be the guy Ernie's using for leverage, so you might need to throw a fist or two to keep him safe."

"Would be my pleasure," said Leathan, smiling broadly. "I haven't been to the gym today."

"So you're going for Gray," said Montbretia.

"Half to protect him and half to stop him selling any other assets he doesn't actually own," said Boniface.

"You'd better explain what you want us to do," said Montbretia.

sixty-one

He checked the clock.

Three PM.

It probably was time to be awake, but he would have preferred to have made the decision himself, rather than have the obligation foisted on him by whoever was knocking at the front door.

And whoever was knocking seemed to be quite persistent.

Gray rolled over, leaving the sheets in a knotted twist, and stumbled for his robe. The robe he had liberated from a hotel in West Germany in 1979 on Prickle's first tour after Danny Featherstone had joined the band. The band had done a series of low-key gigs, mostly playing at American airbases—this hotel was their last stop before they went to France, and because of a late change in schedule, the hotel they were booked into was more expensive than they were used to.

He knew it was more expensive: Unlike their usual hotels, this offered complimentary robes, and so Gray decided to get a low-level refund, and the robe had found its way into his suitcase. He had contemplated taking more, but if he filled his suitcase that wouldn't leave space for essentials such as toothpaste and pornography.

He reached the small landing joining the two upstairs rooms and turned onto the staircase, which descended with a wall on either side, reaching the small passageway linking the front and back rooms of his house. He turned into the front room, turning off the television as he passed, and yanked the front door, which was stuck at the bottom.

As soon as he was earning—as soon as he was gigging again—Gray would replace the door and the frame. He would have some cash, and for once he would get someone else to fix his door—a proper chippy who knew what he was doing. And he'd get someone else to fix up the house, starting with the windows, which had been decaying for far too long and needed to be replaced.

Once the décor was updated, he'd get a new sofa and a decent TV— the current one was fifteen, maybe twenty years old and, to be frank, was pretty embarrassing in the way it filled up so much space for not a particularly large screen. And when the house was finished, then he'd have a holiday—or several. Perhaps he could persuade that Monty girl to go with him?

The frame released the door. "For fuck's sake, can't you leave me alone?" Boniface stood outside. He had a different look on his face. The really annoying, slightly smug PR man had been wiped away, and in his place there seemed to be concern. If not concern, his look was serious.

"Hi Gray." No smartass greeting—it must be serious. "Can I come in?" He leaned forward in expectation, but for once didn't push, and his foot stayed well away from the door. Gray stepped back and tilted his head toward the interior of the house.

By the time he had turned around, Boniface was sitting on the dining chair that Gray had brought in when Boniface and that Monty girl were there the other night. "We need to talk." Boniface's voice was low, but there was a rasp at the back of his throat—the sort of rasp that comes from stressing the voice.

As a singer, Gray knew this usually happened for two reasons: first, the voice getting overused, and second, nervous stress affecting the vocal cords. He suspected it was the latter with Boniface, and dropped onto the sofa. "Sure man, what's on your mind?"

As Boniface continued, the strain remained in his voice. "You need to get out of here for a few days." He reached into his jacket and pulled out his wallet, opening it and taking out some cash. He counted out six £50 notes, showing each to Gray before stacking them on the floor in front of him. "Does that give you an indication of how serious I am?" He paused. "Just in case it doesn't—I'm also going to pay your train fare. You must have friends somewhere—anywhere that's a long way away—that you can drop in on."

Gray reached for the pile of cash. Boniface bought his foot down on the notes, heavily. "You're not having that until you're ready to leave—get dressed, pack some hand luggage, and hurry up."

Boniface seemed dead serious. His usual faux friendliness—more like barely concealed tolerance of someone he clearly looked down on—was gone. Instead, it seemed to have been replaced by concern—what felt like genuine concern to Gray. "What's going on, Boniface?"

Boniface sat back in his chair, keeping his foot on the cash. "Ernie's grand scheme for getting into the music business is in the process of falling apart." For the first time since he had come in, a hint of a smile twitched at the side of Boniface's mouth. "I'm making it fall apart...with a little help."

"You fuc..." Boniface was on his feet before Gray could stand, and pushed him back onto the sofa. "That's my pension you're playing with, Boniface."

The younger man stood over Gray. "There is no pension."

Gray lay where Boniface had pushed him on the sofa, figuring how he could stand without Boniface stopping him. He tried to figure whether he could land a solid kick, but that would be difficult at this angle—and without shoes. And if Boniface had some strength, then he might be outclassed by the younger, taller man. "What d'you mean, there's no pension?"

"Ernie didn't recruit you to front a reinvigorated Prickle or whatever bull he told you—Ernie got you in debt so that you would sign over a bunch of spurious rights that you probably never owned in the first place and almost certainly don't own given how you and Prickle parted company."

"My lawyer," began Gray.

Boniface laughed, letting Gray see that he was laughing at him. Once Gray had noticed, Boniface sat down. His voice was calm, but there was still a hint of anxiety. "You don't have a lawyer, Gray. All you have is some bad advice from a bloke with no legal qualification—a man who owes his living to Ernie." He snorted. "They lied to you. They encouraged you to gamble knowing you would lose. They allowed you to keep playing, knowing you would lose more. Every loss was another debt—and that debt was leverage over you. And boy, have they levered you into position."

Gray felt the breath dragged out of him as his gut clenched.

"Ernie doesn't need you, whatever he told you. You're just as replaceable as any other member of the band—in fact, you don't need to be replaced...you've already been replaced by Kit and then Thad. Ernie just needs to find a new, young, good-looking frontman who can hold a tune, and he's set."

"But..." Gray began before being cut off again by Boniface.

"In fact, if you look at it from Ernie's perspective, once he's got your rights, then it might be easier if you're not around. Permanently. That way all income accrues to him directly, and you can never try to do to him what he's trying to do to Danny and Prickle."

Gray sat up, ready to ask a question.

Boniface kept talking, pulling out his phone and checking the screen. "I see what you're thinking."

"You don't even know..."

"I do. You reckon that all you have to do is nod your head and say 'yes, Boniface, I agree,' take the money, and then everything will be fine."

Gray felt the smirk twisting his mouth. "It's not a bad option."

"It's a dreadful idea. When Ernie thinks you're part of the scheme to break his dreams into a million little pieces, then he's going to come looking for you. Or rather, he's going to send some of his friends to look for you."

"But I'm not part of the plan to break Ernie's dream."

"You are," said Boniface, leaning forward, holding his phone with both hands. "Can we be honest?" His voice was just above a whisper.

Gray shrugged.

"Just between you and me...the rights relating to your time with Prickle...all this legal stuff against Danny, Prickle, and PAD Management...all this stuff instigated by Iain Irvine..."

"Yeah," said Gray.

"Just between you and me...it's bogus, isn't it? It's just your way to pay off your gambling debt, isn't it?"

Gray felt the smirk pushing again at his lips.

"Come on, Gray," said Boniface. "We're big boys—we can be honest, no one's listening. You agreed to claim these old rights just to settle your gambling debt, didn't you?"

"Yeah," said Gray, grinning. "You got me there. But you can't prove anything."

It was Boniface's turn to smirk. He held his phone between his thumb and forefinger and waggled it. "I can prove it—you've just given me the evidence."

Gray lunged forward, grabbing for the phone. Boniface twisted, moving the phone away from Gray and raising his elbow against the other man. Gray's windpipe made contact with Boniface's elbow and the older man slipped, his toweling robe billowing open as he fell to the ground.

sixty-two

Leathan crossed the road about fifty yards up from the black-painted wooden gates with the inset wicket gate. In daylight, from the other side of the road, the entrance under the archway looked quite benign, but still, he didn't see a need to take any risks, so he kept his pace swift and continued to let his gaze scan his surroundings.

The short parade of shops gave way to a row of faceless terraced houses. It seemed that the main way to distinguish between each residence was through a combination of the detritus left in the front yard and the state of the decay of the wood in the doors and windows. One house had a fridge-freezer in front of it, another a shopping cart from a supermarket, and a third a stack of car tires. The woodwork was almost exclusively white—or at least had been white once—and ranged from painted, badly, within the last five years, to not painted in the last twenty years, to the few where Leathan could see the wood rotting and crumbling even from the other side of the road.

He crossed the street quickly to check the front yards—none of them seemed to have anyone sitting in them. In the fifth house, an older woman was struggling to get herself and her shopping cart out of her front door. "Let me help you," said Leathan, starting up her path, watching as a look of fear froze the face of the resident.

Leathan stopped and took two steps back, looking at the gray-permed figure, wrapped tightly in an old raincoat, as she gripped the only shield at hand, her cart. "I'm sorry—I must have given you quite a fright bounding up your path like that." He indicated to cart, wedged in the front door to form a barrier between the woman and who or whatever predator she was avoiding today. "May I help you?"

"Now you've got me in this mess, you may as well," she said.

"I'm sorry," said Leathan, moving toward the door and lifting out the cart, placing it squarely on its four wheels, the handle toward its owner, who had locked her door and was squirreling her keys into the deepest recesses of her handbag, which she then placed inside the square bag held within the cart's cage.

He walked backward along the path, as if withdrawing from an audience with royalty, allowing the owner of the cart to step from her property onto the public path beside the road. As she went to turn, he began. "I wonder if you can help. I'm looking for my brother...younger brother. He's...not really an angel...the family is very worried. We think he might have found a bad lot...and maybe he's even been taking drugs.

We want to get him help."

"Oh dear," said the cart-pusher. "We get a lot of that around here."

"Do you know where they congregate?"

Her face soured and with the slightest bow of her head she indicated the sprawl of housing across the road. "Not that one," she said, pointing to the collection of buildings to the right, "but that one," she indicated the estate to the left, her face souring further. "Won't go in there myself." A small shake of the head seemed to confirm that was all she could offer.

"Thank you," said Leathan, as she started pushing her cart in the direction of the parade of shops around Ernie's club. She was the only person in a street that was comparatively deserted apart the occasional car passing to note that humanity might pass through.

And in this neighborhood, there seemed to be two choices for cars: Either you had a beat-up wreck that was at least twenty years old and probably had a replaced panel or two, which would now be painted a different color from the rest of the car; or you chose a customized high-end German model with a booming bass sound system and tinted glass, so dark that no one could see in, and you probably couldn't see out. Apparently, there were no other options for cars—no family sedans were allowed.

Leathan crossed back to the side of the housing developments. The development directly opposite the cart-pusher's house—the one that drew the less sour face—was probably a 1980s construction, erected at a time when planners understood the mistakes made with the immediate post-war housing and were determined to make a whole new set of mistakes in the name of progress. The freshly painted railings denoted an intention to take ownership of the land, and the recently cut grass—grass, rather than mud—within the fencing and lack of litter suggested a certain level of care.

He carried on up the road, leaving the fenced-in development, delineating the border with its even more down-market neighbor. Where the first development had a certain cohesion, this second and older development didn't. The grass—or more accurately, mud—formed rolling undulations separating the street from the 1950s collection of four-story brown-brick and steel-window housing.

The noise of kids playing filtered through the development, but no kids were visible from the street apart from the occasional passing teenager seeking anonymity under a hoodie, pulled tight to hide his identity. From somewhere in the distance, passing a car standing on bricks rather than wheels, two uniformed officers on foot patrol approached cautiously. Leathan recognized the insignia: Police Community Support Officers. Civilians dressed in a uniform to suggest they were police, but without most of the powers of sworn officers. A political sop intended to reduce antisocial behavior and give people a feeling that there were police on the streets. In reality, they were probably just another authority figure for most of the residents to dislike.

She was tall, blond, and while pretty enough, could probably handle herself in a barroom fight or might just play rugby on weekends. He was short and Asian with a boyish grin—all of his physical attributes thrown into sharper contrast by his colleague.

Leathan stood straighter, and without increasing his speed he began to walk with greater purpose toward the two uniforms, doing everything he could to exude a casual confidence as the gap narrowed.

"Hi," he smiled at the blond. "Good afternoon," he acknowledged the shorter man.

The uniforms—in uniforms that simply didn't look like proper police with a dark shirt instead of white, and a blue band around a pointless hat—acknowledged in a somewhat socially awkward manner. Leathan wasn't sure whether this was them displaying a fear of violence or a fear of actually having to do something. They both made small noises that might have been greetings, but then again...

"This is a slightly awkward question..." Leathan paused, taking in the concerned look that flicked between the two. "I'm looking for where the junkies hang out." A look of shock passed between the officers. "Or maybe just the drinkers."

"Sir," began the Asian man, his accent clearly from London, his attitude one of minor royalty, which didn't seem to match with someone taking a low-qualification job that offered scope for violent attacks and yet didn't allow you to carry a gun, instead offering only a stab-resistant vest.

"I'm sorry. I should have made myself clearer," said Leathan. "I'm looking for my kid brother. We want to get him help. We want to get him off the streets and away from here so he's not a bother to you. I've heard he hangs out around here."

The two uniforms seemed to relax. The blond turned and pointed in the direction from which the two had walked. "To the end, turn left, two blocks over. There's a group of them—they get pretty lairy, so you'd better take care."

Leathan heard them before he saw them, and he soon recognized the distinctive uniform: cheap leisurewear—hoodies, sweatpants, football shirts—all displaying too much flesh for March. None looked healthy— several were overweight, most looked borderline malnourished, and none had the appearance of someone with a washroom in their hostel. Several of the group had already passed out, having probably been drinking since they got up—the rest were seated on a bench, a low wall, and a recently cut log that didn't have a corresponding stump anywhere in sight.

A collection of empty green beer bottles and cheap cider cans was scattered around the group like a ripple from a stone dropped into a pond. A few carrier bags, old but still holding something, suggested that the day's drinking was anything but finished.

In the group of eight that were still conscious, he recognized many of the accents—Eastern European of assorted varieties, although Leathan didn't have sufficient grasp of any of the languages to make a precise geographical location. Nor to engage in their mother tongue...

However, he could engage in the language they all understood and pulled out two £20 notes, rustling them between his fingers as he sized up the drinkers. Unlike the Police Community Support Officers, Leathan didn't feel intimidated—he was sober, fitter than each individual, and fitter than the group collectively. Plus, he was sure he could handle himself if one lunged for the cash, and certain he could run faster than all of them.

He rustled the cash with greater emphasis, increasing the volume as he tried to make eye contact with one of the group. The only one in the group with a jacket—an old, ripped fake leather jacket—stood, walked to Leathan, and held out his hand expectantly.

Leathan placed the first £20, keeping the second at eye level. "I'm looking for a guy called Billy. About thirty. Usually wears jeans, boots, T-shirt, and a sleeveless denim jacket, maybe a green sweater. Black hair." He tried to stare at the other man, but the man's eyes were focused on the remaining cash. "Have you seen him?"

The other man was silent—the remainder of the group carried on drinking. Clearly there was nothing out of the ordinary happening.

Leathan rustled the second £20. The man caught his gaze, held it, then returned to looking at the £20.

Leathan dropped it into the other man's hand without releasing his own hold. "Have you seen Billy?"

The other man momentarily closed his eyes as if affirming, and Leathan let go of the note.

"You've seen Billy?"

The man nodded—a single bow of his head.

Leathan pulled out another £20 and rustled it for the other man to see. "What's Billy's name?"

He shrugged, grabbing at the £20. "Billy Krokodil is what we call him." Leathan released the note.

"You know where I can find Billy Krokodil?" asked Leathan, sliding his hand into his pocket.

The other man tilted his head forward. "I know where he was going."

Leathan pulled out another two £20 notes. "These make one hundred. Where?"

"Home."

Leathan pulled his hand back, taking the note farther from the drinker.

"Prince William Estate," said the drinker. "In Tottenham." He grabbed the notes. "Gone to get more Krokodil, I expect."

sixty-three

When they had passed through in the barge, Montbretia had realized that the Surrey Hills would present a challenging cycling terrain.

When she came through with a bike—a loaded bike that she had taken cross-country—she realized that the terrain was far beyond tough. Indeed, some might start at the word *impossible* and work back from there.

Boniface had insisted that Montbretia take a change of clothes.

As soon as she had given way on that detail, Boniface's demands escalated. Not just a change of clothes, but warm clothes—and something warm if Dawn needed to change—a sleeping bag or two, cooking gear plus food, and lights—but don't switch them on until you've found Dawn. And even then, act with caution—you won't know who's around looking for Dawn, and if we've figured where she is, then someone else could have made the same deduction. It was enough that she had felt like a loaded mule on the point of collapse as she wobbled along the flat roads and pushed the bike up the hills and across the bridleways.

After she had hidden the gear near—but not in—the church, she had found cycling much easier. However, she had to admit—reluctantly, because she hated when he had been so pompous—as she looked at the mud spattered over the back of her legs, the mud she could see up her back as she twisted awkwardly and feel on the back of her head under her helmet, that Boniface had been right: A change of clothes would be necessary if she was going to spend any period of time roughing it—and roughing it without the chance of a shower. Apparently the Normans liked worshiping God but didn't feel the need to clean themselves before praising, and the rivers and streams she had seen as she followed the paths through the Hills looked quite chilly.

Finding a fallen tree, its diameter around four feet, Montbretia stopped, took out her map, laid the bike on its side, and jumped up onto the natural seat offering a view through the wooded hillside and over the valley.

She opened the edge of the map, cursed under her breath, and jumped down to retrieve her other map. That was something Boniface had also insisted on—two paper maps, since the area traversed where the maps met. She pulled out of her phone and found no signal—yet another correct call by Boniface.

Montbretia struggled to hold the maps together, trying to locate where she was and where she had been. Each map was somewhat over three feet wide and three feet deep; the paper had been folded in half and then concertina-folded to make the map a pocketable size. Assuming you had big pockets—big, long pockets.

Pocketable, but not readily open-up-able and spread-out-able, or look-at-next-to-another-map-able.

Montbretia gave up, jumped off the log, and instead opened up each map fully, spreading them across the fallen tree. She worked down the page until she found the railway line and then followed the line along until she found Gomshall, where she had alighted from the train with her heavily laden bike.

At Gomshall, Montbretia had worked out two routes to the church: the main road, a distance of 2.6 miles, or the backstreets and bridleways, a distance of 3.3 miles, plus as Montbretia had discovered, hills. It was obvious that if Dawn was hiding, she wouldn't hide on the main road, so the backstreets and bridleways seemed the obvious route.

And it was only 0.7 miles farther—nothing on a bike, even with a load.

It seemed far less obvious once she was spattered in mud, and as Montbretia traced the path she had followed from the station, she realized it would have been more sensible to take the straighter, flatter route and dump her load at the earliest opportunity.

But regret is part of the learning process, and lesson learned, she returned her focus to the map, trying to figure where Dawn would go and where she should go next to try to intercept Dawn. The main road—the road she should have followed along the valley floor—was the only road going east/west. Every other road—the minor roads coming from the valley floor—went broadly in a north/south direction. The only way to go east/west was to stay on the bridleways and footpaths, and since she was already muddy, that didn't seem to be much of a disadvantage now, although, as she had established, it was far from ideal cycling terrain.

With the map spread out, and now being able to compare the map to the terrain, Montbretia reflected on the task she was assigned: Find Dawn, keep Dawn safe. Don't do anything like try to take her home—find her, keep her safe.

And before Montbretia could keep Dawn safe, she had to find her. Boniface was bullish about where Dawn would spend her nights, but during daylight hours, his theory was that she would keep moving and make sure no one saw her. Montbretia stared at the paths—there were hundreds...and those were the officially recognized paths. If Dawn knew this area as well as Boniface said she did and had decided to disappear, then she would be untraceable. Forget Boniface's theory that you don't find a moving target by moving yourself...this was an exercise in logic, and Montbretia was determined to find Dawn.

And if she couldn't find Dawn, then she was determined to root out any signs of danger, even if she wasn't quite sure what danger looked like.

She looked back at the map, let her eyes follow the intended path, then got back on her bike and started pedaling.

sixty-four

By the time he had spent five minutes wandering around Prince William Estate, he knew what to expect: Leathan was starting to feel like something of an expert in North London low-cost social housing.

The look was familiar: six-story blocks, each intersecting to form something close to an S shape and perched on the top of a slope. In the foreground, the planners had aspired to give the residents some open green space. Clearly the residents had happily taken this space and used it as they saw fit to store old and unwanted furniture—two chests of drawers and one wrecked sofa—and unwanted electrical items, in particular, three unwanted flat-screen television sets.

Leathan scanned the red-brick blocks, the flat surfaces only differentiated from those you might find in Communist Russia by the meager balconies, detailed along their bottoms by concrete plinths that had once had their outside edges painted a uniform white.

A road snaked through the estate, but the footpaths were more akin to cow paths—tracks worn across the grass that had become the accepted route over time due to their usage, usually since they provided the swiftest means to travel from point A to point B. The cars were the mix Leathan was becoming used to: beaten-out wrecks that were twenty-plus years old and customized luxury German cars with very tinted windows and copious amounts of bling on the wheels and anywhere else additional trim could be added.

This combination of cars also had a third variety: those cars that had given their lives so that other cars might live. Leathan counted at least five cars, some on bricks, others just dropped on their bellies, which had given for others. All had given their wheels, some their doors and odd panels, some their glass, most components from their engines, and several their seats, so that the residents of the development could have somewhere to sit if they got too tired walking from one side to the other and the wrecked sofas weren't comfortable enough.

As Leathan surveyed the dead cars, he saw what he had hoped to find: a solitary male, sitting on a vinyl car seat, wearing old boots, jeans, and a blue T-shirt. His hair was a mess of darkish colors, and his skin had the clammy look of the soon-to-be dead.

Leathan approached and hefted another car seat next to the guy, who seemed unaware of the arrival of the other man.

"Hey," said Leathan.

The other man remained silent, his head bowed, his mouth open, the slightest rise and fall of his chest confirming there was life.

"How're you doing?" tried Leathan, dropping into the seat he had just hefted.

Still no response beyond the basic function performed by the autonomic nervous system.

"Billy," said Leathan, reaching over and pushing the other man's shoulder.

The man grunted and continued to assiduously ignore Leathan and the rest of the world as he sat on his car seat in the shadow of the red-brick block.

"Billy," said Leathan with greater force, giving the other man a determined shake.

The other man grunted louder and started to topple away from Leathan. Leathan grabbed his arm and pulled him back to the vertical. "Billy, listen to me."

"Yeah," grunted the other man as he started to flop forward.

Leathan stood and moved behind his seat to pull him straight. "So you are Billy?"

Another unqualified grunt, but this time sounding more positive.

Leathan knelt behind the seat—his head at the height of the other man—and tried to push his hands into the other man's pockets, looking for any form of identification. The other man seemed unaware and unconcerned as Leathan intruded first into this back pockets, where he found nothing, and then into his front pockets, where again he found nothing. Leathan pulled out his hand and looked at the fingers on his right hand, which had acquired a yellowy-brown stickiness. His sniffed his fingers and quickly regretted the action, choosing then to try to clean his hand on the other man's T-shirt.

"Billy." Leathan shook the other man as he returned to his seat, pulling out his phone.

The other man grunted. Again, a more positive grunt.

Leathan stayed on his seat, punching a number into his phone.

The call transferred to voicemail. "Boniface, it's Leathan. I've found Billy, but he's pretty spaced out at the moment. I'll stay with him until he's a bit more lucid, and then I'll get him somewhere else. Call if you need me."

He hung up and lay back in his seat, reaching down with his hands, grabbing for some way to change the angle of the seat.

sixty-five

In the gloom of Ernie's office, Boniface could see Wesley's eyes as the dull light from the brass banker's desk lamp with the green shade glinted off them. With each agitated blink of his eyes, the small teenager's dull mid-toned skin seemed to act as a complete camouflage, hiding him completely in the dark room. With his eyes hidden, the only confirmation that he was still present was his fidgety breathing and his sour breath.

"I hoped you'd come around." There was no joy in the voice—merely an attempt at menace.

"Figuratively or literally," replied Boniface to the would-be music mogul.

The pointed face with stubbly gray skin topped with thinning wiry hair seemed to ignore the question. "You've made the right decision, Boniface. It's so disappointing having to waste time waiting for an answer or expending energy persuading people. You've saved us all the bother by coming to tell me that you've sorted everything out."

"But that's the thing," said Boniface. "I haven't come round to your way of thinking." He sighed. "Quite the opposite, I've come to say thanks for the kind offer, but no thanks."

He tried to divine what Ernie was communicating as Ernie's gaze fixed slightly to Boniface's left with his eyebrows twitching.

Wes explained the finer points of the communication when his fist landed squarely in Boniface's gut.

Boniface remembered the force Wes could unleash. He was smaller than Jojo, but he seemed to be able to transmit a disproportionate amount of power through his right arm—so much power that Boniface instinctively hunched forward as the teenager's fist made contact, but he still fell backwards, unable to argue with the momentum of his body. Now Boniface was lying on the thin and dirty carpet, clutching his hands across his stomach with his legs pulled up in a fetal position. Winded and in pain.

Lying on the floor, Boniface felt that he had some sort of equality with Gray, who had ended up on the floor when he made a lunge for Boniface's phone—the phone on which Boniface had recorded Gray's confession that he knew his legal claim against Prickle was bogus. As Gray had lunged, his windpipe had made contact with Boniface's elbow, and the singer had ended up on the floor, whimpering.

Boniface wasn't sure whether he was whimpering about the pain, the fact that Boniface had tricked him, fear about Ernie's reaction, or distress about finding that the pension he had been expecting now would not be paid. Whatever the case, he was whimpering, and continued whimpering for what felt like an eternity to Boniface, who eventually decided to just ignore Gray and made his way to the singer's kitchen.

To call it a kitchen was probably hopeful. In reality it was more likely some sort of experimental laboratory where they were developing new antibiotics resistant to whatever forms of infection Gray had managed to grow through a lack of basic kitchen hygiene sustained over thirty years.

Boniface searched the kitchen, figuring that boiling water might kill off most bugs if he were to have a cup of tea. But he had been disappointed by the discovery of the milk—or to be more accurate, cheesy yogurt—and it was at that point when Gray decided to give up his whimpering and find out what Boniface was doing.

As Gray had decided to stop whimpering, Boniface had been able to encourage him to get dressed and ready to leave. When Gray had finally appeared, there had been no hint that he had spent any of the 45 minutes he had been out of Boniface's sight washing. He was dressed badly, and he had an overnight bag, although there would have been more dignity for him if he had thrown his possessions into a supermarket bag.

With Gray dressed and packed, Boniface had called a cab and taken him to Euston train station, where he bought Gray a ticket—first class, plus a supplement for a single sleeper carriage, which seemed only fair for the other passengers—for Fort William, the second largest settlement in the Highlands of Scotland, best known for being next to Ben Nevis, the highest mountain in the UK.

Boniface hadn't argued when Gray told him he had a friend who lived near. Boniface hadn't argued because he didn't care. All he cared about was getting Gray on the train and making sure he left London.

Gray had waved sarcastically from the window as the train finally lumbered away from the platform, leaving Boniface relieved in the knowledge that the singer was on board a metal tube with locked doors that would not be stopping for at least ninety minutes. When it did stop, the train would be in Crewe, in the Midlands of the UK, where theoretically only boarding was possible, although Boniface didn't understand how boarding was allowed but disembarkation prevented. Even so, Gray was out of the way for at least three hours, hopefully more, and he had money in his pocket—a stack of cash that Boniface had given him—so even if he didn't make it all the way to Scotland, he should be hard to find for quite some time.

And if he did make it to Scotland, then Boniface had instructed him to call in twenty-four hours.

Having rid himself of the vexation that was Gray, Boniface checked his voicemail. And now, as he lay on the carpet, having been floored by the thuggish teen, the indignity was mitigated by the reassurance that

Leathan had found Billy, and while Billy sounded pretty spaced out, two out of the three were safe, and Boniface was confident that Montbretia would find Dawn, making three out of three.

It was only when he was confident that the extent of the damage Ernie could inflict on him was physical pain that Boniface had walked through the wicket gate inset into the black-painted wooden gate. He had been greeted by Wes, much as a hungry man would greet lunch.

However, the hungry man was disappointed—at least initially—when Ernie granted Boniface an audience, instead of asking Wes to communicate using his well-honed nonverbal talents in the lightless room under the butcher shop. From his perspective on the carpet, Boniface saw that the disappointment had been short-lived, and the frustration had built like a pressure cooker that had just exploded into his gut.

"Get him up," grunted Ernie. Boniface felt his suit jacket being grabbed as he was pulled to the vertical, his legs not feeling ready to hold his weight. He tried standing, but the pain on the side of his head from where his skull had made contact with the floor felt like the sole focus of his concentration.

"Do I need to make you stand up?" The sour breath accompanying the muttered threat was like smelling salts, reviving Boniface's drifting concentration.

"You disappoint me, Boniface. I knew you'd try to pull some stunt—I just hoped you might do something more imaginative than bullshit me," growled Ernie.

Boniface felt a spasm in his thigh and leaned on Ernie's desk, his wrists twisted as he gripped the edge of the flat surface. He kept his voice a whisper to hide any tremble. "Billy's safe. The game's over, Ernie."

The man behind the desk showed his nicotine-stained teeth, the blackened stumps grasping the receding gums. "As I said, I hoped for more than bull." A serenity fell over his bristly face. "I knew you'd want to save Dawn's kiddie—that's why I moved him away from here and got Jojo to babysit."

"Think again," said Boniface, trying to keep his feeling of superiority from showing on his face.

"Really?" asked Ernie. "You really want to try that line?"

"I don't need to try," said Boniface. "The truth speaks for itself."

Ernie moved a crumpled piece of paper into the pool of light under the green shade, flattening out the creases. Boniface strained to interpret the upside-down handwritten characters as Ernie ran his finger along what Boniface guessed was a phone number while he punched the digits on his desk phone with his other hand. "Still got our boy there?"

Boniface lowered himself to be closer to the paper as Ernie withdrew his finger, leaning back on his chair and glaring at Boniface.

"And he's behaving himself?"

It was an address and a phone number—written with the handwriting skills of someone who didn't know which end of a pen should be applied to the paper.

"Good. Good. And you've got that *very pure* heroin?"

Boniface picked up that the conversation was intended for him, not for whoever was at the end of the phone. He let his eyes make a final pass over the address before rising to see Ernie.

"You will be very careful with that heroin. Street junkies are terrible thieves, and his system wouldn't be used to something that pure. You know, if he stole it off you, it could have tragic consequences—he might overdose." Ernie had locked eyes with Boniface as he hung up the phone. "I think you were misinformed about Billy's whereabouts, Mister Boniface. But don't worry, he's safe with Jojo." The lightness in his eyes—the fun an evil child gets from tormenting an animal—disappeared. "What harm could happen?"

Boniface felt the urge to leave the room and call Leathan. "What about Gray?"

"Gray is weak. Your problem is Danny—he is pig-headedly in love, so I need to influence him in other ways."

"Are you sure about Gray?" asked Boniface. "I mean, really sure?"

The older man looked toward Wes and flicked his eyes toward Boniface. Boniface flinched. "Listen. It's time to stop playing the hero—it doesn't suit you, and to be frank, it's embarrassing to watch you go down on one punch." He stood up. "Go away and come back when you've got what I want and what you've said you will provide. I'm holding you personally responsible for anything that's not delivered." He turned to Wes. "Get him out of here. If he carries on like this, you're going to have a lot of fun at midnight."

sixty-six

Leathan liked to think that he could handle himself—even if that confidence was only that he could run faster than the other guy—and that he was prepared to go anywhere, but this place was sapping his soul.

He had crossed the main road from one housing development to another and had found himself transported to a different world. Prince William Estate had a series of joined six-story red-brick blocks and was comparatively compact. Across the road, King William Estate sprawled, seemingly with little logic in its layout.

Four tower blocks—Leathan counted sixteen or maybe seventeen floors on each—provided the only landmarks as he subsumed himself into 1960s concrete, erected with the sole purpose of warehousing the lowest echelons of society, the underclass that no one cared about, least of all any members of that social strata. It was somewhere that caged people with nothing to lose—the cage turned their anger inward, and having nothing to lose offered perhaps the ultimate freedom. And it was that unfettered freedom that scared Leathan: So often it led to the freedom to ignore even the most basic of human obligations and to have no conception about future consequences for present acts.

"You're sure he's not playing with us?" asked Leathan.

Boniface burned his ear off down the phone. He had the right to be angry: He was in pain—apparently Wes hit much harder than Jojo—and Leathan had messed up. Big time.

Leathan had been sitting with the guy on the car seat for about an hour when Boniface called. During that time, the best Leathan had got out of the guy was a grunt that seemed to be an affirmative answer to a question. After the call, Leathan shook the guy—vigorously, but not violently—and then squeezed the back of his neck with a vice-like pinch until he got a reaction: another grunt, but this time a grunt with his eyes open. Leathan asked, "What's your name?"

"What's your name?" said the newly awakened. "I'm Barack Obama."

Leathan increased the pressure. "Play nice."

"Vic."

Leathan released the pressure, taking in the mottled brown hair. Mottled brown, not self-dyed black. "Vic what?"

"Vic what has got a sore fucking neck." Leathan returned the pressure. "Vic Morton."

It was at that point that Leathan dropped Vic's neck, cursed his own stupidity, and started sprinting. He crossed the road and didn't stop running until he found himself disoriented in his quest for Chesterfield Terrace in the middle of the King William—King William, not Prince William—Estate.

The more he looked around, the more the development resembled a set for a TV show about inner-city deprivation. The four tower blocks—layers of beige concrete and white-framed windows with balconies set at each corner whose sole purpose seemed to be to provide a convenient location for satellite dishes—provided no differentiation sufficient to triangulate a location between the blocks.

The lower blocks—again, strata of beige concrete, but layered with open walkways punctuated by boarded-up properties—seemed to have been placed to fill up the gaps between the towers. Their exact location seemed to have been set according to a child's game, and Leathan expected that at any moment a child would pick up the estate and work a silver ball through the maze of gaps between the concrete.

Not that the ball would roll that well with the semi-regular piles of discarded furniture. Unlike the development across the road, these piles seemed to comprise ripped-up chairs, usually stacked in small heaps with bed frames, chests of drawers, all with added household rubbish seemingly sprinkled on top and left to marinate. Instead of being used by the occasional passing junkie, these seemed of interest only to the local rat population, which apparently had no fear of being seen in daylight, suggesting they probably carried knives for their own personal protection.

It took him another ten minutes of dodging through alleyways, avoiding thug-like eight-year-olds, and navigating small rubbish heaps to find Chesterfield Terrace, a sagging four-floor beige concrete-layered block where two out of every three residences seemed to be boarded up or so covered with graffiti that it was impossible to discern whether it was still inhabited.

Leathan took one flight of stairs, side-stepping the urine, feces, needles, vomit, and a dead squirrel as he ascended through the gray rectangle, which opened onto a broad walkway with properties on one side and on the other a low wall with a view over the only patch of open ground he had found on the estate.

He hesitated, stepping back down onto the penultimate step, craning his head to look down the walkway before slowly moving toward his target. Drawing level with the first front door, he checked the number—twice and then a third time, looking for any ambiguity.

Number thirty-six.

What was likely to be number thirty-seven was boarded up.

The next residence had a number eight loosely hanging by one screw. The ghost of the number three preceding the hanging figure suggested that Leathan had found number thirty-eight.

Thirty-nine and forty—if Leathan had understood the numbering system correctly—were both boarded, the heavier thickness of paint from the graffiti on number forty suggesting it had been vacant for longer.

And then he reached the end of the row. Number forty-one. Confirmed by the silver numbers screwed to the right of the mail slot midway up the door. On the walkway outside sat a baby stroller, rusted, probably dating from the 1960s, and two kitchen cabinets.

Gingerly, Leathan put his ear to the first window. Even at this distance, he could feel the vibration of the main road transmitted through the glass, but couldn't hear any sounds of humans in the residence. There was a sound—perhaps the firing of guns in a movie—but no voices, no doors banging, no one walking…nothing actively human.

He moved to the next window, surveying the frosted pane before leaning closer. Again, the only sound was like a movie where every character had more bullets than the whole of the US army, and weapons never jam. But he couldn't be sure whether this was a movie left playing or whether anyone was inside watching.

Leathan moved across the walkway to stand facing the door—two large panes of obscured glass in a wooden frame. One kick, and it would splinter and he would be in. One kick, and he could be dead—he had no idea how many people were inside. And if Jojo was there—or any of his friends—how armed they were.

He stared at the obscured glass, willing his eyes to see any signs of occupation—a lamp turned on, or the shift of light as someone moved across a room. He moved closer, hoping for a raised voice. All he could hear was shooting.

He straightened and looked away from the apartment. There was a group of feral ten-year-olds sharing a single cigarette on the other side of the open ground.

As he exited the stairwell, he started walking toward the young smokers. Initially they seemed indifferent to his approach, but as he got closer heads turned with greater frequency and their voices got louder. "You a cop?"

Leathan shook his head, his mouth reflexively lifting at the edges.

"Pedo?" The questioner seemed to be the alpha-male ten-year-old—the one who took a drag in between each pass of the cigarette.

"Nope," said Leathan reaching the group of five, all around the height of his waist, all with graying skin and a look of malnourishment. "Who wants to earn twenty quid?"

"See! You *are* a pedo," said the alpha, pointing his dirty face under a buzz cut at Leathan.

"If you don't want the cash, that's fine," said Leathan, turning away.

"Didn't say that." His retort was swift. "Just telling you what I won't do."

Leathan pulled a £20 out of his pocket and squatted in front of the group. "Chesterfield Terrace." He pointed to the block behind him.

"We ain't fucking stupid," muttered another in the group.

"One floor up, last door on the right, number forty-one." He waited for the group's eyes to follow. "See it?"

"Yeah." Alpha was back in control.

"Go and find if anyone's in."

"What?"

"Knock on the door—see if anyone's in," repeated Leathan.

"I'll save you ten," said the one currently holding the cigarette. "Give me ten, and you can knock on the door yourself."

"If you don't want..." Leathan started to rise.

"It's not enough," said the alpha, his strained voice reasserting his dominance as he retrieved the cigarette, taking a deep drag with his lips clamped tightly around the paper cylinder.

"Twenty," said Leathan. "And when you get back, I'll buy you a pack of cigarettes."

There was a spark in the eyes in front of him—a hint of excitement as they looked to one another.

"A pack each," said the alpha, seemingly less excited than his comrades.

"Tell you what," said Leathan. "Get whoever answers to come onto the balcony so I can see him from here—tell him there's a car on fire or something—and I'll buy you a carton. That's two-hundred cigarettes between you." He waited, fixing his stare on the alpha. "Deal?"

"Deal," said the alpha, grabbing the note in Leathan's hand. His eyes flicked to the tallest of the group, who wordlessly set off alone across the open space, disappearing into the stairwell shortly to appear one story up, only his head visible above the low wall as he moved toward number forty-one.

The top of his head was barely visible as he banged on the door—the fearless kind of knocking achieved only by kids and drunks. Leathan marshaled the remaining smokers in front of him until he felt sufficiently camouflaged.

The kid was clearly a dedicated smoker—from where he crouched, Leathan could hear when the kid banged for a second time. The head ducked, a sound of a kid shouting, and the head reappeared.

When it opened, the door opened slowly. The kid moved away—he was by the wall almost immediately, pointing at something in the distance insistently, looking back and calling whoever was inside to come out and look.

Leathan watched as Jojo filled the doorframe. Even at the distance, Leathan could see the large teen's vigilance—the way he observed, moved, stopped, observed, moved, stopped, and on. By the time he was fully out the front door, he seemed confident that there was no one waiting in the passageway. But from his body language, Jojo seemed unimpressed with the disturbance, and the kid's backward steps soon turned into a run.

"I believe I am in your debt," said Leathan, returning to his full height. "You'd better show me to the store." The alpha took the lead, walking swiftly away from Chesterfield Terrace, ducking into a narrow alley that wiggled between two blocks. He navigated two piles of furniture and refuse, finally bringing the small group—including the door knocker, who had caught up with them—onto one of the streets that carved its way through the estate.

He tilted his head across the road to a row of five stores: a launderette, a drop-in advice center, two boarded storefronts, and the last, Ali's Convenience, according to the sign in front of the heavy shutters covering both windows.

"Marlborough?" asked Leathan.

The alpha stared into space—a ten-year-old tobacco connoisseur—before wrinkling his nose and saying, "Yeah."

Leathan walked through the aluminum-framed door and straight to the counter. "Two-hundred Marlborough."

"In a carton," said the Asian man behind the counter, pulling out a carton before Leathan could respond.

"Could I also have two lighters and…" he scanned the shelves behind the store owner, "lighter fluid?"

The man Leathan presumed to be Ali placed the four items on the counter. "Anything else?"

Leathan shook his head once and watched as Ali rang up the price, expectantly standing without feeling the need to read the numbers displayed on his till. Leathan handed over two £50 notes and pocketed one of the lighters and the lighter fluid before picking up the change Ali had dropped on the counter without explanation. He pocketed the cash, then grabbed the cigarettes and a second lighter.

As he stepped out of the store, ten hands reached to him. "You earned a bonus," he said to the tall door-knocker and handed him the lighter. "There you…" he said, passing the box of 200 cancer sticks to the alpha. The five were running—moving as a pack, swiftly into the distance—before he could complete his sentence.

sixty-seven

"What do you mean *not there*?"

"What do you want me to say, Ernie? I can't say it any more clearly. I can't make him there when he's not."

Ernie looked up at Iain Irvine, his tanned skin showing a faint glow of perspiration. "I mean if he's not *there*, then where is he?" He felt his volume start to rise as his pitch dropped. "Or let me phrase it in a similar way to how you put the proposition to me... If our cash cow isn't in the field where we left it, then how can we take it to market?"

Irv seemed to get that surly defensive attitude that he took when he didn't want to admit he'd made a mistake. "What can I tell you—he was carrying a bag and left in a cab with some bloke in a suit."

"You mean he left with Boniface?"

"I don't know, Ernie." Irv seemed to be losing interest. "I'm sure there are other blokes that are about six foot and wear suits, but yeah, it sounds like he was with Boniface."

"And who told you this?"

"Next-door neighbor—some city type who thinks he owns the world." Irv sat on the edge of the desk. Ernie stared at him until he stood. Irv shrugged. "Only knows about the cab because the driver knocked at the wrong door—thinks he said he was going to Euston, but it could have been Kings Cross."

"This Boniface is being a right pain up my arse. First he puts Gray on a train, and then he comes round and tries to taunt me." Ernie slumped back in his chair. "Where has Gray gone, Iain?"

"We looked through his place. There was no sign that he planned this."

"Of course he didn't plan this—this is Boniface causing me trouble."

"I mean, he didn't even plan for thirty seconds before he left," said Irvine. "There are no notes; he didn't have an address book. The last number dialed was no use—he called for a pizza two days ago. He didn't leave a single breadcrumb."

"What about the cab?" Ernie wanted to punch someone to relieve his frustration.

"He didn't call them from the landline and whoever he called, it wasn't one of the local ones, but we're trying other firms."

"Try the chains," said Ernie. "It'll be a firm you can summon with a smartphone."

Irvine tilted his head, squinting. Wordlessly asking a question.

"Boniface," said Ernie. "Boniface will have ordered the cab, and he's the sort of git who will have used something flashy on his phone."

"I'll get on it," said Irvine.

"Yeah, and you won't get anywhere—he'll be using a big company used to dealing with celebrities. There won't be anyone we know who we can lean on...at least, not in time." He leaned forward in his chair. When he continued, his voice was quieter, but the emotion had drained. "This was your idea. The day Billy said his mother was famous—you made the link to Gray. You came up with the idea. Tie them up in litigation, cause them so much pain in so many places that either they give way and we win something, or they just offer us go-away money. It's easy."

Irv didn't respond. He just stood with that stupid sneer across his leathery face.

"And have you found the woman yet?"

Irv shook his head. "Not a clue where she went."

Ernie felt his anger burning. "How hard can it be to find a woman whose only talents are having big tits and neglecting her son?"

"It's not that easy—there are too many people around the house, including these two hefty roadies, and Wes and Jojo stick out. There are all these delicate little villages where they all eat cucumber sandwiches with the vicar and date their land back to Domesday. Our boys are the wrong color. They can't even look like tourists or school kids on a day trip."

"I'm not impressed, Irv. Do something fast."

sixty-eight

It seemed to take Leathan infinitely longer to retrace the route back to Chesterfield Terrace than it had taken to walk in the other direction with the ten-year-old smokers desperate for even one cigarette that didn't have to be shared with the others.

As he passed the second heap of discarded sofas, old paint cans, and bed frames, Leathan stopped.

Thinking.

It was a matter of basic logistics and practicality.

For the first journey, he carried three sofa cushions, an old mop, and a handle usually used to hold a point roller. For the second, he hefted a single bed frame. Two journeys each required less exertion than one unsuccessful journey trying to carry the whole load. Added to which he could be more discreet with smaller loads.

He dumped his load at the corner of Chesterfield Terrace, on the corner away from the open space. The heap didn't look out of place, and it was unlikely to be stolen as he completed a quick reconnaissance of the area. As far as he could see, Chesterfield Terrace was simply a lump of concrete, built on a concrete plinth, and was less than one-third occupied—assuming boarded up meant unoccupied.

The unoccupied property that was of particular interest was the one at ground level, at the end of the row. The property immediately below the one where he now knew Jojo Brooks was temporarily stationed, and where, by extrapolation, he suspected Billy Wilkins was also to be found.

The simple solution would have been to go through the front door of number forty-one, but since Jojo was holding a pistol last time he saw him, Leathan felt no urgency to bang on that door.

In any case, he had a much more straightforward solution.

He looked up at the boarding over the back of the ground-floor residence. Two rooms, two windows both covered with OSB—oriented strand board, cheap but effective engineered wood, constructed from glued flakes of wood giving a rough, tough, but cheap material used in construction sites across the globe.

The graffiti told him it had been up for a while. That the boarding was still attached to the window frame told him that the fitter and his nail gun had done a good job.

Leathan examined the bottom and the sides of the OSB. As he expected, nails had been uniformly shot, making a tight seal between frame and board. He guessed that the fitters probably had ladders and platforms—Leathan could only improvise and flipped over the bed frame, laying it vertically on its longest edge, balanced against the wall.

He stepped back and looked at the apartment above—number forty-one. He was sure he could still hear the sound of a movie with a lot of shooting. Stepping forward again, he looked left, looked right, and then climbed on the side of the bed frame, raising his eyes to the level of the top of the window.

There were fewer nails across the top, and the board had been cut short, allowing Leathan to see the top of the frame. Allowing Leathan an opportunity, as he took out the paint-roller handle—a sturdy piece of thin metal, essentially bent in a right angle with an exposed end and a plastic handle at the other. He tried to find a gap to wiggle the thin end into.

Leathan stabbed the point, looking for any gap between the board and the frame, but could find none, so he resorted to trying to hammer the point through a gap. His reward for a hand sore from banging the blunt end was the progress of the point behind the board. When the roller spindle was sufficiently behind the board, Leathan applied his weight to the handle, waiting until he finally heard a reassuring groan from a nail.

And then the board stopped. This nail would not release any further.

He scanned his surroundings again, then pulled himself up on the exposed roller handle to stand on the windowsill and placed his other foot to the side of the window as high as he could get it. Then he pulled and pulled.

The nails groaned, slipping slightly but refusing to release the OSB they were holding prisoner.

He dropped his foot back onto the sill and examined the gap he had created—it was wide enough to fit his thumb. He jumped down, grabbed the mop and climbed back again, inserted the wooden handle from his new tool into the gap, and leaned his weight onto his new lever.

The nails creaked and groaned, the OSB moved, but the nails still refused to give entry. He moved the mop farther down the board and applied his weight, bending his knees to give more purchase on his lever, rocking to give momentum to the application of his body weight.

A groan.

A creak.

A crack.

The nails gave way and released the board, which released the tension on the mop handle Leathan was pulling. He fell backward, managing to get a leg out as he hit the concrete plinth, but was not able to stop his momentum propelling him to the ground, to be followed by a window-sized piece of OSB landing on top of him.

He wasn't sure how long he waited before he moved, but when he did, it hurt.

A lot.

His leg, his ass, his elbow, his knee where the board hit, his head, which hit the deck and then got sandwiched between the ground and the board as it bounced—all hurt. Slowly he rolled out from under the board and got to his feet to admire his handiwork. The window was nothing special: a single-glazed casement window in three sections with an opening window on each side and a fan light at the top of the center section.

Leathan hunted for the roller handle, finding it under the OSB. He positioned the thin end on the glass just outside the handle and smacked the flat side with the butt of his hand; a spider's web of fracture spread across the window as he propelled the end of the roller handle through the pane. "I didn't want it broken," muttered Leathan as he manipulated the window's handle with the painting tool and opened the swinging pane.

With the window open, Leathan threw in the three sofa cushions, the paint-roller holder, and the mop, then jumped onto the bed frame before climbing through the window.

It was probably the smell of urine—stale urine, or at least what smelled like stale urine—that he noticed first. Impatient for his eyes to adjust to the lack of light, he stumbled forward, keen to explore the accommodation, only slowly becoming aware of the crescendo of shooting from above and the sound of stamping feet. He felt a smile cross his face. "I'll never understand computer games," he muttered.

Passing into a small hall he turned into the first room, his hand instinctively flicking the light switch inside the door as he entered. The light remained extinguished. Leathan pulled out his new lighter and flicked the flame into life. In the flickering orange glow, he could make out a kitchen—dirty dishes sat in a now-empty sink, and takeaway food wrappers littered the floor. He looked for an empty space on the worktop and ran his finger along the surface, rapidly pulling it away to inspect the accumulated grease.

He turned and crossed the passage, tugging the pull string inside the door. A click, but again no electric light. He lifted his flaming lighter, keeping his finger pressed, to view what he now knew to be a bathroom. A bathroom with a smell that stung more than the smell he had encountered so far.

Feeling the top of the lighter starting to get hot, he released the trigger and turned back into the passage, taking a left into the last remaining room, which was lit by the light that pushed its way past the OSB still fastened over the window. Two single beds were pushed into the far corners by the outside wall, and what looked like a stack of black trash bags covered the remaining floor.

Leathan returned to the room through which he had entered and scrabbled around, looking for his paint-roller holder. He found it and went back to the gloomy kitchen, pushing a space on the worktop, and climbed up to crouch under the ceiling. Gripping the roller handle as if he were gripping a pick, he waited—listening for shooting to start above—then jabbed at the ceiling, driving a small hole through the skimmed drywall panel. He pushed the horizontal length of the roller handle through the hole, leaving the other end to hang.

There was a burst of gunfire from the game in the apartment above.

Leathan jumped.

He launched himself toward the door, grabbing the handle with both hands, letting his weight and momentum transfer to the plaster ceiling panel.

As he swung, Leathan felt the panel give, releasing his hook as a chunk of the ceiling crashed to the floor, spitting dust in every direction.

As the crash quieted, Leathan listened to the continuing shooting above while he pulled out his lighter to illuminate his handiwork and found a hole, jagged but broadly circular about two feet across, exposing the rafters holding up the floorboards from the residence above. Holding the roller hook in both hands, he jumped, catching the long end in the newly exposed gap above the ceiling panel. He jumped two or three more times, yanking down more ceiling panel.

Having doubled the size of the hole, he moved to the bathroom. On the first leap most of the ceiling panel collapsed. It took three tugs in the bedroom to make a large enough hole and only two leaps in the room through which he had entered.

He bundled up the three sofa cushions and carried them to the bedroom, throwing them over the black trash bags before pulling out the lighter fluid, which he liberally sprayed over the cushions. Then he moved to the kitchen and doused some of the trash still left on the counter, emptying the rest of the fluid over two discarded sofas he found in the lounge.

Leathan walked to the window, pushing it fully open, then returned to the bedroom and ignited the lighter fluid–soaked cushions. The spreading flames momentarily hypnotized him, but the carcinogenic fumes of burning foam caught his throat, forcing him to remember his mission.

He darted into the kitchen and lit one pile of trash, leaving without waiting to see how it burned. As he moved through the hallway and into the living room, wisps of dark smoke trailed him. He lit the two sofas and took the short steps to the window, cautiously climbing out and resting on the bed frame, where he closed the window and looked back at his creeping flames.

He jumped down and manhandled the OSB he had worked so hard to remove from the window, leaning it back in position where it had come from in an effort to keep all of the smoke trapped within the residence and funneled through the ceiling he had just remodeled.

When he was satisfied that the OSB was sufficiently secure, he return to the front of the block and crossed the open space, squatting down where he had talked with the ten-year-old smokers, and watched the door of number forty-one.

sixty-nine

Montbretia had decided—temporarily—to admit that Boniface might be right. It might be a much more straightforward strategy to stay still and wait for a moving target to come to her.

It wasn't so much that she wanted to admit that he had a point; it was more a matter of practicality. She had been riding—energetically riding over rough, hilly terrain—for several hours, and the light was starting to fade. She hadn't found Dawn but instead was returning to the location where Boniface said she would find her. Hard as she thought about it, she couldn't find a way to finesse herself out of admitting that she was doing what Boniface had suggested.

She turned off the road and crossed the cattle grid as she entered the private grounds of Albury Park, passing the sign that confirmed that access was permitted to the land if visiting the Old Parish Church.

The church was less than five-hundred meters away, and although the obvious route was along the tarred strip intended for road vehicles—and probably to the disgust of whoever made the sign at the gate—Montbretia left the track, pulling up about one-hundred meters away from the church, where she dismounted and dropped her bike against a tree with a reptilian-scaled trunk too thick to wrap a bike lock around. If it got stolen—in what was essentially the middle of nowhere—Boniface could buy her a new one.

There were maybe ten or fifteen of the thick-trunked trees. Spaced, but the spread of the branches reached between each tree, which with the thick leaves gave her cover of near-darkness as she moved silently toward the church.

She reached the last tree in the group and stopped, letting her eyes drift across the view: a church more than a thousand years old, surrounded by a low ironstone rubble wall with a semi-horseshoe of trees behind offering some screening from two sides. Screening. Another way of saying "a place for the bad guys to hide if someone had the same idea as her."

Her eyes tracked across the panorama, looking for color, movement, or even smoke. Her ears tuned in for any sound, whether human or animal disturbed by human.

And then she broke cover, moving to the next group of trees, passing into the shadows as she worked her way toward the horseshoe behind the church. Pausing repeatedly to scan and listen, after about five minutes, Montbretia reached the baggage she had jettisoned several hours earlier.

It was untouched—which she had hoped would be the result of hiding it eight feet up a tree. She pulled it down and began to quietly move the small heap to the outside of the ironstone wall.

She checked her phone. Boniface was right again. The Norman church truly did have the same phone coverage that the Normans had in 1066. With no way to know what was happening with Boniface and Leathan, the only option was to continue and get inside before the daylight was lost.

The top of the ironstone wall gripped her ass as she twisted her legs over before silently stepping toward the church, her head in constant motion, like a windshield wiper.

The tower of the church, constructed from yellowed ironstone and sandstone rubble with red-brick battlements, stood in the center. To the left a narrower and lower block had been added with a pitched red-tiled roof. To the right, another block stood—higher than that on the left—with a rendered wall, a steeper pitched roof, and a wood-frame porch topped by a gabled roof.

The handwritten note—*please be sure to shut the grill securely to keep birds out*—explained the function but didn't warn Montbretia of how high-pitched the hinges' squeak would be as it opened. The bird screen screeched again as Montbretia pulled it behind her, reaching for the iron handle, which, although large given the size of the wooden door, seemed insufficient. The spindle had worn loose in its hole through centuries of use, and it took her a moment or two to jiggle the latch up, with a substantial metal click that could be heard from the outside.

The heavy wooden door groaned, cartoon-like, on its hinges as it opened. Montbretia turned to pull the bird shield behind her, missed the step down, and stumbled backward into the church, finding herself drawn to look at her new surroundings. She closed the door with her gaze still being drawn up. The whitewashed walls were topped by a white-washed roof supported by rafters that looked over a thousand years old.

The plaster on the walls was rough, but with occasional nooks with statues and detailing around pictures and memorials. She misstepped on the uneven flagstone floor, unable to draw her attention from looking up until she bumped into a substantial table with local guides and histories on display, together with a notice soliciting donations and giving details of how to make any payments tax-free.

From the airy square of the nave, she walked under the tower, staring up into the darkness of the inside of the unlit tower.

Boniface had mentioned part of the interior had been renovated by the owner of the estate during the Victorian era. As she looked down from the tower, her eyes fell upon what she presumed was the Victorian mausoleum. In the gloom, she couldn't make out much—a tomb, perhaps, a darkened window that was probably stained glass, a decorated wall and ceiling that just looked dull in the gloom—all separated from the rest of the church by a wooden screen to a height of about eight feet.

From the third open side under the tower, Montbretia found the altar. It was simple, little more than a table with a wooden cross, two candlesticks, and fresh flowers. In front of it, a pewter lectern stood—a bird of prey spreading its wings to hold a Bible.

Montbretia turned, returning toward the nave but stopping as she passed the screen separating the tomb, and moved up close to the screen, looking down behind it. A few neatly knotted empty candy wrappers were on the floor with three bottles of water in a straight line.

As she stood, she sighed. "You were right, Boniface."

Cautiously she opened the door and the bird screen, stepping from the chill of the church into the slightly less chilly, but still not warm, late afternoon before making three quick trips to retrieve the luggage that had been strapped to the back of her bicycle, dumping each load behind the door inside the church.

Montbretia picked up one of the backpacks and pulled out a blanket, dropping it on the ground in front of her. She dug deeper, pulling out some socks, clean sweatpants, and a fleece jacket.

She picked up a second backpack and took out a camping light, switching it on and placing it at the center of the nave. She returned to her unpacking and looked back at the light, wrinkled her nose, then returned to the light. "Better not," she muttered, flicking off the switch and placing the lamp next to her small pile.

She put on a jacket, then sat on the blanket, removing her shoes and replacing them with the socks before wriggling into the sweatpants.

"Okay, Dawn," she said under her breath. "I'm here, and I'm waiting for you. Where are you?"

seventy

"*This*? This is it?"

Boniface could hear himself shouting at the minicab driver.

"This?"

He pointed behind him at the housing development, the four beige-striped concrete towers blocking out anything that remained of the natural light of the day.

"This side? Not that side?"

"This side, sir," said the minicab driver, smiling broadly.

"King William Estate?" asked Boniface.

"Yes, sir," said the driver, his thick Bangladeshi accent coming through. His smile undimmed.

"How do you know?" barked Boniface, looking toward the towers and the low blocks. "Where does it say that?"

"That sign there," said the driver, pointing. His smile radiating from his eyes.

"And where's Chesterfield Terrace?" asked Boniface.

"I don't know, sir." The smile remained.

Boniface dropped a bill on the passenger seat before turning and jogging to the sign.

It probably did say King William Estate. There probably was a map of the estate, too. But all Boniface could see were the letters *Kin* toward the top-left corner and a few hints around the edge that the metal sign showed streets and walkways. For the most part, the sign was scratched, gouged, bent, burned, and covered in graffiti. Between the two posts holding it, Boniface stopped counting when he had seen fifteen needles.

The rush-hour traffic thundered down the road, penning Boniface into the beige concrete development. On one side, the smell of the internal combustion engine. On the other, the smell of something acrid starting to burn, fused with deep-fat frying, reached into his nostrils.

Boniface looked up at the low block in front of him. The sign, about ten or eleven feet off the ground, said "Burl..." The remainder had been graffitied over.

Not Chesterfield Terrace.

Boniface ducked to the right and followed the path passing Burl-whatever, which then twisted past some dark-brick two-story maisonettes, before curving away, becoming a narrower alley with a brick wall on one side. The alley passed a heap of abandoned sofas and beds, then turned, opening onto another block.

Croxton something.

The sign, as high as the one for Burl, had been snapped off and was dangling nearly vertically by one screw.

He saw a group of kids—probably no more than ten or eleven years old—smoking and throwing stones at the few cars that dared to pass. He avoided eye contact and turned in the opposite direction, becoming increasingly aware that the smell of burning he had noticed earlier wasn't dissipating. If anything, it was getting stronger.

Boniface looked up to the sky. Somewhere above the towers, there was a gentle breeze blowing, and it was drifting black smoke over his head. Black smoke that seemed to have its origin somewhere ahead.

It was as if a celestial force was leaving him a trail of breadcrumbs to Leathan.

Boniface picked up his pace, starting to jog as he followed another passageway, coming out near a row dilapidated shops. Across the road, he took another path—the smoke trail still in sight. He ducked around some more heaps of furniture and one with paint cans, finally coming out at an open space across from a long, low-slung block.

He recognized the back of the man watching the source of the smoke. "It's not a coincidence that you're here and there's a fire."

"See what happens when you leave me alone with matches."

"Shit, Leathan. You set fire to someone's home."

"Relax," said Leathan, although the look on his face didn't agree with the words falling out of his mouth. "The place was boarded up—it had been used by junkies as far as I could tell."

"But isn't it..." Boniface looked from Leathan's face to the smoke and back to Leathan. His brow was creased, his mouth tightening. "Isn't this a bit...I dunno...a bit dangerous?"

Leathan flinched and half-shrugged. "What did you want me to do? You weren't here, and I don't know who else is in there."

"Where?"

"First floor up—at the end. That's where Jojo is."

"And Billy?"

"Dunno. I only saw Jojo."

Boniface went to speak but stopped, catching Leathan's gaze, which swiftly moved to the funnels of black smoke coming out from behind the block. "I didn't know what weapons they had, so I thought it would be quicker to smoke them out—I knocked holes in the ceiling so the smoke would go through the floorboards." Leathan was speaking, but without commitment as he seemed to be focusing with increasing intent on the smoke. "At least, I hope it gets through the floorboards."

"A place like this will have huge slabs of particleboard on the floors—not stripped-back floorboards," said Boniface. "Then there will be carpets on top. How's the smoke meant to get through?"

The other man didn't reply.

"That's looking dangerous, Leathan."

Leathan winced, clearly not wanting to admit a problem, but seemingly having difficulty arguing with the assessment as he stared at the block.

"The plan was to save Billy, not to kill him in a different way before Ernie gets to him." Boniface moved his view from the side of Leathan's head to the block. "That smoke's getting thick. I'm going to have a look."

"Suit yourself," said Leathan, remaining still as Boniface started to walk toward the block.

Boniface had taken half a dozen paces when he heard footsteps behind him: Leathan jogging to catch up. "You need someone to supervise you," said Leathan, passing Boniface, who picked up his pace, then broke into a light jog.

By the time they reached the bottom of the stairwell, they were sprinting, jostling each other as they ran up the stairs, not noticing the smell in the stairwell—which had been masked by the acrid burning smell—and not paying attention to the vomit and dead squirrel.

They turned out of the stairs, slowing as they moved along the walkway toward number forty-one. "So how are we going to do this?" asked Boniface.

"I dunno," said Leathan. "I thought the smoke would force them out." The thick black smoke drifted around the end of the building. "I thought they'd just come running—look at it...it's much thicker than I expected."

"Are you're sure they're still alive?" said Boniface, feeling the tension in his throat. "We're not going to go in and find corpses?"

"What do you mean go in?"

"I mean you're kicking the door down."

"But we don't know who's in there or how many people are in there." Leathan was gabbling. "Or whether they're armed, or..." He stopped, turned to face Boniface, and continued, his voice simpering. "That's why I tried to smoke them out."

"And how's that working out?" said Boniface, continuing toward number forty-one. "You kick the door, then deal with Jojo and whoever else you find. I'll get Billy. In. Out. Finished."

"But..."

Boniface tried to get the annoyance out of his voice. "We're trying to keep Billy alive. Ernie's happy to waste him, so we don't have any option." He indicated the door. "Kick. Run."

Boniface leaned to the side of the door, leaving Leathan to stand in front of his target.

He breathed in once, shaking his shoulders loose as he exhaled. Inhaled again, more deeply, looking up at Boniface as he exhaled. Broke eye contact as he inhaled, and as he exhaled he lifted his foot, stamping onto the door where the cross-member halfway up met the side-member.

The cross-member flew in, and the left side of the door cracked. The lower pane of obscured glass shattered, with pieces scattering across the walkway and into the residence, and the top pane cracked as the muffled sound of music became clearer.

Boniface frowned, questioning the other man. "It was computer games earlier. He likes it loud—I think he's got trouble with his hearing," said Leathan, standing back and reloading his boot before he launched his foot at the cracked side of the door, which splintered, sending the door flying open. As it slammed into the back wall, the remaining glass in the top panel shattered.

"Go," said Boniface gently, tilting his head to indicate the entrance Leathan had cleared and softly slapping him on the back as he stepped up into the home. Leathan's footsteps crunched as Boniface turned, ready to follow the other man, who was ducking into the first room on the left before swiftly exiting and crossing the passage into the opposite room.

"There's no smoke, Leathan," hissed Boniface, becoming aware of the warm air that was pushing past him as he stepped up into the doorway, his feet grinding broken glass into the fitted carpet.

There was a noise—above the sound of music—coming from the room to the right at the far end of the corridor, and the door opened, rubbing along the carpet as it moved. As the door opened, the sound of a blaring TV—some rapper telling everyone how great he was, against a drumbeat that kicked Boniface in the gut and frizzled his ears at the same time.

Leathan exited the room on the right with a rolling pin in his hand, and the big black presence of Jojo filled the frame of the door at the far end.

"I've got a knife," shouted Leathan, moving toward the teen.

"Not as big as mine," said the oversized teen without a hint of fear. Leathan's bluff had been called.

Boniface caught sight of himself in the mirror just inside the door. His suit was clean and presentable this morning. Since then, he had been to see Ernie, where Wes had manhandled him, although thankfully not given him too much of a pounding. However, the cloth had taken a beating caused by Wes not understanding the subtle nuance between fear and respect. While the suit was probably beyond repair, it wasn't what he hoped to be wearing if he got into a fight in a tight passage.

He ducked into the kitchen and scanned the counter. Some beer—cheap, sharp, and over fizzy. Some peanuts, and that was all that was on display. Boniface opened the first eye-line cabinet and saw a row of squat tumblers. He grabbed the first one, feeling its heft. Then grabbed a second and exited back into the corridor.

Leathan was waving something at the big teen—bobbing and weaving as Jojo tracked his movements, seemingly more amused than frightened. Boniface took the first tumbler and pitched it, letting the weighty glass spin as it left his hand. The rotating object drifted right, clipping the wall and bouncing at a sharper angle than it hit, almost as if it picked up speed in its impact.

The big teen became aware of something fast-moving at head height and twisted to look at the incoming UFO, turning his head into the spinning tumbler as it made contact with his temple.

"Motherfucker!" shouted the teen, looking to the source of the pro-jectile, which had fallen to the floor. Leathan ducked, grabbing for the first tumbler, and Boniface launched the second. The teen swayed out of its way, allowing it to hit the wall behind him and shatter, not realizing that he had moved in the direction of Leathan's wooden baton which made contact first with his cheekbone; Leathan's second blow landed on the side of the teen's head above his ear.

He bellowed as Leathan pushed forward, shoving the teen off balance and knocking him into the room from which he had come.

Boniface rushed forward. Where Leathan and Jojo went right, he went left, opening the door to what might be a bedroom with a figure sprawled on top of a duvet. Billy. Maybe unconscious. Maybe asleep.

seventy-one

A suppressed sound pushed its way through the thick church walls from outside: A latch rattled, followed by the groan and then slam of old wooden gate closing.

Montbretia waited, listening—her eyes scanning the nave of the church in the early evening gloom, which had rendered her surroundings in monochrome. She remained still—sitting on her blanket with her thick socks and warm jacket—pushed into the corner to shield herself from the line of sight of anyone entering the consecrated building.

Another latch clicked—the latch on the bird grill being lifted, and then the sound of the grill opening, the hinges squealing as the large metal mesh moved. Then the sound of the spindle in the wooden door, twisting to lever the latch out of its seat, ending with the latch hitting the stop as it was raised to its maximum level, leaving the sound echoing around the church.

The hinge beside Montbretia's ear moaned—a deep complaint about years of arthritic movement—and the door opened. A figure entered backward—ass first, the sound of the bird grill closing before the ass stepped backward.

A female ass.

An ass that Montbretia half recognized.

An ass that Boniface had admired.

Montbretia watched as the other woman swiftly looked around without looking behind and then crossed the nave, walking under the tower and to the altar, where she stood in silent contemplation for a moment.

Montbretia didn't interrupt the wordless invocation as she stood, moving forward, her socks not making any noise on the flagstones. "We've missed you."

Dawn let out a slight scream, reflexively bringing her hand over her mouth as the yelp echoed against the hard surfaces.

"It's alright—it's Montbretia. We met at Boniface's office."

Dawn dropped her hand but remained frozen, a look that Montbretia took to be fear spreading across her face. The other woman's face hardened, her lips thinning, her eyes narrowing, her head leaning forward. "Stay out of this."

Montbretia felt the aggression hitting her like a heat wave from a furnace. "I'm on your side, Dawn."

"You don't know what's going on, and I'm leaving." Dawn walked straight toward Montbretia, her shoulders pulled in as if readying for a fight. Her footsteps—which had been light when she entered—were now strides echoing around the thousand-year-old building.

Montbretia swiftly moved backward toward the door.

"Get out of my way." There was no softness in Dawn's voice.

Montbretia shook her head—the tiniest vibration. "I can't let you go," she whispered.

"Get out of my way," repeated Dawn, standing in front of Montbretia.

"No." Montbretia kept her voice low.

Dawn reached for the door, knocking Montbretia back against the ancient piece of wood. "Get out of my way." The older woman grabbed for the handle, and when she couldn't reach, she pushed Montbretia.

Montbretia bear-hugged Dawn, holding her arms tight against her body as the older woman struggled. "Let me go."

Montbretia gripped tighter. "We know about Billy."

Dawn's struggling became twisting.

"We know about both Billies."

Montbretia felt Dawn deflate and relaxed her grip while holding tight enough to realize that the other woman was trembling.

"I'm not worried about Billy." Montbretia stared at Dawn—the former model's anger seeming to turn into exasperation at Montbretia's incomprehension. Perhaps she was marveling at the younger woman's stupidity. "I'm worried about Danny."

"Huh?" said Montbretia, finally dropping her grip and stepping back from Dawn to look at her more clearly. "Danny loves you."

"Precisely," said Dawn. "Danny loves me unconditionally. He will do anything for me, so I had to be where Danny couldn't save me, because otherwise he'd give up *everything* for me." She shook her head, holding her bottom lip in her teeth—her eyes defocused and a smile forming on the side of her mouth not clamped in her teeth. "Everything. That man would give up anything and everything for me, and then we'd have nothing."

The older woman looked up, fixing Montbretia in her gaze, her voice soft, warm. "Danny would lay down his life for me—like that." She clicked her fingers. The snap echoed around the nave. "But I want a live husband—I don't want to bury the guy...I love him...and now you're just causing trouble."

Montbretia took two small steps backward, reaching the door and gripping the handle. "We need to talk and I want to eat." She softened her face. "Having looked at what you've been eating over the last few days, I reckon you could do with something sensible to eat, too."

seventy-two

Billy hadn't seen any urgency to get out.

Billy hadn't seen any urgency to even bother with opening his eyes.

When Boniface followed Leathan in, despite the fire downstairs, the residence had been smoke-free. With the front door open—permanently, thanks to Leathan's boot—there was now a through draft creating a vacuum, drawing smoke through the floor...or maybe the smoke was just coming in through the door. Thick, black, acrid smoke that was settling in Boniface's throat.

Boniface shook Billy as he lay on his back on the single bed. Billy grunted but refused to move. Even the racket from the rap video playing in the other room didn't seem to disturb him.

Boniface shook him again, more vigorously. Billy didn't even bother grunting.

"Billy. The place is on fire—it's time to get out," said Boniface.

The man on the bed gave no response. In the next room, there was the sound of skin-on-skin, punches being thrown, kicks delivered, and furniture taking a thrashing as human bodies came into contact. Another crash, and the music stopped.

"Come on, Billy," said Boniface. "Time to move, and if you're not going to do it yourself..." He rolled Billy onto his side, sliding his right arm behind the other man as he slumped onto his back. Slowly, he pushed his left hand behind Billy until it met his right hand.

He pulled his fingers together, tightening his grip on Billy's prone body and managing to grab his own wrists. He leaned back, holding his wrists tightly, and pulled Billy into a sitting position on the bed.

Not that Billy seemed to notice.

"You could make my life easier," said Boniface, releasing his grip, instead taking Billy's shoulder with one hand to keep him in a sitting position while he dragged his legs with the other, dropping his feet onto the floor. Billy half twisted into a sitting position, and Boniface returned his arms to under Billy's armpits, reaching his hands behind the other man's back and gripping his wrists before bending his knees and hefting the junkie to a semi-vertical position.

"I...ohhh." Billy groaned. Boniface felt his wrists slip and guided Billy back to the sitting position.

"Come on, Bill—you need to help me or burn," said Boniface, coughing as he looked at the thickening smoke. In the next room there was the sound of glass breaking—perhaps a window, maybe a mirror.

Boniface returned his arms around Billy, gripped him tightly, bent his knees, and raised him to something close to the vertical, pulling him so he was leaning forward. As the junkie started to topple, Boniface bent, getting his shoulder to the younger man's waist, gripping around the top of his legs and spreading his weight across his back as the other man flopped forward, before Boniface stood with the dead weight of the other man spread over his shoulder.

There was shouting from the other room as Boniface reached the bedroom door, then the now-familiar sound of one human coming into contact with another, followed by the noise of a sharp exhalation of breath. Boniface moved into the narrow corridor, feeling the weight of the man over his shoulder as he watched the smoke blowing out the door—the vacuum sucking more fumes from the floor below.

"Leathan—I've got Billy," shouted Boniface as he staggered through the front door, taking a few stumbling steps before roughly lowering Billy and leaving him sitting against the wall of the walkway facing the boarded front door of number thirty-nine.

Boniface stood outside the door of number forty-one, gulped a lungful of clean air, and reentered, turning into the room where Leathan had disappeared. "Help me, Boniface," said Leathan.

"Where's..."

Before Boniface could answer, Leathan leaned forward, brushing the smoke away to reveal Jojo lying on the floor. "Grab his arm." The two men took an arm each and started dragging the big teen toward the front door.

"There's a lot of glass," said Boniface.

"Better that he's cut than he dies of smoke," replied the other man, pushing through the door, followed by Boniface and the inert body.

They crunched over the glass, sweeping the shards with Jojo, then flopped the body down the front step, and dragged him just past where Billy sat.

"What happened to him?" asked Boniface, looking back at the smoke flowing out of the door from which they had just exited.

"I stopped him killing me," said Leathan.

"We'd better get these guys away from the smoke. Let's go with Billy first." He turned to the junkie. "Billy, meet Leathan. Leathan, meet the right guy this time."

"When you say it like that, I almost feel you don't appreciate me," said Leathan, grabbing Billy's arm as the sound of a siren began to fill the air. "Get his other arm." Boniface grabbed Billy's free wrist. "Ready?" Boniface nodded, and they pulled Billy to his feet, each holding an arm around their shoulders as they started to drag Billy along the corridor.

As they turned into the stairs, Billy changed from letting his toes drag along the ground to trying to get his feet flat. Something in the smell invigorated him, and by the time they reached the open space at the bottom, he was moving his legs, although not taking much weight on his feet.

The two got Billy across the open space and sat him on the open ground at the spot where Boniface had found Leathan. Billy sat, his legs pulled up with his arms wrapped around, his eyes now open and his head moving in slow motion. Boniface squatted next to him. "How're you feeling?"

Billy's skin lacked any tone—it was as if the color had dissolved and the muscle tone had departed. The only variation in shade was given by the bruises, rashes, and bristles. "I need..." he sniffed and continued his slow survey of his surroundings with his bloodshot eyes.

"Alright," said Boniface. "I'll be back soon; don't go anywhere."

Boniface stood up, stretching his back as he looked at Leathan. "Jojo hit you bad," said Boniface.

"I know—it hurt. That's why I had to put him down." He looked down, his voice trembling and only just audible against the sound of the fire engine, which was drawing near. "I think I might have done real damage, Boniface. He was too big for me, and I was more scared of him than he was of me, so I had to hurt him."

"Let's go get him," said Boniface, looking back at the block, flames starting to sneak out from the gaps around the shuttering on the ground level.

The two started jogging across the open space, Leathan then leading through the stairwell. "You can see he's a big lad," said Leathan, pointing his head at Jojo, who was laid out on the passageway, which was filling with smoke. "He was too big to fight in such a tight spot—I could move quicker. It was the only advantage I had."

They reached the big teen. He was still breathing, but it was labored. The bruising on his face was severe, and the cheekbones—previously symmetrical—were now misaligned.

"Let's get him out of the smoke," said Leathan, reaching for a wrist. Boniface grabbed the second, and they both leaned back to pull. Slowly, the friction holding the body—probably aided by blood and glass fragments—started to release its grip and the body began to move, dragging along the passageway.

"How are we going to do the stairs?" said Boniface, breathing heavily as they reached the top of the stairwell. "We don't want to permanently disable the guy by bouncing his spine on the concrete steps."

"One under each arm, and lift," said Leathan. "Let his feet bump." He exhaled. "You ready?" Boniface nodded and they lifted, both groaning as they walked backward into the stairwell.

"Which side was the vomit on?" asked Boniface.

"The opposite side to the piss and the squirrel," said Leathan. "And our friend's not paying attention, so he's likely to find it all."

Boniface stopped counting after the first ten steps, instead concentrating on holding the weight as he turned through 180 degrees on the half-landing.

The two pulled the near corpse-like body out of the stairwell and away from the building. They laid Jojo—dressed in black jeans, a drab olive jacket with breast pockets and hip pockets, and white sneakers, which were now mostly black—on the ground and stood, struggling for breath as they felt the damage the exertion had inflicted on their muscles.

Looking across the open space, Billy was on his feet—he didn't seem to be going anywhere, but at least he was standing—and the first fire engine had stopped, its blue light still flashing, but its siren extinguished.

"Shouldn't they come running?" said Leathan, pointing toward the first few fire crew who were opening up the equipment doors on the engine.

Boniface shook his head. "Risk assessment first." Leathan looked like he had been shocked by 1,000 volts. "They're here to sort things, not become part of the problem. There'll be someone with a clipboard. Let's go find them and tell them what we know."

They started walking toward the fire engine. "Listen," said Leathan, stopping. "Billy's safe, and the fire brigade are here..." He stopped talking but somehow seemed to fill the space with the anticipation of what he was going to say next. "Do you still need me here? I did start the fire and I hurt Jojo pretty bad—if you don't need me, it's a good time for me to be somewhere else."

"Go," said Boniface. "And thank you." He stopped, turned to Leathan, and embraced. They broke and he pulled out his wallet, taking out the cash he hadn't given to Gray or spent encouraging people to tell him about Carmen when he was searching for her that morning. He pulled out a couple of notes and gave the rest to Leathan. "That's all I've got, and I need to keep some back to get Billy out of here." He looked over Leathan's shoulder as the other man took the cash. "And where is Billy?"

Leathan spun. "There. See? Staggering over to give Jojo a kick."

Boniface patted his heart. "He had me scared—there's no point in losing him now." He reached out and shook Leathan's hand. "Again, thank you."

"My pleasure."

"Eurostar and Paris?" asked Boniface.

"I'll get back to Paris in about a week—I'll take the long route home. Go and see a few friends along the way—take it slow in case Ernie really does have friends." He turned and started to jog in what Boniface thought was the direction of the main road.

Boniface checked on Billy—he had reached Jojo and was kneeling beside him. It was as if he were pilfering from a dead body.

"Did I see you up there?" Boniface spun to see a fire officer towering over him. He looked up to the white helmet, following down to the poorly fitting white vest denoting *Incident Commander* worn over his uniform. The officer cradled a clipboard in one arm and held a pen in his opposite hand.

"Yeah," said Boniface. "We got that guy down—he needs a paramedic."

"They're on the way," said the incident commander, making a note. "Where was he?"

"We got him out of number forty-one—that's one floor up, on the right." Boniface pointed loosely; the officer's gaze seemed to follow, and the notes continued. "I think the fire started immediately under." Boniface pointed to the ground-floor apartment where flames and smoke were now freely flowing. "Kids, I guess," said Boniface.

"Is there anyone else up there?" asked the officer.

"Not that we could see—we got the two out. That guy..." he pointed to Jojo, "and..."

Billy was gone. Boniface scanned the open space. A small crowd had congregated, including a group of kids Boniface had seen on the way into the development—all looked to be about ten years old and all were smoking.

"I need to go find him," Boniface said under his breath, turning away from the incident commander before he started sprinting toward Jojo.

seventy-three

"How did you find me?" Dawn looked at the other woman. Twenty-something, slim, good figure—she looked athletic, but perhaps that was more to do with how she was dressed in sweatpants, a fleece jacket, which seemed to be mandatory for every visitor who walked around the Surrey Hills, and with her hair in a plait.

When Dawn had seen her at Boniface's office, the young American woman had come across as very efficient but maybe standoffish, almost disapproving. Boniface raved about her—talking about her in terms of her being some sort of an organizing machine.

Dawn had formed an image in her mind of someone quite bookish, maybe rather withdrawn. But in reality, she was dealing with someone who was prepared to stand her ground—physically and emotionally, she'd already stood up to Dawn and stopped her leaving—and someone who had the gumption to sit alone in a thousand-year-old church when it was getting dark.

"I didn't find you," said Montbretia, the side of her lip lifting. "You came to the place where I was."

Dawn's eyes brightened, acknowledging the humorous rebuff. "Then why did you come here?"

"A guess...by Boniface. He figured it was the place you would feel safe." She pushed out her lower lip. "Sanctuary. The place that first drew you to the area. The place where you and Danny solemnized your vows." She lifted her shoulders. "It seemed pretty logical when he put it like that, but I hadn't thought about it that way until he said it."

She reached for a backpack and pulled out a blanket, spreading it on the ground, then produced two more, keeping them folded as she placed them on the first. "A bit of padding. Why don't you sit down, Dawn?" Montbretia then walked to the corner behind the door and picked up two more backpacks, brought them over, gently placed them on the floor, and then dropped onto a folded blanket, patting next to her to encourage Dawn to sit.

As she lowered herself, Dawn watched Montbretia unpack one of the backpacks. "Are you warm enough?" asked Montbretia. "Dry enough? I've got some sweatpants and a jacket if you want—you can sit on them or wear them." She wrested a lump of mixed fabrics from the backpack, dropped them between the two of them, and dived back into the backpack.

"Hungry?" Dawn watched as Montbretia took out an aluminum pot with an oversized lid held on with a narrow webbing strap. She dropped the strap, flipped off the lid, and pulled out what looked like three pots and a kettle stacked inside one another. From inside the kettle she took an orange polythene bag, which Montbretia revealed to be carrying a small brass pot.

Montbretia took the largest aluminum pot, which was perforated and had a large hole in the middle, and placed it upside down on the flagstones before picking up the brass pot, unscrewing its lid, and dropping it into the large hole in the center. A red bottle appeared from a backpack, and Montbretia squirted some liquid into the small brass pot.

"That's a rather interesting contraption," said Dawn. "It's like a Russian doll of cooking pots."

"That's exactly what it is," said Montbretia, striking a match and igniting the liquid in the brass container before taking the next cooking pot—which, when Montbretia lifted it, Dawn could see didn't have a base—and fitting it on top of the perforated pot, creating a cylinder.

"Cute, isn't it? It's a bunch of cooking pots," she grabbed the larger of the two remaining aluminum pots. "A frying pan," she pointed to the lid, "a kettle, a stand," she tapped the perforated base, "a windshield," she indicated the pot without a base set on top of the stand, "and a spirit burner." She looked at Dawn. "Home away from home. It's very quick, very efficient, lightweight, much safer than gas, and storm-proof. I've been able to make a cup of tea in the middle of a thunderstorm with no problem."

"Impressive," said Dawn.

"There is a downside," said Montbretia, exaggerating a grimace. "There's only one burner, so you're going to have to decide whether you want soup first or a cup of tea."

"Ooh dear," said Dawn, joining the younger woman in the humor.

"And before you make that decision, the soup is tomato—out of a tin, I'm afraid...I can't match your skills—and for tea you have a choice of English Breakfast, peppermint, and rooibos."

"Rooibos?"

"It's South African," said Montbretia, looking down and curling her lip. "Truth be told, I don't like it much—I'm trying to get rid of it."

"Shall we start with the soup?" said Dawn.

"I was hoping you'd say that," said the younger woman, pulling a can from the backpack and a paper bag, which she held up as she continued. "I've got some rolls as well—I'm sure they're not up to your home-baking standard, but they're quite good." She emptied the soup into one of the pots and balanced the pot over the flame inside the windshield before reaching into a sack and placing two yellow melamine mugs in front of her. "I must apologize for not bringing the finest porcelain."

The American woman reached into her bag again, pulling out

something Dawn couldn't make out. She then turned over what she had thought was a lid but now knew to be a frying pan, and placed a tea light on the metal surface, lighting it and immediately returning the matches to the backpack. She turned to Dawn. "Enough for us to see, but not enough to highlight our presence through the dulled glass."

Clearly Dawn had been wrong in her initial assessment. Montbretia wasn't a quiet mouse of a librarian—she was practical, resourceful, and knew she was taking a risk, even if she hadn't expressed that risk directly.

She watched as Montbretia stirred the soup, resting the spoon in the second cooking pot before pulling out a roll of paper towels. "Just in case," said Montbretia.

"How's Danny?"

Montbretia's head swung to face Dawn as if her neck were spring-loaded. She paused, and when she started talking, her voice was soft, with no rancor in the tone. "He's in a bad way, Dawn. He's missing you." She paused. "I don't think he's slept since you left."

Dawn felt her eyes start to sting. "I should call him—can I borrow your phone?"

Montbretia shook her head and stirred the soup.

"I need to call Danny—I need to put him out of the pain I'm causing him."

"No." Montbretia's voice was just above a whisper. "Only Boniface and I know where you are. Another hour or two of worry isn't going to kill Danny, and as you said, if people can find you, then Danny's at risk."

"Please," said Dawn.

"There's no signal."

"I know—but if you cross the park and walk a hundred yards up the hill, there's a spot where you get a perfect signal."

Montbretia shook her head gently, looking back at the soup. "It's nearly ready..."

Dawn went to speak but was cut off by Montbretia. "I know you want to see him, but while people don't know where you are, then they can't force Danny to do anything." Her voice took a more businesslike tone. "We don't know how Danny will react if you call him—you know he'll do anything for you, and we don't want him to play the hero and make a stupid gesture." She picked up the pot of soup and began to pour it into the mugs. "Plus, your dinner's ready, and a church is probably safest place to be—people tend to be twitchy about killing people in a house of worship."

Montbretia placed the fuller mug in front of Dawn and opened the paper bag, offering her a roll. Dawn took a piece of bread and started to tear at it.

They dunked bread and sipped their soup. Dawn broke the silence. "You said you know about both Billies."

"Father and son."

Dawn felt her face flush. "Does Danny know?"

"About Billy...about your son?"

Dawn felt her throat tighten and the tears flow.

"He didn't believe it." Montbretia's voice was calm. "We saw Carmen—Carmen Gallagher—this morning. She seemed certain Billy's your son. Boniface spoke to Danny—Danny said Carmen was wrong."

"It's true," said Dawn, dropping her half-eaten roll as she put her head into her hands, starting to sob.

"Something else Carmen confirmed for us..." Dawn looked up, aware of her appearance and still feeling the tears. "Billy—by whom, I mean Billy Senior—is dead."

"No." Dawn became aware that she staring at the other woman and that her mouth was still open.

"Died in a car crash nineteen years ago."

"What about William?" Dawn fought to squeeze her voice out. "What happened...why didn't they tell me?"

"It's a conversation you need to have with Carmen...but from what I understand, Billy Senior's family took control." Montbretia's voice faded as she took another sip of soup.

Dawn looked down at her roll and the halo of crumbs, which she started to sweep up. When she spoke, she whispered. "How is William?"

"He's alive, but I haven't seen him," said Montbretia. "Boniface has gone to find him and get him somewhere safe. Once Billy's safe, then Boniface will come and find us."

"But he'll bring Billy?"

Montbretia winced. She seemed to be weighing up something. "Billy's not in a good way—there might be drugs, so Boniface might take him to get help." She paused again, still seeming uneasy, then blurted. "And you and Danny need to have a conversation before anything else happens. You need to have that conversation without any of us, including Billy, being around."

Dawn bowed her head, picking at her bread roll and taking an occasional sip of her soup. "Thank you for this," she said.

Montbretia smiled softly, sitting still, seemingly not ready to ask any questions.

"You must think I'm an awful mother," said Dawn.

"I know you've got a husband who loves you totally. Unconditionally." Her face brightened, a note of wonder creeping into her tone. "And he wrote a great song for you."

Dawn sobbed, bowing her head.

Gradually she looked up, wiping her tears with her fingers. Montbretia leaned forward and placed the kitchen roll beside her. "I haven't seen my boy since he was six weeks old. He's thirty-one now—that's older than you."

Dawn ripped off a sheet of paper towel and dabbed her eyes, then blew her nose.

Montbretia put a hand into a backpack and pulled out some black polythene, rustling it open to reveal a trash bag, into which she threw the soup can before placing the bag, open, near Dawn. "We've got all night—don't be shy about filling it."

Dawn blew her nose again and dropped the piece of kitchen roll in the black bag. "I suppose church is the place for confessing—and if there is a God, may he forgive me."

She finished her soup, then tore off a few sheets of paper towel, gripping them tightly in her hand. "I was raped when I was fourteen by Billy...William's dad. He lived near us, so I knew him, but he was quite a bit older than me." Her hand gripped the paper towels, trembling. "And when I say rape...he beat me, ripped my clothes...we're not talking about regret the morning afterward, we're talking about a fourteen-year-old kid being brutalized by a twenty-one-year-old man."

She looked up at the American, registering the shock and the questions on her face.

"Around where I came from, Billy was the scariest man alive. I wasn't alone—there were others, but he usually waited 'til the girls were older. But I had boobs, which made him think it was alright." She sniffed and dabbed her eyes. "That rape led to William." She felt a smile form and her face relax as she said his name. "For all these years, I've always thought of him as William... And he's really alive?"

Montbretia nodded reassuringly. "Yes."

"I'm not proud—I was fifteen when William was born, and only just fifteen. Billy knew William was his—more to the point, his mother and his family knew William was their family. I was a useless teenager without any family to support me, so they forced me to give them the baby." She felt the tears begin to rise. "At first, they said it was best for me—I could go back to school—and best for the baby that they looked after him, and that I could see him whenever I wanted. But that didn't last long. Within two weeks I was cut out of his life."

Montbretia sat silent, watching.

"I still saw Billy. He used to taunt me—'Be nice to me, and I'll let you see little Billy'... He knocked me around, lied to get me into bed, raped me several more times, and I got pregnant again. I was still fifteen." She felt herself go cold. "I didn't keep it—couldn't keep it. I went to a really dodgy place—they scared me so much that I never went for a checkup after, and I'm sure that's why I haven't been able to get pregnant since."

She picked up the jacket Montbretia had laid out earlier and threw it across her shoulders, pulling it like a shawl. "When I turned sixteen, I turned my boobs to my advantage and earned enough money modeling to get out. Billy tracked me down—he was after money; he said it was for William. Then he went after Carmen, thinking it made me jealous... How is Carmen?"

"She's had a rough time," said Montbretia. "But...I've only met her once—this morning—and she seemed like she was trying to sort herself out."

Dawn took in Montbretia's words. "Billy went after her. I warned her, but she liked a bad boy...and then Lorna..." She felt her voice go weak. "After Lorna, we all fell apart. I was lucky—Danny found me, and I never looked back. I put everything behind me and locked the door. I never told Danny about Billy and William—I was ashamed and Danny would have tried to fix that too, but I always hoped that William would find me, and now he has."

seventy-four

It wasn't unreasonable.

He had held Leathan at gunpoint this morning, and a few minutes ago he had come at Leathan with a knife when all Leathan had to defend himself was a rolling pin. That said, Leathan did say he had a knife.

Leathan had acted to ensure that Jojo would pose no further threat. It wasn't unreasonable.

No threat to himself. No threat to Boniface. No threat to Billy.

But as Boniface looked down at Jojo, he recoiled.

The lump above his left eye was probably due to Boniface and a luckily pitched spinning glass tumbler. The gashes could not be attributed to Boniface, nor the broken tooth, nor the displaced nose, nor the cheekbones that now lacked the symmetrical appearance they held this morning. And Boniface was definitely not responsible for the blood, which was spread across Jojo's jacket and was drying across his face and in his hair.

Boniface knew what had happened—Leathan would have used Jojo's disadvantages against him. Jojo was big—in the tight space Leathan would have moved quickly, finding the gaps that the big guy couldn't reach. Leathan would have annoyed the teen. He would have taunted him—called him stupid, gay, ugly, bad with women, smelly—anything childish that would have made the teen disproportionately angry in the moment.

He would have said anything that would've distracted the teen. Anything that would have enraged the teen.

And once the teen was distracted and enraged, then Leathan would have struck. But most importantly, Leathan would have made sure if he got a chance to hit Jojo that it counted.

Looking down, Boniface understood just how much the blows had counted.

As Jojo struggled for breath, Boniface understood how Leathan had to be certain that there wouldn't be any retribution from Jojo while Billy was still in danger. Billy, who Boniface had last seen rifling through Jojo's pockets. Billy, who was now nowhere to be seen.

Boniface knelt down beside Jojo. In the early evening cold, the damp of the ground seeped into him through the knees of the second suit he had ruined that week. "Where's Billy?"

When it came through snatched breaths, Jojo's voice was little more than a strained whisper. "Fuck you and fuck that junkie."

Next to the fire engine, another siren had been switched off. Boniface looked up to see the blue light still flashing on top of the yellow/green ambulance, with a paramedic getting out of the passenger's side. Boniface raised his hand, making sure he caught the paramedic's gaze as she scanned the open space.

"I can still cause you pain," he said to Jojo. "Where's Billy?"

"Fuck you and fuck your psychotic friend," said the teen, without the strength to elaborate on his stream of abuse.

"You'd better take a look at him," said Boniface, standing as the green jumpsuit–clad paramedic approached. "He's not in a good way."

He didn't listen as she put down her bag and started talking to Jojo. Instead, he turned and headed for the stairs.

At the top of the first flight he looked left toward Billy's place. Thick smoke billowed along the walkway, hiding the legs of the white-helmeted incident commander with his clipboard, seemingly so keen to complete his risk assessment.

Boniface turned right and jogged along the walkway going away from the fire, his head in constant motion as he looked for any sign of Billy having passed or gone into one of the other residences. Toward the end of the passage, he turned into another stairwell and ascended to the next floor, completing a quick sweep before ascending to the next floor.

Having reached the top floor, he followed the stairwell down and exited from the back of the building, running for a short while before stopping, and muttering as he panted. "Where have you gone, Billy? Where have you hidden yourself?"

There was a woman pushing a stroller toward him. Bleach-blond hair stacked in a pile, wearing a black tracksuit with pink detailing, and with a cigarette clamped in the side of her mouth, which jiggled the burned end of its ash as she talked into the phone held to her opposite ear. She gesticulated wildly with her free hand when she wasn't using it to jerk the stroller forward, and when the free hand was being used to point at something for the benefit of whoever was on the other end of the phone, she knocked the stroller forward with her large belly.

Boniface leaned into her field of view, raising his eyebrows as if questioning. She kept talking, looking him up and down, her face sneering. "What?" she said, without giving any indication that the person on the other end of the line knew her focus had moved.

"I'm looking for a guy. Blue jeans, white T-shirt, denim sleeveless jacket, black hair, boots."

"I know, I know. Di'n't I tell ya." She seemed to have returned to her conversation.

"Have you seen him?" asked Boniface.

"Why would I?"

Boniface leaned into her field of vision again, pointed to himself and then to her phone.

"You, of course! Why would I see this bloke?"

"Because he..." Boniface inhaled. "Have you seen him in the last few minutes?"

"Nah. I was..." Boniface was jogging before the fourth word—following another rat run, searching in a rabbit warren. He followed an alley past several furniture and trash dumps—the last including two cathode-ray tube televisions—coming out to a block with a row of garages at ground level.

Each door—at least, each door that was still in place—had been graffitied. Most had been attacked in one way or another. Some were a bit bent, as if they had been kicked in the middle. A few had a bottom corner folded up, like a bizarre bookmark. Two had simply been removed from their tracks and were propped against the gaping hole behind them.

Boniface followed the row, opening each closed door—none was locked—and looking through the gaps left by bending, twisting, and mangling the other doors. Most seemed to be full of trash, furniture, old televisions. In one, he found a car, burned out and without wheels. Another was filled with empty metal shelves. Another was filled with car tires.

In none could he find Billy.

He took a path wheeling back in the general direction of Chesterfield Terrace. He passed several clumps of dark-brown brick maisonettes before coming out at the far end of Billy's block, facing the block's rear elevation. A group of firefighters were training a hose on the ground-floor dwelling at the far end, but thick black smoke was still billowing along the length of the building.

Boniface started shuffling in the direction of the fire, his head spinning as he passed boarded-up residences, what seemed to be a storeroom for dumpsters, and then across a back entrance to one of the stairwells. He stopped and jogged back to the dumpster store, pulling its wooden door fully open to reveal a tidy concrete-floored room with eight dumpsters, the two closest both with their lids open, and a third to the side with its lid open seemingly being fed by a large pipe coming in through the ceiling.

He smirked. The room seemed redundant. As far as he could tell, the residents had no need for formal waste-management arrangements—they dumped their trash wherever and whenever they wanted.

He had a quick look, saw something, and rolled out two of the dumpsters. "Billy!"

Boniface looked at the gaunt figure, comatose against the back wall, next to him a syringe, an old tablespoon that didn't seem sufficiently hygienic to go in a kitchen, and a lighter. He pushed his fingers into Billy's throat, just to the side of the windpipe, and felt a weak pulse. "For once in your life try and do the smart thing, Billy, and stay alive."

He turned and sprinted through the bottom of the stairwell and to the other side of the building, stopping as he reached a firefighter. "Where are the paramedics?"

seventy-five

"I know it's not your sort of thing." He listened to the response, feeling the tension in the back of his neck, but realizing that if he let his annoyance become anger he would achieve nothing. "I know. I know. But I'm asking a favor." His face relaxed. "Yeah, *another* favor. But I promise it's the last one today. In fact, I guarantee it's the last one I'll ask for... This week."

He laughed. "You got me. These are the last favors...zzz—not favor, *favors*—that I will ask for this week." He pushed his phone more closely against his ear. "Could you get the short version up on the website within thirty minutes and email me the link?" He winced, holding his tongue between his teeth to remind himself to shut up. "I know. I know. It's not a story that you want or that you would usually cover—but it is something *you* can trade for a favor. You must want someone else to be in your debt?"

Boniface sat on the concrete pathway behind Chesterfield Terrace, leaning forward with his knees pulled up, listening as his former wife, editor of the *European Daily Herald* newspaper, berated him for asking her to abuse her position and publish a story that 999 times out of 1,000 she would ignore.

About twenty yards in front of him, a paramedic securely closed the rear door of the ambulance before jumping into the passenger seat. Slowly, the large yellow and green van moved off, following along a pedestrian walkway unobstructed by traffic before dropping over the curb and onto the highway, and disappearing without flourish. No lights. No siren.

Boniface had been impressed by the paramedics. When he found them and led the first to where Billy lay, there had been no shock, no drama, no panic—just immediate attention and total focus on the person who mattered: Billy. Billy, who by then appeared to be in a deep coma. As the crowd formed and the second paramedic brought around the ambulance, the focus had remained total and the crowd that gathered had not distracted. The crowd that now seemed to lack any focus—the few who were left watched the lone policeman struggle to attach crime-scene tape around the dumpster store room before awkwardly standing guard.

"The sympathetic story needs to come first. There needs to be a focus on the tragedy of continuing estrangement because of the son's upbringing and the son's hard drug use." Boniface became aware that it was uncomfortable and cold sitting on concrete. "It's your turn to call in a favor. Find whoever can do the most sympathetic lifestyle story. This is gonna be all over the press in a few hours, and I can't stop it—but we can make sure that Dawn and Danny's perspective is understood...with your help."

The small congregation of people had started to disperse. Those who remained seemed to be there due to lack of anything else distracting them. Boniface stood up inelegantly—pushing with one hand while keeping his phone clamped on his ear—and looked down at his suit. Thick smoke, broken glass, running and searching, and his struggle to save Billy had all taken their toll: It was time to visit his tailor again.

"Within the next few hours I'll be able to get pictures to whoever you find to publish. The pictures will show that Billy was at Dawn and Danny's property within the last few days." He listened as his former wife noted the detail. "Yeah. Billy will show up on their security cameras. It will confirm the connection."

He watched as the next few people ended their conversation and left.

"Thank you," he said. "I'll leave it with you." He punched the screen of his phone and then returned it to his ear. "Danny. It's Boniface."

Boniface recognized the pile of blond hair before he saw the black tracksuit with pink detailing, and the fat belly being used to nudge the stroller as another small cluster dispersed.

"Danny, listen to me—it's time to bring Dawn home." He wasn't quite sure what Danny said, but he continued. "She's safe, she's with Montbretia—they're in the old church at Albury." He pulled his ruined jacket tight against the early evening chill. "Go now, Danny. But one thing—don't listen to the radio, don't check the internet, and leave your phone behind... Yeah, I know, but there's a lot you need to hear straight from me—not some media fabrication. Find Dawn and stay at the church—I'll be there as soon as I can. I've got somewhere I need to go first."

He dropped his phone into his pocket and muttered under his breath. "Montbretia, I hope you've got Dawn."

seventy-six

"This is how you PR men are dressing these days?" Ernie made a show of looking Boniface over, dishing out a sneer that Boniface guessed had been practiced over many years.

"From Paris to Milan," said Boniface. "If you left this gloomy place once in a while, you'd find that everyone is dressing like this."

"I like it here," said Ernie, his crumpled gray face lit by the banker's lamp on his desk, the only source of light for the room. "So you've got something to tell me, Mister Boniface. Our business is concluded, is it?"

"Our business is definitely concluded," said Boniface. "One or two Is to be dotted and Ts to be crossed...but that's just minor stuff."

"Good. Good," said Ernie in his gravelly way. "I knew you'd see sense in the end."

Boniface snorted. "I always saw sense. I just wasn't sure whether you would see sense."

Ernie went to speak, then stopped, as if his ears had been tardy in conveying the message to his brain. "What?" he barked. "What are you talking about, Boniface?"

"Where's Wes?" asked Boniface. "Jojo's not here. Wes isn't here. You've got a new kid on the door—what's going on?"

"Boniface!" There was a sharpness—a frustration—in Ernie's tone.

"Here's my guess," said Boniface, feeling a slight swagger in his delivery. "By now I'm guessing that you've tried to track down Gray—the lack of Wes and Irvine suggests they're out looking." He couldn't keep the glee from his face; he just hoped it wasn't too obvious in the gloom. "He's gone. Gray is beyond your reach. I'm sure you've broken down his front door by now and have checked his other haunts. Save yourself the trouble and call off your hounds."

"I own him," said Ernie, his teeth clamped together as he spoke, his lips carefully enunciating each syllable. "He has a debt that will be paid."

"No he doesn't," said Boniface, looking around for a chair. In the corner where Iain Irvine usually roosted was an upright 1930s dining chair. Boniface pulled it over and sat in front of Ernie, leaning forward to rest his elbows on his knees, lowering his eye line to match the older man's. "Gray has a debt because you made him gamble."

"I didn't force him..."

Boniface cut him off. "You didn't force him, but you made sure he kept gambling until he lost, and when he did—which I'm sure didn't take long, assuming he's as good at gambling as he is at living the rest of his life—then you lent him more money to gamble his way out of his losses, and then you lent him even more money to gamble out of his deeper debts."

Boniface noticed a slight look of self-satisfaction cross Ernie's face.

"You didn't try to collect because you wanted him to have a massive debt so that when you made your offer, he would only have one option."

"He's a grownup," said Ernie. "He knew what he was getting into, and he will repay his debt."

"Except he can't." Boniface let the statement hang as he pulled out his phone. "What you think he owns—the rights to Prickle—he doesn't, and he knows it. Always knew it. Take a listen."

Boniface tapped a button on his phone and heard his own disembodied voice come out of the small speaker: "the rights relating to your time with Prickle...all this legal stuff against Danny, Prickle, and PAD Management...all this stuff instigated by Iain Irvine..."

"Yeah." It was Gray speaking.

Boniface's voice returned. "Just between you and me...it's bogus, isn't it? It's just your way to pay off your gambling debt, isn't it? Come on, Gray. We're big boys—we can be honest, no one's listening. You agreed to claim these old rights just to settle your gambling debt, didn't you?"

"Yeah," said Gray's voice. "You got me there. But you can't prove anything."

Boniface pocketed his phone. "And before you ask, a copy of that audio file has already been sent to Fiona Aldred at PAD Management."

Boniface made a mental note to send the giraffe-in-training a copy of the file as soon as he got out, and hoped Ernie didn't make him pay for the omission and the lie.

"Let's be clear—what you thought you owned, you don't. Where you might have thought you could tangle Prickle in litigation for years in the hope of them cracking or agreeing to pay you off, they won't." He exhaled. "In short, you've got nothing."

Boniface watched the few dust mites swirling under the banker's lamp, with Ernie's face remaining stony in the background.

"You've got nothing, and that gambling debt you think Gray owes is cancelled."

Ernie slammed his hand on his desk, giving Boniface a look that had been practiced over many years, which probably worked if you were scared of the man.

"If you want to be angry with anyone, then it's Irvine you need to get angry at." Boniface saw a slight crinkle of confusion momentarily flit across Ernie's brow. "He lied to you. He's no more a lawyer than I am... or you. He's the one who has messed up your plans. Not me. Not Danny. Not Gray."

Something flickered in Ernie's eyes as he lifted his hand from his desk.

Boniface wasn't sure what, but some of the certainty seemed to waver—maybe only for a moment, but it was still gone, even in the twilight of the poorly lit room.

His eyes narrowed—some would take this as shiftiness. Boniface knew better; this was Ernie feeling confident. This was Ernie about to play his ace.

"Aren't you forgetting something, Boniface? Or should I say, aren't you forgetting someone? Young William."

Boniface felt his gut twist and the energy drain out of him. He tried to inhale but had forgotten how to breathe—not that his body seemed to want or need oxygen at that moment.

When he spoke, it was a whisper. "Billy's dead. I don't know whether you killed him. I don't know whether he killed himself. I don't know what happened, but he's dead."

Ernie's face was fixed like a palsy sufferer.

"As for Jojo," said Boniface, his voice still subdued. "I don't know. He might be alive—he probably is—but he was in a bad way when I last saw him."

"But there's still the story," said Ernie. "Daniel wouldn't want to see dear Dawn in the press—the neglectful mother whose junkie bastard child died from a broken heart after self-medicating because his mother rejected him."

Boniface felt his face relax. "You're too late on that one, too—it's already in the press." He pulled out his phone and followed a link Veronica had emailed him. "There you are—*European Daily Herald*: Model's tragedy." He held his phone for Ernie to see. "The most sympathetic story you will ever see."

Ernie's face twitched.

Boniface stood. "And now, for once, I'm going to walk away from here without getting a pounding."

seventy-seven

Montbretia pulled the blanket tighter.

When Danny walked through the door of the old church, after the initial trepidation about who was arriving—Danny didn't have the lightest footsteps—Montbretia grabbed two blankets and a jacket, slipped her sneakers over her socks without tying the laces, and made herself scarce quickly.

She knew better than Danny that he and Dawn needed to talk. She knew better than Danny that he and Dawn needed privacy when they talked.

And in her rush to give Dawn and Danny their privacy—not that they even seemed to notice she was there—Montbretia hadn't considered what she was taking. She intended to return and get more, but as she looked back when she reached the old door, she realized that all she held was all she was taking. It was like looking back at a burning building—anything that was left was gone forever, although of course it wouldn't actually burn. It just meant she couldn't finish her cup of tea. If there was a God, then clearly he was sending a message that rooibos was not for her.

She initially intended to wait in the timber-framed porch with its pitched roof, but even with the wooden door fully closed, she could hear Danny sobbing, so instead she walked into the graveyard and chose a tomb. Respectful of what lay within, and with extreme care so as not to cause any damage, Montbretia slipped off her sneakers, lay her first blanket over the top of the waist-high platform, and then checked her clothes for anything sharp that might scratch or dig into the ancient memorial. Satisfied that she would not cause damage, she cautiously mounted the flat platform and wrapped the second blanket around her, soon wishing she had something softer to sit on and that she could light a fire in the graveyard for more warmth.

But whatever discomfort Montbretia was feeling, growing with each minute she sat, that was nothing to what Dawn was going through. The story she had told Montbretia—the story she was now telling Danny—was delivered in a manner that was harrowing, and yet in other ways matter-of-fact. It was a story of choices made, decision taken, and the consequences accepted, and now Dawn had to account to the man who loved her unconditionally for the lie at the heart of their marriage.

Somewhere in the distance—perhaps 500 meters away, near the entrance to the park—car headlights appeared. Two yellow streams hewing a path through the blackness. Two eyes staring into the distance, searching.

She watched the headlights bounce over the low speed humps and follow the road as it gently curved, listening as the familiar sound of the engine—the Teutonic marching song of a Mercedes—became louder, before drawing up where the road ended. The car jiggled backward and forward as it parked: an unnecessary exercise since it was the only car here and was effectively parking in the middle of a field, so there was hardly a need for it to be parked ready for a Le Mans start.

Montbretia sat still as the yellow eyes arced across the church, knowing that she would remain invisible in the shadows created by the artificial light unless the eyes hit her directly. And then the eyes died and the engine silenced. There was a weak light illuminating the inside of the car, which was swiftly extinguished with the sound of a familiar door clunk.

There were footsteps approaching, but Montbretia strained to see their owner with her night vision that had been assaulted by the headlights. There was a rhythm to the footsteps as they approached the gate in the ironstone rubble wall.

Then a foot kicked the wooden gate, and there was a mumbled curse.

Montbretia giggled and whispered: "Turn the handle, Boniface."

There was a rattling of the latch and a click as it lifted, followed by a slow creak as Boniface returned the gate to its closed position.

"What are you doing here?" he asked.

"I thought you wouldn't be that long, and I figured they had some talking to do, so I'm waiting here."

"How are they?" asked Boniface, hesitation catching in his voice.

"There were tears," said Montbretia. "Rivers of tears. Oceans of tears. A biblical flood of tears. I came out to collect wood and round up two of every animal. Then I ran down to the village and banged on the doors, telling everyone to head for the hills."

Boniface reached the tomb Montbretia sat upon.

"I think Dawn might have cried, too."

Boniface grinned. "And how are you?"

"Me?" said Montbretia. "My ass has gone to sleep, but apart from that I'm fine—I haven't cried. I'd like something warm to drink, and I could do with a pee...you know, in a proper bathroom, not behind a bush, but apart from that, I'm great." She looked up. "Pass me my sneakers—they're somewhere down there—and help me get off this thing. That would help."

"You're sure you're okay," said Boniface, bending down and patting the ground around the base of the tomb. "There you go." He stood, placing the sneakers on the flat surface.

"I've been away from you for a few hours, Boniface. I rode around. I had a chat with a nice lady and we had some soup. I've not really been exerting myself."

Boniface nodded. "You may not feel like you did much, but I am grateful. I'm grateful that you found and looked after Dawn." Montbretia looked at him quizzically. "It's been a shitty couple of hours, and I've done a lot that I said I wouldn't do." He shrugged and offered his hand to help her down. "Show me where they are—we need to talk."

Montbretia accepted Boniface's hand and cautiously lifted herself from the tomb before leading him through the graveyard, under the porch, and through the bird screen and heavy wooden door whose hinges announced their arrival. She stepped through the door first and closed it behind Boniface.

"Boniface," said Danny. By the time Montbretia had finished closing the door and turned into the nave, the bassist was embracing the other man like a long-lost brother, the snivel letting her know that tears were flowing again.

Montbretia remained by the door, watching. Dawn sat where she had sat earlier in the evening. The tea light burned low, casting dark shadows across her face, giving it creases Montbretia hadn't seen before. She looked worn, exhausted, emotionally drained, but managed to give Montbretia a nervous smile.

"Sit down, Dan." Boniface's voice had changed. Outside, he had been weary, frustrated, maybe angry. Now he sounded unsure, nervous, almost hesitant.

Danny sat on the blanket next to his wife, their bodies entwining, wordlessly melting to become a single figure. Boniface sat on the flagstones, the low-burning candle still balanced on the frying pan lid in the middle of the circle. Dawn leaned forward, her face drawn but expectation lighting her eyes.

Boniface was silent. Finally Dawn broke the still, "Where's Billy? Where's my baby?"

She heard Boniface sniff, saw him raise a hand to his face.

"Dawn, I'm sorry..."

"Where's Billy? Tell me he's alright."

Boniface sniffed. He voice a whisper. "Billy's dead."

Her roar of pain was animalistic. Prehistoric. The oldest sadness that any one human could endure. It seemed interminable as it echoed around the church. Husband and wife clung onto each other, inconsolable in their despair. Montbretia turned away, unable to watch as the two howled, neither able to be strong enough to comfort the other, but both clinging to the other.

She felt a hand on her shoulder and jumped. Boniface nodded at the door, holding his finger over his lips. She grasped the latch with both hands, lifting it silently, cracking the door sufficiently for Boniface to squeeze through. She winced as he squeaked the bird cage open, then followed him, shutting the door and the bird gate behind.

"What happened to Billy?" asked Montbretia.

"It may have been murder, it may have been misadventure," said Boniface. "My guess is we'll never be able to prove what happened." He shrugged. "But that's only half of it, isn't it?"

"What do you mean?"

"Look at them," said Boniface. "Dawn told a lie, Danny made a choice, and now Billy is dead. Danny is joyful his wife is back; Danny will forgive whatever Dawn said or didn't say—he just wants to support wife—but he met the kid, and he's always going to wonder whether he could have done something. Dawn abandoned the kid..."

"She had no choice," snapped Montbretia. "She got away from an abuser and buried the abuse so deep that she didn't even tell her husband."

"That won't make her feel better—that won't make either of them feel better." He sighed. "I'm not criticizing what she did when she was a teenager—I'm just asking how do you live with that going round in your head?"

seventy-eight

The vicar stood just inside the door, ready to perform the strange ritual of greeting his congregation as they departed.

"Thank you. It was a very moving service," said Boniface as he shook hands with the holy man before passing through the old door, under the timber-framed porch, and into the overgrown graveyard surrounding the church. The grass path between the church and the ironstone wall had been recently cut, carving a neat route to the wooden gate, which Boniface opened rather than walking into, as he had done a week before.

Gradually, the other members of the congregation passed through the gate, leaving the consecrated ground. Dawn and Danny clung to each other—their eyes the color red usually associated with tropical infection. They were followed closely by Carmen and Jilly, both looking far more relaxed than when Boniface had seen them a week ago, but still mopping their tears.

Gray was escorting Montbretia and appeared to be on his very best behavior and trying his hardest to be both charming and a bit of a bad boy—clearly someone had told him women like a bit of a bad boy. Sven and Reuben, the roadies, both wiped tears as they walked, as did the tattooed lady with them who Boniface guessed was Sven's wife. Kit Flambeau—or Christopher Edington, according to his passport—walked with Luca and Mel Grant while Newton Jubb, Prickle's keyboard player, brought up the rear.

Carmen laid a hand gently on Dawn's shoulder. The grieving mother turned and embraced her former bandmate, a new peal of sobs sounding across Albury Park. Danny left his wife and walked over to Boniface, offering his hand in greeting. "I don't think I've ever been to a—I don't know what you call it, a memorial, a celebration...who cares—I don't think I've ever been to a service in a consecrated church where the organ was a Hammond organ played by a keyboard wizard," said Boniface.

"Yeah, that was Newt's idea. He's spent the last few days with Sven and Reuben trying to figure how to get enough car batteries rigged together with a transformer to power a Hammond and the amps." He looked in Newton's direction. "It was a lovely idea of his—he reckoned there would be a lot of singers here, so why not make it more personal? Instead of getting in the local choir, he wanted people for whom the gathering would actually mean something, people who actually care about Dawn—people who love Dawn—and who understand that she has lost someone dear."

He wiped a tear and turned away, pulling a handkerchief out of a pocket.

"I didn't say thank you for handling the press and the fallout—that was a masterstroke you pulled that night. Whoever you persuaded to run that story as it was written, however you persuaded them, I'm impressed." Danny turned back to Boniface. "And now the legal stuff has gone away, PAD are back on side, and our finances will be released, so we can pay you." A mischievous smirk poked out from the sadness. "I'm not sure I should say, but I think tall Fiona quite likes you."

"How's Dawn?" said Boniface in an attempt to hide his embarrassment. "How are you?"

Danny deflated—his shoulders hunched as his head dropped. "It's hard to lose the stepson you never knew you had—it's even harder for Dawn to lose the son she knew she had, and then to find they were so close to reconciliation. Even if he was only after money, at least that would have been a start for communication, and we could have helped him."

He seemed unable to form the words of the next sentence—his mouth moved as if he was talking, and his hands moved as if he were explaining, but words didn't come quickly.

"It's hard to hear about your kid's fifth birthday when you weren't there but you should have been. But even though it's tough to hear, there's a joy in hearing what he was like as a kid. And from the people we've talked to who knew him more recently, obviously he was troubled, but he seems much more than just a plain junkie. He was as much a victim of his situation as Dawn. In fact he was more of a victim—Dawn escaped."

His gaze seemed draw to his wife, who was still being consoled by her former bandmates. He turned back to Boniface, mopping his eyes again.

"What happens next?"

The bassist sucked air through the side of his teeth. "Not much. We can't bury a body until the coroner has released it, and since there are murder charges being contemplated, that might take a while. As far as we know he didn't leave a will, so there's the question about who has rights—it should be Dawn as next of kin, but the family who never supported him sense there might be money, so I've asked Fiona to get a good lawyer for us." He shrugged. "So for now, we do the charity gig, which with all the publicity—it's a long time since I've been on the front pages of the nationals—has sold out."

Boniface winced. "Who's going to sing?"

"No one can replace Thad," said Danny. "No *one*. But many can pay tribute to a fallen comrade. So I'm going to take lead vocal for a couple of songs." He looked in the direction of his bandmates chatting with the musical theater singer. "Kit's going to join us for a few songs—don't forget 'Tattoo Your Name on My Heart' was written when he was singing with us, and the song was written with his range in mind."

The bassist's gaze seemed to wander, stopping when it found Montbretia, who was still humoring Gray.

"And Gray will sing a couple of songs."

"Gray?" Boniface could hear his pitch rising. "After he tried to destroy you."

"He's family, Boniface. The prodigal father has returned to our heart and will return to the stage with us. Kit is family, Gray is family, and it's one gig." He stopped, his eyes narrowing as if questioning. "Anyway, didn't you make his gambling debt miraculously disappear?"

"I felt bad—I lied to him, and I knew the debt was bogus." He stifled a naughty schoolboy smirk. "If I'm honest, I don't feel that bad that I lied to him, but I hope I didn't blow his last chance of earning money from music."

"You didn't," said Danny. "We need to act like a family and help him find some work. He's a good singer; he shouldn't be running a painting and decorating business."

Dawn looked across and smiled at Boniface, still keeping hold of her bandmates' hands. "See, Boniface," said Danny, following Boniface's gaze. "Family."

"Family still grieving over the one they lost when they were teenagers," said Boniface.

"You spoke to Carmen and Jilly, didn't you?" asked Danny.

"They both helped," said Boniface, looking at the three women. "And helping them will help Dawn."

Danny seemed unsure of what Boniface was suggesting.

"Jilly needs a friend. She needs someone she can talk to. Someone to help her when she feels overwhelmed with her grandkids. Let her come and stay and bring the kids with her." He remembered his first experience of the three. "They're a handful.... And it will hurt, seeing what Dawn will never have, but it will help."

"You think?" said Danny.

Boniface nodded slowly. "As for Carmen, she needs help to get on her feet and stay clean. It wouldn't be the first time you've come across someone in that situation. She needs a job—she needs to work to earn a living. She needs self-respect and a pension. She doesn't want charity—she wants a chance, and she'll prove herself fetching and carrying."

"Is there a suggestion in there, Boniface?" Danny seemed to have twigged where Boniface was pushing.

"You must have friends and contacts that hire people with unconventional backgrounds—perhaps PAD could take her on for a short while. You just need to make a few phone calls and call some favors."

The bassist pushed out his bottom lip.

"Think you can make that happen, Danny?"

Boniface Books

You can check out the latest Boniface books at simoncann.com/boniface.

The Murder of Henry VIII (Boniface #1)

As Boniface said when he took the job, how hard can it be to handle the press and publicity for the launch of a book about England's most famous Tudor monarch?

But when the author is murdered, Boniface realizes the job demands more than he expected. And when the man he is talking with is shot, then he witnesses as a third person is forcibly drowned, and he finds he is being pursued by a former Russian Special Forces soldier, Boniface runs.

He delays his death by trading the only thing of value he can offer his would-be assassin: proof of a 500-year-old cover-up. The only difficulty in making the trade is that Boniface can't prove what he knows is true—yet.

If he finds and hands over the proof, the murderer has no incentive to keep him alive. If he lives, he has to explain the transaction for his life to his capricious paymaster.

Boniface needs to unwrap what the dead author found, figure out why he was killed, protect his client's interests, and stay alive.

Pollute the Poor (Boniface #2)

The first Boniface knows about the dead body in the next room is when he is arrested for murder.

The lack of evidence against Boniface doesn't seem to concern the police—they are sure they have the right man—they just need to prove his guilt, and while they do, Boniface is bailed, allowing him to return to work with his client.

His client, a shipping company, couldn't care less that Boniface is distracted. The client has its own problems: News is about to break that one of its ships dumped toxic waste in East Africa, leading to painful and lingering deaths, as well as widespread disability and illness. While the company privately acknowledges its role in the dumping—and its ongoing responsibility for the welfare of the victims—it is insistent that Boniface keeps the story out of the public domain until it has fully assessed how it can most effectively deliver support to those affected.

Boniface knows he has been set up for the murder—and that somebody is trying to destroy him, his business, and everything he holds dear—but he doesn't know who has set him up, or why. He strips back the layers, discovering who the dead man was, why he was killed, why the body was dumped in his office, and why he was set up in such a clumsy manner until he finds who has endangered his livelihood, his liberty, and his friends.

This leaves Boniface with only one conclusion: He must neutralize the threat, permanently, while at the same time trying to protect anyone affected by the dumping.

About the Author

Simon Cann is the author of the Boniface series of books.

In addition to his fiction, Simon has written a range of music-related and business-related books, including the *How to Make a Noise* series, the most widely ready series about synthesizer sound programming, and *Made it in China*, about entrepreneurs building businesses in China. He has also worked as a ghostwriter on a number of books.

Before turning full-time to writing, Simon spent nearly two decades as a management consultant, where his clients included aeronautical, pharmaceutical, defense, financial services, chemical, entertainment, and broadcasting companies.

He lives in London.

Keep in Touch

If you want to know more about Simon, his books, the background to his books, and what he's up to, then check out:

- His website: simoncann.com
- His Facebook page: simoncann.com/facebook
- His Google+ profile: simoncann.com/gplus
- His YouTube channel: simoncann.com/youtube

The swiftest way to find out when Simon's next book will be published is to join his mailing list at simoncann.com/mail.

www.ingramcontent.com/pod-product-compliance
Lightning Source LLC
Chambersburg PA
CBHW021232250626
47155CB00008B/2980